BEN
BETRAYED

A NOVEL BY

GARY BAXTER

Cover Design: Nifty Ness Designs

Interior Design: Cecily Potter

Printed in Australia

Edition December 2023

Paperback ISBN: 978-0-6458751-6-4

E-Book ISBN: 978-0-6458751-7-1

ACKNOWLEGEMENTS

These people deserve my heartfelt thanks for helping to bring Ben Woolford's continuing story to life.

For starters, to those friends and readers of my first action novel, who kept asking for the next book!

Terry Schultz – for his name as a skilled pilot – once again.

Madeline Ash from Creating Ink, for your thorough and thought-provoking editing – Thank you.

To Vanessa (Nifty Ness) for the cover design and patience.

Cecily for the imaginative and quick formatting.

Bob – my enthusiastic Beta reader, for your attention to detail.

To George Elliot – as a mate and fellow author, I value your encouragement.

I must mention the two Qatar pilots who willingly answered my questions about the Airbus A330 just before their flight to Doha from Adelaide.

Piers Hunt for his extensive knowledge in guns and policing terminology.

Kathleen Grosser, for a last-minute 'final eyes' read.

And Kate for her tireless help and running around to make this book happen.

Thank you

GARY

CHAPTER ONE

Ben Woolford sat back in the window seat of the Qantas Airbus A380. There was only about an hour left of the fourteen-hour flight from Dallas, Texas. The coastline of Australia would soon come into view, probably around the same time the sun would rise and warm the start of the rest of his life. Rebecca's bright red hair covered his chest as she slept soundly on his shoulder. He thought about the last month of his life—what an adventure. He looked down at the woman he now adored and knew in his heart that she was to be a big part of whatever lay ahead.

It wasn't long before he felt the throttles ease back and the huge plane begin to slow, and then, the welcome feeling of the start of the decent. Rebecca stirred when the flight attendant requested everyone prepare for landing at Sydney's Kingsford Smith airport. She lifted her head from his shoulder and tried as best she could to stretch out in the cramped economy class seat. He watched her and a smile formed on his face. Could she possibly look more beautiful?

'Good morning sleepyhead,' he said, as her eyes slowly opened to see his welcome smile. She smiled back momentarily as the pain of her awkward sleeping position taunted her.

'Morning,' she replied in a croaky pre-coffee voice.

'We're nearly home, well, the big part of the trip anyway,' Ben said.

They were soon to land in Sydney, collect their bags, pass through customs and immigration; then catch the domestic flight to Alice Springs where she, at least, would pick up her life as a local police constable. Ben on the other hand had some hard thinking to do. He had a wad of money in the bank from his last job and an apartment in Adelaide but he'd since fallen completely for the young woman now sitting by his side. Would he move to Alice Springs to be with her as she worked her way up to being a detective or would she move to Adelaide to be with him? It really didn't matter in this moment.

The plane touched down without effort and they were soon in the queue with the other four hundred plus passengers to wade through customs. Ben looked around as any private detective does when in a foreign place and a feeling of uneasiness fell over him. Was it his imagination or were the Australian Federal Police officers looking at him? He tried to dismiss it but as he looked at the other side of the exit, he saw another two AFP officers that were fully armed, also looking in his direction. He appreciated that he was probably the tallest person around him and sure he looked a little scruffy, but it wasn't that. He didn't want to worry Rebecca and he tried his best to dismiss the concern.

They passed through the official counters without issue and proceeded to the domestic terminal. When the bus that transferred the international passengers to the domestic terminal arrived at the transfer gate, he again noticed an excess of armed AFP at the terminal. Could it be that word was out that he alone saved eighteen American lives at the Pine Gap facility, and he was now a bit of a celebrity in the policing community?

No, something wasn't right, he could feel it. His days as an SAS sergeant told him that.

They boarded the flight to Alice Springs and the concern that he had in Sydney calmed but was not forgotten. It was a relatively short flight compared to the previous and the 737 landed from the west and taxied up to the small terminal. They were seated in the middle of the plane, so it was quite a wait as everybody slowly made their way to the front door. He noted that on this occasion, the airline didn't use the rear stairs to hasten the process of turning the aircraft around for the return flight.

Rebecca led the way and Ben had a feeling he was walking into enemy territory. When the first armed AFP officer made eye contact with him, he knew something was wrong. Seriously wrong.

He leaned toward Rebecca and said, 'Bec, don't react but something isn't right, just keep walking and act natural.'

Rebecca slowed and looked back at him. 'What do you mean?' she asked, a serious look on her face.

'Keep moving babe, I might be wrong but I'm sensing something.'

Rebecca turned and quickened her pace to catch the other passengers. They reached the baggage carousel and Ben could see that the AFP were at every exit.

'Bec, I don't know what's going down here but I think we might have a problem.'

Rebecca then noticed the excess of armed AFP, all with their attention focused on the two of them. Her heart sank, but she herself was a police officer, stationed in this town. What possibly could be wrong?

As the luggage from their flight filed out along the conveyor belt, it was no surprise that their bags didn't appear. The entire belt was empty and the airport almost deserted when their bags finally appeared from under the rubber slats. Ben knew that this was a tactic the police use to keep a suspect back till the airport was clear before they approached in case a scuffle broke out. He looked at the bags and then to the approaching AFP, their fingers firm on the triggers of their DD Mark 18 short barrel automatic rifles.

They weren't here to welcome them back. The police stopped about five metres from them, and a sergeant stepped forward.

'Ben Woolford, place your hands on your head and kneel on the ground.'

Ben did as he was instructed as Rebecca yelled at them. 'What are you doing? I'm a Northern Territory police officer!'

'We know who you are Miss Reed, and we were instructed that if you give us any trouble, we are to arrest you as well.'

Ben looked at her and shook his head slowly. Rebecca stayed silent.

'Benjamin Charles Woolford, you are being charged with the murder of Marcus Chen.'

'Call Jones, then Greg,' Ben said to Rebecca as his arms were forcibly pulled behind him and cuffed.

The officers ignored her from that point. She knew better than to say anything more. She collected the two bags from the carousel as she watched her man, her hero, being placed into the caged AFP van.

She quickly took out her phone.

CHAPTER TWO

Senior Sergeant Tim Jones ran the Alice Springs police station. He had six months left before retirement, where he planned to move back to Darwin with his wife to enjoy the simple life. The past couple of months had been particularly trying with Constable Reed being shot, kidnapped and then rescued both times, not by the police but her now boyfriend. Then, there was the take over at the Pine Gap joint defence facility by a Chinese spy who nearly blew the place to kingdom come and almost killed eighteen American hostages. But that was all behind him now and a calm had settled over the station. Constable Reed was due back this week and the station would be fully staffed again.

There was a knock on his door and Constable Will Jackson burst in.

'Sarge, its Reed, line one, it sounds urgent.'

Jones's stomach churned; he knew the peace would be short lived.

'Reed,' he said with a note of seriousness.

'Sarge, the AFP have arrested Ben, they've charged him with murdering Chen.'

'That can't be right,' Jones said.

Jackson was busting to know what was going on and left Jones's office slowly, trying desperately to hear what was going on with the girl he was totally infatuated with. Will had fallen for Rebecca Reed back in the police training academy when they were both cadets. He was devastated she'd fallen for the ex-military vigilante, Ben Woolford. The man had saved her life and now they'd just returned from an overseas trip that they took straight after he became a hero, saving the day at the American Pine Gap facility. Jackson knew his chances with Rebecca were slim, but he wasn't one to give up.

'Let me make a call and see what I can find out,' Jones said, already flicking through his old-fashioned Teledex for the number of the AFP at the Airport.

'Australian Federal Police,' answered a capable sounding officer.

'This is Senior Sergeant Tim Jones from Alice Springs police; I would like to speak to your sergeant please.'

'Yes sir, I will put you through now.'

'Tim, it's Martin Robbins, I've been expecting your call,' the much younger man said.

'Expecting my call, why is that?' Jones said suspiciously.

'All I was told was to arrest Woolford as he and Reed arrived at the airport and await instructions. They also said to expect a call from the local authorities,' Robbins said.

'And what did they tell you to tell me when I called?'

'Basically, what I just told you. Arrest him on a murder charge and await instructions.'

'And where did that instruction come from?'

'The commissioner's office in Darwin.'

'Don't you report to Canberra?'

'Yes, but although the airport is federal jurisdiction, the Northern Territory Police Commissioner certainly outranks me.'

'Okay, thank you Martin.'

Jones knew exactly who to call next. Russell Scott, the detective from Darwin who was sent down to take over the case of four abducted women and found himself hating Ben Woolford who was always one step ahead of him... That was until Woolford became useful. Now it suited Scott to throw Woolford under the bus for reasons still unknown. Jones dialled his number.

'Deputy Commissioner's office.'

'Russell Scott please. Tim Jones, Alice Springs police,' Jones replied.

'Yes sir, Mr Scott is expecting your call.'

'I bet he is,' he said softly.

'Jones,' Russell Scott said.

'So, you got the promotion I see,' Jones said with a sense of sarcasm. 'Is that because of the job that Woolford did for you?'

'Now Jones, it's not that simple.'

'Well let me tell you what *is* simple, Scott; Woolford did all you asked to prevent a huge political blow up and saved the lives of those Americans at the facility, and now he's been arrested for it. Tell me what's not simple about that?'

'Jones this is way over our heads. It turns out that the Chen fellow is the nephew of the Chinese president and if they find out that the Americans put out a hit on him, well, it'll put a massive amount of fuel on a fire that's already simmering between the two countries. It's best if you and Reed just forget it happened and consider Woolford "collateral damage" for the better good.'

'I'll give you collateral damage, you prick,' Jones barked back.

'You can't talk to me like that, I'm the deputy Police Commissioner!' Scott exclaimed.

'Look here, you arsehole, do you think for one second that Reed is going to sit back and say, 'Oh well, that's unfortunate,' and move on? Well, neither am I!' Jones yelled down the phone.

The phone was silent as Scott let Jones calm a little before he delivered his next statement.

'Jones,' Scott said softly, 'For Reed's own good, and yours, you need to let this go. Believe me, this is way bigger than you can imagine. It could mean war between China and the US. Millions of people could die.'

That startled Jones. If Scott was right, everyone involved with this could be in serious danger. Not only Woolford but himself and Reed as well. He'd watched enough documentaries to know what the CIA were capable of.

Jones had to get the advantage back in his court.

'So, what happens from here?' Jones asked in a much calmer tone.

'I believe Woolford will be handed over to the CIA, who I imagine will sacrifice him to the Chinese.'

'They'll torture and kill him,' Jones said, only just keeping his anger under control.

'Who knows, but if that can prevent a war… Look, Jones, I know it's a shit situation and that you and Reed have developed a liking for this chap.'

'A liking? He's Reed's bloody boyfriend; she isn't going to sit back and accept this.' Jones's voice was rising again.

'Tim, do I need to say it? The American's will do *whatever* they need to do to fix this, do you get what I'm saying?'

Russell Scott went on to tell him more about the process and that the way they'd taken out Chen had everyone very nervous including the Police Commissioner himself; alluding to his approval of the hit without going through all the proper channels.

The realisation flooded over Jones.

'Okay, I get it,' Jones said as he comprehended the enormity of the situation. He ended the call without another word. His mind was filled with visions of black suited CIA agents following him in black Chevy Suburbans.

He called Rebecca Reed.

'Sarge, what the hell is going on?' Rebecca said before he could get a word out.

'Where are you?' Jones asked.

'On my way from the airport, my car was in the long-term carpark.'

'Don't come here, I'll meet you at the showgrounds,' Jones said, trying and failing to keep the alarm from his voice.

She arrived first and parked near one of the corrugated iron pavilions that housed the arts and crafts during the annual Alice Springs show. Rebecca looked up at the deep blue sky, finding it hard to believe what was happening. She turned when she heard a car approach from the direction of the entrance gate, the gravel track crunching beneath the tyres of the speeding vehicle. At first, she wasn't sure who it was but soon realised the sarge had driven his own personal car. That in itself was strange, as he only ever drove a police car.

Sergeant Jones pulled up next to her and a second later a cloud of dust that trailed the car blew over her. That didn't matter. Information from the man that she admired most, and could trust, was all she cared about.

Jones hopped out of the car and into the drifting dust. Rebecca was desperate to see his face, desperate to see a sign in his eyes that told her that he could fix this problem. The look Jones gave her was anything but what she was hoping for. He walked briskly up to her and without any greeting, took her arm, steering her inside the empty shed.

'Sarge, what the hell's going on?' she demanded, holding back tears.

'Reed, this is bad, really bad.'

'But he only did what you asked him to do. He saved those people's lives.' Her voice was breaking, and Jones could see that tears were imminent.

'Reed, now listen carefully. If we're to save him, we need to take all emotion out of it because this is way over our heads, and I only know a tiny bit of what's really going down.'

Jones placed both his hands on her shoulders and she looked up into his eyes. Reed was like the daughter he never had; he'd watched this beautiful woman blossom from the fresh cadet into the constable she was today. He'd been there when she was nearly killed in front of him at a shoot-out at the Vipers motorcycle club, and later kidnapped and drugged by Russian people smugglers, and in the middle of it all, he'd watched her fall in love with the only man he considered good enough for his Reed. But now, he would see her heart be broken as the man she loved was condemned to death or worse.

'Reed we'll fix this, alright? But we need to be smart. Chen was the Chinese president's nephew and the Americans have found themselves in a very sticky situation. The Chinese have demanded the head of the person who killed him.'

'But Chen took eighteen people hostage —at gunpoint! We only did what any police force in the world would've done in that situation,' she said with tears now trickling down her face.

Jones's heart broke as he watched her.

He swallowed the dry lump in his throat. 'The trouble is that we did it, evidently without any permission from above. There is no TV footage or reports to any police. The Chinese don't believe, or won't believe, what they've been told. They are saying that the Americans thought that he was a spy, which they are denying, and assassinated him.'

He ran his hand through her dusty red hair and pulled her to his chest as she cried uncontrollably.

Then, almost as if a switch had flicked, she straightened, pulled back from him and with a look in her eye that scared the shit out of him, said, 'What else do you know, Sarge?'

'Reed, I don't like that look. These aren't just a bunch of bikies or even a drug cartel, this is the CIA. Who knows, they're probably listening to us now.'

'You know they can't hear us in here, that's why you brought us into this tin shed.'

'Reed, don't do anything stupid, they will squash you like a bug.'

A calm instantly came over her as if a spirit had taken over her body.

'Sarge, you know there is no way I am going to just sit here and not contribute.'

'Yes, I know,' he said slowly. 'Okay but let's do this together and carefully. We'll need to outsmart the most ruthless organisation in the world. They told me that this could start World War Three if it got out that the US put a hit on Chen.'

'I don't care about World War Three, just Ben. The Americans can worry about wars—my job is to save my man.'

Jones thought he almost saw a smile come over her face. *Oh shit,* the last time he saw that look put her in hospital for a week.

Rebecca turned and rushed to her Subaru. She opened the door and turned back to Jones still standing in the doorway of the large empty shed. A worried look sat on his face.

'I'll be in touch, boss,' she said as she started the engine and roared off toward the showgrounds gate, all four wheels spinning on the little Subaru XV.

Rebecca knew what to do. Ben had told her. She took out her phone and called Greg Sheppard.

.

CHAPTER THREE

Greg Sheppard was sitting back on the couch of the extravagant Dallas mansion that was owned by the new love of his life, Jennifer Madison. A beautiful woman he'd met by chance on a cruise in the Caribbean and had fallen for instantly, and she for him. Once Ben and Rebecca left, Greg had stayed in Texas to help Jennifer tidy up the financial mess after her husband was charged with her attempted murder. It should only take a few days and then both he and Jennifer could settle in Australia and live happy and peaceful lives. The television was on but being the middle of the day back home in Australia, he was checking emails on his computer that rested casually on his lap. His phone rang, which wasn't unusual at this time of night. He answered it without looking to see who it was.

'Hello, Greg Sheppard speaking.'

'Greg, it's Bec, sorry if it's late there but we have a big problem. I don't want to say anything on the phone but Ben asked me to call you.'

'I see. On a scale of one to ten, how big is the problem?'

'Ten,' Rebecca replied without hesitation.

'Right, I see, so I need to get back?'

'Yes,' was all she said.

'Will we need help?'

'Yes, same team.'

'Okay, I'm on my way.'

The call ended and Greg called both Steve and Dan, the two ex-SAS who fought under Ben in Afghanistan and again by his side only last month on a rescue mission of a Darwin millionaire's daughter. Greg wasn't a soldier, not even a boy scout—he was a businessman, film producer and racing car driver. He was initially a client of Ben Woolford's, but when Ben asked him to drive a car to escape with the kidnapped woman under heavy gunfire, his value became obvious. Ben knew he would be the person to help him this time as well. Greg booked the next Qantas flight and would be in Alice Springs in just over twenty-four hours. Steve and Dan would be there in six.

Greg had arranged the hardware for the assault on the Mexicans last month and before he boarded the plane, he ensured the same equipment was on its way to Alice Springs again. Greg gave Steve the pickup instructions, Stuarts Well, south of Alice Springs, 9.00 p.m., Northern Freight Road train, same as last time. Jennifer was in the kitchen when Greg walked up behind her. He placed his hands on her waist and his chin on her shoulder. She moved her head so her face was against his.

'Babe, are you happy if I head home tomorrow? There's been some trouble, I just had a call from Bec.'

Jennifer broke from his embrace and turned to face him. 'Is everything okay?'

'Ben's in some trouble. I don't know what but Bec said it's pretty big.'

'Well, of course, we are all done here,' Jennifer said in her strong Texan accent.

Greg leant forward and kissed her.

Deputy Police Commissioner Russell Scott called his boss, Peter Warner. Warner didn't get to the top job due to his ability—he stepped on anyone and everyone he needed to get the Police Commissioner's job, including undermining his boss at the time. He thrived on television exposure and any chance to wear his elaborate Police Commissioner's uniform. He would appear at any event that he was invited to. He was the ultimate attention seeker. He would probably have made a good politician.

'Russell, do you have that problem sorted?' were Warner's first words.

'Peter, Jones and Reed aren't going to roll over on this.'

'They're fucking police officers and I'm their boss; they will do what they're told.'

'I'm sure they know that, sir,' the formal reply felt better to Scott. 'What will happen to him?'

'I'm guessing the CIA will silence him and hand over the body to the Chinese with a sorry note from the US ambassador.'

'And kill him,' Scott said firmly.

'None of us need this story getting out. You are in this too Scott, so let the CIA do their job and we can all get on with life.'

The line was quiet as Russell Scott took in the information.

'Scott, don't get emotional about this. He was an out-of-control vigilante, you told me that yourself. It needs to be done. The CIA will be here tomorrow and we need to hand him over to them… Do you hear me?' Warner's voice rose to consolidate the message.

'Yes, sir, I hear you.'

Scott ended the call and placed his head in his hands. He knew what he had to do. He left his office and drove his government appointed car to Smith Street in the Darwin CBD. He walked into the post office and purchased a cheap off the shelf phone.

Ben Woolford sat in the holding cell at the AFP station that was just next to the airport. He could see that the sun must have risen, as the hallway had a golden glow about it. He ran the whole scenario around in his head. The one thing he was sure of was that he was in a great deal of trouble. This was not something he was going to get out of alone.

Ben closed his eyes and laid out the picture of events as he saw them. A whiteboard appeared in his imagination. He drew out the situation like an army general planning an assault. He put his name at the bottom and drew two lines away from it. AFP and NT police were at the end of each line. *Why did the AFP arrest me and not the local police?* This would be a local matter normally. He thought about how the whole Pine Gap hit was arranged in the privacy of Sergeant Jones's office. *Something must have gone wrong and they need a scapegoat.*

The whiteboard in his imagination faded as he heard footsteps coming down the passage. An AFP officer appeared into view carrying a paper bag that he passed casually through the bars of the cell.

'It's just something from the airport, we don't have guests very often,' the officer said.

Ben looked at the officer's name tag.

'Faulkner, what's going on? You were there, at Pine Gap, I remember you.'

Faulkner looked at him and Ben saw a look of guilt in his eye.

'Tell me something,' Ben pleaded.

The AFP officer looked at him like a man on death row.

'You know I can't say anything, I'm just following orders. I know you're ex-military, so you understand what I mean.'

'What happens from here?'

'You'll be taken to Darwin, that's all I know,' Faulkner said as he turned and quickly walked away.

Ben sat back on the small bunk that was pushed against the wall of the two-metre square room. He opened the bag to see a sandwich in a clear plastic triangle and a bottle of orange juice. He opened the drink and consumed it all. He returned the empty bottle gently into the paper bag and fell back against the cell wall. He closed his eyes. He thought of Rebecca and how close to perfect his life had been just yesterday.

CHAPTER FOUR

Steve and Dan collected Greg from the Alice Springs airport just after 11.00 a.m. They shook hands. Steve was tall, dark and huge, where Dan was shorter, blond but every bit as tough as Steve and Ben. 'Looks like you've recovered well after that nasty stick injury, Steve,' Greg commented.

Steve just nodded with a small grin in reply, remembering the gunshot wound from their last mission.

'What do we know, Greg?' asked Dan.

'Absolutely nothing, but I guess because it was Bec that called that means Ben is in trouble. She's waiting for us in the old Arts and Craft pavilion at the showgrounds.'

The three men arrived at the Blatherskite Park showgrounds in their white Toyota Corolla hire car. Greg pointed from the back seat when he saw her car parked at the furthest pavilion from the gate. They pulled up quietly next to the dark grey Subaru. A worn-out looking Rebecca Reed walked out from behind the pavilion to hug them all. Seconds later she was near dragging them inside the shed. Rebecca explained all she knew, and what she did know wasn't much.

'The AFP nabbed him as soon as we landed. They threatened to arrest me too if I tried to stop them. All Ben said was to call Jones and you, Greg. From what Jones has uncovered, Ben's been blamed solely for the Pine Gap hit. The sarge is furious and says he will help.'

'Can we trust him?' Greg asked.

'Yes, I think so,' Rebecca said, wishing she sounded more confident.

They all looked at each other.

Greg was first to speak. 'Well, I think we're going to have to because we know very little and he's the best chance to get information.'

They all nodded and Rebecca took out her phone.

'Sarge, it's me… We're going to rescue Ben,' she said quickly. 'Can you help us?'

'My God, Reed, you could get yourself killed, but yes, I'll do whatever I can.'

'Can you meet us now at the showgrounds?'

'Who's us?'

'A couple of friends.'

'Okay, I'm on my way.'

Sergeant Tim Jones reached for his keys and phone. He noticed an unread message from an unsaved number and ignored it for now. He hopped into his police HiLux and switched on the ignition. The car synced the phone and an electronic voice stated that he had one unread message. He reversed the car out of the parking spot and selected drive. He held his foot on the brake and reached for his phone. He opened the message from the strange number.

> He is to be handed over to the CIA tomorrow.
> To be silenced.

Jones read the message again and roared off to the showgrounds.

Five minutes later the police car joined the little Toyota and Subaru that were parked at the pavilion. Jones stepped out. His eyes swept the horizon and he made for the half open door.

The sight of a fully dressed and armed police sergeant walking in took the three men by surprise. Immediately the two ex-SAS took a step back with their right leg, instinctively initiating a defensive stance. Rebecca walked up to Jones and thanked him for coming. Greg reached out to shake his hand which Jones shook with apprehension. Jones quickly took note of the two men who hadn't come forward; assuming correctly that they were military men. He nodded an acknowledgement to them. They nodded back, their eyes glued to him.

'I just received a text,' Jones said, breaking the awkwardness of it all. He took out his phone and showed it to Rebecca. Greg, Dan and Steve gathered around to see it as well.

'That's our best chance,' said Steve. 'Hit them as they leave town.'

Greg looked at Jones. 'Sergeant, can you tell us what you know? Every detail, one piece of a jigsaw puzzle means nothing but when you put a few pieces together, a picture forms.' Greg remembered Ben saying those exact words to him.

Jones straightened and said, 'Okay, in for a penny in for a pound.'

He told them how the US had asked the NT Police Commissioner to quietly deal with Chen and not involve the AFP or state police. It was technically on US granted soil. A private contractor, namely Ben, was used and the problem solved. The big hiccup was that Chen turned out to be the president of China's nephew and now he'd gone missing. The US told China that he was killed accidentally by some vigilante who had been shooting up the town recently and that the culprit had been arrested.

'The Chinese don't believe the Americans. They believe he was assassinated, murdered without a trial by the US. There was no CCTV footage of the incident where Chen held eighteen Americans hostage so telling the Chinese that story can't be proven.'

'But there is footage,' Rebecca said. Everyone looked at her. 'Peter's drone, it would all be recorded on the memory card in the drone. That would save Ben.'

'The US won't want that coming out, it would show that they lied to the Chinese.' Greg said.

'We need to get that card from Peter, now, first job. Is he still working for you, Sergeant?' Dan asked.

'Yes, a couple of days a week, sometimes more. He's become a real asset.'

'Let's get Peter and the drone involved as well, he could be really handy,' Greg said.

'Is there anything else you can tell us, Sarge?' Greg asked.

'Other than the text I just got, that's it.'

Jones shook hands with the three men and Rebecca reached up and hugged him, something she'd never done before. Jones hugged her back and said softly, 'Please don't get yourself killed.' He looked at her for a moment longer and turned to walk out of the shed.

'Sergeant,' Greg called out and Jones turned around. 'Would you be able to talk to Ben and warn him?'

'I doubt it, but let me see what I can do,' he said and disappeared from the corrugated iron showground pavilion.

Rebecca looked at the three men in turn and said, 'What do you think?'

Greg was first to speak. 'We don't have any choice—we have to get him out and fast.'

'We can't storm the AFP station with weapons. If it goes wrong, we would all spend the rest of our lives in jail,' Rebecca said.

'No, you're right, but taking him from the Americans, now that's a different story,' Steve said.

'Rebecca, the drone will be handy, and we need that memory card. Can you get onto Peter?' Greg asked.

'I don't have his number but he lives only five minutes away.'

'Okay, let's plan this out,' Greg said.

'What we know is that the CIA will collect him tomorrow from the AFP. We can assume they'll head out of town to some deserted location and waste him,' Steve said.

Rebecca felt sick, the reality of this event now making her head throb. Greg noticed her turning pale even in the darkened shed. He put his arm around her and guided her to an empty milk crate that lay on its side. She took a seat and Greg asked her if she wanted to go but she refused.

Greg returned and Steve continued, 'There will most likely be only two of them, armed with pistols, a hire car and an excuse to the AFP that they're taking him for questioning. I suggest we follow them out of town, force them down a dirt road somewhere and I'm sure with some resistance, we can overpower them.'

'Sounds simple enough,' Greg said.

'That will depend on how much of a fight they put up,' Dan said.

Greg turned to Rebecca. 'Bec, do you want to be involved with this part?'

'Try and stop me. I feel my days are numbered as a police officer in this town anyway, what the hell.' Rebecca stood shakily and joined the circle of men.

'Steve, you received the hardware from Stuarts Well okay?' Greg asked.

'Yes mate, all checked and good to go, radios on charge. We'll need a few boxes of shells though.'

'We will need four V8 LandCruisers, fast enough to keep up with whatever the CIA have and good for off road if we need it. They don't need to be all the same... In actual fact, try and make them different colours so we don't stand out too much,' Greg said. 'Let's get Peter with the drone along as well, that might be handy... and that bloody memory card with the Pine Gap vision needs to be priority one. Okay, Bec, why don't you go and see if Peter is happy to help and get that SD card and protect it with your life. Do you have Ben's rifle?'

'Yes, it's under my bed, not the safest place but we did leave in a hurry,' Rebecca replied and Greg nodded.

'Steve, do you want to get the ammo we will need?'

'Will do, I know that gun shop in town has what we want.'

'Dan and I will secure the four cars. Let's see if the sarge can get to Ben to tip him off about our plan. Bec, can you check that too?' Greg said.

'Will do,' she said, excited that a plan was coming together. She turned and took out her phone. She walked slowly from the boys as she dialled her sergeant. 'Sarge, any chance you can talk to Ben?'

'Yes, I think so, it won't be on my own though. The CIA are in town and plan to collect him at zero eight hundred tomorrow the feds have said.'

'Okay, thank you, stand by for what we need him to know.'

'Alright, and Reed, keep your head down.'

'That's my plan, Sarge. I'll be back in touch soon.'

When Rebecca returned, the group had drawn a rough plan in the dirt floor of the pavilion. She could see how the four hire cars would surround the vehicle and force it off the road. She had missed the finer details but was sure she would find out soon enough.

'The CIA are in town and the sarge believes he can get a message to Ben. It may need to be cryptic as he won't be with him alone,' Rebecca said. 'Also, they plan to collect him at zero eight hundred tomorrow.'

'That's great to know but we can't trust that. Okay, let's get going, if they decide to collect him early, we will miss our chance.'

Steve dropped Greg and Dan back at the airport to collect the four-wheel drive vehicles they would need. Rebecca headed for Peter Watkins's house.

Peter's front door was open and the fly wire screen torn from the frame when Rebecca arrived. Immediately suspicious, she walked cautiously up to the small red painted verandah. The flyscreen appeared to be freshly torn and held the flimsy door semi ajar. She wished that she had her service firearm with her.

'Peter!' Rebecca called out. 'Peter, are you here?'

Without touching the doorknob, Rebecca pulled the mangled fly screen door further open and stepped carefully inside. The place had been ransacked, every chair on its side, every shelf cleared, with books and papers everywhere.

'Peter?' she called out again.

Confident that no one was there, she quickly checked each room. Every cupboard and drawer had been up ended on the floor. The drone box was in the middle of his bed, the drone itself lying on the floor, battery removed and the little cover that held the SD card open and empty. Rebecca took out her phone and called the station.

'Alice Springs Police—,' a familiar voice said.

'Jackson, get me the sarge quick!' Rebecca said, not letting him finish his greeting.

'Reed, what's up?' were Jones's first words.

'Sarge, Peter Watkins's house has been ransacked and he's missing. It's got to be the CIA.'

'Don't jump to conclusions, Reed.'

'His drone was upside down on the floor and the memory card gone. It's not some random robbery, Sarge.'

'Okay, I'm on my way.'

Rebecca walked out onto the verandah and looked up and down the street.

Someone must have seen something.

She walked over to the neighbour opposite and knocked on the door. A lady in her thirties answered the door and Rebecca asked if she'd seen anything but she had only just arrived home. It wasn't until the third house opposite that an old lady said that she had seen a white van pull into his driveway earlier that day.

'There was a lot of noise, smashing things and then they dragged him out. I think they were detectives. He used to be a bikie you know.'

'What made you think they were detectives? What did they look like?'

'Young, tall and strong, like in the movies,' the elderly lady said.

Yeah, American movies, an anger was building inside her.

'Okay, thank you. The police will be here soon and may want to ask you some more questions.'

As she turned from the lady, she saw a police car turning into the street. Constable William Jackson and her sergeant jumped quickly out as it pulled over only just short of a skid.

Rebecca turned to Jackson. 'Will, get a statement from this lady here.'

She then turned to the sergeant. 'And you need to see this, Sarge.'

Jackson looked at the sergeant to confirm that he should do as Rebecca had instructed. The sarge nodded in the direction of the elderly lady and Jackson took out his note pad from his back pocket.

'Sarge, we need to find Peter quick. He could well be in danger.'

The sarge rubbed his chin with his thumb and forefinger as he looked at the up-turned drone, the same drone that Peter had used many times to help the police solve local crimes. Although Peter wasn't a police officer, Jones considered him one of their team. He felt a heat start to boil through him. His arms started to tingle and almost start to shake; the heat in his chest felt like it could explode at any second.

He softly said, 'Go and help Jackson, Reed.' He reached for his phone.

She had never seen him like this and left without a sound.

Sergeant Jones took out his phone and called Russell Scott in Darwin. After being transferred from the reception desk, Deputy Commissioner Scott answered the phone.

'Tim,' he said nervously.

'Listen here Scott, it looks like the Americans have taken Peter, my drone pilot, after ransacking his home. Why would they do that?'

'Trying to find that drone footage from the Pine Gap incident, is my guess,' Scott said cautiously.

'Well, you listen to me. If anything happens to that kid, World War Three will be starting here in Alice Springs, do you hear me?' Jones said, his anger burning the deputy commissioner's ear.

'Fuck, alright, alright, let me see what I can find out,' Scott said, and the phone went dead.

'Reed!' Jones called out from Peter's doorway.

Rebecca heard the urgency in his voice and ran to him.

'I want to know exactly what your team have planned and what we can do to help. Those pricks up north have just crossed the line.'

Greg, Steve and Dan had a plan worked out and rehearsed, well, as best they could when Rebecca called Greg from Peter's front yard.

'Greg, Peter Watkins has been taken, we assume by the Americans. His place has been trashed and the drone SD card gone, it's probably not the one they were after as that was weeks ago.'

'Shit, I hope the little fella's okay. Can I talk to the sarge?'

'I'll go get him, stand by.' Rebecca handed Jones her phone.

'Yes, Greg?'

'Sergeant, we appreciate your help.'

'I can't help directly but tell me your plan and let me see what I can do.'

'First, I need you to go to the AFP and find out all you can, and if you can get a cryptic message to Ben that we are here to help and to be ready for anything.'

Greg went on to explain the plan in a little more detail, including how the four hire cars would run the CIA vehicle off the road and hopefully rescue Ben without any shots being fired.

'I think with my help, we can make that all so much easier,' Jones said.

The two men discussed the plan for the next few minutes before Jones gave Rebecca back her phone.

Jones walked out of Peter's front gate a determined man.

'Jackson' he called out. 'To the airport, AFP.'

CHAPTER FIVE

Peter Watkins's new life as a police contractor was a dream come true. He'd been raised in a bikie family, the Viper Motorcycle club. The club was started by his father's brother and quickly resorted to crime to fund itself, becoming very profitable with drug manufacture, theft and prostitution. But when they decided to take on Ben Woolford, their empire came crashing down; all members found themselves either dead or in jail. All except Peter or 'Skunk' as he was known then. Ben took a liking to him, saved his life and helped him on the path he was on now. He owed his life to Ben.

Peter was watching television when a heavy knock rattled his front door. The flyscreen door was locked and he opened the main door cautiously. His immediate thought was that it sounded like police but they would ring him, he was 'sort of' one of them. As his faded blue front door opened, he was confronted by two tall men, dressed in black with baseball caps and dark sunglasses.

'Peter Watkins?' a strong American voice asked.

'Yes, why?' Peter asked, wishing the door between them could do more than keep flies out.

'Can we come in?' the second man asked.

'No, what do you want?' His voice was now quite shaky.

The first man reached for the handle, and finding it locked, he 'stepped back and kicked in the fly wire that gave very little resistance. Peter stepped back, desperate for an option but before one even started to come to mind, the first man had him by the shirt and pushed him against the wall. He felt the plasterboard crack as his head hit the wall hard.

'Where is the footage of the Pine Gap incident?' the second man asked.

'I don't have it,' was all he could think to say. The man holding him stepped back a little and planted an uppercut into his solar plexus. Peter would have doubled over but the hold on him was much too powerful. The second man started pulling the place apart. He started in the kitchen, emptying every drawer onto the floor. Peter tried to yell in protest but was hit again, knocking the wind out of him.

'Tell us where it is and we'll leave you be,' the man holding him said to his face. The man's spittle added to the sweat that was now streaming down Peter's face. Peter could hear his bedroom being destroyed before it fell silent. Obviously the second guy had found the drone under his bed. He returned holding a black SD card.

'This has August written on it. Where's last month's card?' he demanded as he held it millimetres from his face.

Peter saw the card move away from his vision only to return as a closed fist and hit the side of his face. He saw stars and was hoping he would just pass out and wake up with the two thugs gone, but the volume of the man's voice increased as his consciousness improved.

'There's an old lady watching from over the street. Let's take him for a ride,' Peter heard one of them say. Next the wire door flew open and he was dragged into the white Hyundai iLoad van. After what seemed like a few minutes, the van pulled into a roadside parking bay about twenty kilometres out of town. The two men dragged Peter out and threw him to the ground just out of sight of any passers-by. Peter looked up to see the taller of the two pull out a black pistol. He recognised it as the same as the nine millimetre Glocks that the police use. The man pointed it straight at his face.

'Last chance Peter Watkins. Tell us where that memory card is or you die now.'

The man racked his weapon and straightened his arm to fire.

Peter in this moment didn't care if he died. It would be a relief to leave the pain in his chest and swollen eyes behind. He watched the man slowly pull back the trigger. He closed his eyes and heard the gun fire.

It was mid-afternoon when Will Jackson swung the police HiLux into the carpark of the AFP station at the airport. Tim Jones was almost out of the car before it had stopped. He walked into the station with purpose, Jackson struggling to keep up. Constable Faulkner approached the counter.

'Yes sergeant, what can I do for you?'

'I want to see Ben Woolford, now,' Jones said with all the authority of a senior sergeant of police.

Constable Faulkner puffed his chest out and said, 'This is federal jurisdiction, you have no authority here, Sergeant. You can't come in here demanding anything from me.'

'Look here you piece of shit, you *live* in my jurisdiction so if you don't want a police car to follow you to work every day, I think we better find a way to quickly work together,' Jones said, staring him down.

Faulkner's puffed chest deflated as he took in the threat. 'Well, you can't, he's not here. They picked him up half an hour ago.'

'I was told zero eight hundred tomorrow,' Jones said, shocked.

'They arrived here half an hour ago and they left from the rear gate.'

'Which way did they go?' the sergeant asked, his phone now in his hand.

'I didn't see, but he's meant to be going to Darwin.'

'He won't get to Darwin, you fool,' Jones said, turning for the door before stopping. 'What type of vehicle were they in?'

'White iLoad, rental I'd say.'

Jones turned, tapped a number into his phone and waited for Rebecca to answer.

'Sarge?'

'Reed, they took him half an hour ago, you better rally the crew,' he said as he stepped back into the police car. 'Jackson, get onto traffic and find out which way that white Hyundai iLoad went.'

Will Jackson made the call to the traffic camera division and within minutes had the information they needed.

'They went west down Larapinta Drive only ten minutes ago, Sarge.'

'Not the road to Darwin!' Jones said.

'Reed, they headed west along Larapinta, if you don't catch them by the Namatjira drive turn-off you'll need to split up.'

'We're on our way,' Rebecca said in an authoritative tone that concerned Jones further.

Rebecca, Greg, Dan and Steve all had coms so they could talk to each other in real time. Steve and Dan were fully armed with automatic assault rifles, Bec had her police issue Glock and Greg had a M17 9mm Beretta pistol. Rebecca told them that the road split about fifty kilometres out.

Greg was the first away and was driving the fastest vehicle. The V8 Diesel LandCruiser tray top was just topping out at around 180 kph.

'If we haven't caught them by the turn off, I will continue straight on with Steve following, Bec you and Dan take the turn off to the North. Let's hope these radios reach the other party when we find them.'

Greg was passing cars coming in the other direction at a closing speed of over 300 kilometres per hour.

Greg had only just passed the Namatjira drive turn-off when a large white van appeared in the distance.

'I think I have them,' Greg called over the radio.

'We haven't turned off yet so confirming we stay on Larapinta Drive,' called Dan.

'Yes, stay on Larapinta,' Greg replied back.

Greg dropped his speed to keep as far back as he could and still keep them in sight. He didn't need to spook them until the others arrived. Rebecca had tried to call Jones but she was now out of phone range. Greg saw the first of his team starting to fill his mirror and within a minute the four V8 Toyota hire cars were tightly nose to tail so they would look like one car in the rear revision mirror of the iLoad van.

'How well do you know this area, Bec?' Greg called.

'Not very, to be honest.'

'That's okay. Team, we will go back to plan A, the one we discussed in the showground shed. Balaclava's on, any questions anyone?'

'All good,' came back from the three behind him.

Greg increased his speed slightly to look like nothing more than someone in a hurry. The other three vehicles followed close behind. Greg indicated to overtake and watched the driver's window till he was alongside—he was sure this was the vehicle. The rear windows looked as if they had been painted out in a hurry with probably a pressure pack spray can. Greg looked away from the van as he passed to not create any suspicion yet.

Greg pulled in front of the van, indicating as you would. Steve pulled out to overtake as well, and when he was alongside, Rebecca pulled right up behind the van almost hitting its rear bumper. Greg braked, rapidly decelerating, and each of the team followed. Steve now had a sub-machine gun pointed at the driver's head who was busy trying to avoid a crash from in front. Dan slipped his vehicle down the passenger's side of the van, gravel from the roads verge rattled under his vehicle, his gun now only inches from the passenger's window. Greg hit the brakes hard on his LandCruiser and the white van slammed into the back of him hard. All five vehicles stopped and Steve jumped out, running to the front of his car, his Heckler and Koch MP5 pointing straight at the driver's head.

'Hands where I can see them. Now!' Steve yelled. Dan had the passenger covered. There was a moment that seemed to last forever as the two men considered their options. The driver's eyes were fixed on Steve's through the balaclava, the arrogance of the American obvious. Steve saw his lips move and both men slowly raised their arms. There was an air of relief as the two men decided surrender was their only option of survival.

Rebecca received a nod from Steve and ran for the rear door, her breath held in a mix of panic and desire as she opened it quickly. She gasped in relief at seeing her man was still alive and well but cuffed and lying on the van's white painted floor. His smile confirmed he was okay. His feet were bound with silver duct tape. Her first reaction was to kiss him, and she did. Holding back tears, she feverously tried to tear the tape from around his feet, but it was too strong. She resorted to unwinding it, which she performed as quickly as she could. Before she'd managed to free him, Greg called out.

'We need to go, right now!' He knew it could all turn to shit at any second.

Able to move, but with the tape still stuck to one leg, Ben climbed out the rear door. His hands were still cuffed and with no keys, he would need to travel that way for now.

'It's great to see you babe,' Ben said to Rebecca with a grateful smile and a wink.

Despite his restraints, Ben manoeuvred into the passenger seat of Rebecca's LandCruiser as she started the car and backed away from the van. She turned it full lock, selected first gear and dropped the clutch. The rear of the V8 Toyota spun in a half circle. After a moment of over correction and snaking, Rebecca had the car under control and was speeding away down the highway back to Alice Springs. She radioed the team a few minutes later to tell them that Jones had traffic blocked on Larapinta.

She waved as she sped past the police car that was parked sideways across the road.

Greg and Dan had moved their vehicles and turned them in the direction of the city. Dan had jumped out of his car and turned Steve's car around as he kept his gun pointed at the two Americans. Dan ran back and with his six-inch knife put a hole in the side of the rear tyre of the van. The explosion from the tyre making the Americans jump. Steve lifted the rifle higher to remind them not to move. With Greg's car gone from in front of them, Steve ordered them to drive off. The driver's left hand reached for the gear selector. He clicked it into drive and the van moved forward, the flat tyre flapping on the road. Steve and Dan ran to their vehicles and headed at speed back toward Alice Springs. It wasn't long when the flashing lights of Jones's police car became bright in the fading light. Steve could see the sergeant and another officer standing by the caged HiLux and slowed to talk to them.

Steve pulled up and Jones came to his window.

'Is anyone hurt?'

'Just a tyre, Sergeant.'

'I can live with that; do you need me to hold them up?

'No, it'll take them a while to change that tyre.'

We'll need to talk when we get back,' Jones said stepping back from the LandCruiser.

'Yes sir,' Steve called out as he put his foot down and sped off. Greg and Dan waved as they followed Steve past the sergeant.

Jones called for Jackson to move the police car and release the held traffic.

Peter Watkins opened his swollen eyes to see the two men climbing into the white van. The driver didn't even look back as the van sprayed him in dust and gravel from the rear wheels before pulling back onto the deserted highway and speeding off. He tried to sit up but his chest screamed with pain. He rolled onto his side and then to his hands and knees.

His face was now only inches from where the bullet went into the ground next to his head. That, he was thankful for. He pushed back with his hands and managed to get to his feet. He was disorientated and not sure where he was. His senses were coming back to him slowly. He knew with the sun in the northern sky, mountain range on his right and the fact that the van would have driven off back toward the city, he had a pretty good idea where he was. He struggled to take a deep breath and figured he had a broken rib or two. He staggered out onto the road and started what he figured to be a long walk back to town. Each step was painful, his chest top of the list. His right eye had pretty well closed over, and he was grateful he could even see at all.

A car sped past; a beat-up Holden Commodore full of residents from a nearby settlement. It was almost another hour when a car and caravan drove past and stopped a short way up the road. The driver hopped out, trying to assess whether he should help from the safe distance he had. The man could see that Peter was injured and soon ran to his assistance. The man's wife followed soon after.

'What happened, young man?' the man asked as he put an arm around him to help.

Peter wasn't sure he could talk, so he didn't.

The older couple laid Peter on the bed of their caravan and headed for the hospital, the lady riding with him.

'Were you thrown from a car?' she asked.

God it's all such a blur.

But what he did know was that someone wanted the footage from the Pine Gap hostage rescue and that they were prepared to do anything to get it.

'I was mugged and dumped out here,' Peter said through his swollen lips.

'You poor thing, we will have you to the hospital soon.'

Peter needed to talk to Ben—he would know what to do. He had no idea where in the world he was although he did know Rebecca was due back this week. As soon as he could, he would need to tell Ben where the SD card was hidden.

'Boy, am I glad to see you, my darling.' Ben said. He was leaning forward in the passenger seat with his hands still cuffed behind his back. 'No chance you have keys for these things? Who the bloody hell uses real cuffs these days?'

Rebecca looked at him with an exhausted grin, shaking her head with an almost guilty 'no'. They both knew that was the least of their worries.

'They were CIA,' Ben said. 'What have you found out, Bec?'

'The sarge has been digging and apparently Chen was the Chinese president's nephew and the Americans spun them some story about a vigilante taking him out. You are their scapegoat. So, if you or any of us let the truth out, the Chinese will know they've been lied to, and supposedly, World War Three will start. The CIA arresting you, and your unfortunate death before you could talk, would have at least given China the body of Chen's killer.'

'What about you and the sarge? And Peter, shit, he has it all on the card from the drone.'

'The Commissioner feels that because we are police officers, we'll keep our mouths shut as per instructions and as long as you are safe, I'm happy to do that,' Rebecca said, looking at him with a look of approval.

'So, they were taking me out there to kill me?'

'I'm afraid so. Not what we expected on our arrival home, hey?'

'That's for sure.' Ben sat quiet for a moment as the LandCruiser sped along the outback road. He replayed the last forty-eight hours in his head.

'You got the team together quickly, my dear,' Ben finally said.

'Well, you told me who to trust. I called the sarge first, then Greg. They were great, Greg was still in Dallas, but he was here in twenty-four hours and had arranged the guys and firepower before he left the US.'

'That's just amazing, well done. First let's get these cuffs off and have a meeting with all interested parties. I'm guessing this is far from being over.'

'Having the CIA after you is not ideal, my love,' Rebecca said as the lights of Alice Springs came into view.

'No, but this is our back yard, not theirs and I'd be damn sure the Northern Territory police aren't going to want any part of this. If this gets out, there will be some heads getting chopped,' Ben said, uncomfortable that his hands were still bound behind him.

'Where to babe?' Rebecca asked.

'Your place, I'm pretty sure there's only two of them and we only have the time it will take them to change that tyre. Although, I doubt either of them had ever changed one before.'

Rebecca pulled up at the front of her house. It was fully dark now. She ran ahead of Ben to get the door open so that the neighbours wouldn't see a handcuffed man waiting at her door. They entered and she quickly found the handcuff keys that were in the pocket of her uniform that was still draped over a chair in her bedroom. She removed the cuffs and Ben kissed her.

'I was wondering if I would ever get to do that again,' he said as he touched both her cheeks with his fingers. 'Do we have a plan?' he said, rubbing his wrists.

'Not really, the plan was to save you from being executed and with the time we had, we would worry about the rest after that.'

'Great, well you did that and did it well,' Ben said.

'Okay, we need to meet the team and get a plan before the Americans regroup. Chances are the AFP could be around here any minute,' Ben said, looking toward the front door.

'The boys are staying at the Northern Star motel on the road out of town.'

'Let's head there and meet them. I'll need to go into hiding for a while 'till we see how serious they really are,' he said, reaching for the small suitcase that he last saw on the carousel at the airport the day before.

Rebecca reached under her bed and retrieved Ben's rifle.

'Thanks babe, I might be needing that.'

The police radio crackled with a call from the station as the HiLux came into range.

'Sarge…' Crackle… crackle… '—kins… hospital.'

Jones looked at Jackson. 'Did you get that?'

'Something about the hospital, I think he said.'

After another kilometre had passed, the car was close enough to town for the radio to work properly. 'This is Jones, say again.'

'Sarge, Peter Watkins has been admitted to hospital. He's been beat up real bad, what do you want us to do?'

Jones looked down the road that the police car lights poorly illuminated and took a deep breath.

'Sarge, are you there?' came back from the police station.

'Yes,' he said. 'I'll send Jackson around for a statement, leave it to me,' Jones replied in a scarily soft tone.

'Roger that,' came back over the radio.

Jackson looked at his sergeant and said, 'What do you think happened, Sarge?'

'I know exactly what happened and there is going to be trouble, mark my words.'

Jackson continued to drive on without another word, the silence deafening. Nothing like this was taught at the academy. Although he didn't know a lot about what was going on, he knew that Ben Woolford had been arrested and was to be taken to Darwin on some pretty big charges and as far as he was concerned, treated like the criminal he was.

He pictured the distraught Rebecca Reed that he himself would console and eventually, she would see him as the man he was and that she truly needed. The police car pulled up in front of the station. Sergeant Jones hopped out and turned back to Jackson.

'Go home and get a statement from Peter first thing in the morning,' he said, slamming the door of the car. He had a call to make.

Jones fell into his office chair, his head swirling. He reached for his office phone that sat on his desk. *No, let's see what Peter tells us.* Jones needed time to calm down and of course maybe, Peter did just get mugged—but he doubted it.

When Ben and Rebecca arrived at the Northern Star motel, the three other LandCruisers were parked out of sight.

'Greg's in room 21,' Rebecca told him as she pulled up. They rushed to his room and knocked with a sense of haste. Greg was on the phone to Jennifer in Dallas and quickly said, 'I'll call you back babe, I have visitors.'

Ben went straight to Greg almost before the call had ended, holding out his hand and offering a big thank you. Rebecca had gone to get Steve and Dan. They both arrived with huge smiles, hugs, and pats on the back.

'Looks like you pissed off some mean dudes this time Ben,' Steve said.

'Yeah, looks that way buddy.'

A seriousness came over their faces as they all knew this was not over by a long shot.

'You'll need to go into hiding mate, those yanks will be back as soon as they change that tyre,' Dan said.

'What're the chances of them knowing how to change a tyre?' Ben said, smiling.

'Well, even if they drive the whole way with it flat, they'll be back here soon and I bet it will be a shoot first, ask questions later arrangement when we catch up next time,' Steve said.

'That's for sure,' Ben agreed.

'We need to get you somewhere safe where they can't find you. Keep your head down while we find out what the hell's going on,' Greg said.

'I have an idea,' Rebecca added in. Everyone looked at her. 'What about the bikie fortress that we raided? It's empty and has huge walls around it.'

'Needs to be further away than that, these fellas will be turning over every stone,' Ben said.

'Okay, what about that old farmhouse that those Russians were camped up in before they moved to their new government supplied accommodation? They won't be needing that again for a few years,' Rebecca said with a wry smile; her eyes searching the group for approval.

'That's perfect,' Ben said. 'It's two hundred k's away—that's a big radius for them to search.'

'Okay,' Greg chimed in. 'Time is precious. Let's get supplies and get you out there before those bloody Americans turn up. They're going to be really pissed that we messed up their party.'

Rebecca took out her phone and opened her notes app, 'Okay, what do you want, babe? Once we get you out there, you won't be ordering takeaway.'

'That's true,' Ben agreed. He reeled off a list of supplies and Rebecca and Greg set off to purchase what they could before the shops closed. Ben went to the cupboard in Greg's room, grabbed two spare pillows and all the blankets from the shelf, and lugged them out to the LandCruiser.

CHAPTER SIX

Greg and Rebecca soon returned with three bags of food and essentials. Ben agreed with Greg, Dan and Steve that he would stay out at the farmhouse until it was clear beyond doubt that the CIA had gone, and he was no longer America's most wanted. Greg, Dan and Steve would hang around town, keep a low profile and learn what they could. But all they'd done was buy some time, they all knew that.

With the Toyota full of fuel, Ben and Rebecca headed north out of town. Ben kept an eye in the mirror and was confident they weren't followed.

'Will you be alright out there on your own?' Rebecca said, looking over to Ben as he drove.

'Yeah, I'll be right. But it's pretty shit, isn't it? I helped the police and this is what I get.'

'We'll sort it out but it's best you disappear until we get to the bottom of it,' she said with her hand now resting on his leg. She was busting to tell Ben about Peter being missing but she knew if she did, he would turn the car around and make it his mission to find him. It was best for the police to follow it up. Ben needed to be in hiding and that's all that mattered for now.

They turned onto the dirt road. It would be slower now, kangaroos were everywhere and although the LandCruiser had a bull bar, a big roo could still do some serious damage.

'How will we communicate; how will I know what's going on?' Ben said, looking at her pretty face that was dimly lit from the dashboard lights.

'We will come out, one of us, whoever is not being tailed. We will bring more supplies and whatever good news we have but you must stay out here for now.'

'I know, I will. Anyway, it's not like you're leaving me with a set of wheels.'

'And that would stop you?' she said with a smile.

It wasn't much longer before the outline of the farmhouse came into view. Ben noticed Rebecca go quiet, wondering if it was the memory of the Russian people smugglers who'd drugged her and locked her up here after she was caught by them on a solo stake out.

'Are you okay, Bec?' Ben asked.

'I can't believe it was less than four weeks ago I was here and thinking that I was going to die. Can you believe those Russians were kidnapping young women and flying them out from that airfield out west? If it wasn't for you, I would've been sold off as a sex slave to a middle eastern millionaire.'

'I know. But if you hadn't found them, those poor women and more in the future, would be gone,' Ben offered gently.

Ben pulled the LandCruiser up at the back door to the house. It was completely dark. He left the engine running and the lights on high beam. The first thing he noticed was an overhead wire that ran from a flimsy power pole to the side of the house. He could only hope that there was power still connected to the house.

He took out his torch, turned it on and stepped up the two steps to the verandah. He opened the fly wire screen door and it squeaked like they all seemed to do. The main door was a dark mission brown with faded and flaking paint. It was stiff and required a firm push to open it. He reached around the door frame and found a light switch. *Moment of truth.* He clicked it down and a dim kitchen light lit the room.

'Well, that's a big plus,' he said, turning back to Rebecca.

'Yeah, it sure is. I had my doubts.'

The smell of cigarette smoke was thick in the air. An ashtray was full in the middle of the kitchen table and beer bottles were scattered in several places, one still half full.

Ben turned and hugged her, squeezing her tighter than he really should. He knew she would be close to crying and he would too— if he had time to think about it all.

'You better get going. I'll be fine here, honest. Electricity and running water, it's going to be a holiday,' he said with a smile, trying to ease her pain.

'I'll fix this Ben, I promise. The sarge and the boys, we'll fix it,' she said, a tear now obvious.

She kissed him and went back to unload the car of his things. He probably had enough food and supplies to last him a couple of weeks. He took out his rifle last and stood next to the car. He worried about Rebecca driving back in the dark—without a way to know if she got home okay.

'Drive carefully and don't worry about me, this a bloody palace compared to some places I've been.'

'I'm sure it is. I'll be back when I can. I love you,' she said, jumping in behind the wheel of the LandCruiser. Ben quickly glanced at the fuel. She had just over half, plenty to get her home.

'Hey, just remember there are lots of eyes and ears out there. More than usual. So be careful, beautiful.'

She nodded, looked at him with glistening eyes, then swiftly put the car into gear. She turned it around and with a wave, headed off along the two-wheel track back to the highway. He stood there watching until there was no sound from the big V8 diesel and the tail lights had long disappeared. The silence and the starry night would have been breathtaking had the circumstances been different.

He stepped inside the house, closed the door and removed his rifle from its padded felt bag. He filled the magazine and clicked it back into the rifle. Next was to see if the fridge worked and given that the past owners had left in a hurry with the assistance of Northern Territory police, he was a little concerned about what he might find in there. He was pleasantly surprised to find that just the milk, juice and a half container of yogurt was all that urgently needed to be removed. The freezer was full of frozen supermarket microwave dinners. Although a little out of date, they were a good find. He placed in the fridge what he needed and decided that given he hadn't slept in a real bed since he was in Dallas, Texas four days ago, that was to be his next priority. He flicked on lights. There were three bedrooms, all smelt of the sweaty Russian men, but he was past being fussy. He went and gathered up the blankets and pillows he'd taken from Greg's motel room and made a bed in the biggest room. He desperately wanted a shower, but sleep was what he needed most.

It was daylight when Ben woke, his Tikka T3 loaded and laying by his side, the barrel facing the open door and the stock just inches from his head. He took a second to take it all in, the room, the smell, and his solitude. He pulled away the blankets, hopped out of bed and slung the rifle over his shoulder. He hoped he didn't need it but just in case, he certainly didn't need it leaning against a wall inside if he found trouble outside. He carefully pulled back the scrim curtain of the kitchen window. Everything was calm, birds chirped, and the sun had lit the homestead's building with a golden morning glow. He then went to each room that had a window, checking outside in all directions. Having scanned North, West, South and East and studied each view closely, he was comfortable that he was alone.

He stepped outside, surveying the location he would for now call his home. He tried to stay only one step from cover in case someone was out there with a long gun and scope. There were quite a few old cars scattered around in various states of repair. He figured they would have been there pre the Russians moving in. There were farm tools in the various sheds and a 44-gallon drum almost full of diesel fuel. To the right was a row of stone shearers quarters with barred windows and doors. That was where the Russians held the girls they'd kidnapped before the international buyers arrived in their Learjets to buy them at auction at the somewhat nearby airfield.

Ben felt confident that he was safe, at least for the time being, and decided he'd take that shower he desperately needed. He wandered back inside. The bathroom was filthy, not only from the Russians but years of bore water and recent non-use. He pulled the bathroom window curtain back so he could still see outside and placed the Tikka where he could reach it from the shower. He turned on the hot tap and stood in hope for the water to warm. It didn't.

'Well, that would have been just too much to hope for,' he said out loud.

He went to the back door, stopped, and again surveyed the horizon. All quiet. He walked around the house to the bathroom window. Two large gas bottles lent unrestrained against the white weatherboard wall. One was connected to a flimsy bundy tube that led to what looked like a pre-war hot water service. He shook the connected bottle and it felt empty; however, the second appeared much heavier and hopefully was full of gas. He gave the valve a quick turn and a welcome white spray of liquid propane burst from the outlet. The connected bottle tap was turned on, so he could assume it was probably empty.

He went to the shed that he'd found earlier where he'd spotted some tools, and grabbed a rusty shifting spanner. He swapped over the flimsy fitting and when he turned on the tap, he heard the rush of gas fill the system. That was a good sign, but he knew such an old system wouldn't have a self-igniter. He removed the outer cover, exposing the inner gizzards of the water heater.

The pilot light would've gone out once it used all the remaining gas in the old cylinder and would need to be re-lit. Surely a house full of smokers would have a lighter or box of matches somewhere? He found some easily in a bedside table. He lit the pilot and went back inside, turned on the tap and heard the water heater ignite the main burner. A smile formed on his face as the hot water started to flow from the rusty showerhead.

With the bathroom curtain pulled all the way back, he undressed, his eyes not leaving the only road leading in from town. The shower was amazing, the water hot and plentiful, but being naked in a small room while the American Central Intelligence Agency was trying to find and kill him, had him soon out and dressed.

His next major task was to create exit options should any uninvited guests turn up. He stood on the verandah in front of the back door. The yard had a few scattered vehicles that had been driven until they'd stopped or a better one had come along.

He inspected each and decided an army green Toyota 4runner was probably the best option as his base to assemble a vehicle. The plastic rear canopy was smashed, three of the four tyres flat, and the diesel engine didn't look like it had been started in years. He found a container and put some of the fresh fuel from the drum into the tank. The inside of the fuel cap wasn't rusty, which was a good sign, it meant that there wasn't any water in the fuel tank.

He collected every battery he could find from the wrecked cars and connected them all together using the starter cable wiring from each vehicle and aligned them so the sun would heat them. With a makeshift test light using a globe and wires from one of the other cars brake lights, he tested which batteries still had some charge. He hoped the large bank of batteries joined together would give him enough to spin the engine fast enough to start. He cracked open the fuel feed pipes to the four fuel injectors and used the hand primer to pump the fresh fuel to the engine.

The moment of truth—he walked around to the driver's seat of the rusty Toyota and turned the key to the first position. A healthy set of lights lit up the dash. He turned the key and the engine turned over, not fast enough to start but enough to prove it probably would. He headed back inside the house to try to find either some Epsom salts or aspirin to add to the better batteries. Combined with the heat from the sun he was confident that he would have a running vehicle. He found a small pack of aspirin in a bedside table and placed one tablet into each cell of the best four batteries.

While the aspirin was doing its job of making voltage, he found four wheels with pumped up tyres that would fit the little Toyota and went about changing those. He removed the broken rear canopy, making the 4-runner look a lot like a sawn-off cab HiLux. He checked the oil and water and both were at their upper levels.

The sun was now high, and the batteries felt warm, especially the four with the added aspirin. He hopped into the cab again and turned the key. The engine only turned a few revolutions before the first cylinder fired closely followed by another and then the other two and a cloud of smoke drifted past his door to mark his achievement. He smiled, probably only the second time since arriving back home to Australia.

He disconnected the battery bank, only leaving the original battery to charge by the Toyota's alternator. He jumped back in, gave the clutch a couple of pumps and selected first gear. The rusty clutch shuddered and groaned but the vehicle moved. He did two laps of the yard before deciding to add more fuel. He wanted to see if the battery might keep some charge if he left the engine running. He filled the small tank to the brim and then left it to idle away while he planned a better way to start the engine should none of the batteries prove workable.

He slung his rifle over his shoulder and headed up the hill that surrounded the house from the northern side. If he could make a clear path, he could park the car on top of the hill and roll start it should he need to leave in a hurry.

He spent the rest of the day clearing his roll-start runway and occasionally driving the 4runner around to get some air through the radiator. By dark, he had put together a car, which he now affectionately called a 4Lux, made a roll-start track and given himself a way out should he need it.

With the light fading, he sat back on a slatted wooden chair that was probably as old as the house itself and admired his vehicle perched at the top of the hill, its rusty spotlights filling the roo bar that adorned the front of the car. In different circumstances, this could have been an amazing break from reality—he just needed a cold beer in his hand and his girl at his side. In the peace and quiet, he could hear hundreds of birds chirping, an occasional rustle in the bushes by bearded dragon lizards and the thumping of kangaroos. The gentle breeze filtered through a huge ghost gum that laced the air with a soft eucalyptus scent. But this wasn't a holiday, this was a life-or-death situation and he couldn't afford to let his guard down. He touched the rifle that sat by his side and tried to imagine what might happen from here.

CHAPTER SEVEN

Constable William Jackson stood in shock as he looked at the young drone pilot that he'd worked with on many police cases. He'd seen dead people look better.

'My God,' he said as he approached the hospital bed.

'They did a job on me Will,' Peter said in a muffled tone, trying to smile. His face was bruised and purple, an oxygen tube up his nose and another larger tube exited from the corner of his mouth. Jackson took out his note pad.

'Can you talk mate, are you able to tell me anything?'

'If you can understand me, I can,' he said in a dampened reply.

Peter went on to explain how he'd answered the door to government looking men with American accents who ransacked the house looking for the SD card from the drone and then took him out east and threatened to kill him.

'Luckily, an older couple with a caravan drove past and picked me up. I'd be dead meat for sure if they hadn't.'

'I'll get their details from the reception desk,' Jackson said as he wrote down the last of what Peter offered.

Jackson knew it was time to leave him be. Touching Peter's hand, he said, 'We'll catch them mate, glad to see you'll be okay.'

Jackson left. He knew whose fault this all was—Ben Woolford. If he hadn't turned up in town two months ago, life for him and Rebecca would be just fine. She would be all his by now and he'd be able to hold that beautiful woman in his arms.

Woolford had to go, one way or another and there were people in town wanting to do that.

Sergeant Jones wasn't surprised by the information Constable Jackson gave him. He was calm now and this situation required careful thinking and no rash actions. Woolford, he guessed was safe, hell he had two ex-SAS babysitting him. Peter was alive and should recover fully. He figured the tip off had come from Deputy Police Commissioner Russell Scott, so he could well assume him an ally, or at least not an antagonist.

When Rebecca arrived at the Alice Springs police station for work the next morning, Jones called her into his office.

'Close the door, Reed,' he said as she entered. 'Is Woolford safe?'

'Yes sir, for now.'

'Okay, good. We will need to assume our duties as if nothing is going on. Tell your SAS mates to keep their heads down and out of the way. We need the dust to settle and see what comes out the other side.'

Rebecca nodded and he went on.

'I want you to report back to me when you see anything. You can bet they'll have a tail on you so just go about your normal life and duties. Try not to be alone if you can, take Jackson with you on jobs and if you can get someone to stay with you, it might be a good idea. We already know how serious these Americans are.'

'Yes Sarge, but I feel we have the upper hand now,' Rebecca said with far too much confidence.

'Reed, don't underestimate these people, they won't like being beaten by a few country town cops. Oh, and limit your phone calls to only a few seconds. No talk of Ben or any word about your friends by name.'

'Yes, sir,' Rebecca said, and she left his office.

Jones fell back into the worn-out fake leather office chair and stared at the door Rebecca had just closed. He took in a deep breath and tried to appreciate the lull before the ensuing storm he knew was coming.

Jones took out his phone and typed a text to Russell Scott.

Thanks.

No reply would confirm he was the sender of the message. No reply came.

The next week proved that the American agents hadn't gone anywhere. They were still scouring Alice. Rebecca was constantly followed by different cars with tall single males driving. She figured they were on a vehicle rotation at the rental car companies at the airport.

Peter had improved significantly and was due to be discharged. A broken jaw was now the worst of his injuries. Steve had moved into Rebecca's spare room, while Greg had flown back to Adelaide and Dan to Melbourne, both ready to be back in Alice Springs at a minute's notice.

Through the station and community chatter, there was talk of strange men searching empty farmhouses around the town and Rebecca guessed it wouldn't be long before there were more men here, likely searching further and further out. At least for now, without any more clues, for all they knew, Ben Woolford could be long gone.

'It's good to see Peter is going home today,' Jackson said to Rebecca as they drove around the Alice Springs streets on patrol.

'Yes, I really feel sorry for him, this had nothing to do with him,' she offered, not taking her eyes off the road in front of her.

'Is Woolford hiding?' Jackson asked her.

She looked at him with no reply.

'I'm just asking, that's all.'

'Yes, for the time being he should fine,' she replied.

'Must be a good hiding spot. Those Americans seem to be doubling in numbers.'

'I don't want to talk about it, Will.'

'I get it, just tell me, is he still in the NT? I won't tell anyone.'

Rebecca looked at him for as long as she dared take her eyes off the road. She couldn't decide if she could trust him but a simple yes or no wouldn't tell him much.

'Yes, but say nothing to anyone, okay?' She looked at him again.

With a smile on his face, he said, 'Sure, who am I going to tell?'

Rebecca immediately regretted it. She remembered what Ben and her sarge had said about 'eyes and ears everywhere'. She knew Will hated Ben, but thankfully she hadn't revealed anything specific. The Northern Territory was a big place.

That night, Will Jackson sent a text.

He is still around Alice, will keep following up.

The four CIA agents sat around a table in a room at the Hilton DoubleTree hotel. The most senior agent, and in charge of the hunt for Woolford, was Charles 'Chuck' Wilson. He'd just got off the phone from Washington.

'This is how it is. We need to find this Woolford fella and that footage from the Pine Gap incident. Apparently, he's still around here somewhere, and I bet he's busting to see his little lady. I want someone on her 24/7. He will need supplies, wherever he is, and we need to be ready.'

'Is the instruction still to terminate on sight?' one of the men asked.

'No, take him alive if we can, he could be the only one who knows where that footage is. I don't think the weedy drone pilot still has it,' Wilson said. 'The other thing is, there's an A330 sitting at the airport, apparently arrived yesterday, no markings but Chinese rego. We could well have company.'

Rebecca tried her best to go about her work. The CIA agents following her were nothing more than a pest, but it was no surprise. Getting out north to see Ben was going to be near impossible. She missed him badly and felt sorry that he had to live like a hermit until this all was sorted. The part that really made anxiety dig into her gut was not knowing how they could possibly make it out the other side of this.

The sarge had been told that a Chinese wide-body plane had arrived in Alice Springs apparently for servicing, which was suspicious. No one believed it. He'd alerted her that China may be on the warpath as well and she didn't need World War Three starting in her hometown. She knew that if the CIA and the Chinese Ministry of State Security were looking for Ben, the world would not be big enough for him to hide. If the Chinese were following her, they were doing a much better job than the Americans.

She took out her phone and called Greg.

Greg was in Adelaide having dinner with Jennifer who had also arrived back in Adelaide from Dallas, when his phone rang.

'Rebecca, how is it going there?' were his first words.

'Greg, the Chinese are here, I haven't seen them, but an unmarked plane is at the airport under the guise of servicing.'

'Long way to go for a service, do you suspect they are looking for Ben as well?'

'Definitely. They're good though, I haven't noticed anything.'

'Okay, we will be there tomorrow, we may need to get him out of there,' said Greg, his mind racing for options. After swiftly explaining the situation to Jennifer, he called Dan in Melbourne who agreed to be back in Alice Springs as soon as possible.

CHAPTER EIGHT

Ben had explored the place thoroughly. He'd found unopened bottles of chloroform that the Russians had used to subdue or knock out the girls they'd kidnapped, the cable ties used as handcuffs, and women's clothes that the girls had been made to discard. He felt a kind of sick relief that he had been a big part of putting an end to that.

Ben had been hiding out at the farmhouse for almost two weeks now. His beard was scruffy, hair a mess and the process of washing his clothes was, you might say, primitive. He sat on the verandah with a glass of orange juice, the last of it. The bore water wasn't really drinkable but would do if he didn't drink too much, and the rainwater tank was empty. He'd finished the few cans of beer the Russians left behind and the food was running low. He'd hoped to see someone by now but understood that the heat must be on back in town. He swallowed the last of the juice and looked at the 4Lux parked on the hill and the cleared runway in front of it.

He mused through his options. He could hit the highway and go north to Aileron, a small town basically inhabited by Aboriginal people and the occasional traveller that didn't have enough fuel to make it to Alice. If they had someone there watching, he would stand out. If he went to Alice Springs he could attempt to blend in, get his supplies and just maybe get a glimpse of his girl. Boy, he missed her. He wanted to know she was okay.

He didn't need to think for long. He decided to dress up like a homeless man and hope the 'scrap-built Toyota' would make it the two hundred kilometres into Alice. He looked at it again. It seemed to smile at him, and he smiled back. It was getting dark and from the various pre-Russian owned clothing, he selected his wardrobe for the trek to town.

Next morning, he woke with a mix of excitement and nervousness. He knew he shouldn't be going; he could easily live on what he had. Boil the bore water and fresh meat was in abundance while he had a gun. But he knew the real reason—he desperately wanted to see Rebecca and the fact she hadn't been out to see him told him that they must be watching her every move.

The 4Lux couldn't lock, hell it didn't even have a back window, so he decided to leave his rifle at the homestead. He connected the battery terminal, checked the water and oil again and closed the bonnet with a slam. The flimsy dark green bonnet rattled as the catch locked in. He turned on the ignition and two welcome red lights lit up. He turned the key back off. He selected second gear, leaving the clutch in and released the handbrake. The 4Lux started down the hill slowly building up speed. He knew the faster he went the more chance he had of it starting. He turned on the ignition and once the glow plug light went out, he dropped the clutch. The back skidded then gripped, turning over the high compression four-cylinder diesel. The engine roared to life as he reached the flat area in front of the house. He fed in the throttle and started the three-hour drive into town. The suspension was so stiff that he worried the car may break in half, but it didn't, and it wasn't long before he arrived at the bitumen. He turned right and wound the little 4x4 up to a hundred kilometres per hour.

Once he reached Alice Springs, he refuelled the car and bought a new battery at the first petrol station he found. He didn't need to be making a run for it and having a car that wouldn't start. He parked the car in the shopping centre undercover carpark, finding a spot close to the entrance and backed it in. He knew a car chase in his spare part special wouldn't end well for him, but it was all he had. He took off for the supermarket and gathered another two weeks of supplies including a six pack of beer. He probably stood out wearing dark sunglasses inside, but he had no choice. He shopped quickly, filling the trolley in under ten minutes. He only had limited cash that was left in his bag from before his US trip. He didn't want to use a card in case the CIA were monitoring that. He put the shopping in the 4Lux and against his better judgment, headed for the café that was opposite the police station on a diagonal angle to the north. He walked slowly, with a slouch and head down, playing the homeless person role as best he could. He ordered a coffee and took a seat furthest from the counter, the only one that gave him a view of both the police station and café front doors. His coffee arrived and with manners not fitting of the average homeless person, he thanked the waitress. His head was turned toward the window and eyes glued to the police station opposite.

The café door squeaked open and without moving his head, Ben's eyes darted to see a large man enter. He was tall, shaved head, overweight, and heavily tattooed. He was most likely a bikie, or a 'wanna be', and walked with slow confident steps. It was obvious he got his way through intimidation. The man glared at Ben from the second he set eyes on him. Ben immediately saw the man as a problem; too obvious to be one of his hunters, but just someone looking for trouble that he didn't need any of.

Ben turned his eyes back to the window but in his peripheral vision, he watched the man. He saw him pointing in his direction, at the same time raising his voice to the waitress that had only just served him coffee. Ben carefully turned his head toward the guy, who was now yelling at the girl, demanding she move the man from his usual seat. The girl threw swift glances between the irate customer and Ben. She scrambled from behind the counter, her steps slowing to a trepidatious tip-toe by the time she arrived at Ben's table.

'Err, excuse me sir. I'm so sorry, but would you mind sitting in another seat? The gentleman at the counter is a regular—he always sits in this spot. I hate to ask… but…' She shot a fearful glance back toward the man, his chest out and arms folded across his chest.

As she turned back to look at Ben for his reply, something about him caught her attention. He had a presence and strength that was much more than his initial outward appearance portrayed.

This made her even more nervous. The other guests in the café could see that this could go one of two ways and there was a quick flurry of gulped last mouthfuls and scraping chairs by other patrons who suddenly decided it was time to leave. Two Asian men, likely tourists in their Hawaiian shirts, didn't move, intent on finishing their coffee and watching the 'entertainment' unfold.

Ben looked at the young waitress' name badge, and said in a calm quiet voice, 'Mel, ask the gentleman to come and ask me himself.'

Ben could see the girl was incredibly scared and now clearly shaking, and figured this was not the first time she had been through this scenario. He quickly thought that the smart thing to do was to just move to another spot and not attract any attention, but this was the only seat from where he had a chance of seeing his girl. That was something he wouldn't give up—definitely not to some thug.

He sat firm, sipping his coffee as the man approached.

'Do yourself a favour shitbag and sit somewhere else,' the man said, towering over the seated Ben.

'Look mister, I want to sit in *this* seat and I don't need any trouble, okay?' Ben said, sliding his coffee mug away from in front of him.

'Well, you've now got trouble because if you don't move in the next three seconds, I'll move you and it won't be to another seat.'

Every eye in the place was watching now, everyone that hadn't already left anyway.

'Look, I won't be here much longer, as soon as my coffee is finished, I'll be off,' Ben said, trying not to make a scene.

'You'll be off alright, you shitbag,' the man said as he grabbed a handful of Ben's shirt above his right shoulder.

The man barely started to pull Ben from the seat when Ben's right arm exploded up from the table and over the chunky tattooed arm locking the man's hand in Ben's armpit. Ben's forearm flew up from beneath, and the crack of the man's elbow was a sickening sound heard by all.

The man pulled away screaming, his left arm broken. Following a look of shock and horror, rage filled his face. He lurched at Ben, winding up a right-hand hook punch that took so long in coming, that Ben could've had another sip of his coffee. The punch was aimed at his head and without any trouble Ben ducked the massive fist. With the man now open on his righthand side, Ben drove the second knuckle of his right fist into the man's temple. He watched as his assailant's eyes rolled back in his head and he fell unconscious onto the timber floor with a thud, his left arm bent at an unnatural angle.

The café was silent. Not word was said, not a chair moved, it was as if everyone was holding their breath. The two Asian men looked at each other and smiles formed on their faces. Ben reached for his coffee and drank down the last mouthful. He stood up, quietly stepping over the unconscious man, and walked up to the counter without the slouch he'd had when he'd arrived. He needed to get the hell out of there before anyone official arrived. With a little nod of acknowledgment to Mel the waitress, he handed over a ten dollar note, and said, 'He'll need an ambulance, luv. Thanks for the coffee.'

He then turned and left through the front door.

The two Asian men followed a moment later.

'Rebecca, there's been some sort of incident across the road at Rosie's café. Are you able to go over and see what it's about?' Jackson said from the police station switchboard desk.

'Sure, I'll head over now.'

Rebecca placed her police cap on, checked for her badge, gun and accessories and headed out across the road. The ambulance was already there loading a stretcher into the back, its blue and red flashing lights ablaze.

Rebecca entered the café and was greeted by Mel who she knew well from her coffee run each morning.

'What happened, Mel?' Rebecca asked as she surveyed the room. People were wanting to leave and she held up a hand to Mel, signalling she'd be a few minutes and asked the patrons for their contact details before they left.

'So Mel, what can you tell me?'

'Tom Simmons came in for coffee and demanded a homeless guy get out of his favourite seat and the homeless man flattened him,' Mel said.

'A homeless man did that to Tom Simmons?'

'Yes, he was fast, like a ninja, didn't even get out of his seat. Once Simmons was down, he casually drank the rest of his coffee, gave me a tip and left.'

'Wow, what did he look like?' Rebecca asked.

'Tall, ratty clothes, messy hair and beard but his eyes were focused and sharp. He was a bit different 'cos he was polite. Not your average homeless person you see around here.'

'Have you seen him in here before?'

'No, he's never been here that I've seen.'

Rebecca wrote down the details. Tall, polite, ninja like, not afraid of a thug. He sounds like a hero. Then a sense of warmth and familiarity came to her. She only knew one hero.

'Did he by any chance have light brown hair, almost red?'

'Yes, I guess so.'

Rebecca reached for her phone, flicked through it for a moment and showed Mel a picture of Ben.

'Could that be him?'

'Yes, that's him, I think. But this guy was much scruffier,' Mel said, seeing the mystery man in a completely new way.

'Did anyone follow him out? Perhaps suits?'

'I don't think so. Two Asian looking men in flowery shirts left soon after him, but they'd been here for a long while.'

'Asian, like Chinese?' Rebecca said, horror flooding through her.

Mel nodded.

Shit, that's not good. Rebecca drew in a breath to stay composed.

'Thanks Mel. Sounds like it might've been just what Tom needs. I'll catch you later if I need anything more.' Rebecca closed her notebook, turned and raced back to the station.

As soon as she got to her desk with no-one around, she took out her phone and messaged Greg.

Chinese could be close.

When Jackson finished the conversation on the phone about a missing dog, he turned and asked, 'Rebecca, what's the deal at Rosie's?'

'Someone gave Tom Simmons a hiding.'

'Whoa, who was it? He needs a medal.'

Rebecca didn't reply, just stood up and went to Sergeant Jones's office. She knocked on the door and he called her in. She entered and closed the door behind her.

'Sarge, I think the Chinese are onto Ben, we have to warn him.'

'What makes you think that?'

'He was in Rosie's across the street and the waitress said two Asian looking men followed him out.'

'Do I need to ask if that had anything to do with the disturbance over there?'

'No sir, best you don't.'

'Alright, let me see what I can find out about that Chinese Airbus that's parked at the airport.'

CHAPTER NINE

After the altercation with the thug at the coffee shop, Ben knew he had to get out of town. He headed quickly back to the shopping centre carpark and jumped into the 4Lux, turned the key and the engine spun over beautifully with the new battery. He cursed himself for the way he'd handled the problem at the café but no harm done other than he didn't get to see his girl. He was out of town in minutes and again on his way back north. A constant look in his mirror confirmed that no one was on his tail. He reached for a beer; they were still cold.

It isn't quite lunchtime yet but what the hell.

The bottle was finished in a matter of seconds and a sense of calm enveloped him. He thought back to the last few weeks that he'd shared with Rebecca, the drunken flirty-ness of their first meeting and of course their passionate lovemaking that same night. He pictured her asleep and naked, lying on her bed after that first time together, her red curly hair framing her beautiful face. He sighed as that memory sent heated blood bursting from his heart.

He hadn't checked his mirror for some time and his eyes sprung to the wobbly centre mirror. There was a car a long way back, white, maybe a small hatchback. He pulled into a rest area and left the rattly diesel running as he watched the car drive by. Two men in colourful shirts sat in the front—could be locals, hard to see through the tinted windows. He waited for them to be almost out of sight before he pulled back out onto the highway.

The rest of the trip went quickly, his mind constantly torn between finding a solution to his problem and Rebecca, his prize at the end. He soon turned toward the back of the farmhouse and had his groceries unloaded and another beer in hand. He cursed that he had only bought a six pack but his time in the supermarket had been limited, and anyway, he was starting to feel far too comfortable in the farmhouse. He left out one of the steaks that he'd bought, deciding that it would be his dinner tonight.

Greg called Rebecca as soon as he received the message.

'What can you tell me, Bec?'

'Apparently Ben was in the café across the road from the station and somehow got into an altercation with the town bully and reportedly was followed out by two Asian men.'

'Do you think they have anything to do with that Chinese plane at the airport?'

'The sarge is trying to find out why it's here but I'm guessing the Chinese want him as bad as the CIA. Greg I'm worried, I need to warn him.'

'It's a three-hour drive and let me tell you, no one will get near that farmhouse without him being all over it. Let's not worry about that now,' Greg said, hoping he sounded more confident than he felt.

'If they get him on that plane, he'll be gone forever,' Rebecca said with a panic in her voice.

'I have a plan. What type of aircraft are they in?'

'Airbus, the sarge said, a big one,' Rebecca said nervously.

'Two or four engines?'

'Two, I think.'

'Okay, leave it with me. Don't do anything till you hear back from me.'

'Alright, but please let me know what's happening.'

'I will,' Greg said, and hung up.

He immediately called Terry Schultz. Terry was an ex-military pilot who served with Ben, Steve and Dan in Afghanistan. Terry was short and thin with a friendly face and was now working as a pilot for a Singapore freight company called Singfreight. He did a thrice weekly flight to and from Australia to Changi airport. He'd first met Greg a few weeks ago when Ben had arranged for Terry to pick him up in Adelaide and drop him in Alice Springs at short notice.

'Hello,' Terry said, answering the phone.

'Terry, it's Greg Sheppard. I'm not sure if you remember me, Ben Woolford's friend, are you free to talk?'

'Hi Greg, of course I remember you. How is that troublemaker?'

'In trouble.'

'No surprise there. How can I help?'

'Long story for later but we suspect the Chinese could grab him and if they do, he'll be loaded onto their waiting plane as soon as tonight and flown to Beijing.'

'Mmm. Yeah, that does sound like trouble.'

'How can we stop that happening?' Greg asked.

'Well, you could fill the cockpit with bullet holes, that will delay them. What type of aircraft is it?'

'Airbus, big, two engines, is what I got from Bec.'

'Okay, so it's either a A330 or A350. I doubt they would be still using the A300 or A310. Can I call you back?'

'Sure,' Greg said, and Terry was gone.

Greg raced down to the airport. Having flown himself as a private pilot, he had no problem recognising in the dark that the Chinese plane was in fact a A330-300. That may help Terry when he called back. It was the same aircraft that Terry had flown when Greg got the lift with him from Adelaide.

Greg's phone rang, 'Terry.'

'Greg, I have a plan. It's pretty crazy, what help do you have there?'

'Steve and Dan are here.'

'Those bloody maniacs, I don't know how they're still alive! Greg, I will be there in two and a half hours, all of you meet me at the airport.'

'That's amazing, thank you Terry. By the way it's an A330-300.'

'Perfect, and Greg, bring some fire power.'

'Okay, you've got it, see you at twenty-two hundred,' Greg said, looking at his watch.

Greg's phone rang again—it was Rebecca.

'Do we have a plan?' she asked without waiting for Greg's greeting.

'Well, yes, we do. I actually don't know what it is, but it's arriving from Adelaide in two and a half hours.'

'What do you mean?'

'Terry Schultz, a pilot friend of Ben's, is on his way. I think he's going to disable the plane so they can't leave.'

'Really? Okay, I guess that's good.'

'I'll tell you more once he gets here. Remember the CIA are still all over you, so act normal.'

'Thanks Greg,' she said, still a little concerned.

Greg called Steve and then Dan who was now back in Alice. He told them all he knew and Terry's request for weapons.

Dan and Steve arrived early and they watched the Qantaslink Flight arrive from Adelaide.

Terry Schultz was starved of adventure nowadays so when a call came in from Ben Woolford or one of his fellow soldiers, he jumped to attention. Terry had flown one of only two Lockheed P3C Orion Maritime Patrol Aircraft that supported the ground troops like Ben, Steve and Dan during the middle east conflicts. After he left the RAAF, he'd secured a cushy job flying a freighter for a Singapore owned company that paid him well. The aircraft were retired passenger planes and overriding fault warnings were just a normal day at the office.

The best part was that none of the freight complained if he was running late or the ride too bumpy. It was a well-paid, boring job. So, when Greg called, he easily managed a swap of shifts and was in Alice Springs on the next flight out.

Terry smiled as the three men walked up to him at the terminal. He hugged Steve and Dan.

'It's been a while, fellas,' Terry said.

'A few years now, mate,' Steve said.

Terry shook Greg's hand and said, 'Fill me in.'

'Sure. Come with me.'

Greg turned Terry and guided him toward the exit. Once in the car, he explained everything from the AFP arresting Ben, the consequent rescue from the CIA and the latest news that the Chinese were in town and might've spotted him and followed him to his hideout.

Terry remained speechless as he listened. Once Greg finished, the three of them stared at Terry for his plan to disable the Chinese aircraft.

'We could kill two birds with one stone here, gentlemen,' Terry said with a smile. 'Greg, is it that A330 out there with the Chinese registration?'

'We believe so. Apparently, it's here for servicing but it hasn't moved.'

'Well, that's perfect because that's the same truck I drive for my deliveries.' Terry was bursting from his skin. 'Do you expect something could happen tonight?'

'Impossible to tell, but likely, they would want to grab him and get him out as fast as they can,' said Greg. 'How can you disable it?'

'Oh, I've got a much better plan than that!' Terry said.

Just then Greg's phone rang. It was Rebecca, calling from her desk at the police station.

'Greg, what's happening? I want to know, it's killing me. I need to warn Ben.'

'Bec, it's too far, too late and we apparently have an amazing plan, I just don't know what it is yet.'

'But the Chinese will get him tonight, I just know it. He can't secure that whole farmhouse with one rifle. We don't know how many of them there are, and once he's on that plane, there's nothing we can do.'

'Bec, I know you're concerned. Meet us at the airport viewing carpark as soon as you can, and we can run through Terry's plan.'

'On my way.'

Rebecca called out to Will Jackson, 'I'll be back in a while.'

She didn't see him pick up his phone.

The four men stood looking at the unmarked A330.

'See the nose wheel gents, there's a small hatch just in front of it that leads to the avionics compartment. It's pressurised and heated the same as the cabin, so if someone were hiding in there they wouldn't freeze to death.'

The three men looked on, confused, 'So?' asked Steve.

'There's also a hatch from the avionics bay into the cabin—pops up just behind the captain's seat.'

'Go on,' Greg said.

CHAPTER TEN

It was 8.45 a.m. Monday morning when Sam Taylor quietly walked into the NZSIS government building in the middle of the New Zealand capital, scanned his ID and fingerprints and headed to his office. The small space where he worked was as simple and unassuming in appearance as he was. The e-projection screen, with an AuthaGraph world map which filled one wall, was the only notable feature. Sam was thin, lean and not muscley at all. Barely five feet tall with dark hair and brown eyes. He wore the same style dark jeans and jumper every day. This thirty-two-year-old looked just like any other computer geek.

At 9.00 a.m., he sat down at his desk. With one click of his mouse, the multiple screens which filled his desk booted into action. He adjusted his dark-rimmed glasses before focussing on the first email of the day. A picture of his wife Tanya and his two children, Jack and Bethany, sat at the right of a computer screen and was the only personal item on display. Even then, his coffee mug obscured most of the picture. Nothing about Sam or his office reflected his skill or authority. He was a contractor to the New Zealand government, heading up their cyber security and intelligence services department. He was one of the best in the world, and a lot of other countries knew it. He would often travel, advising friendly countries of the latest ways to combat foreign interference, espionage and underworld terrorism. He was paid handsomely for his knowledge and the new Red GT3 turbo Porsche that sat in the underground carpark was proof of that.

He'd travelled around the world mostly to English speaking allies like Australia, UK, Canada and USA. However, this morning he'd received an email from the Serbian Special Anti-Terrorist Unit. It stated that they would like to have him present to a small team and were willing to pay all costs including the usual six figure sum that he now received easily for his services. A smile formed on his face as he quickly added in his head that his supplementary income would now exceed a million NZ dollars for the year, and it was only June. He emailed them back, asking if they had a date in mind. He knew it would be about 11.00 p.m. in central Europe, so he didn't expect an answer back till much later that day. Surprisingly, there was an instant reply.

We would like you here as soon as possible. There are flights via Dubai that can have you here in less than twenty-four hours.

He checked his diary, and seeing that he could make his next week free, he messaged Tanya. Like most people, he'd never been to Serbia and a few days either side of his meeting would be a chance to admire the many sightseeing locations around Belgrade.

He emailed back. *I can leave next Monday, back the following Friday please.*

It was only about thirty minutes later when a reply came back with a first-class flight booking, departing Wellington for Sydney, Dubai and then Belgrade. He would leave the New Zealand winter and be in the central Europe summer twenty-four hours later. He blocked the dates out in his e-calendar and left the office to get a fresh coffee, a sense of excitement buzzing through his body.

Ben had finished his fourth beer when he turned off the gas from cooking his Scotch Fillet steak. He let it rest as he mashed the two potatoes that he'd boiled. A couple of scoops of the coleslaw he bought off the shelf, a microwaved mushroom sauce and his dinner was ready.

I'll sleep well tonight. He savoured the meal, the best by far since he'd left the US. He imagined Rebecca there with him, appreciating his gourmet cooking and making eyes at him that suggested he would be rewarded as soon as they made it to the bedroom. Ben knew in that moment, he had to come up with a plan to sort this out. He couldn't keep living like this alone—as a fugitive.

He washed the meal down with his fifth beer and was feeling more relaxed than he had in a long time. Far more than he should. He needed to stay alert, despite this isolation. He reached for his rifle and went outside, careful not to stand where the kitchen light lit him up.

His listened to the silence. He heard a crack of a stick and he jumped, instinctively swinging his rifle off his shoulder and then heard the thumping of a kangaroo jumping away. The stars were immense and with no moon, millions of them filled the sky. He felt such a small part of the milky way that filled the southern sky. A lonely part, like a solo spaceman millions of miles away from any other person. A lost soul floating through space. He started to sing the Elton John song 'Rocket Man'.

When he reached the limit of his knowledge of the lyrics, he went back inside, placed the rifle against the wall and cleaned up the mess from dinner. He grabbed his rifle, turned off the kitchen light and went to the bedroom that he called his own. It had taken some time to erase the smell of the last owners, but he was feeling at home now.

As he turned on his bedside light, he wondered how long the electricity would stay on. *Who the hell is paying for it?*

He was only one page into his book when he reached over and turned out the light, well aware of how dangerous it would be to fall asleep with it on.

Ben didn't hear the back door open or the first squeak of the old jarrah floorboards, but he heard the second. He opened his eyes. It was still pitch black, he reached for the Tikka T3 that lay next to him. The next thing he saw was the red laser light on the middle of his hand as it touched the rifle's stock.

'Don't move, Mr Ben,' a man with a strong Asian accent said. 'I have night vision, I'm not here to hurt you but I will put a hole in the middle of your hand if you pick up that rifle.'

'Okay,' Ben said, lifting his hands up beside his head. 'What do you want?'

Ben knew full well how night vision googles worked—although he could hardly see an outline of the intruders, the room would be like daylight to them. He also knew if he could turn the light on, they'd be blinded for a few seconds. But then what? Bullets would start flying, all of them in his direction.

'We would like you to come with us. We want to protect you from the Americans.'

Well, that's nice to hear.

'Okay,' he said as he sat up further, with his hands still around his head.

The light came on, but both the Chinese had their googles on their foreheads. Ben quickly sized them up. They were military, probably MSS, the Chinese equivalent to the US Secret Service. He doubted that they wanted to kill him or that would've already happened; obviously they wanted something first. He pulled the blankets back and slowly reached for his pants.

'Mr Ben, please don't try anything stupid, we are instructed not to kill you, but I will fire to injure you if I have to.'

Ben knew that was true, that was why he had a red pistol laser sight aimed at his hand and not his head or chest, which gave Ben some comfort for the time being. He dressed, the red laser never leaving some part of his body. The second man produced a heavy cable tie and zipped both of his hands tight together behind him.

He looked back at his messed-up bed and his faithful rifle that lay on the bed next to him each night. He wondered if he would ever see it again.

The Chinese were gentle and courteous, quite a contrast to the rough treatment he received from the Americans.

Ben was guided into the back seat of the same white Corolla that he'd seen drive past him that afternoon. He scowled at himself for letting his guard down.

'What can you tell me? Where are we going?' Ben asked calmly as the car took off down the rocky road back to the highway.

'Mr Ben, you are like us, a past sergeant in your Australian armed forces. We couldn't tell you even if we did know. Our job was simple, collect you with minimal harm. If we wanted you dead, we would have left you to the Americans.'

Ben didn't answer. He wasn't going to learn any more from these two.

'By the way, Mr Ben, that was, how do you say — 'cool'? What you did at the coffee lounge.'

'Yeah, well it seems pretty stupid now,' he said, just loud enough for them to hear.

It was slow going, the Corolla didn't have the ground clearance for this road and Ben doubted that the driver had ever driven on a dirt road before in his life.

Somehow, the little Toyota made it to the highway without getting a puncture or ripping out the fuel tank on the sharp rocks.

They were only ten minutes down the highway when two black LandCruisers flew past them at well over the speed limit. Ben turned and saw the brake lights come on around where the road to the farmhouse was.

'Looks like we got you just in time, Mr Ben,' the MSS agent said.

Ben ignored the comment. How in the world had he ended up with the world's two biggest superpowers after him? He was just a retired SAS soldier, now private detective that wanted a normal life, make a few bucks and spending time with his girl. *Hell, will I ever see her again?*

As soon as they were in phone range, the passenger—who Ben was now sure was the only one of the two that could speak English—made a call. It was in Mandarin and more of a command than a request. Ben wasn't fluent, but what he did recognise was 'wheels up in twenty.'

Chuck Wilson sat in the passenger seat of the first LandCruiser as it powered along the dirt track that led to Ben's hideout.

'We're going in loud,' he said over the radio. He knew the element of surprise would be a luxury he didn't have time for. To find the homestead before Ben heard them coming would take time, lots of time that they didn't have.

The homestead came into view and the two black cars roared up to the back door. The four men jumped from the cars and stood either side of the door, waiting for shots to fly through the old timber. When all was still, Wilson pushed open the door, reaching inside and finding the light switch. He nodded to one of his men to enter, then the second.

Within twenty seconds, one of them shouted, 'Clear!'

'Shit! We missed him; he could be anywhere out there in the bush!'

'I doubt it, sir,' one man said. 'His rifle is still here on the bed.'

'The Chinese must have him. Shit, we need to stop that plane!' Wilson yelled.

CIA special agent Chuck Wilson reached for his sat phone, grabbed his note pad that had the details of the Chinese aircraft, and called a number he knew well.

'Target is going to be on a Chinese A330, Bravo, niner, niner, one, alfa, most likely enroute to Beijing from Alice Springs, in about one hour. It can't get to China, is that clear?'

'Yes sir, understood. Sir, we have six F35's at Tindal, a terrible accident could happen if that airliner happened to stray into our wargame airspace.' And the call was finished.

Wilson considered the consequences of what he'd asked. The collateral damage would be minimal—a couple of pilots, a couple of Chinese agents, a two hundred-and fifty-million-dollar aircraft and one problem pest sorted. A stray missile from a war game exercise would be sad and unfortunate news but it would crash in the middle of nowhere; there would be no casualties on the ground and only one Australian on board that no one even knew was on the plane—he would just be a pile of ashes. It would be forgotten soon enough.

He turned to the driver of the car. 'I need a drink, Rick.'

CHAPTER ELEVEN

Ben wasn't at all surprised when they drove straight through the town and out the other side to the airport. The white Corolla turned into an aircraft maintenance hangar and the two Chinese quickly alighted the vehicle. Ben turned his head from side to side, desperately trying to learn what he could. It was pretty clear to him that in about ten hours' time he was going to find himself in China with no passport or way to get home and *that* would be the best outcome of this situation.

The English-speaking MSS agent opened the door.

His only words were 'Quickly, come… come.'

Ben could tell the man's strength by how tightly he held onto his arm.

'Mr Ben, could you please hop into this freight container? It's just for the trip across the tarmac.'

Ben cooperated and the driver of the Corolla joined him, a gun in his hand. It was pitch black in the container and he felt it start to move and bump its way toward the waiting Airbus. Ben knew he could head butt this fella easily in the dark. *But what would that really achieve?*

The vehicle stopped and immediately the hatch opened. They'd parked aligned to a vehicle driven staircase, to which Ben was directed to climb the stairs. The man with the gun remained close behind. Ben reached the top step and felt like he was stepping into Airforce one. There were numerous first-class looking seats, a polished timber conference table and what must be a luxurious bedroom at the back.

Ben was directed to sit, and his non-English speaking friend sat next to him. The port engine started to spool up and then the starboard. The second MSS agent appeared through the doorway and the big door closed behind him. *How the hell can a foreign country just fly in, apprehend an Australian citizen, and take off—without anyone the wiser?*

The engine thrust increased and the big Airbus started to make its way toward the taxiway and the hold point of runway one two.

Mark Breeden was on for tower duty this morning at the Alice Springs Airport. He was a short, twenty-eight-year-old, with dark bushy hair. He had been married to Teri for two years and had a one-year-old daughter who'd already been awake at 5.30 a.m., when he left home to start his 6.00 a.m. shift. It was 5.55 a.m., when he'd sat at his console with his coffee. He could see the strobes flashing on the Chinese Airbus on the far side of the airfield. It was the only aircraft active at the airport.

Being a small airport, Mark would handle ground movements along with the approach and departure frequencies.

'Alice Spring tower this is bravo, niner, niner, one, alfa request taxi clearance for runway one two, in receipt of ATIS,' the pilot of the A330 said in a heavy Chinese accent.

'Bravo, niner, niner, one, alfa, we don't have a flight plan in the system for you as yet. What are your intentions?' Mark responded.

'Bravo, niner, niner, one, alfa, we will send a flight plan through once airborne. Plan is, track a heading of three, five, zero direct Alice Spring to Beijing, and climb to flight level three, six, zero, over.'

'Bravo, niner, niner, one, alfa, proceed to hold point runway one two and standby,' Mark said as he quickly read through the NOTAM's -notice to airmen- for the day.

'Bravo, niner, niner, one, alfa there is a NOTAM for your track due war games in the Darwin and Tindal areas. I can approve a heading of three, three zero then ATC will direct you from there, clear for take-off runway one two.'

'Bravo, niner, niner, one, alfa, heading three, three, zero,' the Chinese pilot replied.

Mark watched the A330 turn onto the runway and without stopping, apply full power and accelerate toward the east. With the sun almost up, the eastern sky was a gorgeous orange colour as the large bird climbed into the cool morning air.

Mark Breeden lived for these moments. He took another sip of coffee and his supervisor Jeremy Hall gently squeezed his shoulder as he walked past. It was his way of saying, 'Great job mate.'

Mark would monitor the Chinese airbus until it reached his 'top of climb' and then hand him over to Air traffic control in Brisbane who would monitor it until it left Australian airspace.

'Bravo, niner, niner, one, alfa turn now onto a heading of three, three, zero and climb to flight level three, six, zero,' Mark said in a casual voice.

'Bravo, niner, niner; Heading three, three, zero, flight level three, six, zero, over,' the Chinese captain replied.

Mark watched the Airbus turn onto the new heading and he sat back in his chair and took another sip of coffee with both hands wrapped around the mug. He watched the plane climb through ten thousand feet on his radar screen. It was almost daylight outside and he could see a student doing a pre-flight check on a Cessna 172 at the flight training school.

It was tight in the Avionics Bay of the A330-300 for the three stowaways.

Terry was between the nose wheel storage compartment and the side of the fuselage. He would be the last one to enter the cockpit. Steve and Dan were armed with G19X nine-millimetre Glock pistols. They knew that the chance of needing to discharge them was extremely low, but they would need to get the pilots' full attention. The engines were still at climb power and both pilots would be wearing headsets, so there was little chance of the pilots hearing them enter through the avionics bay access hatch that opened behind the captain's occupied seat. Steve would have his Glock pointed at the co-pilot long before the man saw him in his peripheral vision.

Terry gave Steve the nod and he turned and started to open the hatch to the cockpit. He opened it slowly and Steve checked to see that the cockpit door to the main cabin was closed. As expected, it was. The co-pilot was busy working on what looked like a flight plan as Steve climbed into the cockpit. He was completely inside before the first officer noticed. The co-pilot's head snapped around and he shouted something in Chinese. The captain turned to see the barrel of a nine-millimetre Glock pointed at him.

'Don't touch anything. Is the autopilot engaged?' Steve said, knowing all pilots around the world speak English. Dan had now climbed in as well and was standing behind the captain, his gun held on the first officer.

'Yes, the autopilot is on,' the captain replied slowly, desperately trying to consider options that he really didn't have.

'Okay, no one needs to get hurt, just do what we ask and everyone can get back to their families soon enough,' Steve said.

'What do you want?' the captain asked.

'Captain, we apologise for this, but you have taken something that doesn't belong to you and we would like it back, nothing more, nothing less. Please hop out of your seat.'

The captain looked confused. 'Why, what are you doing?'

Steve just tipped his head away from the seat and the captain understood.

He looked over to the first officer and said, 'your aircraft.'

'Yes captain, my aircraft,' he replied.

The captain stepped over the console and Dan secured his hands with a cable tie. The cockpit was tight but Terry had managed to climb in, secure the avionics bay hatch and climb into the captain's lefthand seat. Terry quickly assessed the cabin layout and instruments. The altimeter was climbing through twenty-five thousand feet and on a heading of three, three, zero.

'My aircraft,' he said to the first officer, who didn't answer back.

Steve looked through the cabin door peephole and could see Ben and only two MSS agents. Neither were holding weapons. He looked over at Dan and held up three fingers, then two, one and he flung open the cockpit cabin door as they burst into the main cabin holding a gun at each of the Chinese agents.

'Don't move gentlemen and we will all get to go home,' Steve called out.

Dan went straight to Ben, throwing him a quick wink as he reached into Ben's lap to undo his seatbelt. Ben stood and turned to let Dan cut his wrist restraints, his gun's aim not leaving the man's head.

'Don't hurt them boys, they were good to me,' Ben said.

Ben reached into the jacket of the man who had been sitting next to him, removed his weapon, then signalled for the man to stand. Ben quickly secured his wrists with a tie that Dan handed him.

Steve had done the same to the other man.

'Is there anyone else aboard?' Steve asked Ben.

'I don't think so, but let's check,' Ben said, making his way aft with the Chinese QSZ-92 semi-automatic pistol he had now borrowed from his captor. It was raised as he opened what appeared to be a door to a bedroom. He opened the door slowly; the lights were off and there didn't appear to be anyone there. He entered and with the same caution, checked the bathroom. 'Clear', he called out, loud enough for Steve and Dan to hear.

With the two MSS agents secured, Ben walked into the cockpit.

Ben smiled when he saw his old mate Terry Schultz sitting in the left-hand seat.

'Mr Schultz, I can't tell you how happy I am to see you.'

'Likewise, Mr Woolford.'

'I can't wait to hear how the hell you lot got on this plane but I've never been happier to see anyone in my life,' Ben said.

'Well, my friend, that's for later. I suggest you find yourself a comfy seat and please make sure everyone has their seatbelts on. We have a hell of a ride coming up.'

Mark Breeden had given the take-off clearance for the flying school Cessna and was nearly ready to hand over Bravo, niner, niner, one, alfa to Brisbane air traffic control. He decided to wait till they were at their cruise altitude and the flight plan had been lodged before making the call.

He cleared the training school Cessna to land and could see that the Chinese plane had levelled out at thirty-six thousand feet. It was now five hundred nautical miles from Alice Springs airport and on a heading that he believed would keep them clear of the Top end war games.

'Bravo, niner, niner, one, alpha contact Brisbane on 1-1-8 decimal 1-5.'

Mark listened for the reply and he said again, 'Bravo, niner, niner, one, alpha contact Brisbane on 1-1-8 decimal 1-5.'

Still no answer. He looked at his screen. The aircraft was passing through twenty-six thousand feet and dropping at nearly ten thousand feet per minute.

Mark called for his supervisor. 'Jeremy, I've got a problem with that Chinese A330.'

Jeremy came running over.

'Bravo, niner, niner, do you read?'

Still no reply.

'He may have a pressurization problem and is getting to ten thousand as is the standard procedure,' Jeremy said.

'At ten thousand feet per minute? It'll rip the wings off!' Mark replied.

They watched the plane descend through fifteen thousand, fourteen, thirteen, ten and continue plummeting to the ground.

'Bravo, niner, niner, do you read?' Mark called out a last time.

They both watched in horror as the plane passed through five thousand, four, three, two thousand and then disappeared from the screen.

'They've fucking crashed. Oh my God!' Mark screamed, turning away from his desk and ignoring the call from the Cessna trainee for a second take-off clearance.

'We don't know that Mark,' Jeremy said without any conviction.

Mark spun around after hearing the Cessna call again.

'Bravo, foxtrot, Oscar clear for take-off,' Mark said in a rushed voice.

Jeremy was on the phone to SAR—the 'Search and Rescue' team who would have a helicopter in the air in minutes.

CHAPTER TWELVE

Terry knew the Airbus A330 well. The big advantage of not having any passengers and only freight meant that he could play a little, try things that are outside the aircraft's rules and regulations, but safe enough to break up a bit of boredom on the seven-hour flight to Singapore three times a week.

Terry pushed the talk button for the cabin and said, 'Hang onto your lunches, fellas.'

He pulled the throttles back to idle and the first officer screamed, 'What are you doing?'

'Gear down,' Terry called to the first officer.

The first officer looked at him and reached over and lowered the undercarriage.

Terry watched the speed drop and then pushed the stick forward, turning the plane into a slow spiral dive. The airspeed indicator rose sharply, dangerously close to VNE, the red line that the aircraft was to never exceed.

'You will tear the plane apart—you crazy fool!' the first officer screamed.

'Relax, my friend, and just do what I say,' Terry replied in a calm voice.

The aircraft felt like it was free falling from the sky, the ground appearing closer and closer at an alarming rate. They'd passed through five thousand feet and were still descending at eight thousand feet a minute. Terry looked at the transponder and it was still squawking the assigned frequency. He started to raise the nose and with the engines still at idle, the speed dropped away quickly. He lifted the nose further and introduced some throttle.

'Kill the transponder,' Terry called and the first officer obliged.

The engines started to spool up and at one thousand feet he had the plane flying straight and level.

'Gear up,' Terry called, and the clunk of the undercarriage retracting confirmed it was all tucked away. Terry set a heading into the autopilot and wiped a bead of sweat from his brow. He looked over to his co-pilot who looked back at him, a look of shock on his face.

'I just killed us without killing us,' he said, before cancelling the continuous ground proximity warning that was blaring. He increased the power to seventy five percent, and they were travelling just above the desert at six hundred kilometres an hour. Terry pulled back the throttles slightly, lifted the nose and called for the gear to be lowered. At two thousand feet, the big wide-bodied Airbus overflew a well-maintained gravel runway. Terry checked the windsock which confirmed he would land in the direction he'd planned for.

'We can't land there,' the first officer called with panic in his voice. 'We are too heavy; we need to dump fuel.'

'Believe me, you'll be happier if we keep the fuel on board,' Terry said, banking the plane around onto a short final for landing.

'It's not long enough,' the first officer called again.

'We have no passengers and no freight, it'll stop on a dime, you watch,' Terry said to his very nervous first officer.

Terry touched it down as gentle as a leaf falling from a tree. He knew he was well over the maximum landing weight and the runway was short; he stood hard on the brakes to pull up the two hundred tonne aircraft. The main undercarriage was already braking hard well before the nosewheel had even touched down; the thrust reversers were now on full. The runway was all of a sudden looking a lot shorter than what Terry thought it would.

The antilock braking system was doing its best on the loose surface as dust filled the air behind the plane.

Terry looked down. They were still travelling at one hundred knots and the runway was fading fast in front of them, but they were going to make it. Terry shut off the thrust reversers and the aircraft came to an abrupt stop. A huge cloud of dust drifted past the cockpit windows. For the second time, Terry wiped a bead of sweat from his brow.

Terry reached for the tiller, turned it left, applied throttle to the right-hand engine and turned the aircraft almost in its own length. The aircraft taxied back down the gravel runway. Terry could see Greg and Rebecca outside the little one room departure lounge, two white LandCruisers parked side by side, one with a rickety set of stairs that appeared to be made from a six by four trailer.

Terry pulled the big A330-300 to a halt and shut down the engines. He suggested his co-pilot open the cockpit door and join the others. When Terry appeared in the main cabin, he received a soft clap from his Australian passengers. While none of the Chinese were particularly impressed, the captain did seem to have a look of disbelief and admiration.

Greg was reversing the portable stair trailer toward the aircraft when the large front cabin door opened. Rebecca guided him back and then climbed the stairs and entered the elaborate Chinese corporate jet.

Rebecca ran to Ben and hugged him tight.

'I've missed you so much,' she said, not wanting to let him go.

Greg stood just inside the plane and waited for what he thought was enough time for Ben and Rebecca to squeeze the crap out of each other.

'Ben, can I have a word?' he asked and nodded for Terry to join them.

'Of course.' He kissed Rebecca before stepping out onto the top of the rusty steps.

The four Chinese men waited nervously as their fate was decided by the three people who stood outside the aircraft on the staircase which swayed gently in the southerly breeze.

Steve and Dan could see the more senior of the MSS agents considering his options—how he may overpower the two gunmen, secure the aircraft, and fly back to Beijing a hero.

'Don't think about doing anything stupid,' Steve said to the agent. 'If it all goes to plan, we will all walk away with what we need. Do you understand, my friend?'

The agent nodded, but he was clearly not used to people making decisions for him.

Ben stepped back into the cabin and walked up to the senior MSS agent.

'I have a proposition for you, my friend. I want to thank you for treating me as courteously as you did, and I want to return the favour.'

The MSS agent bowed his head accepting the compliment.

'The runway here is six thousand feet long and with the fuel you have on board and the day getting hotter by the minute, you will need at least six and a half. So, I propose that you sit here till this evening and the cooler air will give you the lift you need to get off the ground with the fuel you need to get home.' Ben looked to the pilots who didn't appear to disagree. Terry handed Ben a map that he had taken from the captain's flight case. He looked at it and showed it to the handcuffed captain.

'I want you to fly a heading of two, nine, five degrees which will take you north of Broome and avoid you passing any towns or settlements. I want you to fly at no more than fifteen hundred feet and with the transponder off until you are well out of Australian airspace. Then, lodge a flight plan using a different registration number that will get you into Beijing.'

The agent looked at the two pilots for their opinion. The captain didn't have any questions, just nodded, accepting that it was possible.

'Why would we do that? Why would we not get into the air and declare that we were hijacked and have the authorities arrest you?' the MSS agent said.

'Because if you do what I ask and the CIA think we all died out here, especially me, I will give you footage of what happened at Pine Gap.'

'How can we trust you will do that?' the agent asked.

Ben looked around to everyone.

'The other option is that we kill you all now, burn the plane so it's almost unrecognisable and we drive off.'

The agent stared at him and then softened his expression before he spoke. 'I prefer the first option,' he said calmly.

'Do we have a deal?' Ben asked.

'Yes, we will do what you ask. I will trust that you will also do as promised.'

Ben reached into the waist band of his pants and removed his hidden Leatherman; he flicked out the three-inch blade and walked toward the agent. A look of shock appeared on the agent's face as Ben approached with the glinting stainless blade. Ben reached behind him and cut the restraints and then took a step back. The agent rubbed his wrists and Ben held out his hand to shake on the agreement. The agent stood giving Ben a slight bow before offering him his hand. They shook hands and Ben gave a small bow in return.

Ben turned to the captain.

'Captain, are you confident that you can take off as we have planned with all the fuel you have on board?'

'I will do the calculations, but yes, the cooler air will help us greatly.'

'Okay, thank you gentlemen, good luck on your flight home,' Greg said as he left the aircraft. Ben was the last to leave.

'How do we contact you, Mr Ben?' the agent called out.

'I'm sure you'll find a way,' Ben replied.

'Yes, we will.'

Greg started the LandCruiser and pulled the stairs away from the aircraft once his team had disembarked. He looked back to see the agent standing in the large open doorway, a mixture of disbelief and relief on his face. Greg disconnected the stairs from the rear of the LandCruiser and Ben, Rebecca and Terry joined him in the first car.

Ben and Rebecca were in the rear seat hugging each other when Ben said, 'What a brilliant plan, you two!'

'We're hoping it's enough to send the Americans home,' Greg said.

'It was simply perfect. So where were they hiding that they could just take over the plane?' Ben asked.

Greg went on to explain that Terry had come up with the plan. They'd had no idea whether the Chinese would be able to find him, but if they did, the guys figured they'd be moving quickly. He explained how Terry got them airside at the airport by shuffling his Singfreight security pass and then into the avionics bay. How they'd just waited till the aircraft was at 'top of climb', taken it over and then dropped it like a rock from the sky.

By flying out undetected, everyone, including the Americans would think the plane crashed. This would give them precious time to regroup. It could take many days for the Chinese to realise that the government plane that landed with an incorrect registration was in fact the missing plane that Australian search and rescue are looking for. Ben knew that the MSS would be back again soon to collect the footage and knew that the footage probably wouldn't tell them anything they didn't already know.

It was a masterful plan as long as the A330 could sneak out without anyone seeing it. Rebecca had told Greg and Steve about the old mine site runway that was used by the Russians to sell kidnapped girls to middle east people smugglers. Terry figured that if rogue pilots could easily land private jets there, he'd find a way to get the big Airbus on the ground, even if it meant mowing down a few bushes at the end of the runway. It was normal procedure for the over run of the runway to be cleared in case an aircraft did overshoot but luckily, he hadn't needed it.

CHAPTER THIRTEEN

Sam Taylor sat back in seat 1A as the B737 lifted off from Wellington airport. A sense of entitlement and satisfaction filled him as he sipped on the champagne he'd been offered just after he'd found his seat. In Sydney he did an international transfer and was soon relaxing in the Emirates A380 first class suite. First class had an on-board shower, spa and lounge bar should you need a change of scenery from the plush suite. He knew as long as he could keep ahead of the cyber bullies, this would be his way of life.

A swap of aircraft in Dubai had him enjoying the luxury of a Boeing 777-900 first class.

The B777 landed at the Nikola Tesla airport in Belgrade, using every inch of the three thousand five hundred metres of runway one two right. He was pretty sure it was the biggest plane that could land here.

Sam was almost the first off and met outside by a tall man in a black suit.

'My name is Goran,' the man said with no expression and in reasonable English. 'Please follow me.'

Goran took his case and Sam followed him in a different direction to the hundreds of other passengers who would soon be queuing for the immigration terminals. It was late in the night but Sam had slept soundly on the plane—it would now be morning back home in Wellington. The man opened a side door and an official behind a small counter asked him pleasantly for his passport. It was quickly scanned, stamped and handed back with a smile; no questions were asked.

'Welcome to Serbia, Mr Taylor,' the man said, and then immediately looked at Goran. Sam saw Goran nod to the man.

An automatic door opened to a long narrow walkway and next thing he was outside the terminal and looking at a black Mecedes S500. The back door was open and waiting for him. The driver closed the door behind him, then hopped into the driver's seat. Goran jumped into the passenger front seat.

Sam felt a slight uneasiness about how simple his entry into the country had been. In a western country there were strict rules and very little corruption, but these people appeared to be above the law, which concerned him somewhat.

The big Mercedes pulled in front of the Square Nine Hotel after only a short ride from the airport. It was a modern new building flanked either side by nineteenth century classic architecture. Goran opened the door for Sam, and the driver collected his case from the boot. The opulence of the hotel was obvious as the front door was opened by a uniformed doorman. The use of walnut was tastefully adorning one complete wall and scattered forms of lighting gave the entrance a warm feel of exclusiveness. Sam followed Goran to the reception desk and without a word, a credit card sized key was handed over to the tall Serbian and they headed to the lift. The deluxe junior suite was on the top floor of the five-story building and Sam was pleasantly surprised.

Goran handed the key card to Sam and without any expression said, 'I will pick you up in the morning at 9.00 a.m.' He then turned and closed the door behind him.

Sam looked at his watch that had automatically changed to the new time zone, noting it was just after midnight. He slid the curtain back and looking out, he could see the Danube River on the far side of a small park. He decided that when he was free, he'd take a stroll along the path he imagined must be there along the bank.

He wasn't the slightest bit tired as he'd slept for most of the Dubai – Belgrade leg of the trip. But he didn't want to be yawning when he met with his clients tomorrow.

His alarm went off at 7.30 a.m. and he showered and dressed for the day. He ordered breakfast, arranging for it to be delivered to his room.

At 9.00 a.m., Sam was in the lobby and ready with his laptop bag when Goran arrived. Again, the same black Mecedes pulled up in front of the hotel and Goran jumped out to greet him and open the rear door. The trip progressed in complete silence, neither Goran nor the driver spoke which suited Sam, he was content just to take in the sights of the city. The car pulled up in front of a large white sandstone building, much like the hundreds that fill the centre of Berlin. There was a large, pillared frontage with a dome on top and two wings that stretched out about a hundred and fifty metres on either side. Goran opened Sam's door, gesturing toward the entrance.

'This way please.'

Sam followed Goran into probably the biggest building he had ever been in. The foyer was almost entirely marble and stretched in every direction. They turned right, following a long, wide hall that was no less lavish than the entrance. Goran stopped at a door, opened it and they entered a room that consisted of a large polished timber boardroom table with probably thirty timber chairs with green velvet seats and backs. The bottom half of the walls displayed carved dark timber panels which had probably been there for hundreds of years. The plush carpet matched the green of the seats perfectly and was adorned with the Serbian emblem, evenly spaced out every metre or so.

The door opened and three men entered.

'Colonel Milovan Simovic,' Goran said as the first man held out his hand. This was the person Sam recalled he'd received the email from.

'Colonel, it's nice to meet you.'

The next two men were introduced as well, but Sam had no chance of remembering their names. They were obviously the cyber security people in this country but looked very young for their positions, certainly no more than mid-twenties.

'Thank you for coming, Mr Taylor,' the colonel said in a richly accented voice. 'The payment has already been transferred to your account.'

'Thank you, Colonel, Belgrade is such a lovely town,' Sam exaggerated. They both knew he'd seen very little of it.

'My men here are to learn from you and you keep them for as much time as you need.'

'Colonel, I will see what you already have and show you the latest cyber protection that the world has today.'

'Thank you. If I don't see you again before you leave, I hope your time in Serbia is a memorable experience for you.'

For the first time, Sam had to try to teach cyber law, ethical hacking and cyber defence to people who had little English. He also realised that these people were so far behind the rest of world; a whole new system really needed to be implemented.

By the end of the second day, he felt he'd given the two Serbian cybersecurity men all he could. He uploaded a program for them to use as well as providing detailed instructions on their procedures from here on.

He left the two men tapping away on their computers as he packed up and headed for the exit. He hadn't seen Goran again since the meeting with the colonel.

The same driver was waiting for him and took him back to the Square Nine hotel. He found it strange that the colonel didn't want to discuss his opinion of where his country was at in regards to the security or whether more needed to be done. That didn't matter, he figured, he had done what he came to do, and what he was paid for.

The black Mecedes dropped him back at his hotel and he thanked the driver as he alighted the vehicle. On entering his room, he simply fell onto the bed. He lay there exhausted, exhaling the intensity of the past two days. After a few minutes, he sat up. Now he needed a drink. He rose and grabbed a beer from the well-stocked minibar.

Kicking off his shoes, he checked his watch, then decided to have a shower. It would be another three hours before Tanya would be awake so he could tell her about his trip and how the job had gone.

He showered and dressed casually in jeans, t-shirt and white Nike runners. He went upstairs to the rooftop bar and asked the Maitre'd for a table. He ordered a Burek, a traditional Serbian pie made with thin flaky pastry and very spicy mince. It was served with sliced boiled potatoes and tasted far better than he expected.

He couldn't help but notice a young woman arrive. She was seated just slightly to his left. She was probably in her late twenties, with long dark brown wavy hair and was absolutely gorgeous. Her nose was petite, her lips thin, but her mouth was wide. Her brown eyes were narrow, with long dark lashes. In all, she was very seductive. She wore a black dress, thin straps over each shoulder and a gathered neckline that was appropriate for the summer night without being too casual.

She'd ordered and was sitting quietly, waiting for her meal. With her seated facing Sam, it made it near impossible not to catch each other's eye each time they looked up. Eventually after the many glances at each other, she smiled back at him.

Sam finished the pie, drank down the last mouthful of an elegant French Syrah and headed for the downstairs bar. The woman looked up as he walked past and smiled at him again. He smiled back before checking his watch to see if Tanya would be awake yet. *Probably another hour.*

The bar was much like most of the Serbia he'd seen, with a heavy use of timber. The bar itself looked as if it had been made from one huge piece of walnut. It was stunning, with the back wall filled with every type of alcohol imaginable. He grabbed a seat, ordered a bourbon on the rocks before taking out his phone to search 'must see' places in Belgrade. He first smelt the waft of her sweet fragrance and turned to see the lady in black from the rooftop taking the seat next to him. She glanced at him, threw him another smile before turning to the waiter to order a cocktail. The bartender served her drink, a clear liquid that was probably vodka with an olive and piece of lime hooked on the rim of the glass. He watched her take a sip and as if she knew he was watching her, she turned, held out her hand and said, 'My name is Milena.'

'Sam,' he said. 'Pleased to meet you.' The two glasses of the French Syrah ironing out any nervousness.

'Where are you from Mr Sam?'

'New Zealand. I'm here for work.'

Milena had now turned to face him, and with her this close, she was even more beautiful than he had first thought. She drank the second half of her drink down in one mouthful, placing the glass back on the bar.

'Can I buy you a drink Mr Sam?' Her smile was a cross between cheeky and sweet innocence.

'Okay, thank you,' he said, and finished the rest of the bourbon in one gulp.

Milena again had finished her drink before Sam was halfway through his and ordered two more drinks. Milena moved her chair closer and with the effects of what he assumed was vodka or gin, began touching his arm each time she spoke.

Sam had lost count of time or the drinks when Milena said she needed to use the bathroom. She stood, slightly losing her balance and fell into his arms. Her delicious, sweet-smelling hair filled his senses as her lips kissed his neck. She moved back slowly. 'Sorry, but mmm, you taste so nice.'

Sam was enveloped by the awe of this woman, her touch, her smell and her beauty. She was totally overwhelming. Milena walked off wobbling slightly as she made her way through the bathroom door.

'Whoa,' he said as he rose from the bar stool, suddenly feeling very lightheaded and wondering how many drinks he'd actually consumed. He decided he would leave the remaining one, and head back to his room, as soon as Milena returned and he could say goodnight.

He felt her hand on his back and her lips near his ear.

'Mr Sam, could you please walk me to my room, I think I have too much drink?'

'Of course,' he said, giving him the excuse to leave as well.

Milena put her head on his shoulder and her arm around him, as the two of them disappeared into the elevator.

'What floor are you on Milena?' Sam asked, his words slurring.

'Five… room is five, oh, three,' she said, and kissed his cheek.

Her lips were soft on his skin and he closed his eyes as he took in her consuming touch.

The elevator door opened and they staggered toward her suite which happened to be only two doors down from his. They reached her door and she fumbled the keycard and dropped it.

Sam reached down, collected up the card and swiped the lock. He pushed down on the handle and Milena fell into the dark room, dragging him with her. The door closed abruptly and the room became completely dark. Sam felt Milena's arms wrap around his neck and her perfume and feminine scent totally overwhelmed him. He felt her lips touch his and although he didn't encourage it, he didn't resist. Her lips were delicious, her hands ran through his hair and although it was dark, he closed his eyes. He felt his resolve fail and he let this gorgeous creature devour him.

Inhibitions were discarded along with their clothes when Milena lay back on her bed and switched the soft bed side light on. He could see her now, naked with her dark wavy locks spilling across her pillow. She held out her hand for him to join her, and he did—he was a long way past the point of no return. He fell between her spread legs and found her easily. It was the beginning of a moment he would never forget.

Sam was riding the wave of indescribable pleasure when the door burst open and three men walked in. The main lights came on and Sam detached himself from the woman. He spun around to see who the hell the intruders were. A man in a suit and two uniformed police officers stood at the foot of the bed looking down at the naked pair.

'Get dressed, my dear,' the suited man said to Milena.

Milena jumped up off the bed, now apparently not under any influence of alcohol at all. She pulled her dress over her head quickly, her knickers, bra and strappy black shoes in her hand.

Sam watched her walk past the three police officers and leave the room without looking back at him.

'Please dress,' the suited Serbian said to Sam.

'What the hell's going on here?' Sam demanded.

Sam's head was spinning. He fumbled finding his clothes that Milena had almost torn from him. They were scattered all around the floor.

'Mr Taylor, you do realise that soliciting a prostitute is illegal in Serbia?'

'No, no, she isn't a prostitute!'

'Mr Taylor, she is well known to us.'

'I didn't pay her any money. What's going on here?'

The man pulled out an iPad, tapped the screen and turned it to Sam.

Sam could see himself with Milena below him, his pale arse rising and falling between her legs. He looked over at the wall to see the pinhole camera that had taken the footage.

'You've set me up!' he yelled, still fumbling to dress.

'Mr Taylor sir, this a very unfortunate position you have found yourself in. The penalty for such an offense is sixty days in prison, and there is no negotiation.'

'But I paid no money, she was just a girl at the bar.'

The man sat down on the bed next to Sam and signalled for the two uniformed officers to leave.

'Mr Taylor, what will Tanya think if she sees this?' he said, holding up the iPad, the picture of him frozen on top of the beautiful dark-haired woman.

His eyes shot up at the man. 'No, you can't do that, and how do you know her name?' he demanded.

'Well, Mr Taylor, if I could make this unfortunate incident just… go away, what would you be prepared to do?'

'Anything! How much do you want? I have plenty of money, name your price.'

The man smiled and calmly said, 'What we would like won't cost you any money at all, just some of your time.'

'Okay, you name it, I'll do it, and then that will be erased?' he said, pointing to the iPad.

'Yes, you do us one favour, and this never happened,' the man said, standing. 'We will be in touch Mr Taylor, please enjoy the rest of your time in Belgrade.'

The man turned and walked out the door, Sam watched as the door closed behind the detective.

He collected the remainder of his clothing and headed back to his own room. He knew he'd been set up, but they had something on him that he needed gone. He couldn't imagine what they would possibly want but whatever it was, he would do it.

CHAPTER FOURTEEN

The track from the old mining airfield was about three hours further along the same road as the old Russian hideout where Ben had been residing.

It was early afternoon when the old homestead came into view and as they approached Ben called out, 'Stop!'

Greg hit the brakes hard, suspecting Ben had seen something that may have them driving into an ambush. The car skidded to a stop and a large cloud of dust swallowed the car. Steve and Dan pulled up behind them and with guns in hand, hopped out stealthily from the second LandCruiser.

'Stay here and keep the engine running, Greg.'

Ben jumped out of the first car and followed the dust cloud toward the homestead, his eyes scanning from side to side. Steve and Dan were now by his side.

'What did you see, mate?' Dan asked.

'When the Chinese agents took me, we passed two black cruisers coming this way, so let's make sure we aren't walking into a trap. They may well be expecting me to return here.'

Ben stopped and looked at the tyre tracks that were outside the back door of the farmhouse.

'It looks like they were here alright, these heavy tracks were here after the Corolla.'

'Looks like they turned around and headed back,' Dan said.

'Yeah,' said Ben, 'four footprints got out and four back in, so we can assume they didn't leave anyone here, but let's make sure they didn't leave any surprises for us.'

The three of them checked for boobie traps and it appeared to be clear. Ben was relieved and surprised to see his rifle right where he'd left it on the bed. He reached for it carefully, assuming that they would figure he would go for it first. It was clear.

It was time to think. *Where to from here?*

Ben called everyone over and the six of them sat around the little wooden kitchen table that Ben had dined solo at for the last two weeks.

'Firstly,' Ben said. 'It sure is nice to have visitors.'

Everyone laughed except Rebecca. She was almost in tears, so full of mixed emotions, she couldn't believe Ben could see the funny side of such an unbelievable ordeal.

Ben's smile faded as he said, 'Gentlemen and gorgeous lady, thank you so much for the amazing efforts these last couple of weeks.'

Everyone nodded acknowledgement and Rebecca hugged him.

'So, from here, let's see what we know, what we suspect, and what we plan to do.'

'I think we can assume the Chinese will play ball. It will be all over the news whether the plane is found or not, so we will know where we stand there.'

'We can assume that the CIA think I was on that plane and that it crashed, taking me with it,' Ben said. 'It may be best if I lay low here for a couple more days and see if the CIA goes home. Who knows, they might already be on their way.'

'I don't know Ben, they now know about this place,' Greg said.

'It might be safer to hide out in Alice,' Steve suggested.

'If you stay here, I'll stay with you,' Rebecca said.

'No Bec, you need to get back to work and act normally till it's clear,' Ben said firmly.

'I'm not leaving you again. They'll think you are dead, we should be safe here,' Rebecca said.

Ben considered this and remembered the many times he stood out in the warm desert breeze staring at the millions of stars and wished she was there with him. He looked around at the four other men and there didn't appear to be any significant opposition to the idea.

'Alright, we can consider that option,' he said with a grin. Her smile back told him that there was no considering to be done.

'Okay, moving on,' Ben said, looking slowly away from Rebecca. He was selfishly looking forward to the time with her.

'Bec and I will stay here, we'll keep one of the LandCruisers. It'll be getting dark soon, so you four head back to Alice and return the other cruisers to the hire company. Greg, maybe contact Jones and tell him Bec and I are safe and hiding out until the coast is clear. Find out what you can about the Americans and let's get that SD card from Peter,' Ben said.

'Ben,' Rebecca said softly. 'I need to tell you something.'

Ben turned to her, her lowered tone concerning him.

'The CIA beat Peter up pretty bad searching for that memory card.'

'The pricks. Is he okay?' Ben asked.

'He was in hospital for nearly a week, but he seems to be on the mend.'

'That's shit, this has nothing to do with him,' Ben said.

'Did he give up the card?' Greg asked.

'No, I don't think so,' Rebecca said, feeling guilty about not telling Ben sooner.

'I already know why you didn't tell me, so I'm not going to ask that question,' Ben said.

Steve, Greg, Dan and Terry all hopped into one of the LandCruisers and headed back to Alice Springs. Rebecca and Ben watched them leave; standing together with his arm around her, they waved like two parents watching their kids drive off.

The sun was setting in the west and lit the back of the car as it drove off with a golden glow. They both stood there until the car was out of sight and a familiar warmth came over Ben. He knew that not only was he about to spend some precious time with the love of his life, but tonight, he wouldn't just be sleeping with his rifle. He turned to her and kissed her, softly at first as he took in the heavenly moment. It wasn't long before it became uncontrolled. He picked her up and carried her to his bedroom. They made love like never before—passionate, fervent and somewhat aggressive, just what they both needed.

Ben lay back, his hands behind his head, a feeling of complete satisfaction filling him.

'You shouldn't have stayed, but I'm really glad you did,' Ben said, smiling at his exhausted lover.

'You would've needed to shoot me to stop me, mister!'

'Well, I didn't have my rifle, did I?'

They both smiled and Ben hopped out of bed and headed for the kitchen, still naked. Rebecca appeared soon after, only wearing a t-shirt. He looked at her and smiled. He knew he would be tasting her beautiful flesh again before morning.

Chuck Wilson and the three CIA agents sat with their bags packed, waiting for the call they needed.

His phone rang. He listened for ten seconds and hung up without saying a word.

'Confirmed, the Chinese plane disappeared from radar about five hundred miles north of here, our job is done, guys,' Wilson said, standing. 'There's a C-17 waiting for us at Tindal that will get us stateside. We were never here.'

The four men collected their bags and headed for the black LandCruiser. Their bags not only included clothes but weapons and body armour. They would sneak through the U.S. military hangar at Tindal airport and onto a huge C-17 Globemaster. All their equipment had come from the States with them and would return the same way, no passports needed. They were just part of the war games.

Wilson sat in the front passenger seat of the big black Toyota as it headed north in the dark of the early evening from Alice Springs. He didn't say much. The job was messy, no body to account for and although the plane had crashed, he really didn't know that Woolford was even on it. It was all just too easy; he didn't like it. He hoped by the time they reached Tindal, SAR would have found the wreckage and photos would be all over the news.

Next morning, Greg walked into the Alice Springs police station to let Rebecca's sergeant know that she wouldn't be back at work for another couple of days. As he walked through the front door at 8.30 a.m., he saw Jones leaning over the desk of a young constable. They both looked up as he walked in.

'Hi Greg,' Sergeant Jones said.

'Good morning, Sergeant.'

'Bec wanted me to tell you that she is going to have the next two days off.'

'Is she okay?' Jones asked, now standing fully upright.

'Yes, perfect, staying with a friend out of town.'

'I see, well she actually does have a job, so I hope she's back soon.'

'I'm sure she will be and hopefully much happier than before,' Greg suggested.

Jackson's eyes were burning into the side of Greg's face.

'I've heard that the Chinese plane has disappeared,' Jones said suspiciously.

'I'm sure it will turn up, Sergeant,' Greg said with a smile.

'I hope it does, young man,' Jones offered back. 'There's a lot of people looking for it, costing a lot of taxpayers' money.'

'Probably looking in the wrong place, but how would I know?' Greg said, looking at the constable sitting at the desk, now realising he may have just said too much in front of him. The intent expression on the young man's face concerned him.

'Okay, I'll see you later,' Greg offered, turning toward the door, trying to shake his unease.

The black LandCruiser pulled into the BP service station at Tennant Creek. It was daylight now. Wilson's phone beeped with a message, then another. He was assuming it was confirmation of the ride back home on the Globemaster.

He opened the message app—an unknown number, not unusual. He tapped on it.

Lightning did not fire on target.

'What the fuck!' Wilson said.

'What's up, boss?' the driver said, the two agents in the back just waking up.

'Message says that the F35 never shot down that plane.'

'Well, where did it go?' said a voice from the back seat.

'Fucked if I know… Turn the car around!' Wilson yelled.

He opened the second message.

Woolford must be at Russian Farmhouse.

Wilson dropped the phone onto his lap and rubbed his face with both his hands. 'I fucking knew it was too easy. How the fuck do these hick town cowboys keep outsmarting us? They are making us look like fools.'

Wilson pounded the dash with his fist. Everyone was now fully awake.

The car had been refuelled and with a squeal of tyres, it left the fuel station. It was now on its way back the way it came.

CHAPTER FIFTEEN

Ben woke softly, his eyes still closed. His left arm and shoulder were covered in golden red curly locks. He didn't need to see them. He could feel his girl's face on his bicep. It didn't matter where he was, a two thousand dollar a night beachside apartment or some deserted farmhouse in the middle of 'Shitsville', as long as this lady was by his side, he was at home. That's just how he felt now.

Her naked body was pressed against him and his love for her had now hit a new high. He opened his eyes to look at her and she stirred. Her left arm that was across his chest pulled tight and he put his hand on hers. He turned slightly and kissed her forehead. She looked up at him and smiled, her head still laying on his left arm. He brushed her hair back from her face and caressed her cheek with his right. He looked into her deep blue eyes, and he knew he could never love her more.

He made her a simple breakfast of scrambled eggs with whatever he could find thrown in. Today he would show her around the farm, especially the picturesque surrounds, although he knew she'd want to see the cells that the Russians had used to hold her and the other women just a few weeks ago. He was surprised at how analytical she was about revisiting the stone rooms, more grateful that they'd found the place and saved lives.

He showed her the 4Lux that he'd built up to get into town and even though they had a brand new LandCruiser hire car, he took her for a ride in the 'spare parts special'. It was a pretty rough piece of gear, with no back window, all different sized tyres on different coloured rims and an exhaust that finished somewhere halfway along the car. They headed out for a short way on the same road that led out to the airfield where Terry had landed the A330.

Ben showed her a small mine site he had found during his two weeks there. They walked around the area picking through old bottles and rusty cans from many years ago. Ben had his rifle over his shoulder when out of the vehicle, and always within reach when in the car. He was careful not to let Rebecca distract him too much from keeping his guard up, but he was feeling pretty safe now.

It had been a lovely warm winters day and the two of them bathed in each other's company. Ben had put together plans for a nice dinner; it would probably be their last night there as he knew she had to get back to work. He cooked up some chicken sausages that he had grabbed on his quick trip into town and mashed some potatoes. Some boiled frozen peas and corn and the meal was served. They'd missed lunch, so this early dinner added to the enjoyment of Ben's rustic, yet tasty food.

'I wish we had a bottle of wine to have with the meal and then we could finish it off on the verandah. I want to show you just how beautiful it is out here at night,' Ben said.

'We'll have plenty of time for that,' she said as she pictured them on a balcony overlooking the ocean somewhere.

They cleaned up the dishes and went outside and sat on the two rickety chairs that had spent many years in the desert weather. The floorboards of the verandah had shrunk, the gaps twice the size of their original fitment. The ends were splintered and there was only enough paint to see what colour it used to be, clearly still the original boards from when the farmhouse was built. There wasn't any moon yet and it was pitch black—they felt a part of the millions of stars that saturated their vision. The verandah faced south and from where they sat, they could see the southern cross in the milky way. Ben leant forward to take a sip of his cup of tea, when a pane of glass in the kitchen window behind him exploded. It was followed a millisecond later by the sound of a gunshot, then another two.

'Get down!' Ben yelled as he dived over the edge of the raised verandah, pulling Rebecca's chair backwards with him. Ben ducked down behind the timbers trying to help Rebecca from her up-turned chair. Rebecca was still in a perfect seating position but on her back, her legs had fallen under the base locking her in and preventing him from dragging her free.

'Bec, get down here!' he yelled.

Two more shots fired and he ducked as he scrambled to help her get to cover.

Then he realized—even before he looked again. He stopped, moved closer, and saw an entry hole above her left eye.

Her eyes were open; he knew she was dead. No praying, hoping or medical assistance could help her. He'd seen it before—the bullet had gone through her skull and was imbedded in her brain. There was no surviving that. He'd witnessed people die in front of him before, roadside IED's that blew his mates and close friend to pieces, but this wasn't his mate, she was his girl, his lover, the woman he wanted to spend the rest of his life with. He wanted to scream and run carelessly toward them firing wildly, but he knew that would just get him killed too. When the next round of bullets ricocheted off the side of the building next to him, he knew he had to leave her. He grabbed his rifle and ran along the side of the house and up the hill to where he had built the roll start runway for the 4Lux. If they had night vision goggles, they would see where he went but if not, the darkness was his friend. Tears filled his eyes and anger his heart.

He only had nine shells in the T3 and he had to assume that there were four of them. He couldn't afford to waste a shot because getting back into the house to reload was an unlikely option. He hid behind a downed tree trunk that overlooked the house from a raised position. He would just have to wait till they made a move.

This time he would be shooting to kill.

Waiting was something he had done a lot. He had been the designated marksman of his platoon, so he'd sit for hours until someone showed themselves, and then take them out. Those were his orders. But he'd never done it with the hurt and anger that burned through him at this moment. This was a personal mission and these men would pay with their lives.

He had to focus, but it was hard, at times tears blurred his vision. All around fell completely silent as if each were waiting for the other. It seemed they had no idea where he went. He figured they only had pistols or he'd already be dead. He would have preferred that, his life for hers but that choice had been made for him.

He knew where they must be, so he kept his scope on that area. He saw a movement. He clicked two notches on his scope. As he saw a figure run toward the house, he fired, and the man went down. He didn't move again, likely a chest shot. He pulled the bolt back slowly and the empty cartridge ejected and landed beside him. The next bullet sprung into the breach, and he actioned the bolt for the next shot. That man wasn't wearing NV goggles, so he hoped that was the case for the rest of them.

A volley of shots fired in his direction but none were close. Ben knew the moon would rise soon in the east and that would change the circumstance. He knew the area around the house well and he had now changed from the hunted to the hunter. He climbed the remainder of the hill and headed east along the lee side of the ridge. Another round of shots was fired at where he had been. It gave him an idea of their location.

Still fighting back the grief of his loss, he forced himself to stay focused. These four men were going to die tonight. He thought he saw movement, but he couldn't waste a shot. It had to be clear. He put the rifle barrel into the fork of a tree and his cheek to the rifle butt. He focused the scope to a closer distance and there they were, three of them as he suspected. Handguns only, no rifles. He couldn't shoot all three. He knew the two survivors would head for their vehicle as soon as the next one went down. He'd have to plan for that.

He lined up for a headshot on the closest man and squeezed the trigger. The man went down, collapsing like a rag doll. The two others spun around, realising that Ben had come around behind them. There was panic between them. Ben reloaded and the two men disappeared from sight. He swung the rifle over his shoulder and headed further east toward where their vehicle must be. It must've been parked a long way out and they'd walked in.

He reached the track and crossed it; they wouldn't expect that. The full moon had just appeared, and the desert would soon be lit almost like daylight. This would work to Ben's advantage.

He set up behind a rock that sat just one metre in on the southern side of the track. His scope focused on the distant spot where he figured he would see them first. He was now between them and their exit. Two men dressed in black came running fast down the road hugging the northern side as tight as they could.

Ben lined up one man in the crosshairs and let a round go. He immediately reloaded and was back on the scope. The first man went down, squirming and crying in pain. The other had dived into the bush.

'Come on, show your face, you arsehole,' Ben whispered.

The lighter it became the more advantage he had.

Nearly an hour had passed since the first shot that killed Rebecca, and the man on the road had stopped moaning and was now lying still. *Just one to go.*

He heard footsteps slowly crunching the undergrowth about fifty metres in on the other side of the track. Ben spun and turned the rifle in that direction. He could hear the steps louder and faster now—his target was running. Ben jumped up and ran along the track. He would be much faster not having to run through the bush.

A shot was fired from the last agent, the flash giving Ben an exact location. He stopped running, raised the rifle and waited for the next round from the agent. Ben saw the flash and a bullet hit a branch just to his right. Ben fired at the flash and again quickly reloaded. Another two shots from the agent were closer this time—the agent must be able to see him. He knelt down on one knee and watched. He heard the crack of a stick and closed his eyes. Another branch broke and he turned the rifle to the noise. His eyes were now perfect for the dark. He opened them and saw a movement and fired. The 303 projectile would have little deflection in the light outback bush and at only about forty metres it would cause catastrophic damage to someone, wherever it hit them. Ben heard him fall, a thud in the undergrowth. There was no crying in pain—it must have been a kill shot.

He listened for a few more seconds and then walked toward the agent. The man was face down, an exit wound in the middle of his back. Ben turned and headed down the path back to the homestead. He passed the dead man on the path and pushed him onto his back with his foot. A sat phone fell from his hand and he kicked it, hard. It flew off into the bush. He was probably in his thirties, dressed in a black jacket but no body armour. They were obviously expecting a quick easy hit.

It was now time for grief, the anger had gone and by the time he reached the farmhouse and could see his girl still unceremoniously sitting in the upturned chair with her feet pointing to the sky, the tears flowed. He'd never cried before, not like this. He laid his rifle down and lifted her lifeless body into his arms. There was almost no blood, she was still in perfect condition, with just a small hole in her forehead. He pulled her tight to his chest and his tears streamed into the beautiful red curls that he would never again wake up next to.

He sat there holding her until daylight. By then, he had no more tears left to shed.

He'd never felt so alone, but he was a soldier, and he would fight on. He placed her gently on the verandah and went inside to collect one of the motel blankets that he'd taken from Greg's room. He wrapped Rebecca in it and placed her on the back seat of the white LandCruiser. He collected his rifle and personal stuff. He wouldn't be coming back here.

The CIA's black Toyota was parked nearly a kilometre down the track, He didn't stop to check it out, he knew who they were and for now, they were no longer a threat. The drive was long and the sun had risen well in the eastern sky. Strangely enough, he still felt comforted by the fact that his girl was with him, but that comfort was shallow. He turned onto the highway and let the V8 diesel have its legs. He was in no rush but somehow the faster he went the less pain he felt. At one hundred and sixty kilometres an hour he was soon driving into Alice Springs.

With Rebecca wrapped in the blanket on the back seat, he pulled up in front of the police station. He locked the car and walked inside. Will Jackson froze, staring at him in disbelief. There was no one else around.

'Can I speak to the sergeant, please?' he said to Jackson, whose eyes never left him.

Jackson picked up the phone and after pushing just one button said, 'Woolford is here to see you, sir.'

Almost immediately, Jones appeared.

'Ben,' he said, wondering why he was here.

'Sergeant, Bec and I were attacked last night by four American agents.'

'And Reed, is she okay?' he said slowly.

'They killed her.' Ben's voice broke as he said it.

Jackson's head fell onto his desk, his hands either side of his head as if blocking his ears.

'I see,' Jones said, only just keeping it together. There was a pause as Jones closed his eyes and his head dropped to his chest. Jones finally looked up and said, 'I'll have them hunted down; I promise you.'

'No need, they're all dead.'

Jackson looked up in shock.

'Sir, someone must have told them we were there, and when I find out who it was, I'll kill 'em too,' Ben said.

That sort of talk to a police sergeant would normally have an individual thrown in jail, but not today.

Ben noticed the look on Jackson's face and he stared at him.

'Where is she now?' Jones asked.

'In the car outside, sir.'

Jones nodded in the direction of the door and Ben turned, leading Jones to the car. Ben opened the rear door and looked at Jones as the sergeant looked at the blanket that covered his beloved constable. He reached in and lifted the blanket from her face. Ben had closed her eyes and she looked so peaceful. Jones looked at her for longer than he needed, but eventually covered her face again gently with the blanket.

Jones took in a deep breath and said, 'She will need to go to the morgue at the hospital, Ben, I will call ahead. Jackson will meet you there. I then want you to come back and tell me what the fuck happened, including what you know about a missing Chinese aeroplane.'

'Yes, sir,' Ben said. He closed the rear door and opened the front. The hospital was only a few hundred metres away and Ben beat Jackson there. He waited the few minutes for Jackson to arrive and watched him walk inside to arrange for Constable Rebecca Reed to be transferred to the hospital's morgue. A heat was building inside him that he wasn't sure he was going to be able to control. Someone had told the Americans he was there and there weren't many people who knew. A nurse approached and asked if he could drive around to the loading bay at the rear of the hospital's main building. He started the car and did as she asked.

The ramp led to a roller door that was below ground level and he reversed up to it as the door started to open. He stopped with the car still on a steep angle. He jumped out and opened the rear door. He reached in and lifted Rebecca's body easily in his arms. Jackson had arrived and was walking slowly down the ramp, a look of shock and despair on his face.

Ben laid the lifeless body on the gurney and placed his right hand on her chest. This is not how he wanted to say goodbye to the woman he loved but just in that moment, nothing seemed right. He placed his other hand at the side of her face through the blanket and held it there for a second or two. He took a breath and turned away. His closed the rear door of the car and looked at Jackson who had stopped halfway down the ramp. Jackson broke eye contact and looked away.

Ben called Greg.

'Greg where are you?'

'Hi mate. I didn't expect you in town so soon. We're at the Gap Hotel waiting to drop Terry at the airport.'

'I'm on my way,' Ben said.

Ten minutes later, Ben walked into the bar at the Hotel, a sombre look on his face.

'Is everything okay?' Greg asked.

'Bec's dead. CIA found us out there and they hit her trying to get me.'

It was silent for a second as everyone took in the tragic news.

'Oh mate, I'm so sorry,' Steve said first, and the others all followed with their condolences.

Dan was first to say what everyone thought. 'Let's go and kill every fucking one of them!'

'I got 'em, there were four of them, I shouldn't have let her stay,' Ben said, shaking his head.

Terry returned with a beer and handed it to Ben, who drank down half a pint in one mouthful.

Ben put the glass down and looked at each of them. 'Someone tipped them off, there's no way they could have known we were there. They'd been there, they knew the Chinese had me.'

'The four of you were the only ones who knew I was there. It doesn't make sense,' Ben said.

'It might have been me,' Greg admitted. Everyone looked at him. 'Bec asked me to tell Jones that she was having two days off.'

'So?' Ben asked.

'He asked if she was okay, I said, yes.'

'Jones wouldn't do that, he helped us, he's on our side,' Steve said.

'That constable was there,' Greg said.

'Jackson?' Ben said.

'I don't know his name, but he was listening to every word. I was careful not to say exactly where you were, but my God, I think I fucked up.'

Ben put his hand on Greg's shoulder. 'This is not your fault Greg, but I think we now know who it was.'

Ben drank down the second half of the pint and slammed the glass on the table, attracting the attention of everyone in the bar, including a security guard.

'I need to go and see Jones,' Ben said. He reached for Terry's hand. 'Thanks for everything Terry, I'll call you.'

CHAPTER SIXTEEN

Tim Jones went into his office and slammed the door. He fell into his seat and rubbed his face with his hands. Losing the young lady he adored, in the prime of her life was one thing, but finding a way to explain to her parents that she'd been killed by four American CIA agents by mistake who weren't even officially in the country, was another. He picked up the phone and called the Police Commissioner's office in Darwin.

'Russell Scott please, this is Tim Jones,' he said to the woman who answered.

The line clicked as the call was transferred.

'Tim, I'm guessing you aren't calling to ask about my wellbeing?'

'Russell, your CIA killed one of my constables.'

'You're fucking kidding,' Scott replied. 'Who was it?'

'Reed, she was with Woolford and was shot, I assume by mistake.'

'Fuck, I'm really sorry, I know you were close to her.'

'Yeah, well, I've had enough of this Russell. What the hell do I tell her parents?'

'We'll handle that from here, leave that to me,' Russell Scott said as calmly as possible.

'And apparently, your four CIA boys are lying face down at that farm where we caught the Russians.'

'Oh shit, that's really bad. Let me call you back.'

The line went dead, and Jones rested back in his chair. He looked around his small office and a grief that he had never felt before burned hard in his chest.

His phone rang and he picked it up.

'Tim, I spoke to the commissioner, and he will take care of everything,' Scott said.

'Russ, this is fucking bullshit. This isn't America where people just go around shooting each other and a cop dying is just part of the job.'

'I know, Tim. I agree, there's something going on here that stinks, and I think it's coming from the office next door.' Scott said. 'Tim, I'll try and find out what's going on.'

'Okay, thanks,' Jones said, and hung up the phone.

It wasn't long before there was a knock at his door. He wiped the corner of his eyes. 'Come in,' he said tersely.

Ben appeared, walked in and sat down opposite Jones without waiting to be invited.

'Ben, tell me what you know, starting with the missing Airbus.'

'We landed it at that runway where the Russians were selling the girls.'

'Is it still there?' Jones asked.

'I doubt it, they had instructions to fly it out that night at low level with no transponder 'til they were clear of Australian ATC and file a new flight plan with a different registration and origin to land in China.'

'So, the plane that everyone is looking for is in China?'

'That's my best guess.'

'How was Reed involved?'

'She picked me up from the airfield,' Ben said.

'What happened last night?'

Ben didn't answer straight away. He looked up at the ceiling and thought of the amazing day they had shared together only yesterday.

'We spent the day at the Russian's farm. I guess you know that's where I was hiding?'

'Yes, I figured that.'

'We'd had dinner and were sitting on the verandah …' Ben had to stop; tears were appearing in his eyes. 'It was just so beautiful…' He wiped his eyes with the back of his hand, before continuing. 'I leant forward to have a sip of tea and a volley of bullets exploded around us. I dived for the ground grabbing Bec as I went, but she'd already been hit. She died instantly. I grabbed my rifle and ran to a fallen tree that was on the hill behind the house. They were firing indiscriminately, and I picked them off one by one. I found their LandCruiser parked down the track.'

'So, there's four bodies still out there?'

'Yes, where they fell.'

'Okay, I'm going to need a statement from you, at some stage, so don't leave town.'

'So, what do you know, Sergeant?'

'I know the four men are CIA but you already know that. They snuck in with the war games and there's no official record of them being in Australia.'

'Well, there's going to be four bodies that are going to need names and a place of death,' Ben said.

'I know, I will send someone out there to pick them up and let's see what Darwin wants to do about that.' Jones could see Ben was waiting for more. 'Russell Scott said there's something fishy going on up there, high up.'

'Commissioner?'

'I think so, but don't do anything, okay? Let's just see what happens here first, promise me.'

'I promise you one thing, Sergeant, and that is someone is going to pay. But yes, I'll keep my head down for now.'

Ben stood and walked to the door. When he reached it, he stopped, turned to Jones and said,

'She was a good kid.'

Jones just said, 'I know.'

Jackson wasn't at his desk when Ben walked out.

Jones made a call and sent two rangers in a coroner's van with a camera and four body bags to the farmhouse. This would normally be a crime scene and need to be left untouched till detectives arrived from Darwin but he couldn't just leave dead bodies laying out in the open.

Ben took out his phone and called Peter.

'Peter, it's Ben.'

'Ben, I'm so glad you're okay. I heard you were arrested for the shooting at Pine Gap.'

'Yeah, and I heard you were beat up by the Americans. I'm really sorry.'

'They wanted the SD card from Pine Gap really bad.'

'Do you still have it?'

'Yes, I think I convinced them I didn't though.'

'Can we meet?'

'Sure, same place as last time?' Peter suggested.

'Perfect,' Ben said. 'Five minutes.'

Ben drove the white LandCruiser hire car into the Hilton DoubleTree carpark and nosed the car into the most northern parking spot. A young man still sporting two black eyes appeared from the bushes and jumped into the passenger side seat.

'God, they did a job on you alright!' Ben said.

'This is nothing, you should have seen me before.'

'Is that SD card safe?' Ben asked.

'Yes, it's safe.'

'I'm going to need you to get it for me, can you do that?'

'Of course, I'll call you when I have it,' Peter said.

'Thanks Peter,' Ben said, deciding not to tell him about Rebecca yet.

Peter disappeared back through the bushes, and Ben called Greg.

'Where are you guys? We have some work to do.'

'We're still at the Gap. Are you okay?'

Ben took a breath, anger still burning in his stomach. 'It's time to do some digging, see you soon.'

Ben arrived at the Gap hotel and this time ordered his own beer. He sat down with his team and they could see he was a different man to the one that had been there only two hours prior.

'Steve, can you find out what you can about Constable William Jackson? How he's associated with the Americans, phone records, bank accounts, stuff like that. Dan, see what you can find on the NT Police Commissioner. Apparently, he's involved in all this. Greg, I know you will want to get back to Jennifer, but I'd love it if you can hang around for a few more days.'

'Sure,' Greg replied.

It was late when Sergeant Jones was greeted by the rangers that had been out to the farmhouse with the four body bags.

'What did you find out there?' he asked as they walked in the rear door to the station.

'Nothing, that's what! We spent an hour looking around, so we were either at the wrong place or it didn't happen.'

'You went to the same place where we caught the Russians, right?'

'Yes sir, same farmhouse, someone has been there alright, but no sign of any bodies or even that there'd been a disturbance.'

'I see. Okay, thank you for going out there.'

Sergeant Jones rubbed his chin. *What the hell is going on here?* He sent Ben a message.

> Please come and see me first thing in the morning and don't plan anything for the rest of the day.

A reply came back soon after.

> I'll be there at 8 a.m.

CHAPTER SEVENTEEN

Sam Taylor woke early next morning, his head sore from the bourbon he had consumed the night before. He stared at the ceiling as the events from last night blurred across his memory. *The girl, so pretty, played me and I fell for it, hook line and sinker.*

He needed some fresh air, so he dressed, went downstairs and ordered a takeaway coffee from the restaurant. It was a beautiful day; the sun was still low in the sky but the ambient temperature was pleasant with still a little crispness in the air. Despite the lightness of his surroundings, a dark cloud hung over him. He headed down Studentski road toward the river.

He crossed the park and found the walking track that followed the Danube. The summer sun was getting higher now and the temperature was heading quickly to its 30-degree maximum. Sam wasn't taking in the view as much as he had wanted at this end of the week. His eyes were focused on the path just a metre or so in front of him.

How could I have been so weak to fall for a pretty girl? He'd never even been tempted to be unfaithful to Tanya before.

Tanya. My God, that's right, the detective had named her! How did the police in Serbia know my wife's name only minutes after the event? This was planned from the start. Milena, or whatever her real name is, must have been drinking water instead of what I thought was vodka. So, the barman was in on it too.

'Oh shit!' he said to himself as he stopped and looked around the city he no longer wanted to be in, or ever see again. The two cyber analysts that he had spent the last two days with were just actors who obviously knew nothing about cyber forensics. It all made sense now. It was all a set up for the one favour they now wanted. He checked his account; the balance had increased by the one hundred and twenty thousand dollars that was agreed as his fee. The first-class flights and the Square Nine accommodation added up to a pretty big favour.

His head throbbed from the hangover as his mind went crazy considering what they could possibly want.

Maybe I could go to the Director of NZSIS? Hell, no! That's my job gone for sure. Maybe I could find the NZ embassy and explain my case? But there's no time and Tanya will be asking questions if I'm not home in three days' time. These people could create the charge and have me locked up for two months. How would I explain that? God, they know about Tanya. Could they get to her too?

He just wanted to get out of there, be home and away from these evil people.

He approached a rubbish bin and stopped to throw away his empty coffee cup. His head turned back the way he'd just come and saw the answer to his next question approaching.

Two men in black suits were fifty metres down the path he had just walked. He recognised one as Goran. He stood and waited for them to approach.

'The colonel would like to see you,' Goran said.

'I'm sure he would,' Sam said, now fully resigned to his fate.

Not another word was said as the three of them walked toward the same black Mercedes S500 that was idling down the road behind them.

There was no driver opening the door for him this time. Goran sat in the front and the other man sat next to Sam in the back.

It was a short trip back to the big Government building where he had performed the bogus cyber training. Flanked by the unknown man and Goran, he was escorted back to the same conference room that he had been in the day before.

'The colonel will be with you shortly,' Goran said, and left the room.

Sam walked to the window and looked out over the elaborate gardens. *What a mess.*

The door opened and the colonel entered and closed the door behind him.

'Please take a seat, Mr Taylor.'

'Colonel, this is bullshit, you set me up,' he said, crossing his arms and not moving.

'Mr Taylor, I need your help. My country needs your help.'

'Yeah well, I gave you the help that you paid for.'

'Mr Taylor, you have found yourself in a compromising position, an illegal position and all I want to do is help you.'

'You set me up and now you're blackmailing me.'

'Let's not debate the finer details. Let's find a simple solution to the situation and we can all get back on with our lives,' the colonel said in a calm, soft voice.

'What do you want for that video to vanish?'

'We need a program that will give us access to a neighbouring country's secure network.'

'Are you kidding? If I was caught, I would spend the rest of my life in jail. I'll take the sixty days in your jail thanks.'

Sam was calling his bluff; he needed that video destroyed. He stood firm with his arms folded tight.

The colonel didn't talk for a moment, then said, 'Mr Taylor, the unfortunate video footage would be upsetting for your wife should she happen to see it. I'm a man, I know these things happen, but the women…' The colonel shook his head and then looked straight into Sam's eyes. '…the women—our wives—they don't see it that way.'

Sam was getting angry. How dare he threaten to hurt his wife. But the colonel was right, there would be no excuse that Sam could possibly come up with that would prevent Tanya from being devastated. It could end his marriage—and his life as he knew it. Sam pulled out a seat and sat down, covering his face with his hands.

'What do you want me to do exactly?' he asked.

'We want to get into the Kosovo government mainframe, particularly their military.'

'That's not as easy as it sounds.'

'But you can do it, right?'

'I could probably write a Malware program, a trojan that would sit buried in the software, but someone would need to get onto a high clearance government official's computer and load it without being detected.'

'We can do that—we have people in there.'

Sam looked at him. He shouldn't be surprised.

'And then we are done, right, that video will be erased?' Sam said, almost desperately.

'I give you my personal guarantee,' the colonel said.

Sam didn't put a lot of faith in that guarantee but what choice did he have?

'Okay, it will take me two weeks.'

'Mr Taylor, I will let you leave the country and I will give you two weeks to have this ready for us. I will send Goran to New Zealand to collect it. We will not be happy if it's not ready.' The colonel was staring at him. 'You understand what I am saying, right?'

Sam nodded his head.

The colonel stood and left the room without another word. Goran appeared almost immediately, beckoning his hand for Sam to follow.

'Where would you like us to drop you, Mr Taylor?' Goran said.

'The hotel will be fine,' he said, defeated.

Sam had spent hundreds of hours fighting against invasive trojans and spyware, so creating one shouldn't be so hard. Once back in his hotel room, he started drawing out a software map that could slip in behind the toughest firewall and be almost undetectable. He worked throughout the night, desperate to put this job behind him. He finally grabbed a couple of hours sleep, only after his creation had the ability for the Serbians to be able to read any file on the Kosovo government's network, no matter how highly classified.

He spied the airline tickets on his bedside table, which confirmed his exit the next morning. A small sigh of relief finally escaped him.

His flight home was economy and nothing like the special treatment he'd received on the way there. He could afford the upgrade of course but decided to punish himself. He didn't deserve it, nor would he enjoy the luxury.

Tanya and the kids picked him up from the Wellington International airport with smiles and hugs. Sam did his best to act as normal as possible. He'd never been so glad to be home.

He had the malicious software program done in a few days, all the while spending hours questioning his morals about what he was doing. It was everything he was against.

He'd programmed in an expiry date and a single use application that would guarantee that in sixty days all trace of the software would be erased and any reference back to him gone.

It was two weeks to the day when Sam drove into his secure, pass-only car park beneath the NZSIS building. The GT3 rumbled in the underground carpark, the race exhaust he had fitted letting everyone know when he arrived. He turned into his private park and to his shock, a tall man with his arms folded stood right where his front wheels would sit. The Porsche skidded as he avoided hitting the man.

Goran stared at him and then slowly moved to the side to let him park fully in the bay. Sam hopped out of the car, his eyes not leaving Goran.

'You have what I need?' Goran said without any expression.

'Yes,' Sam said, reaching in behind the driver's seat to retrieve his computer bag.

Sam took out an envelope that contained a flash drive and a typed-out instruction sheet. Goran reached for the envelope and started for the exit. Sam knew he would need to scan the gate so he could get out. He didn't need him waiting and sneaking out behind the next person coming in, which he assumed was the way he got in. Sam tapped his pass on the sensor and the gate opened. Sam hoped, but doubted, it would be the last he heard from Serbia.

CHAPTER EIGHTEEN

Ben arrived at 8.00 a.m. sharp and asked the older lady at the front counter, 'Please tell Sergeant Jones that Ben Woolford is here to see him.'

Jones soon appeared and shook hands with Ben.

'How are you going, Ben?' he asked.

'Been better, I guess.'

'Yeah, me too,' Jones replied. 'Ben, do you have a few hours? A few things aren't adding up.'

'Sure, what's the problem?'

'Come for a drive,' Jones said as he led Ben out the front door of the police station. 'I sent a couple of rangers out to the homestead to collect the dead CIA agents and apparently there's nothing there, no bodies, no blood, no car, no bullets.'

'So, they cleaned that up quickly,' Ben said.

'Or something else,' Jones said, looking at him over the roof of the police HiLux. They both jumped in.

Ben fitted his seatbelt. 'What do you mean, something else?' he asked.

'Well, I have your story and no evidence to back it up other than a dead constable.'

'Yeah, I can see that.'

Ben knew this was pointless discussing further until they got out there. It didn't matter how well they cleaned up, there was always a trace left behind—there had to be, he just had to find it.

Jones called into the Ampol fuel station on the way out of town, knowing they'd need a full tank for the trip there and back. While Jones was inside paying for the fuel, Ben's phone rang.

'Ben, Steve here, looks like our friend Mr Jackson has had a little fund injection into his bank account of ten thousand dollars, two weeks ago.'

'Might have sold something?'

'US dollars,' Steve said.

'That little prick! Great work Steve. I'll be out of town for today, tell you about it tonight.'

Jones hopped back in the car after paying for the fuel and headed north out of town.

'I could've had you arrested for coming into a police station with that handgun that's tucked into the back of your pants,' Jones said, not looking at him.

'It's just a Chinese thing that I took from the MSS agents after they kidnapped me.'

Jones's head spun around. 'The Chinese kidnapped you?'

'Yeah, bundled me into their jet and were taking me to Beijing, I assume on a one-way trip.'

'So, you escaped from the missing Airbus mid-flight and then after making the plane disappear, you're sitting back at the farmhouse on the verandah with Reed that same afternoon?'

'Yeah, pretty much,' Ben said. A vision of Rebecca lying dead on the verandah brought a fresh stab to his heart.

'You better keep talking because unless you can show me your cape, I'm finding this pretty hard to swallow.'

Ben went on to explain to Jones the exact details of how Terry had taken over the aircraft and how the Chinese had left in the cool air of the night in order to get it off the ground with almost full fuel.

'Why would they do that for you?' Jones asked.

'Because I promised to give them what they wanted.'

'And what's that?'

'The true story about what happened at Pine Gap.'

'Is that a good idea?' Jones said, looking over to him.

'I figure that once the truth is out, there will be no need for the CIA to hunt me down.'

'I can see that,' Jones said.

It wasn't long before the police car was travelling down the dirt road that led to the homestead.

'This was about where the black LandCruiser was parked, here… here,' Ben said as Jones pulled the HiLux up to a sudden stop. They both jumped out of the car and Ben led the way.

'It was parked here, in the middle of the track, I had to drive around it when I left.'

'There's no tyre tracks that suggest that, Ben,' Jones said, studying the area.

'Whoever cleaned up here has done a bloody good job,' Ben said.

They both hopped back in the car and continued on to the farmhouse.

Ben first noticed that both the chairs that he and Rebecca had been sitting in when they were attacked were now upright and neatly sitting on the verandah against the wall. Ben didn't say anything. As soon as the car stopped, Ben jumped out and went to the window where the first bullet had just missed his head. The broken glass that had shattered when a bullet had gone through it was gone, just a square hole with no glass remaining. Ben studied that and then went inside to see where the slug had lodged itself into the wall. The hole had been dug out, the slug removed and the timber made to look like anything could have made the hole. It was fresh damage at least.

'This is where the first shot went through the glass and into the wall.'

Jones studied them both and could see that there wasn't much to go on.

Ben went outside. 'This is where the first one went down,' he said.

The site had been swept and aged with leaves, not a drop of blood to be found.

'They've done a thorough job,' Ben said, not looking up from the ground. 'Only thing is, these leaves are from a different tree.'

Jones looked up at the gumtree and nodded in agreement.

'I hit the second one here,' Ben said. He then went on to show him the other two kill sites and again they had been cleaned perfectly.

'If what you say is true, they've done an amazing job in a very short time,' Jones said. 'I guess my job is not to find dead bodies that don't exist but find out who killed Reed and only what can be proven. So far, there seems to be little or no evidence that these four Americans were even here. From the outside looking in, it looks like there was only the two of you here and one of you is dead,' Jones said, looking at Ben to study his reaction.

'Okay, I get it, Sergeant, these cleaners were good but no one's perfect. The only way they could have got in and out so quickly is by chopper so let's explore that option. There aren't many places around here a chopper could've landed.'

Ben took off up the hill, along the runway he'd used to start the 4Lux. 'This is where I ran to first.'

He squatted down behind the fallen tree that he'd used for cover and dug around for the casing from the first shot. He found it and held it up for Jones to see.

'Still doesn't prove much, Ben.'

'Okay, come with me.'

They appeared at a clearing that he would have used if he had to land a chopper out there. There were no footprints, but also no leaves.

'This must be the way they came in and out. They've swept behind them wiping their footprints as they left,' Ben said, pointing to crisscross brush strokes.

Jones just stood back letting the private detective do his job. Ben could see that the downdraught from the rotor had cleared an almost perfect circle but that's tough evidence. He walked to the centre of the clearing; they couldn't sweep the ground where the skids had sat. The helicopter would've weighed over a tonne with the amount of people aboard that they would've needed to do such a thorough job.

'Here Sarge, look at this.' They both studied the impressions on the sandy ground. It was evidence enough that a military sized helicopter had been there recently.

Jones took out his phone and took four pictures of the imprints.

'Well done, but this will mean bugger all in court.'

'Yeah, I know.'

They walked around the property for another thirty minutes and found nothing that would prove who the shooters were, or more importantly, who murdered Rebecca.

Ben walked despondently back to the police HiLux as Jones started the engine. Ben closed his door and Jones headed off back toward Alice Springs.

'Stop!' Ben yelled and Jones hit the brakes.

'There was a sat phone on the one that was just up here on the road. I kicked it as I walked past him,' Ben said, jumping out of the car, Jones followed.

Ben walked along the edge of the road, pushing back the saltbush with his boot.

Jones watched, as he kicked through the scrub.

'Here you go Sergeant,' Ben said as he reached down to pick up the black phone.

'This should help,' Ben said, holding up the phone by its aerial.

'A bit late now to get prints off it,' Jones said.

'I only touched the aerial, but I think the last number called will be much more use to us,' Ben suggested.

The battery still had some charge and Ben flicked through to find the last number called, hit the dial button and held the phone between them so they both could hear.

'Who is this?' was how the receiver answered, after only one ring.

Ben and Jones looked at each other as Ben hit the cancel button.

'I know that voice,' Jones said looking at Ben. 'It's Peter Warner.'

'The Police Commissioner?'

'Yeah,' Jones said as they hopped back in the HiLux, started the engine and drove off.

CHAPTER NINETEEN

It was mid-afternoon when Ben and Jones arrived back in Alice Springs. Ben called a meeting with his team.

'Okay, this is how I see it,' he said. 'Looks like Jackson is our mole and I'll be giving him a visit tonight to see who he's reporting to, although I'm pretty sure I already know. I think the commissioner is in pretty deep. I found a sat phone that was left at the very well sterilized farmhouse and the last number called—was his. We need to find out why he's involved in this.'

'They could still be after you, Ben, they're going to be pretty pissed that you wiped out their entire team,' Greg said.

'Yeah, I know, and I think that the sooner the truth is out, the safer I'll be.'

'What's the plan with that?' Steve asked.

'I need to get the footage from the Pine Gap hit and hand it over to the Chinese agents. That should get the Americans off my arse and give them something bigger to worry about, not to mention that Police Commissioner needs to be exposed. Any info on him yet, Dan?'

'Nothing so far, no large cash deposits in Australian accounts but we are looking overseas at the moment.'

'Okay, thanks Dan. Now, the way it seems is, those four men were never formally in Australia and their bodies, I'm guessing, will turn up somewhere in the US. So that leaves two options for Bec's murder. First one is they frame it on me, as I was the only one officially out there with her. This makes it hard for me to prove that four men appeared from nowhere, killed her for no reason, and then disappeared. Or the alternative is that they go with the simple view that this was just an extremely unfortunate accident, where her sidearm discharged while she was cleaning it or something like that.'

'Bit hard to prove from the coroner's report that would state a horizonal entry at low velocity,' Steve said.

'Yes, but I'm sure Warner can have that document say whatever he wants,' Ben said.

'Well, that's the best option for you Ben, for sure,' Greg said.

'I know, but if Warner can get me locked up for twenty years, it might just suit him better. Anyway, I'm off to have a little chat with a certain police constable.'

'He gets home just after six and takes his dog for a walk soon after. He heads west from his drive toward the park and comes back through a laneway that short cuts the route back,' Steve said.

'Good to know, thanks Steve.'

Sergeant Tim Jones picked up the phone to call Deputy Police Commissioner Russell Scott at the Darwin police headquarters. He'd figured that Scott was probably an ally now, and to be honest, he didn't have a lot of options. He also banked on the fact that if Warner went down, Scott would step into the top job.

'Russell Scott speaking,'

'Russell, it's Tim, can we talk?'

'Sure, I'll call you back.'

It was only a few seconds when Jones's phone rang from the same phone number that the message had arrived from a few days ago.

'Tim, what the hell's going on down there?'

'I have a constable laying in the morgue that those American's killed, that's what.'

'That hasn't been proven,' Scott said without confidence.

'Well, I'm pretty sure the cleaners were straight in there after the incident and did a very good job—only they missed two things.'

'What were they?'

'Fresh marks on the ground from a helicopter's skids.'

'That's not much. And?'

'A sat phone that was in the bush. The cleaners missed it.'

'That doesn't prove much either,' Scott said.

'At around the same time as Woolford claims the incident happened that phone made a call to Darwin,' Jones said.

Scott was holding off on asking the obvious question. After a few seconds he asked it, waiting for the answer he already knew. 'Warner?' Scott asked slowly.

'Yes.'

'Arh shit, this is going to get messy. What is Woolford doing now? Don't let him stick his nose into this, let's sort it from here.'

'I can't promise that, but I'll talk to him.'

Ben decided that he would confront Jackson out of uniform as assaulting a police officer didn't need to be added to his list of problems. He parked down the street, watched Jackson arrive home, and waited for him to emerge with his dog. His dog was a pug that he had named 'JB' after the Pug in the film *Kingsman*. Rebecca had told him during a light-hearted conversation about how people look like their dogs.

At least with a small dog, he wouldn't need much more than a few blocks to stretch its legs. If his route was as Steve had described, Jackson would reach Ben just before the exit of the lane. He drove around, passing the streets but not entering them. Ben saw Jackson enter the lane, and he quickly drove around to the opposite end. He parked, climbed out of his vehicle and timed his entry. Jackson was only five metres from the exit when Ben turned into the lane, walking with purpose toward him.

'You stay away from me or I'll have you arrested,' Jackson protested at his first sight of Ben. Ben didn't say anything, he just walked up, grabbed a handful of Jackson's shirt, then slammed him against the corrugated iron fence. The fence swayed, absorbing most of the force.

'You piss weak arsehole, Bec is dead because of you!' Ben yelled into his face.

Jackson was trembling as Ben pulled him forward and slammed him against the iron fence again. The dog's lead fell from Jackson's hand and the pug continued out of the lane without a care for his master.

'Leave me alone, I'm warning you,' Jackson protested, trying desperately to convey some authority. Ben pulled out the Chinese handgun and pushed it hard into his forehead just above his left eye.

'This is where the bullet went into Rebecca's head, you know that? She's dead because of *you*!' he screamed at him again, his rage soaring hotter than he'd intended or needed. Not a good emotional state for a man holding a gun.

Ben was now almost holding all of Jackson's weight; the young constable had turned to water.

'I loved her,' Jackson said meekly, hoping he could get that out as his last words before he joined her in the morgue.

'Who were you reporting to?' Ben asked.

'Warner, he's my boss, he made me report everything I could find out about you.'

'I promised I would kill the person that ratted us out,' Ben said as he pushed the gun harder against Jackson's forehead. Jackson's legs collapsed beneath him and Ben let him fall to the dusty laneway track.

Ben looked down at the defeated man, instinctively bringing his right leg back to kick him hard in the ribs. He stopped himself. He knew that Jackson did what he did because of his love for Rebecca, the same woman he himself had loved.

He also knew that if he hadn't fallen for her, she would still be alive. He was as guilty as anyone for her death. He lowered his leg, then tucked the gun in the back of his pants. Without another word, he turned and walked back out of the lane.

Ben spied 'JB' the pug two houses down, who started to run as Ben approached. Ben sprinted, caught the lead that was dragging behind JB and hooked the loop over a fence post so Jackson could find him once he recovered. He knew that Jackson was just a pawn in all of this—he was, after all, following orders from his superior.

Ben met with Jones the next morning in his office. Jackson wasn't at his desk in the front of the station.

'I had a chat with Jackson last night,' Ben said.

'Is he alright? He's asked for the day off.'

'Just wet his pants, I think. He admitted that he was reporting direct to Warner with everything he heard from this station.'

Jones was silent for a second, then said, 'Well, that is disappointing but it explains how they were a step ahead of us.'

Jones thought more than he said, but he would deal with that later.

'I spoke to Russell Scott. There appears to be more to this than we first thought. Why did the Americans want Chen killed on the quiet and not officially through the police?' Jones asked.

'Yeah, I thought about that too. Chen must have known something that the Americans didn't want leaving Pine Gap,' Ben said.

'Now Ben, we need you to lay low on this, let Scott and I handle it now.'

'Okay, but I don't need the cops chasing me down for murder, being that for Chen, or Bec either.'

'I understand that, and I know you're completely innocent there. I will do all I can, but I think it best that you disappear again for a while.'

Commissioner Peter Warner sat at his mahogany desk; the leather armrests of his chair pushed up hard against it. He was a control freak and knew the situation down in Alice Springs was out of control. The one hundred and fifty thousand American dollars sitting in a Canary Island bank account didn't seem enough for the shit that was going down now. The Americans had sent a team down from Tindal to clean up the mess at the farmhouse and recover the bodies. Their black LandCruiser had been driven deep into the bush and burnt, the driver picked up by the chopper with the other cleaners aboard.

However, the dead constable was a big deal and he needed to fix that and quickly. He knew Woolford couldn't prove anything about the CIA. The Americans had the gun that would match the slug that killed Reed, forensics would have recovered that. He could plant the gun on Woolford and after months, if not years of unprovable defence, Woolford would be locked up for her murder. But Warner wanted this tidied up and quickly. There was only one option. He picked up his phone.

'Russell, can you come to my office please?' Warner asked.

It was only a few seconds before Russell Scott knocked on the commissioner's door and walked in.

'Grab a seat, Russ.'

Scott sat in the leather chair opposite his boss. He could see that this wasn't just going to be a chat about what each of them were having for lunch.

'Russell, this problem in Alice Springs, we need to sort it so that we can get back to doing the jobs we are here to do. I'm first to admit, we shouldn't have got involved with the American problem at Pine Gap, but we did, and now we need to tidy it up. I understand that the police officer getting shot was unfortunate…'

'Unfortunate? Getting a parking ticket is unfortunate,' Scott said, sitting up in his chair.

Warner held up his hand in defence. 'Yes, of course, bad choice of words.' He paused for a second. 'Russell, we don't know what happened out there in the bush and how that tragic accident happened.'

'I do,' Scott interrupted.

'You weren't there Russell, there's no evidence to prove anything other than that Woolford and Reed were there and she's now dead.'

'There is evidence,' Scott said slowly.

Warner looked up at Scott with a concerned look on his face.

'Jones has pictures of helicopter skid imprints in the sand to the north of the farmhouse and not a leaf in a fifty-metre circumference of them, suggesting a chopper had been there not long before he arrived.'

Warner looked a little relieved. 'Doesn't prove anything.'

'And an American sat phone.'

Warner's mouth fell open as the two men stared at each other.

'And do you know whose number it called last?' Scott added, leaning forward in his seat.

Warner remembered the call from the CIA agent's phone that had hung up when he answered it. The two of them sat in silence for a time.

'You're complicit in this whole thing, sir,' Scott said.

'We all are Russell, that's why we need to find a solution that is good for all parties.'

Scott wanted to argue the fact that he wasn't in any way involved with the death of Constable Reed, but he let it go for now.

'I suggest we convene a meeting with all affected parties and come to an outcome that's best for all. We can't bring that poor girl back, Russell.'

Scott stared at him; knowing full well that Warner was only concerned with covering his own arse. But he didn't want an innocent man going to jail for twenty years either.

'Tell me what you are thinking,' Scott asked after three deep breaths.

'The way I see it is, no one can prove with any solid evidence that anyone else was there on that night. If the death was caused by a tragic accident and the coroner agrees, then Woolford won't need to go through years of hell proving his innocence.'

'Let me talk to Jones, he's old school, I'll see what he thinks,' Scott said, standing from the chair and heading for the door. He turned the knob, opened the door and closed it again, with him still standing inside the room.

'I'm not going down for any of this, this all needs to come from this office,' Scott said.

'Of course,' Warner said.

Ben called Peter. 'Hi mate, have you got that SD card?'

'Yes,' he said.

'Okay, I'll come around now,' Ben said, and hung up.

Ben pulled up at the front of Peter's house in his old faithful black Jeep that had been repaired from the many bullet holes that the Russian people smugglers had fired into it. Peter's front door had been replaced with an almost unbreakable screen that stood out significantly in the shiny new black powder coating.

Ben heard the heavy lock disengage as Peter unlocked the door. They shook hands and Peter instinctively looked down the street. Ben noticed and smiled. 'You don't need to worry about the CIA guys, let's just say they got their justice.'

Peter looked at him suspiciously. 'You killed them?'

'Peter, you can't kill people that never existed, but they certainly won't be visiting you again.'

'Okay,' he replied, still not really sure what that meant. 'I heard about Bec. I'm so sorry Ben, I know she meant a lot to you.'

Peter could see Ben's resolve disappear at the mention of her name.

'Yeah, I'll miss her alright…' Ben said, digging deep to move past the sadness.

'What will you do now?' Peter asked.

'Jones wants me out of here and I guess once we have the funeral, there's no real need for me to stay. I might go to Bali, Noumea, or Fiji. I'll see. I need to get out of here anyway, I need a break.'

Peter took out the infamous SD card from his pocket and handed it to Ben, who took it and held it up between them.

'It's caused a lot of drama, this little piece of plastic. I expect the Chinese agents will turn up any day to collect it and it'll be out of our lives. Thanks for everything Peter, and I'm so sorry that you were beaten up over this.'

'Let's just say we're even, shall we?' Peter said with a smile as he remembered Ben saving him from dying in a vehicle rollover.

Ben leant forward and hugged him, turned, and started back to his Jeep.

'Ben,' Peter called out. 'If you go on a holiday, Bali or wherever, can I come? I want you to teach me how to be a PI.'

'A PI, really, after all the shit I've been through?' Ben said, stopping and turning back to him.

'Yeah, I think it's my calling,' he said with a smile.

Ben smiled. 'Okay, I'll let you know.' Ben opened the Jeep's door, hopped in and waved as he drove off.

Ben was only two streets from Peter's house when his phone rang.

'Hello,' Ben said as he turned onto the Stuart highway.

'Ben, Tim Jones. I've just had a call from head office and they want to declare Reed's death as accidental.'

'The coroner will dispute that bullshit.'

'Apparently, they can sort that.'

'This is just Warner covering his arse, that's all it is,' Ben said, starting to get angry.

'Ben, we can't bring her back and although I agree with you, this is by far the best option for you. We have almost no evidence to prove the truth and if it got out that you shot four American citizens, you would spend the rest of your life in court or jail.'

'That prick needs to go down, there's so much more to this, I'm sure of it,' Ben said.

'Ben, you know I'm a 'by the book' kind of bloke and with them wanting this, it tells me you are completely right. Take it and get on with your life. He will get what's coming to him.'

'Yeah, fuck it, I know you're right. Let me think on it. What happens from here?'

'They want the funeral as soon as possible and after that I suggest you disappear.'

'Thanks Sergeant, I'll be in touch,' he said, and cancelled the call.

Ben drove past the motel that he and his team were staying in and continued north out on the highway. He could always think straight when he was driving. He thought about how Rebecca had tried to shoot him the first time they met and how he'd saved her from a shootout she'd brazenly found herself in. He thought back to the first time they'd made love and how she stole his heart. The tears were starting to flow, and he let them.

He was almost at the turn off to the farmhouse. He lifted his foot from the accelerator pedal and looked at the fuel gauge. He had enough.

'Fuck it,' he said. He braked hard and swung the car onto the dirt road, the front wheels skidding on the gravel as they left the bitumen. The Jeep was fast down the two-wheel track and he soon arrived at the place he'd called home; the place the love of his life was taken from him. He pulled up and hopped out of the car.

He stood there almost in a state of shock. It was the first time he didn't have his rifle in reach and he didn't care. His tears had started to crystalise in the corner of his eyes and he wiped them away. He went inside to see if there was anything he wanted that he'd left and there wasn't. He took a can of drink from the fridge and walked out onto the verandah. The two old chairs that he and Bec had sat in just a few days ago, were neatly positioned against the wall. He took them and placed them exactly as they were on that night. He sat in his chair and placed his arm over the back of the chair that his lady had been in. He took another mouthful of the icy coke and was sure he could feel the warmth of her body on his arm.

'I'm so sorry, Bec,' he muttered softly.

A sense that he wasn't alone engulfed him. Then a creak from the far end of the verandah's rotten floorboards had his head spinning around, instinctively ready to grab for the Chinese pistol that was tucked into the back of his pants. It was getting closer.

It was then that a warmth he'd never felt before flooded his body. He fell limp, and his arm fell from the back of Bec's chair. It was like he was twice the size inside his skin, somehow strange at first, yet so soft, and radiant. Then he caught it, completely.

It was love he could feel, Bec's pure love. She was here.

He closed his eyes and let the beautiful feeling take over his body. He could feel her touch every nerve in his body, caressing him like a mother to a sleeping infant child. He was with her again. He wrapped his arms around himself as if to hold her in. He squeezed her tight, so tight as to not let her go. Every feeling he had ever had for Rebecca Reed rushed through him. He could see her face as clear as day, only inches from his, her smile and her red locks that framed her perfect face consumed his vision. Her blue eyes penetrated his soul and he was sure his heart would explode. She wore an expression of complete happiness and contentment. And then she whispered, 'I love you.'

It was such a heavenly feeling, if he needed to die to stay in this moment, he would without hesitation.

And then he felt her start to leave, the vision of her slowly drifting away from him, up from the verandah and into the sky.

'Don't go,' he yelled, but her face had started to fade in the distance, and then slowly she was gone, leaving him soothed and somehow at ease, just him and the songs of the night birds.

She had said goodbye the only way she could.

'Goodbye sweetheart,' he said looking toward the setting sun. Tears were streaming down his face. He just sat there, staring in the direction that she had gone, somehow hoping she would return but he knew she had now left this world. The sunset colour seemed to be the exact colour of her hair and a smile that started in his heart made its way to his lips. All anger and sadness had seemed to be gone and he sat there exhausted till the sun had set.

He stood and placed the two chairs neatly back against the wall and closed the door to the farmhouse. He closed the flywire door, lifting it so it fitted neatly into the frame. He stepped down from the verandah and turned back to look again at the chairs. A smile formed on his face. The hurt that had been burning in his heart for the past three days was now gone and an unusual feeling of closure had replaced it.

Ben Woolford was a different man to the one that had driven north on the Stuart highway only a few hours before. It was pitch black dark now, but everything just seemed so clear.

He pulled up at the motel and his team came out to meet him one by one when they heard the Jeep arrive. Greg was the first to greet him and was desperate to find out where they were at and the next course of action.

Ben met him as he alighted the vehicle, placing his hand on his Greg's shoulder and said with a smile, 'It's over mate, we can all go home.'

'What do you mean?' Greg asked as Dan and Steve now gathered around, forming a semi-circle around him.

'The cops want to write it up as an accident and push it under the carpet,' Ben said.

'Bullshit,' Steve yelled. 'That commissioner needs to go down.'

'And he will, my friend,' Ben said, still smiling.

'Are you drunk?' Dan said.

'Guys, the only other easy option for them is to blame it on me.'

The three men nodded, still finding it hard swallow what he was saying. There was a delay as they waited for him to speak.

'And she came to me,' Ben said.

'Who?' Greg asked.

'Bec. I was at the farmhouse, and she came to me, I know she's okay.'

Steve shivered as if shaking off a hundred spiders.

'That gives me the heebie geebies,' he said.

'For those of you who want to stay, her funeral will be in the next couple of days and then we can all get the hell out of here,' Ben said softly.

There was only silent agreement amongst the three at the mention of a funeral. They were all going to stay, of course.

'I've just got to make a call, and what say we head to the Gap for a beer and dinner? I'm starving,' Ben said.

He took out his phone and dialled a number.

'Tim Jones speaking.'

'Sergeant, let's go with the plan as presented.'

'Thanks Ben, I will let the relevant people know.' And he was gone.

Ben dialled another number.

'Hello?'

'Peter, it's Ben. Mate, do you still want to come on a holiday?'

'Yes, of course.'

'Okay, after Bec's funeral we're off to Fiji, my shout.'

'That's so good, I can't tell you how excited I am.'

'Hey, we're going down to the Gap for dinner want to come?'

'Yeah sure, see you there,' and he hung up.

CHAPTER TWENTY

As each day passed following his horror trip to Serbia, Sam Taylor felt calmer and began to slip back into his normal life. He'd decided to book an impromptu 'surprise' week-long trip to Fiji for his family. Being only a three-hour flight directly north from New Zealand, it allowed an escape from winter to summer in one relatively short flight while staying in the same time zone.

Sam booked them into a four-star beach front resort on the Fijian mainland just north of Nadi, avoiding the tourist soaked Denarau Island. Tanya and the kids were so excited about getting away from the cold Wellington winter, but even more about the resort, beaches, and time together as a family. Tanya, being a compulsive planner, had a rough itinerary quickly planned out. The floating bars that sat far out to sea, with Kayaks, snorkelling and water slides, and of course a bar and restaurant.

In contrast to his usual workaholic tendencies, Sam also counted down the days until the holiday that he desperately needed. He was looking forward to the relaxing distraction, and putting more distance from the memory of his last overseas trip.

The family were packed and all excited about the Fijian trip. None of them had ever been there before but had shared many pictures of the sandy beaches that would soon be their life for a week.

They arrived at Wellington's international airport by taxi and were unloading the four cases when Sam's phone beeped with a message. That wasn't unusual and it wasn't till they were inside waiting to check-in that his world fell apart again. He opened the message from the unknown sender to see the picture of him between Milena's legs.

The message read:

> We need to talk. Goran will meet you.

The Taylors were in the airport security line and no one looked more suspicious than Sam did, his head continuing to swivel, checking in all directions.

'Are you okay, Sam?' Tanya asked him.

He just smiled and said, 'No, I mean yes, all good.'

Sam had noticed security officers looking at him a couple of times. Anxious and on full alert, his mind became his own worst enemy. He guessed it was only the fact that he had his family with him that prevented him from being pulled aside for questioning. He was fighting with himself to stop sweating and not alert Tanya or the kids to his fears. It was all very real again.

Sam eventually relaxed a little once the Air New Zealand A320 had lifted off. The two drinks at the Air New Zealand International lounge before they left had helped immensely as well. Another two beers on the plane had Sam relaxed enough to somewhat enjoy the flight. Immigration was a long, drawn-out process at Nadi airport and again he felt himself looking nervously around each queued line.

Sam and Tanya finally checked into the hotel and the kids begged to get to the pool.

'Come on, Dad… It's wicked—we have to see the pool now! Bethany and me can go and you can come later…' insisted his seven-year-old, Jack.

'No! You stay right here young man!' Sam nearly yelled his reply, so tersely that all three just stopped, held aghast in their tracks.

Tanya turned to Jack and Bethany. 'Darlings—you need to go and find your hats and sunscreen first and we all need to stay together. This is a very different place to home.'

As the kids headed to find their bags, Tanya turned to Sam and touched him on the arm. 'Are you alright, darling?' she asked.

The look on her face slapped Sam's heart.

'Oh, I'm sorry, it's the security part of me, I'm still caught up in the last job. I didn't mean to snap. Clearly, I need some pool time myself! I'll apologise to Jack. Let's get them to those sun lounges, shall we?' he said, mustering as much levity as he could.

Poolside, Sam resisted looking over his shoulder as best he could until another message came through. A picture of Milena in his arms at the bar, her head buried into his neck, appeared on his screen.

The message read:

Goran will meet you tonight.

Sam's heart froze. He dropped the phone and Tanya asked who it was.

'It's just work, a problem I thought I had sorted but has reappeared,' he replied.

He wanted the earth to swallow him up.

It was nearly time for dinner, so Tanya was finally able to extract the kids from the pool and head back to their room to shower and change. Sam suggested he book a table in the hotel restaurant, before returning to their suite upstairs to dress for dinner.

As the family headed back to change, he took out his phone again and read the message.

Tonight? How do they know where I am? What more can they want? Maybe they found that the virus only had a sixty-day limit? No, that isn't possible.

He put the phone back in his pocket and walked up the three steps into the restaurant. His head was a mess, he couldn't think straight—he needed help. This had now gone too far to handle on his own. He knew he was in deep, way over his head.

He'd just invertedly written a program that was intended to infiltrate and spy on a country's government and military. A penalty paid by hanging or firing squad in some countries. He shuddered as he started to think of all the things that could happen to innocent people as a result of his actions.

He booked a table for four with the smiling young lady who greeted him. His head was somewhere else and he realised he had probably appeared rude.

He walked slowly back to his room and went upstairs, knowing he couldn't do anything until he found out what they wanted. The kids were soon dressed and they headed to the restaurant for dinner. The kids ran to their seats once they were told the table number, and Sam insisted Bethany move from the seat that faced the hotels reception. He again was overly assertive and direct when she started to argue. Tanya's suspicions that something wasn't right began to peak.

Tanya watched Sam closely all through dinner. When he decided to stay back to have a drink at the bar on his own, leaving her to put the kids to bed, she became worried. Sam could see the concern in her eyes and said, 'Sorry hon, I just need to run this problem through my head while it's fresh.'

'Okay. I understand. I love you,' she said, as she walked off after their two children.

Ben and Peter sat at the bar of the Club Fiji Resort in their shorts and t-shirts. They'd only arrived a few hours ago, checked in and were acclimatising to the tropical weather. Peter was excited, he had confessed to Ben that he'd never been overseas before when the question of a passport arose. With Ben's contacts and a little financial encouragement, it wasn't long before a shiny new blue covered book graced his palms.

'When's my first lesson, Ben?'

'In what?' Ben asked, placing the beer glass down gently on the bar.

'I want you to teach me to be a Private Detective.'

Ben smiled and said, 'There's not that much to learn. It's more about keeping your eyes and ears open, taking nothing at face value, and asking the hard questions.'

'Like what, what do you mean?'

'Okay, look around the bar, what do you see?'

Peter sat back casually, trying not to attract any attention.

'Young couple, names are Tim and Lauren, probably first time away, all over each other.'

'Yeah, probably right, no rings, not married,' Ben said, having another swig of his Fiji Bitter and nodding to the next couple.

'He's a doctor, I heard him tell someone, she's here at the same conference as well.'

Ben smiled. He *was* a doctor, confident and loud, Indian origin with a strong English accent, she was from Slovakia, blonde and pretty, probably a couple of years older than him.

'And what do you see there, Peter?'

'As it seems, I guess,' he said, concentrating on them.

'How do you read the body language?'

'Neutral, no touching or flirting.'

'That's because he's married. He was talking to a young child on the phone earlier.'

'So, I'm right?'

'No, I don't think so, see how close they're sitting, sharing the same bottle of wine, they are very comfortable with each other. There's no flirting because they don't need to. That job's done. I'd be surprised if there's any conference here at all.'

'So, his mistress?'

'You've got it. Now, that fella?' Ben nodded toward a geeky looking man with dark-rimmed glasses sitting on his own, nervously playing with a drink coaster.

'His name is Sam. I heard him tell the barman. Think he's waiting for someone 'cos he keeps looking toward the reception desk,' Peter said with confidence.

'I'm not so sure. Yes, he's waiting, but he's *very* nervous. I'd say he's hiding from someone. He's here with his family—wife and two kids. Kiwi accent, drinking in gulps, head spinning around at every sound.'

Ben then saw him look to the desk in shock, almost fall from his bar stool and disappear around the far side of the bar. Ben looked toward the reception desk and noticed two men, middle or eastern European, tall, dark and with olive skin arrive to check in. They both had thin, perfectly shaped black beards, a number four buzz cut and were clearly fit. They both carried small black duffel type bags which they placed carefully on the ground as they spoke to the pleasant Fijian receptionist.

'Well, this is interesting,' Ben said to Peter.

'The New Zealand chap disappeared pretty quick,' Peter said.

'Yeah, sure did, and I don't think it's because he forgot to buy them a drink at the last hotel.'

'What are you thinking?' Peter asked with almost juvenile enthusiasm.

'They aren't here on holiday Peter. Did you see how gently they put their bags down? There's more than bathers and sunscreen in them.'

'Guns?' he said, nearly falling off his stool.

'Maybe, but what I can tell you is that our little Kiwi friend might be in some serious trouble.'

'Do you think they're here to kill him?' The excitement was bursting from Peter.

'Peter, we don't need to get involved, let's order dinner,' Ben said, drinking down the last mouthful of his beer. He knew the young Kiwi was very afraid of the two new arrivals. He looked around to see where the man had gone, but he seemed to have disappeared.

Ben felt as much as he saw a man slide gently onto the stool next to him.

'Mr Ben, it's nice to see you again.'

Ben turned his head, recognising the voice.

'What took you so long?' Ben said.

The MSS agent smiled. 'It took some time to find you. Well, not really.'

'How was your flight?' Ben asked.

The agent knew which one Ben was referring to. 'I think we mowed down a few bushes at the end of the runway, but we got home.'

'I appreciate you doing what I asked by sneaking that plane out.'

'I trust you are an honourable man, Mr Ben?'

'Yes, we have it here for you.'

Ben watched the two new arrivals walk through the dining area, past the bar and toward the two-story resort accommodation blocks.

'I saw them too,' the MSS agent said, catching Ben glance at the two passing guests. 'Looking for trouble, I think.'

'Yeah, you can say that again and I think I know who's about to receive it.'

Ben could see the short Kiwi hiding behind the toilet barricade as the two men walked past.

'Peter, can you please go back to our room and collect the SD card… and see what rooms our friends are staying in, if you can?'

'Yes, boss,' Peter said as he took off after the two men.

'Mr Ben, my name is Tao Deng. I am a special agent in the counterintelligence section of the Ministry of State Security of the Peoples Republic of China,' the agent said, holding out his hand.

'That's a mouthful,' Ben said, taking his hand.

'Mr Ben, I much sorry for your friend, Miss Rebecca.'

Tao may as well have punched him in the face. It wouldn't have hurt as much as the vision of her on her back still in the chair on that verandah.

He drew in a breath and exhaled slowly. 'Thank you. Are you staying here, Tao?'

'Yes, Mr Ben, two rooms from yours.'

'You're good, Mr Tao,' Ben said, smiling. He looked over Tao's shoulder to see that the New Zealander had left his hiding spot.

'What do you make of that?' Ben said as they both watched the Kiwi run between two buildings.

'Serbians or Croatians my guess, young man have big problem,' Tao said.

'Yeah, going to be interesting to see how that plays out. Hey, we were about to have some dinner, would you like to join us?'

'That would be nice, thank you, Mr Ben.'

Ben picked up his beer and room key and walked into the dining area, selected a table and a seat that gave him a good view of the accommodation section. He was starting to wonder why Peter was taking so long when he finally showed up.

'They are in rooms 104 and 105,' he said as he pulled out the seat next to Ben.

Ben and Tao smiled at the young man's enthusiasm. Peter handed Ben the SD card. Ben looked at the tiny piece of plastic.

'So, Tao, why are the Americans willing to kill to prevent me and this falling into your hands?'

'Marcus Chen was a double agent and it got to the stage where neither side could trust him. He had told us that NASA had launched a satellite that can shoot a laser to earth called 'Atlas'. They claim that it is for geographic mapping purposes, but Chen was in the process of confirming its true purpose and capabilities. We had received significant data telling us that Atlas could fire a laser to earth and destroy anything it was pointed at—and it was operated solely out of Pine Gap. But we didn't know how reliable that information was or if it was just intended to throw us off track.'

Tao continued, 'So, we ordered Chen to blow up the section of the facility that controlled that satellite, and if he did that, we would know that the information was reliable.'

Ben sat there nodding his head in thought, looking at the table in front of him. Peter's mouth was open as if he couldn't believe what he was hearing.

'So, Mr Ben, we believe that the card you holding might tell us if Chen actually tried to blow up the facility or if he was escaping to save himself.'

Ben did know the answer.

'We believe, Mr Ben, that the footage of Marcus Chen being killed, or, you as the man looking through the rifle scope, would reveal the true answer. An answer the Americans desperately don't want us to see or hear.'

Ben knew America was an ally of Australia, and China certainly wasn't. Ben fought side by side with American soldiers in Afghanistan and although the CIA had been trying to kill him, it wasn't a reason to give such important information to China.

Ben handed the SD card to Tao. 'As per our deal,' he said. Ben had watched the footage and it didn't show anything that would be any use to Tao.

Tao took the card, his eyes not leaving Ben. He could tell that Ben knew more.

Ben recalled the vision through his scope of Chen reaching for his pocket after the first bullet hit him. And then the second head shot that saved the complex and the eighteen Americans that were held hostage. Jones had later found a detonator switch in Chen's pocket, confirming he was certainly ready to blow the place to kingdom come. So that meant that a weaponised laser *was* sitting out there in space that the Americans didn't want the Chinese to know about.

'Thank you, Mr Ben, shall we order?' Tao said, picking up the menu.

Sam's heart was racing. This was too close to home. *How the hell did they know where I was and get here so fast?* He stopped in a gap between the two main accommodation blocks. The sun was setting. He had nowhere to hide. He should never had trusted that colonel. How could he have been so stupid? It just seemed like he was making one dumb decision after another. He needed help and he would seek it out as soon as he got home; providing he lived that long. He should've said no to the offer and did the sixty days. He should have just told Tanya about what happened and rode that wave, but now he had evil people after him who knew that he himself was the writer of a secret virus that had likely already penetrated a country's government computers.

Sam heard a noise and looked up to see Goran approaching from the beach side of the gap between the buildings where he was hiding. A natural reaction had him look for an escape, only to find the other Serbian agent coming in from the other end. He turned toward Goran, the one he, in some fashion, knew.

'I did what you asked, we are finished!' Sam yelled much louder than he intended.

'The colonel wants another favour,' Goran said, stopping one meter from him. The other agent, also dressed in black, stood close behind and towered over Sam.

'No, no more favours, I shouldn't have done what I did.'

'The colonel is very concerned that you are not taking his calls,' Goran said as he took out his phone to dial a number.

'The colonel can go fuck himself!' Sam said with false bravado.

Goran's hand flew from the phone and slapped Sam across his face. His head spun and his body followed, sending him to the ground at the feet of the second agent. Goran continued to make the call as the other agent picked him up as to not attract any attention from passers-by.

As they waited for their meals to arrive, Ben, Peter and Tao watched the two Serbian men walking around the tropical resort in their black clothing; they were clearly looking for someone.

Ben and Peter listened to all Tao could tell them about the Atlas laser while they ate dinner. He told them that the Chinese believed the US would be running the project solely from the Pine Gap complex, making Australia a military target. He shared that Chen had given them conflicting information that led them to realise he was no longer reliable. He also explained that it was only because Chen was related to the Chinese president that he hadn't been taken out earlier by them. All the while, Ben was also starting to get concerned for the Kiwi when he heard someone yell.

He said to Tao, 'Want to take a look?'

'Yes, Mr Ben.'

Ben knew that Tao would be every bit as trained as him. The MSS agents were masters in martial arts and could hold their own against the best.

Ben heard another noise and nodded, signalling they head toward the gap between the buildings. They walked around the corner to see one of the men in black holding the small Kiwi against one building and the other typing into his phone.

'Why don't you pick on someone your own size, big fella?' Ben called out.

Tao stood next to Ben with Peter tucked in behind.

'Fuck off, tough boy, and save yourself a lot of trouble,' the man with the phone said then looked back at the screen.

'Definitely Serbian,' Ben muttered to Tao.

Ignoring the Serb, Ben said, 'So what have you done to piss your mates off, Sam?'

Ben could see the side of Sam's face was red where he had been hit and he wore dirt and grass on one side of his clothes.

Ben suspected that they would be armed and he knew if that was the case, he would either need to be closer to them or further away. He stepped forward and Tao matched his steps.

The man looked up again from his phone. 'Are you people stupid? Fuck off, this has nothing to do with you.'

Ben took another step closer, a workable distance from him now.

'Well, you see, Sam here is a friend of ours, we just met him at the bar and, you know, it's his buy.'

The two men suddenly turned their attention fully to Ben, Tao and Peter. One man held Sam with one hand, his t-shirt scrunched in his fist. The closer man, who'd been on his phone, quickly reached behind him, leaving no doubt he was about to pull out a pistol. The brown anodised weapon came into view and Ben was shocked at how quickly Tao stepped forward and kicked the pistol from his hand with a front snap kick. The kick had hurt the man's wrist badly and he rubbed it as he stepped back into a defensive stance. The second man threw Sam to the ground and reached for his own pistol.

Ben didn't wait to see the weapon before kicking the man in the solar plexus with a solid sidekick. The man fell forward from the winding impact as Ben used his left leg to kick him in the face. The man's head flew back and his body followed as he collapsed flat on his back. Tao had delivered a beautiful one step back kick to the chest of the first man which also sent him to the ground. Ben picked up the two pistols and looked at them.

'Serbian made Zastava PPZ,' he said to Tao. Ben ejected the magazines and de-cocked both weapons and handed them to Peter.

The defeated Serbian went to stand.

'Just stay there for a minute,' Ben said, taking a step closer. Goran held up a hand in agreeance.

'We just need to talk to this man, it's business,' Goran said, holding his possibly broken wrist. Ben doubted the other man could speak English, his nose was bleeding profusely through his fingers and down the front of his shirt.

'Well, that's fine but wouldn't a seat at the bar have been more comfortable? Then you pulled guns on us, now that's not very friendly,' Ben said, before looking at Sam. 'Are you okay?'

'Yes, thank you,' Sam said, dusting off the grass and dirt from his clothes.

'Can we have our weapons back? My government does not accept us losing such items,' Goran said in a defeated tone.

'So, you Serbian government agents?' Tao said.

What would the Serbian government possibly want with this man? Ben thought.

Goran nodded, as the second man clearly tried to work out what was being said.

'I'll tell you what,' Ben said, 'I'll give you back your weapons when you're ready to leave.'

'Why don't you two head back to rooms 104 and 105 and get cleaned up and we can talk again tomorrow.' They looked surprised that he knew their room numbers; that he was already onto them and that he wasn't just a good Samaritan who happened to be walking by. The two beaten men looked at each other, turned and headed towards their rooms. Goran was holding his wrist and the other had his bleeding nose still cradled in his hands.

Sam was still leaning against the wall of the building when Ben turned to him.

'Sam, you have some nasty friends there. I'm Ben, this is Tao and this is Peter.'

Peter nodded, still standing there holding the two pistols.

'Thank you for helping me out there,' Sam said, and then looked at Ben. 'Hey, would you like a job as my bodyguard, just for this week?' Sam asked in a near pleading tone.

'No, no, no, I'm here to relax with my friend Peter.'

'I'll pay you twenty thousand dollars,' Sam said desperately.

'Whoa… Well Peter, it looks like we have a job.'

Tao started to laugh, he then bowed to Ben and Peter and then turned to Sam. 'Good decision, Mr Sam,' he said, as he turned and walked off.

'Look, I need to get back to my family, but can we talk in the morning?' Sam said.

'Yes, I'm going to need some information.'

'Sure, okay and thank you so much,' Sam said as he ran off.

'Follow him to his room Peter, see that he gets there okay and note what room number it is. I'll catch you at the bar.'

'Yes boss!' he said, handing Ben the two guns and running after the New Zealander.

Ben took off his shirt and wrapped the guns in it. He didn't need to be causing a panic in the resort. He went to his room, closed the blinds, pulled a chair over beneath the ceiling inspection hatch and slipped the two pistols and magazines into the roof cavity. He then returned to the bar to see Peter sitting there, the excitement bursting out of him.

'That was amazing! You and Tao clobbered those dudes,' he said.

'Yeah, this time. I think our little friend is in some pretty deep shit to have a government send armed agents to rough him up. Go and see if the rooms are free either side of him and if they are, tell them we want to change rooms.'

'Great idea, boss,' Peter said, taking a mouthful of the fresh beer before heading for the reception desk.

Ben sat at the bar and looked around. The doctor and the Slovakian blonde were cuddling in a hammock on the beach and what he imagined was a few drunk locals playing pool were the only patrons left at the bar. He took a sip of beer and thought a week of looking after Sam was easy money and a good distraction from thinking about Rebecca.

He tried to imagine what Sam had got himself into. *Drugs, weapons? No, he didn't seem the type. They had said they just wanted to talk, so some sort of information.*

Peter returned, reporting he'd secured one room next to Sam.

'Okay, Peter, you move into my room and I'll move into the one next to Sam.' When Peter looked confused, he added, 'The guns are hidden in my room, best you're in there.'

Peter nodded that he understood.

Sam woke early, knowing that the colonel would be sending him a message, and he had.

For the first time, Sam decided to message back to him.

I have paid my dues. I did as I was asked.

A message came straight back.

He sent the reply and turned off his phone.

Sam looked out his window and could see Ben and Peter sipping takeaway coffee on a bench seat that had a view of his door. He felt a lot better knowing they were there; the twenty thousand dollars was a good investment. He ran his fingers over his right cheekbone. It was sore but no bruising had appeared yet.

'I'll go get coffee,' he called out to Tanya as she was busy getting clothes ready for Jack and Bethany.

Sam nodded to Ben as he headed for the stairs and the two coffee drinkers walked to meet him at the bottom.

'I'm just getting coffees, I can't be long, but Tanya and the kids are going to the Garden of the Sleeping Giant this afternoon and I told her I had to work, so we can talk then.'

Sam ordered two coffees and then Ben said, 'Sam, could your family be in danger?'

The look on Sam's face spoke volumes. He hadn't thought of that. 'I don't think so, but I can't be sure.'

'I'll send Peter on the same bus to the gardens.'

'Okay,' Sam said slowly.

Ben and Peter went back to the bench in the park, watching while Sam delivered the coffee to his wife.

'Okay mate, your first P.I. job. Keep them in sight, don't make eye contact with the wife. The first sign of trouble, call me.'

They watched the four of them leave the apartment and head for the pool. Ben saw Tanya for the first time, noting she was surprisingly taller than her husband and walked with confidence and purpose. She was pretty with sandy coloured shoulder length hair that was tied back in a ponytail. She looked fit and strong but still had a lovely feminine shape. Not at all the type of woman who he'd expected to be Sam's wife.

Ben and Peter positioned themselves at the restaurant where they could watch the family and ordered breakfast. There was no sign of the Serbians yet and that worried him. He figured Tao was gone, first flight out.

The Taylors' soon left the pool area and headed back to their room to change for the trip to the hilltop gardens. Peter had arranged a seat on the bus and a ticket for the gardens. He would already be on the bus when Tanya and the kids arrived, lessoning any chance of suspicion.

Ben and Sam watched the bus leave from separate locations and once it headed down the dirt road and out of sight, they both met in the far corner of the bar area.

'So, Sam, what can you tell me? These government agents are not just a bunch of hoods looking to steal some cash.'

'I work in cyber security and they want me to provide them with illegal software.'

'That's it?' Ben asked.

'Pretty well.'

'Pretty well? There are a lot of cyberterrorism experts out there. Why you and why so heavy handed?'

'Because I'm the best, that's why,' Sam said, looking at him.

Ben could tell he was only getting a small taste of the real story.

'Okay, you are paying me to be a bit of muscle should and when the Serbians come back and they will. However, for me to try to be a step ahead of them, I need the whole story.'

Sam put his face in his hands and leant on the table.

'This Serbian Colonel Milovan Simovic is blackmailing me,' he said as he sat back in his seat.

Sam took out his phone and turned it on for the first time since the last messages from the colonel. The phone beeped with several new messages which he ignored and scrolled through to a picture and handed it to Ben.

Ben looked at the picture of a dark-haired woman with her face buried in his neck. *Not that big of a deal.* He flicked to the next picture and saw Sam naked between her legs. *Okay, that's a bigger deal.*

'They set me up. They paid me to deliver a cyber anti-terrorism program and give them the latest protection. But it was all just a set up to get these pictures from the start and blackmail me.'

Ben nodded. 'It's a pretty common trick.'

'That's not all of it,' Sam said. 'They wanted me to write a worm virus that would get in behind Kosovo's military firewall.'

Ben looked at him. 'You didn't do that, did you?'

Sam bowed his head, nodding. Ben was momentarily speechless but realised the poor man didn't need a lecture on how stupid that was.

'Alright where are we at?'

Sam picked up the phone and showed him the messages from the colonel, some he hadn't read himself yet. Ben flicked through them, at first glance, there was nothing incriminating there, just requests for his professional assistance.

Peter was playing the part of private detective perfectly. He kept his distance far enough that Tanya couldn't see him, but he knew where the family was at all times. He could hear the kids as they walked through the dense tropical garden. Some of the paths were completely enclosed by the gigantic palms, orchids and the mossy tiles that would never see a ray of sunlight at any time of the year. At the far end of the garden was a path that led to a lookout and the Taylors started on the climb.

Again, Peter stayed back and only climbed high enough that he could see where they were. He waited at the halfway rest point till he could hear the trio making their way back down the hill. He found a seat back in the gardens and smiled at them casually as they all walked past. He could hear that they had stopped at the toilet block which was situated halfway back to the office and café at the entrance. As the palms swayed, he caught a glimpse of Tanya and Bethany presumably waiting for Jack. Peter heard Tanya call out Jack's name and he stood, awaiting the response. A few seconds later her call was not so calm.

Peter took off running and arrived at the panicked mother a few seconds later. 'Where is he?' Peter said in almost as much panic as the mother.

'He went to the bathroom and hasn't come out.'

'Let me check,' Peter said as he burst into the little concrete building.

'Jack, are you in here?' he called. He checked each cubicle—they were all empty. He could see the building had a back entrance and he ran through the other doorway and a little along the adjoining path. He stopped and listened, but there was no sound.

'Jack!' he called out again and both Tanya and Bethany soon joined him.

Peter took out his phone. *Damn! No service in the gully.*

'He may have come out the wrong door and headed along this track,' Peter said in a bit of a panic himself.

'Stay here in case he comes back, and I'll follow the path.' He didn't wait for an answer and took off along the path calling out Jack's name every few seconds. He kept checking his phone till he had a signal.

Finally, signal! Peter quickly messaged Ben.

Jack's missing.

He reached the carpark and there was no sign of anyone, just a handful of cars. He called out Jack's name again and the young boy appeared from between two white vehicles. Peter ran to him and knelt in front of him.

'Are you okay, Jack?'

The boy just nodded, clearly shaken from the ordeal. Tears were running down his cheeks. Peter picked him up and carried him quickly back through the office and down the main track to where his mother and Bethany were waiting. Tanya screamed when she saw them and ran toward her boy with her arms outstretched, dropping her bag and its contents all over the path. Bethany stopped and picked everything up, clearly thinking it was all a total overreaction.

Peter handed Jack to her and she squeezed him so tight, Peter feared for his safety. Tanya placed the boy on the ground and hugged Peter next.

'I can't thank you enough,' was all she said.

Peter felt like a million dollars. His first job as a private investigator had been a success.

CHAPTER TWENTY-ONE

en's phone beeped and he casually picked it up to read the message.

'Shit, Jack's gone missing!' Ben said, jumping up from the table and bolted to the reception desk.

Sam struggled to keep up with his new security man.

'We need your courtesy bus with or without a driver. It's an emergency.'

'I'll just ask the boss,' the young Fijian girl said.

'No time for that,' Ben said as he raced out of the foyer to the minibus and was into the driver's seat in a split second. Thankfully the keys were still in the ignition; he started it and had the bus moving before Sam had closed his door.

'Google the location and watch every car we pass for those Serbians and Jack.'

Sam could hardly hold the phone. 'Follow the road past the airport,' he called out.

Ben was going as fast as he could. The road had started to tighten and narrow, the potholes getting bigger the further they climbed the hill. Ben's phone beeped—he handed it to Sam.

'Check that.'

'They found him, he's all safe, they're on their way back!' Sam yelled with relief.

Ben braked hard and quickly turned the van around. It was important that they beat the bus back to the resort. He didn't drive as fast, but still with haste.

'Did it say anything else?' Ben asked.

'No, just: Jack found, all safe, leaving now.'

'Okay, good news,' Ben said.

'Do you think the Serbians had anything to do with it?' Sam said.

'Don't know, but let's just act normal when everyone arrives back.'

No sooner had Ben parked the bus back out front of the hotel that he was confronted by the manager who insisted Ben and Sam will be charged for having stolen the hotel's vehicle.

Ben quickly explained that a young child had gone missing and that because of the manager's bus, the child was now safe. The manager was taken aback by Ben's words, not having thought of an emergency situation, muttering that he accepted their actions were justified. He removed the keys from Ben's hand, placing them safely in his pocket. It was only a few minutes later that the other minibus arrived and by this time Ben and Sam were at the bar, on different sides but close enough to talk.

Tanya was the first one off the bus holding Jack's hand and Bethany followed close behind. Next was Peter, Tanya's new best friend. She had already decided that she would buy him and his friend dinner tonight. Jack ran to his dad and Sam picked him up and squeezed him excessively tight for the second time that day.

'Well, that was an adventure I don't need repeated,' Tanya said.

'What happened?' Sam asked, doing his best to sound like it was fresh news.

'Jack the idiot got lost, that's all,' Bethany blurted out, rolling her eyes.

'And this man found him,' Tanya said, turning to Peter.

Sam reached out his hand and said, 'Thank you…?'

'Peter,' Tanya said, 'and I've invited him and his friend to have dinner with us tonight.' She looked over at Ben.

'Thank you, that would be nice,' Ben said. She was even prettier than he'd first thought. He knew getting closer to the family like this would make his job much easier. Ben nodded an approving look to Peter.

Ben asked what time they might join them, and Sam said, 'How about six, as we need to eat early for the kids.'

'Perfect, I missed lunch,' Ben said, and Sam thought the same.

Peter and Ben walked off to their rooms and Ben said, 'What do you think happened?'

'I'm not sure, the kid hasn't said anything and I didn't want to freak his mum out by asking.'

'Well done, great job with that,' Ben said, patting him on the back. 'A bit too much of a coincidence for my liking.'

Ben suggested they go to Peter's room; he wanted those guns a lot handier than they were. He took them from the ceiling hatch. As he handed one to Peter, he asked, 'Do you know how to use it?'

'Point and pull the trigger?'

Ben smiled. 'Yeah, just make sure it's not pointing at me when you do.'

He went back to his own room and lay on the bed. He could hear the Taylors next door. The drama of the day had obviously been put behind them and the kids were yelling and playing as kids do. He closed his eyes and tried to piece together the full picture. Although he was sure he could keep Sam alive for the next few days, there was a much bigger picture here and he was sure that Sam would have no protection once he was back in New Zealand.

The Serbians would get what they wanted from him and then dispose of him, one way or another. He was potentially a dead man walking and Ben didn't want that to happen. He needed to find a way quickly that would make the Serbians back off.

Ben heard the Taylors' door bang closed as they headed for the restaurant area. He looked at his watch—it was five to six. He waited a little and went downstairs to get Peter. Ben tapped on his door and a man wearing a big smile answered it.

'I love this P.I. shit, Ben,' he said.

As Peter turned, Ben could see the outline of the 9mm Zastava in the back of his pants.

'Hey there Mr Magnum P.I., if you go out there with that pistol on display as you have it, someone will call the cops and P.I. Peter will spend the night in jail.'

Peter reached around, touching the pistol through the thin shirt. 'Can you see it?'

'I can practically see what calibre it is. Leave it home, Rambo, I think we'll be okay at dinner.'

Peter slipped it from his waistband, careful not to shoot himself and slid it under his pillow.

'Well, no one will look there,' Ben said sarcastically. 'Let's go get dinner, I'm starving.'

As Peter followed Ben, he could see Ben's head surveying the whole area, the setting sun and the whole resort was lit with a golden glow. It was just so beautiful and he imagined having his drone here to film the image as the sun sunk into the Pacific Ocean and coloured the cirrostratus cloud in the west.

Tanya's eyes lit up when Peter arrived at the table with Ben two steps behind him. After all, he was the man of the moment. The table was set for six, Tanya and Bethany on one side and Jack and Sam on the other. Ben sat next to Sam, with Peter next to Bethany. Ben could see that Sam already had a beer, the two kids had something that looked like lemonade and raspberry and Tanya a cocktail with an umbrella and straw adorning the side.

Ben looked at Peter and said, 'Beer?'

'Yes, thank you,' he said, and continued talking to Tanya.

Ben soon returned with two pints of Fiji Bitter and sat down just as Sam's phone received a message.

He slipped it out of his pocket and swiped it on. It was obvious to everyone including Tanya that it wasn't good news. Ben didn't have to guess. *It's from the colonel.*

'So, what do you do for a job, Peter?' Tanya asked.

Peter glanced at Ben before replying, 'I work for the Northern Territory police as a drone pilot but now I'm training to be a private detective.'

Ben resisted the urge to laugh but contained it to a smile.

'Oh, no wonder you knew exactly what to do today! We were so lucky you were there with us,' Tanya said with relief. Ben was satisfied that it wasn't too much of an exaggeration. Tanya saw Sam look at Ben and if her frown was any indication, she seemed to suspect they knew each other far better than just meeting at the bar. Ben finished his beer and so did Sam, while Tanya and Peter continued talking about his drone and some of the jobs he had done for the police.

'Let's grab another beer,' Ben suggested, and he and Sam stood and went to the bar.

Tanya watched them—the familiarity was obvious. She watched them order their beers and then saw Sam put his phone on the bar and slide it over so that Ben could read it. She knew something was going on and she had an awful feeling it wasn't good.

Ben watched Sam place his phone on the bar, a message on the screen. Sam had turned it so he could read it.

Children go missing all the time, Mr Taylor, your last chance to talk to me.

Ben carefully pushed the phone back toward Sam and looked at him. This problem had just escalated to a new level.

Tanya watched them both walk back with serious looks on their faces. She hadn't heard a word of what Peter was telling her about the lost tourist he found with his drone on a mountain top back in Alice Springs, but she now suspected Peter turning up when he did today was no coincidence.

Sam caught Tanya's stare. He knew full well he was going to need to tell her something. If the Serbians were prepared to kidnap his children, then he was going to need a plan and first thing in the morning he would discuss this with Ben.

Their meals arrived and other than a few comments from the children, they were consumed in silence. All through dinner, Ben noted the way Tanya was looking at Sam. She was rightfully becoming suspicious.

Ben finished first—he had been ravenous after skipping lunch. He excused himself and went to the bathroom. On his return, he went to the reception desk and asked if his two friends from rooms 104 and 105 had checked out yet. The receptionist confirmed the rooms were now vacant and he returned to the table.

'We'd better get these kids to bed,' Tanya said, looking at Sam.

'Thank you so much for dinner,' both Peter and Ben said at almost the same time. Ben stood as Tanya rose, an automatic reaction from his strict upbringing.

'Dear, do you mind if I stay back for one more beer?' Sam said.

'Sure, come on kids,' she said as she herded them toward the exit.

Ben looked at Peter and nodded in the direction that Tanya and the kids were going. Peter nodded back that he understood and rose quickly from his seat.

Ben sat back down and faced Sam. 'You're going to have to tell her, Sam,' he said.

'I know, but tell her what?'

'Tell her everything. That will give them no leverage with the pictures, although, I guess you don't need her actually seeing them.'

'I can't, it will kill her!'

'Mate, these people are serious. They proved today that they will do much more than just show her some pictures. Sam, your family is in danger, she needs to know what's going on, it will make it so much easier for us to help. Besides, she already suspects something, she's not silly.'

Sam stared at the fresh Fiji Bitter that sat on the bar in front of him, trying to imagine how that conversation would go. 'Okay, I know. She's smart and I know she's worried. I'll do it tomorrow. I'll find a chance to get her alone and tell her everything.'

Ben put his hand on Sam's shoulder. 'It's the best way, Sam.'

Sam just nodded and drank down half of his beer.

'Then I suggest you and I have a chat with this colonel fella.'

Sam jolted. 'What will we say?'

'I don't know yet, that's what I'll be working on tonight.'

Sam swallowed down the rest of the beer and stood up, looking at Ben. 'I've really fucked up, haven't I?'

'We'll sort it out. Get some sleep, Sam.'

Sam walked off with the world heavy on his shoulders. Telling Tanya was not going to be easy. He really didn't know how she would react and that surprised him. Would she scream with her arms flying around hitting him with all she had or would she just collapse onto the ground in disbelief, their marriage over as they knew it? He just didn't know.

He walked up the two flights of stairs like an old man. When he reached the top, he saw Peter sitting at the little table between Ben's room and his. When Sam reached his door, he mimed to Peter a 'Thank you' and entered his room.

Peter heard the lock engage and the safety chain rattle against the timber frame.

Tanya was in the bedroom with the kids when she heard Sam arrive. She immediately turned out their light and closed the door. She walked up to him.

'What's going on, Sam?' Tanya's eyes burned into his.

He placed his hands on her shoulders and said, 'My darling, you're a smart woman. I'll tell you everything tomorrow, I promise. I won't say any more tonight because if I only tell you half the story, you'll worry more.'

He knew that wasn't true, he just didn't want to be up all night answering a million questions.

'Is our family in danger?'

'No, not really. Leave it 'till tomorrow.'

'Not really?'

Sam held up his hand. 'Not at all, for now.'

'Okay, she said, looking concerned.

CHAPTER TWENTY-TWO

Tanya Taylor had grown up in the small town of Palmerston North, situated just over an hour north of the New Zealand capital. Her family were farmers and her father, Frank Hall, brought up his three daughters as if they were the sons he never had. They worked the farm, herding sheep on motorbikes and rode horses bareback—they'd even had a few goes at shearing. Tanya went to an independent school in the town as did her two younger sisters. She would mix with the boys in the lunchtime Rugby games, bearing her share of bruises and the occasional blackeye.

Her father felt that he had raised a well-balanced young lady and together with the feminine touches from her mother, she would be the perfect wife for any man. But like most fathers, he thought that no man would be good enough for his eldest daughter. When Tanya finished school, she went to university in Wellington and shared a two-bedroom flat with a fellow high school friend who was studying at the same campus.

Tanya loved her time studying in the big city and away from the many chores the farm demanded. The night life was great and her list of friends grew immensely. Tanya met Sam Taylor at the Victoria university law school. He was quiet, yet something about his contrast to her other friends, held an alluring appeal, like the desire to find what was behind a locked door. It wasn't long before his obvious smarts and gentle, yet somewhat serious demeanour, had swept her off her feet.

Frank Hall had learnt from his wife, Alison, that his eldest daughter had a man, her first ever and that she was very keen on him. He'd pictured someone that would be a mixture of Clark Kent and Bruce Wayne. However, when Sam Taylor, the short computer nerd was brought home to Palmerston North to meet the family, Frank couldn't believe his eyes.

Despite her dad's doubts, Sam and Tanya's bond held strong, marrying four years later in her high school chapel. A year later Bethany was born and little Jack arrived two and a half years after that. Sam was making great money and so Tanya gave up her legal career to raise their two children. Their life was almost perfect. Until now.

Sam woke to the sound of Bethany and Jack playing in the other room. Tanya was already up and he assumed she was with the kids. He didn't sleep very well, running over and over in his head what and how he should tell her about the Serbian problem. Ben's voice 'Tell her everything' kept ringing in his ears. He stepped into the shower, stayed there longer than he needed and then dressed. He emerged, joining the noise in the main room. Sam peeked out the window and could see Ben and Peter on the same seat they'd been in yesterday. He told Tanya he'd go to fetch coffee, and she nodded with a grateful look.

Ben met Sam at the bottom of the stairs. Peter stayed to watch the family's front door.

'Did you tell her?' Ben asked.

'Not yet, this morning away from the kids. I just have no idea how she will take this, we've never been through anything like this before.'

'How do you think she will react?' Ben asked, as Sam ordered the two coffees.

'Well, my best guess is she'll punch me in the face and knee me in the nuts.'

'Okay, I can see why you're in no rush to tell her then. Why don't Peter and I watch the kids while you two have a walk along the beach?'

This threw Sam. This would be a true moment of trust in the two men he hardly knew. Sam looked at Ben with grateful surprise.

'Sam, we are both private detectives. I'm an ex-soldier and Peter works for the NT police.'

'I know, I checked you out, okay, sure that's a good idea. It's probably best, thanks.'

Sam returned with the coffees and the kids were dressed, ready for the pool. Sam mentioned the idea of a quiet 'walk and talk' to Tanya, reassuring her that they would only be a couple of hundred metres away on the beach at any time. She agreed.

'Hey Jack! Bethany! Peter and Ben are going to keep an eye on you while Mummy and Daddy take a walk on the beach. We won't be too long,' Sam said.

'Okay, whatever!' Bethany called out.

Ben and Peter watched Sam and Tanya walk off, a noticeable distance between them.

'I wonder how that's going to go?' Ben said to Peter.

They were well clear of the resort when Sam started his story.

As you know, I got an email from a Colonel Simovic in Serbia asking me to come over, install the new Cyber program and train his people,' Sam said and Tanya nodded, her eyes fixed on the sand in front of her feet.

'I went over, first class everything, and completed the training in two days. It was strange that only two people attended the training but what did I care? My flight home wasn't until Friday and by Tuesday night I was done and as the flights were locked in,

I would use the two spare days to catch up on some work. I got back to the hotel and wanted to call you but it would've been 4.00 a.m. in Wellington so I had a shower and headed to the restaurant for dinner.' Sam took a deep breath before he started the next part.

'On a table near mine was a pretty dark-haired woman.'

This had Tanya look up at him, but she didn't say anything.

He took a breath before continuing. 'Anyway, once I finished my dinner, it was still too early to call you, so I went to the bar for a drink and decided I would call you after that.'

Tanya nodded.

'The woman came and sat next to me and offered to buy me a drink. Sure, I said. Before I know it, I'm as drunk as a skunk and she could hardly stand. She asked if I would walk her to her room.'

Tanya's head turned slowly to him but refrained from saying anything except, 'Go on.'

'We got to her room and opened the door and she pulled me in and started kissing me. I can't really remember what happen next but then three police burst into the room wanting to charge me with soliciting a prostitute and put me in jail for two months.'

Tanya looked back toward the resort and from the distance could see the kids jumping into the pool from the side.

Sam continued. 'Then the girl jumped up, completely sober, and the police told her to go. I was confused as hell. The room was spinning. The senior policeman told the other two to leave and he showed me a video of us on the bed and threatened to show you unless I did something for them. I said no, and offered to pay money to have the video gone but they insisted on a favour.'

'What favour?' Tanya asked looking at him like he was a stranger. Sam hated it, but he had to get it out.

'They wanted me to infiltrate the Kosovo military computers with a virus so they could spy on them.'

Tanya stopped walking and he had to turn around to look at her. 'Tell me you didn't do that?' she said.

'What, the woman or the virus?'

'The bloody virus.'

Sam dropped his head. 'I would have done anything to not have you hurt.'

'So, what's going on here?'

'The Serbians want more, and two of them are here and were roughing me up when Ben, Peter and some Asian dude beat them up pretty bad. I then asked Ben if I could hire him to watch us while we were here.'

'So, the Serbians took Jack and that's why Peter was there so quickly?'

Sam just nodded and went to hug her.

She stopped him and said, 'Sam, what you have done is punishable by death in some countries and I bet Kosovo is one of them.'

'I know, I stuffed up really bad. I just didn't want you hurt in any way.'

'How hurt do you think the kids will be when you are standing in front of a firing squad!'

Sam now had tears running down his face and Tanya let him collapse into her arms. She patted his back and said, 'Okay, we'll sort this out. Do you have some sort of plan?'

'Ben is trying to work it out. He insisted I tell you the full story so we can all work it out together.'

Ben watched the pair walk back, hand in hand. *That must have gone well.*

The kids were still splashing around in the pool when their parents sat down at the table with Ben and Peter.

Tanya looked Ben in the eye and said, 'How bad is this?'

Ben looked at Sam.

Sam nodded, saying, 'I told her everything.'

'Pretty bad,' Ben said. 'This is a real David and Goliath thing, so we need to be careful and sensible. Sam, we will need to talk about what to do when you get home because this will not be over by the end of the week and we now know that the Serbians are pretty keen to acquire your services.'

'Yes, I thought the same. Can you come to New Zealand?'

'Give me another twenty-four hours and I will make some calls and hopefully come up with a plan. Whatever we do, we need to do it right. We'll only get one chance.'

'Can you really fix this, Ben?' Tanya asked.

'We're taking on a government, and not a very diplomatic one. Let's just gather all the information we can and decide what we do. Chances are that may be decided for us,' Ben said.

Sam felt ashamed he'd got his family into this. He now wished he'd called the colonel's bluff and risked the sixty days in jail.

'Okay, we have a day trip tomorrow on the Seventh Heaven platform. It may be best if the two of you come along,' Tanya said.

'We will, I'll book that now,' Ben said picturing a shootout with the Serbians out at sea.

Next morning, the six of them caught the same minibus that Ben had highjacked two days before to the Denarau Island wharf. It was a good change of scenery from the resort and the first stop was to the bakery. Ben watched every person board the small ferry that would take them the eighteen kilometres out to sea to the floating hotel. The ride took about an hour. It was slow with just the slightest rock from the smooth Pacific Ocean.

Ben decided that they would call the colonel tonight and find out exactly what he wanted.

When they arrived, they all found sun lounges on the northern side of the bar area. Once they were settled in, Ben did another walk around the platform. He could see no threats. Ben and Peter also enjoyed the relaxing event—it would be near impossible for the Serbians to arrive unannounced. After lunch and another beer, it was soon time for the ferry to shuffle the much louder customers back to Denarau Island. Sam and Ben sat at the rear of the boat watching the amazing floating bar and restaurant disappear in the distance and the wake from the single diesel engine boat soften the tension.

'Sam, I think we should call the colonel tonight and find out what he wants. It'll give us time for you to finish your holiday and give us time to formulate a plan.'

'Okay, let's wait till the kids are in bed.'

The ferry docked and the six sunburnt bodies headed for showers before dinner. The kids were especially exhausted and the sun hadn't been down long before Tanya, Bethany and Jack headed for bed. Peter sat outside Ben's room and kept a close eye on the family's door. The sun had been hard on him today and a touch of sunstroke made it hard to stay awake.

Sam and Ben strolled out onto the beach. It was low tide. They could walk far enough out that no one would overhear their conversation. Sam took out his phone and looked at the screen. The number he had now almost memorised sat waiting for the call button to be pressed. He looked at Ben, who nodded in reply. Sam hit the button.

'Mr Taylor, it is nice to hear from you.'

'How dare you threaten my family you piece of shit,' Sam blurted out and Ben signalled to keep calm. Sam took a breath and said, 'What do you want?'

'Are you alone, Mr Taylor?' the colonel asked as Sam looked up at Ben. Ben nodded 'yes'.

'Yes, I'm on the beach.'

'Who is the man standing next to you? I believe the same man who viciously attacked two of my staff. And tell him I want the two pistols back.'

Ben's head spun around scanning the beach. He couldn't see anyone; he had already performed a full scan on their walk out.

'He is here to protect me from your thugs.'

'Mr Taylor, we have delicate business to talk about and it needs to be in the strictest confidence. Ask the man to step away and then we can talk.'

Ben nodded and stepped slowly away, taking three large steps back, his eyes straining in the dark to see who was watching them. The Serbians' bags could have easily had automatic guns in them and suddenly, he felt very vulnerable. He gestured to Sam to move as he talked, making it a little harder for a novice rifleman to hit him especially one with a broken wrist and the other with a broken nose.

'Mr Taylor we would like to make a commercial purchase of your talents. We are not expecting your services for free. We will pay you handsomely for the same as you did before.'

'What do you want exactly?'

'We would like the same program for the Bosnia and Montenegro military computers,' the colonel said casually almost as if ordering a new office chair.

'You're crazy. You can't expect to infiltrate every surrounding country's computers. Who are you, Hitler?'

The colonel laughed. 'My friend, this is only for us to ensure peace in the area, not war.'

'Let me think about it. How much are you offering?' Sam said, a touch of greed flickering through his body.

'You come back to us with a price, Mr Taylor.' And the phone went dead.

'Let's get off this beach,' Ben said. His gut was tight with unease—someone was out there but he couldn't figure out where. It reminded him of the night Rebecca had died, the stealth of the CIA agents, and he rushed Sam off the beach as if he could outrun the horror of that attack.

Sam told Ben the details, which were exactly as he expected.

'Sam, do you think you can cut this holiday short? I want to get you somewhere safer than this.'

'I'll talk to Tanya but yes, I think she'll agree.'

'Let's meet in the morning and discuss this while Jack and Bethany are in the pool.'

Peter was asleep in the chair when Ben and Sam reached the top of the stairs. They both looked at each other and smiled—it had been a big day. Sam knocked softly on the door for Tanya to open it which startled Peter, who nearly fell off his seat.

'Sorry Sam, I'm bloody knackered.'

'That's okay, I'm sure you would have sprung to your feet at the first sound.'

Tanya opened the door and Sam disappeared inside.

'Ben, the sarge called and wants me back in Alice as soon as possible. There's been a spate of car thefts that he needs help with.'

'That's fine. It looks like we are going to cut this trip short anyway. They were watching us on the beach—they're still here and I don't like it.'

'Shit! Really? There's been no sign of them.'

'I know, and that worries me the most. Go to bed. I'll see you on the bench at seven with coffees.'

Peter saluted him and made his way to his room.

CHAPTER TWENTY-THREE

Ben sat on his bed with his computer out, intent on finding out what he could about Lt. Colonel Milovan Simovic. It was the type of dossier Ben expected. Hard, tough, decorated and ambitious.

The now sixty-three-year-old colonel started in the Military Police and soon transferred to the 'Cobra's,' an exclusive detachment for Special Operations in the early eighties. Then a promotion to Major, in charge of the sniper, explosives, and biological warfare 'D' section. He was then promoted to colonel and the commander of the Serbian Special Anti-terrorism unit, holding this position for the last ten years. Ben suspected he had earned some pretty high-level clearances and authority. There was little info about his personal life or interests, other than he had a wife and two children, boys —now in their twenties. Ben was taking notes, writing every detail down hoping that something would start to form into a plan.

The next morning Sam and Tanya walked over to the little wooden seat that Ben and Peter had their coffee at each morning.

'We've changed our flights to this afternoon,' Tanya said.

'You can't go back alone—they'll find you,' Ben said.

Sam spoke up. 'We would like you both to come to New Zealand, just till we get this sorted.'

'Peter can't, the NT police need him back, but I can.'

'Okay, we will pay you of course,' Sam said.

'Let's get you safe first, money later,' Ben said. 'Is there somewhere you can stay, not at your house or another town even better?'

Sam and Tanya looked at each other. 'My parents have a farm just outside Palmerston North,' Tanya said.

'A farm is perfect. Is there somewhere for me?' Ben asked.

'Yes, of course,' Tanya replied.

Ben changed his flight so he could travel with the Taylors. Peter decided to stay on for another day and fly back to Alice Springs on his original flight. Ben and the Taylors were again in the resort's minibus on the way to Nadi airport, which was not much more than walking distance. They soon boarded the Air New Zealand 787 for Auckland at 2.00 p.m., and with a quick change would have them in Wellington by 8.30 p.m. Ben knew it would take a few days before the Serbians found where they'd gone.

It was dark and cold when the A320 Airbus touched down in Wellington. Sam had the family M class Mercedes in the long-term carpark and Ben hired a 4x4 Mitsubishi Pajero from a hire company. Given his past experience he took out the full insurance option. The Taylors called into their home before heading North to Tanya's parents' farm. Some fresh and much warmer clothes were needed. Ben figured that he would need to do some clothes shopping the next day.

He was glad to see the farmhouse was a considerable distance down a dirt track from the main highway. He knew full well that it wouldn't be 'if' but 'when' the Serbians turned up. The Mercedes and Pajero were greeted by Frank and Alison Hall along with two tail wagging border collie sheep dogs as they pulled up at the rear of the house.

Frank was surprised when he saw the big man alight the white Pajero. He was quickly trying to paint the picture as his grandchildren ran to hug their grandparents.

Ben walked straight up to Frank, offering him his hand and a friendly smile.

'Ben Woolford sir,' Ben said, admiring the farmer's firm grip.

'Call me Frank, and this is my wife, Alison.'

Alison uttered a soft 'hello' and offered a surprisingly firm handshake as well.

Frank knew full well that Ben wasn't here as an invited friend. He had a presence about him. Frank was also confused as to why his daughter's family would be arriving late at night, at short notice and with no return date.

Frank was never the person to not say what he thought, so he grabbed Ben's arm as they followed the rest of the family in through the back door.

'What's going on here, Ben?' Frank said.

Ben was surprised at the strength of the older man, easily stopping him in his tracks.

'Sir, let's talk about it once the children are in bed.'

Frank knew straight away that Ben was Australian and probably military or police. *What the hell have they got themselves into?*

It was late, and Alison and Tanya went about getting Bethany and Jack to bed. It had been a long day for them.

Sam finished bringing in the remainder of the cases and Ben his one bag that only contained shorts, t- shirts and essentials. He hated that there was no way he could have brought the pistols with him, having left them with Peter to dispose of safely in Fiji.

Once Ben had been shown his room, and all the moving in had taken place, the three men stood in the kitchen looking at each other. Frank clearly waiting for someone to tell him what the hell was going on. Sam figured it was his place to start.

'Frank, I have a foreign government wanting me to create illegal software which I have declined, and we have reason to believe that they might threaten our family.'

'Is that why you cut your holiday short?' Frank asked.

'Yes, they found us there and started to get heavy with me when Ben here moved them on.'

Frank stood motionless, staring at the floor as he took in the information. The he looked up, rubbed his chin as he took a step and walked around the table; clearly one of those people who need to walk while they thought. He stopped and looked up at Ben.

'Do you think they will come here, Ben?'

'Yes sir,' Ben said without hesitation. 'It will take them a few days to find us but I believe they will.'

'Why don't you call the police, get the army involved? We can't fend off a whole foreign country.'

Ben stepped forward. 'Sir, unfortunately the work that Sam has already performed for them with relative innocence and naivety would be considered extremely illegal.'

'I see,' he said looking at his son in-law.

'Sir,' Ben started again, 'I believe they're only trying to intimidate Sam into giving them what they want, and if we stand firm they may well just go away and leave him alone.'

'And if you're wrong?' Frank said.

'Sir, if I'm wrong, I will come up with another plan, one that I'm working on at the moment.'

'Righto,' Frank said, 'What do we need to do?'

'Do you have any weapons here?' Ben asked.

'Yes, of course, I have four rifles. We don't have foxes like in Australia, but weasels and ferrets are a big nuisance. Do you think we will need them?'

'I certainly hope not but I'd rather be overprepared than under. May I see them?'

Ben was surprised at the relaxed gun laws in New Zealand and that Frank had them casually sitting in a wardrobe. There were two leaver action Winchesters that he'd inherited from his grandfather, a small .22 bolt action that he said the girls used to play with when they were children and a Remington 783 with a simple scope and a box of .22-250 Remington shells.

'We might need to go shopping tomorrow,' Ben said.

'Sure,' Frank said, handing the Remington over to Ben. He reached to the bottom of the wardrobe and handed him a box of shells. 'Let's hope we don't need them.'

'It's just precaution, sir, I'm sure we won't,' Ben said, not believing a word of what he just said.

The Remington was a much lighter rifle than the Finnish Tikka he owned and certainly nowhere as powerful but it would surely slow a person down when the small calibre .22 slugs started flying.

Next morning Ben was up early and went for a walk around the farm. His first point of interest was an uncleared parcel of land to the south that he assumed was a wind break for the house. He figured if the Serbians were to sneak up on them, they would come from there. Next were the sheds, a small one for the drive cars and a big shed that housed several trucks and farm machinery. He strode up the long driveway to the front gate and assessed where any intruders might park, where they might come from and try and get back to. The scrub to the south was the only real concern. He was walking back when he saw Tanya walking out to meet him, carrying two cups.

'I thought you might like this.' She offered him a coffee.

'Thank you, just what the doctor ordered,' he said, not sure if that was a common saying in New Zealand, but he figured she got the idea.

'How serious is the trouble we're in, Ben?'

'I'm not sure, it could all just be a bluff and they'll give up soon, but what Sam has proved he can deliver would be worth many millions to a country if they were considering a conflict.'

Tanya looked at him in horror. 'Are you able to keep us safe on your own when a whole government is after us, Ben?'

Ben stopped and looked at her. They were still a long way from the house. She had a frightened look on her face.

'Tanya, I'm a soldier, I have fought against the Taliban in Afghanistan and they never had any rules of fair play. The Serbian government would not be approving this and I seriously doubt they even know anything about it. I think this is a small group putting together a war plan to present it further up for approval once they have a fail-safe plan in place.'

A slight look of relief crossed her face. 'I have started a plan for the worst-case scenario and I have men back home, ex SAS who would be by my side in less than twenty-four hours if I need them. If that eventuates, it won't be cheap but we can avoid Sam spending the rest of his life in prison for espionage.'

'Oh my God, life was so perfect, and just like that it's all gone.'

'My guess is, they will try and grab one of you if they can't get Sam and force him to do their dirty deeds.'

'That can't happen Ben, my children need to be safe!'

Ben could see she was now shaking, and he reached to hug her. She fell into his arms and let the comfort of his large chest warm the side of her face. She felt safe in his arms and was reassured by his next words.

'I will protect you all with my life,' he said, she hugged him tighter and then pulled slowly away.

'Thank you, Ben. I'm so glad you're here; our lives are in your hands.' She looked at him in a way that she meant what she said. A sense of obligation strengthened inside him. *I will do whatever it takes to protect her and her family.* As he walked back, he couldn't help but remember that the last woman that hugged him was now dead, and that was his fault. *I won't let that happen again.*

They were met by her father when they arrived back at the house. Tanya looked at him and headed for the back door.

'So, what's the plan, Ben?' Frank asked.

'The farm is not perfect for us to protect them sir, but much better than the city.'

'Well, I guess we didn't build it as a fortress. It's a sheep station.'

Ben smiled. 'Of course, it is. The way I see it, that scrub is where they might come from. What's the easiest way for them to get there?'

'Down the neighbour's driveway and then come in around the back of it, but it's pretty dense in there, it's been untouched since the beginning of time.'

'Yes, I saw that, I went and had a look this morning,' Ben said, still struggling to get out of his mind how Tanya felt in his arms. He shook away the thought and asked, 'Frank, can we buy some hardware in town?'

'Hardware?'

'Sorry, a rifle, with a good scope, just in case.'

'Yes of course, the prime minister is trying to change the gun laws after the massacre in Christchurch but at the moment it's still as easy to buy here as in the US. There's a gun shop in Manawatu.'

'That's good—good that they are changing the laws that is.'

'Shall we go after breakfast?' Frank suggested.

Frank liked this man, feeling that he was probably a good person for the job. Ben had assured him that the Serbians would come and so he was going to be ready. Frank looked at it all as a bit of excitement in contrast to his rather mundane 'day to day' sheep farming life.

The drive into town was only thirty minutes, and Frank was fascinated with Ben's military career. Ben didn't like to brag or even talk about it, but winning over the confidence of the man of the house was important. So, he told him a couple of war stories.

The sports store only had limited rifles, but Ben managed to secure a nice .270 Winchester 70, that just happened to be the most popular hunting rifle in the country. He adorned it with a Tasco Varmint scope plus a pair of Bushnell 10x44 binoculars and of course a nice warm army green jacket. He was now set.

Ben spent much of the day firing off rounds to tune the scope to the rifle, something that had Jack particularly interested. Tanya brought Jack down to watch Ben, she herself having fired many rounds at cans and bottles when she was younger. Ben turned to see Tanya and Jack standing behind him.

'Hello, I hope I haven't been making too much noise?' He knew it was a relatively low powered rifle and it didn't make half the noise of his Tikka 303.

'No, Jack was fascinated. He hasn't been involved with guns at all.'

Ben looked at Jack. 'Would your mum let you have a shot?' he said, looking up at her. Her eyes did that thing to him again.

She then said, 'Do you want to have a shot, Jack?'

'Yes please,' he said excitedly.

Ben wrapped the boy in his arms and placed the gun so he could see through the scope.

'Can you see the fine lines, Jack?' Ben asked.

'Yes.'

'You need to put the can in the centre of the lines where they meet.'

'Okay, I got it.'

'Now very slowly, keeping the can in the middle and find the trigger.'

Ben placed his hand on top of Jack's and could feel his finger inside the trigger guard.

'Now, just slowly squeeze the trigger.'

The gun fired and a splinter of wood flew off the post that held the cans.

'Well, that proves it, the scope still isn't right,' Ben said, smiling.

Ben released Jack from between his arms and he ran back to mother, excited.

'Thank you, Ben,' Tanya said, and she again gave him a smile that said more than words. Ben sat down on the fallen log that he'd been using to shoot from.

Ben had never had many women in his life and Rebecca was the first he'd really loved. But Tanya was giving him a warmth that he didn't need right now. He loved the feeling, there was somehow a piece of Rebecca in it all, but he had a job to do and his head needed to be straight and clear. Besides, she was his client's wife. He also understood her fear and how much she wanted a hero, whomever it was, to protect them now.

He fired off three quick shots removing the last three cans from the fence post. He was happy with his new weapon.

At dinner that night, Jack told his father that Ben had let him fire his new rifle and Sam wasn't too impressed. He told Jack that guns are for killing and that is their only purpose. Ben, nor Jack's Grandfather, entered into the conversation. They could both tell Sam was passionate in his belief.

'I'm sorry, Sam,' Ben said.

'No don't be, Ben, this is a farm and sometimes you need to shoot feral animals to protect our pets and livestock,' Tanya said, defending him.

Sam didn't respond. He didn't need an argument starting in front of the children.

It wasn't long after dinner when Ben's phone rang. It was Peter. He excused himself from the table and answered the call.

'Ben, I was just checking out of the resort and the two Serbians cornered me, wanting to know where you and the Taylors had gone. Ben, they started roughing me up and I just said that the family had gone home and I didn't know where they lived. I'm sorry Ben, I just didn't need to be beat up again.'

'That's absolutely fine, my friend. At least I now know to expect them. Are you okay, they didn't hurt you?'

'Just a blood nose. After the CIA broke it, it bleeds just at the thought of being hit.'

'Where are you now?'

'I'm at the airport, flight is in an hour.'

'Mate, I enjoyed our short holiday, let's hope we can work together again soon. Hey! I'll send you some money for your half of the P.I. job.'

'Not going to argue with that,' Peter said.

'Have a good flight, Pete.'

Ben slipped the phone into his back pocket and walked back into the kitchen. Ben caught Frank's eye and offered the gentlest nod indicating that he wanted to talk. Ben headed out the back door and Frank stood saying, 'Ben, those binoculars you bought are still in my car.' And followed him outside.

'What's up?'

'I think they're on their way. It'll take them a day or two to find that Sam is here and not in Wellington but I'm pretty sure they'll find us.'

'Alright son, let's teach 'em a lesson. How many of them?'

'I'm pretty sure there were only two in Fiji and they were government agents, I'm guessing they would be too embarrassed to call for back up when all they are after is a computer expert. But… we can't assume that.'

'Tanya can shoot, she has quite the eye for it,' Frank offered.

'Okay, let's get her up to speed tomorrow with that .22. It might not kill much but it'll slow them down.'

The two men returned indoors, Ben with the binoculars in his hand.

'Thank you for dinner, I'll have an early night,' Ben said. He wanted to continue to work on his worst-case scenario. It was going to be complicated and dangerous and would need to be actioned quickly when and if the time came. Peter and his drone would possibly play a big part if he was available.

There was a soft knock on his door.

'Come in,' Ben called out. The door opened slowly and Tanya stood in the opening.

'This was my room you know.'

'Really? Well, it's a very nice room and your parents are lovely people. I bet growing up here on the farm was pretty good?'

'Yes, it was.'

Tanya took in a breath and said, 'I saw you nod to my father to meet you outside, what was that about?'

Ben took a moment and looked up at the ceiling. 'I was going to wait till tomorrow morning. Can you call Sam in?'

Tanya disappeared and returned with her husband; they closed the door behind them.

'I think they're coming; they roughed up Peter today in Fiji, insisting he tell them where you'd gone. I imagine they would have left today or first thing tomorrow and I guess it will be two days until they find us.'

'Shouldn't we run and hide?' Tanya said.

'To where, and then what? If it was just you, Sam, sure, we would hide you in Australia somewhere. But for now, let's stay put. We'll hide all the evidence that you're here—cars, toys and we lay low inside. Hopefully they watch the place for a day then move on. Look, I know it's a short-term fix but there aren't many options on offer yet that will keep you safe and out of jail, Sam.'

'All right, how long have we got?'

'We could see them as soon as tomorrow night.'

Sam turned and left the room. Tanya stayed for a second longer, a worried look on her face.

'They won't come in if they don't think you're here,' Ben said.

'Thank you, Ben,' she said, turned and left the room, closing the door behind her.

Shit, I wish I had some back up here. He knew he could get Dan and Steve there but didn't want to be calling then in for every job he had. He went back to working on his 'Plan C' for this mess.

Next morning it was about hiding the family Mercedes and any other sign that they were there. The two kids were kept inside with games and endless TV watching. Ben deduced that the rear facing bedroom window would be the best to watch the uncleared scrub from. He checked and it would be a 22.4% waning crescent moon that night and would rise soon after sunset, which would be a slight advantage.

He removed several globes from the kitchen so it would only light the room slightly. He doubted they would come tonight but he had to be ready. Frank was a little too excited for Ben's liking, although he appreciated the danger, the thrill of such an adventure for him was overwhelming.

Ben went back to his computer once he felt the farmhouse was ready.

'Sam,' he called from the other room.

'Yes Ben?'

'How would someone find the virus that's on the Kosovo computers? What would they look for?'

'They would need to look in the programming files that are deep in the hard drive. It will be in two parts, one is the trojan that opens the doors for the worm virus to enter and the second is the worm itself. Once it's in, it works its way into every computer that the infected computer sends an email to. The file would be program1.exe. the second program2.exe.'

'How would you delete them?'

'Easy, click on the file and hit delete. It will remove it from the host computer and then that would need to be done to every infected computer as well, or you just wait till the sixty days are up and it will self-dissolve with no record of being there on any of the infected units.'

'Okay, let's just keep that information between us.'

'Let me know if you need more,' Sam said as he turned and walked away.

That was all crucial information for his backup plan. The day went quickly, and the children didn't complain at all about having to spend the day inside. Alison had cooked up a simple pasta dish that everyone except the grandparents ate in the low lit loungeroom with the inside blinds and outside shutters securely closed. Ben knew the two border collies would be the best asset he had.

'Frank, will the dogs come to your command, no matter what?' Ben asked him.

'Yes, of course, they're sheepdogs. They'll come when I call.'

It was around 10.00 p.m. when the dogs started barking. Everyone jumped up and took up the positions that Ben had laid out. Alison joined the sleeping children in the back room, Ben and Tanya would be at the first bedroom window facing south and Frank and Sam in the second bedroom facing east.

'Casually call the dogs in,' Ben called out to Frank.

It was just a few seconds later that the dogs both flew in the rear door of the farmhouse, their first time being inside. Frank closed the door as if all was normal and then took up his post at the dark bedroom window. The dogs occasionally let out a growl.

Ben scoured the bush for movement and wondered if he was wrong about which direction they would come from. Then through the binoculars he saw a man, dressed in black, a Kevlar bullet proof vest and a pistol drawn. Then a second man, dressed the same. It was hard to tell if they were the same men from the Nadi resort but he guessed they were. Neither man was advancing from the cover of the uncleared bush.

'What are they waiting for?' Ben said almost to himself.

'What can you see Ben?' Tanya said, walking up behind him and placing her hand on his back and her face next to his.

'They're here, in the scrub.' He pointed to their position and she found them with her own pair of binoculars.

Ben jumped up and went to the window that Sam and Frank were at. 'Do you see anything on this side?' he asked.

'No, all clear.'

'We have two in the scrub with pistols and flak jackets,' Ben said, his binoculars searching the neighbour's property for a car or cars. That would help tell him how many of them there were.

'They must have a car somewhere.'

'If they drove down Bill's driveway with their lights off, we wouldn't see them,' Frank said.

'Okay keep me posted if you see anything.' Ben said and returned to the window with Tanya.

'Are they still there?' Ben asked.

'Yes, haven't moved.'

'It doesn't make sense. The way to do this is to be in and out quick, it lessens the risk,' he said.

A scream from Alison had Ben with his rifle quickly on his feet. He reached the main passage only to see a man in black fatigues dragging Bethany out the front door. He heard Tanya scream as she also saw the pair disappear through the open door. Ben caught her as she tried to push past him to chase the man that was disappearing with her daughter. Ben knelt, not only blocking the doorway for Tanya but taking aim at the fleeing man.

In the partially moonlit front yard, he could see the man's bullet-proof vest that covered most of his torso. Ben knew the small calibre .273 would only be an itch to the Kevlar protection. He aimed for the man's left shoulder—the same arm that was dragging Bethany. He was now at about the range that he had tuned the scope for. Bethany was well under the man's shoulder height and would be safe should he be off with the shot. Ben fired and saw the shirt of the intruder tear open as the small slug went into his shoulder. He let the girl go and she fell to the ground. The man also hit the ground as the pain of the smashed shoulder blade hit him. Tanya tried to push past him and he again needed most of his strength to hold her back.

'Stay here!' he yelled at her and belted out the door. The two border collies had passed him and were now barking and snapping at the fallen man.

The man was rolling over, his left shoulder bleeding badly. Ben could see the familiar looking Zastava PPZ pistol in his right hand as the man raised it to fire at him. The pain from his left shoulder and the dogs attacking was all the delay Ben needed to get to the man before he could aim the pistol. Ben launched into a flying sidekick that hit the man square in the face. The man flew back with such force that Ben flew straight over the top of him and landed on his feet two metres past him. He turned and scooped up the curled-up Bethany, swinging her around and carrying her as fast as he could on his chest to cover her from any gunfire. He ran through the doorway and closed the front farmhouse door. Not a single shot was fired from the Serbians.

He placed Bethany on her feet and her mother had her safely embraced. Ben ran around to the window where he'd started. He watched two men from the bush run out and collect their fallen teammate.

'We could take them out, they're in the clear,' Frank said over Ben's shoulder.

'No, let them collect their friend, they'll need to get him to hospital. They didn't shoot at me when I carried Bethany back, so we will show them the same courtesy. They're no more threat to us for now.'

It was only a few seconds later that Ben saw the black X5 BMW roar down the neighbour's driveway toward the main road. 'I doubt we will see them again tonight,' Ben said. 'But leave the dogs out and I will stay here by this window.'

Ben inspected the front door to see how the third man had entered so easily. The glass had been cut perfectly and silently. It made sense now. The two in the bush were the distraction while a third snuck in from the front. This confirmed that there were more than just the two. The man he hit was neither of the men from Fiji and he now suspected these men could have already been here in New Zealand and could have followed them to the farmhouse on the first night. Ben knew that this was far bigger than what he could handle on his own. These were professionals who were fully armed with what appeared to be unlimited resources. His 'Plan C' would now need to be completed quickly.

It wasn't long before the house was settled again and the children in their beds after their parents' repeated reassurance that all was safe. The house was calm and Ben could just hear the occasional footsteps and the kettle boiling. He sat on the bed of the south facing bedroom. The only light was from the passageway. Tanya walked in with two cups of tea and he stood as she placed them on the bedside table.

'Ben, you were a hero tonight, I can't thank you enough.'

She stepped forward and hugged him. He'd only done what he could, and this time it was enough. Tanya was taller than Rebecca and fitted the place against his chest perfectly. She clearly didn't want to let him go, and he felt the same. It had been a scary and emotional evening, and being able to hug someone, somehow was a pleasant release. It was several deep breaths of that perfumed scent when Tanya finally pulled back—but only a little. Her hands still on his waist, she looked up at him, the look in her eyes making his heart start to beat harder. And then she kissed him. He didn't resist, he needed it as bad as she. Her feminine smell, her taste and her touch, consumed him and Rebecca was alive in his arms again. The moment of what was real or right or wrong was inconsequential—it was just them. The kiss became more passionate as each second passed and their hands explored each other.

'What the fuck?!' Sam screamed out from the doorway.

The two pulled apart instantly.

'It's not what it looks like,' Tanya said without conviction.

'Be fucked it's not! Ben Woolford, you are out of here, now, I want you gone now, tonight.'

'Sam be sensible, this was nothing, we need Ben here,' Tanya pleaded.

'Five minutes, be in that Pajero and gone!' Sam screamed as he turned from the doorway.

'I'm so sorry, Tanya,' Ben said, picking up the binoculars from the bed.

'I'm not,' Tanya said, and walked out after Sam.

Ben could hear the heated discussion that was loud enough for all in the house to hear but not enough to wake the children. He packed his bag and wrote his phone number on a page torn from his notebook and left it on the bed. He knew Tanya would be the one to find it. He walked out through the kitchen and to the back yard without seeing anybody. *How the hell did I let that happen? These people need me. They have no other options; I have a plan that is now ninety percent complete on how we could solve this.* He knew it wasn't Tanya he was kissing, it was Rebecca, but to a husband, there were no excuses.

He banged the steering wheel with his palm in frustration and then started the car. He would stay close by in Palmerston North for a few days and hope that Sam would change his mind and let him fix this. He parked down the street from the farm's long driveway and watched for any strange cars that might approach the house but he soon fell asleep.

He was woken by the sun filling the windscreen of the Pajero as it rose in the eastern sky. He jumped up, raised the seat back and started the engine. It was freezing in the car, probably close to zero. He turned the heater up and drove up to the farmhouse driveway. Everything looked quiet. He then drove into town, bought some breakfast and coffee and headed back out to watch the farmhouse from a distance.

As he approached, he had an idea, and drove down Bill's driveway. He could see where the BMW of the Serbians had parked and left in a hurry the night before. He continued down toward the much older looking building and pulled up to the sounds of dogs barking. A man, thin, with a weathered face and wispy grey hair appeared. He was easily in his seventies. The man walked out with a suspicious look on his face. Ben jumped out of the Pajero and with a smile approached the man.

'Bill?' Ben said with a smile.

'Yes, what can I do for you?' the man said, still cautious.

'Bill, I've been staying with Frank and Alison next door and I don't know if you heard it but there was a bit of a disturbance last night.'

The man relaxed and said, 'Yes, I thought I heard a gunshot.'

'Yes, we had thieves and fired a shot over their heads to scare them off. I was just wondering if I could just park in your driveway to make sure they don't come back?'

'Of course, that's fine young man. Are they okay?'

'Yes, Tanya and her family are there now, I just want to make sure they're all safe.'

'Stay as long as you like, let me know if you need anything.'

'Will do, thank you Bill.'

Ben parked his car behind Bill's side of the uncleared bush and took the binoculars and his coffee and found a spot in the foliage where he could watch them.

He was only there an hour when Sam started packing the Mercedes to leave. Most likely they were going home to Wellington. He watched Tanya walk between the car and house, wearing jeans, boots and a western check long sleeve shirt. Her hair was in a ponytail and fitted the farm look perfectly. He thought of the kiss and how Tanya had become Rebecca in that moment. Although it was for just a few seconds, it reminded him that the beautiful redhead had embedded herself into his heart. But for that, the Taylor family would have to pay the price of it.

He walked back to the Pajero once they were packed and had said goodbye to Tanya's parents. He tucked in near the entrance of Bill's driveway and watched them leave, turning south toward their home.

The trip home for the Taylors was quiet. Both Tanya and Sam had a lot on their minds. There was no desire for meaningless chat. Tanya felt guilty that Sam had seen her kissing Ben, but it was just an uncontrollable urge that overwhelmed her in the moment. He was everything Sam wasn't, but that didn't make Sam a bad husband or father, quite the opposite. Sam was the only man she'd ever had or loved, and for the first time in their married life something inside her screamed a desire for someone else.

Sam decided he would contact a security team when he got home—two armed professionals to take him to work and bring him home. He'd have the same car take Bethany and Jack to school and pick them up after he was at his office. Surely the colonel would figure that he didn't want to play this deadly game and might just leave him alone. Or, for a program he could write in a few hours, he could make millions and retire.

He looked over at Tanya and wondered why she did it. *Was the rich cyber security expert boring to her now? Did she want more from Ben than just a kiss? What if I didn't turn up when I did?* He thought of Milena and how he'd felt with her in his arms. *Was that really any different?* Tanya seemed to accept what he'd done without question; maybe he needed to do the same. He reached over and put his hand on her leg. She looked up and when he smiled at her, she slowly smiled back. He knew then that they were both ready to move on.

CHAPTER TWENTY-FOUR

Ben followed at a distance to make sure they arrived safely to their Wellington home and that no one ran them off the road or was waiting for them when they arrived.

He decided he'd stay on for another day to see how Sam went about protecting his family. The next morning when a black car with two heavy security guards arrived, he could see that he had it covered. Ben felt he'd done all he could for now.

The next thing was to book a flight back to Alice Springs, collect his car and things from Rebecca's house and head back home to Adelaide. It was time for him to think ahead as well.

The flight back was a convoluted affair with a stop in Sydney, then Adelaide and then onto Alice Springs. Peter picked Ben up from the airport and Ben gave him a much-shortened version of the events in Palmerston North.

'How is the work for the police going, Pete?'

'Good, we caught the thieves, the drone was able to follow them without the police chasing them and causing a risk to other motorists.'

'Listen to you, risk to other motorists,' Ben said.

Peter laughed. 'Okay, the other stupid bloody drivers.'

'That's more like it.'

'Where are you going to stay?'

'Not sure… Actually, I might stay at Bec's place, that's if her parents haven't cleaned it out yet. My Jeep and rifle are still there anyway. Hey, yeah, drop me off there, and I want to go and see the sarge before I go. I'll probably hit the road tomorrow, it's been a while since I was home.'

'Sure thing, boss.'

Peter dropped Ben off and could see it was a little difficult for him. He watched him walk up, unlock the door and disappear inside. Peter released the brake and moved off to his own home. He thought about how Ben had saved his life, in more ways than one and just hoped that he'd get a chance to see him again, and moreover get a chance to repay the favour.

Inside, the smell of the woman he loved hit him hard, her perfume, the Dove soap she used. It was intoxicating, he expected her to just appear from the kitchen or bedroom, but of course she didn't. The fragrance was a reminder of love and passion and he wished he could bottle it. Her things were just where she'd left them. He picked up her shirt and bra that hung over a chair and covered his face with them. Nothing in his life would ever smell that good again. He wondered if she might come to him again tonight, but he was sure she had moved on, to wherever that other place was. It was still so vivid—the memory of the last time he felt her came crashing back in waves, when she'd entered him and he felt her forgiveness and farewell.

He managed the sadness better than he expected, yet was still afraid of what triggers might change that. He was quite aware that smell was the strongest of the senses that recall memory and how it had near overwhelmed him when he first walked in. He'd held it together, but realised the smell of her on the sheets could well be his undoing.

He changed into some clothes that suited the warmth and headed for the police station. He parked out front and walked in the door to see Constable Jackson at the counter. The man sprung to attention. Sergeant Jones was talking to a couple of rangers and did a double take when he looked up and then offered a warm welcome.

'Ben,' he said. 'Hold on just a minute.'

Jackson's eyes never left him, a look of effrontery on his face. Ben just smiled back at him, confirming that their beef was over.

'Come into my office Ben,' Jones said, walking away from the two rangers who also turned and headed for the police carpark.

'How have you been?' Jones asked.

'It was tough staying at Bec's place last night.'

'I'm sure it was.'

'As you probably know, Peter and I went to Fiji for a quiet little holiday but somehow we managed to find some trouble to get involved in.'

Jones laughed. 'Yes, Pete did tell me a little of it.'

'Well, it got a lot more exciting after that, let me tell you.'

'Now Ben, the way I see it, is, that you have a free dance card now. Would you be interested in a contract basis detective job? I've okayed it with Darwin and you've already proven that you're better than that mob we have up there.'

Ben smiled. He loved the idea, part time detective, much better pay than a private investigator, surely.

'Sarge, thank you, but without Bec here I have no reason to stay. Adelaide's my home and to be honest, I need a bit of a rest. I'm not going to take on any jobs for at least a month.'

'Well, the offer stands. We could certainly use someone like you here.'

Ben reached out and shook his hand. 'Thank you for everything sir, I really appreciate how you have supported me.' Ben paused for a second. 'And, I really miss that cheeky little redhead.' Tears started to well as he said it.

'Me too, Ben, me too.'

Ben smiled knowingly, nodded and turned to make a quick exit from the station. Within seconds he was in his Jeep and heading for the 'drive through' bottle shop to grab a six pack of beer, before driving back to Rebecca's place. He didn't stop for food. The hunger to just be back at her house, quietly on his own, was more than his rumbling need to eat. Once back, he rummaged through the kitchen, finding some cheese and biscuits which he consumed while he went through the many emails he had ignored in the past week.

He was soon tired of that and couldn't wait to get to bed and smell her for the very last time. He stripped off and slid into the side he had always slept on when he stayed there. He put his head on his pillow and reached for hers and buried his face into it. The scent of her was immense, he hugged the pillow tightly and the tears again started to mix with that precious fragrance.

He woke the next morning, both his arms wrapped around her pillow. He hugged and kissed it before he rolled over to leave the bed and head for the shower. She was there again, the smell of that soap, the same one that they had washed each other with the last time he'd stayed there. He let himself be consumed by the memories that the fragrance that he would never forget afforded him. He took in the vision of her beautiful naked body against his and how different she looked with her red curls wet. He recalled how he'd washed her hair, massaged her head with his fingers, and then all over her body, ending with them making love again right there in the shower. The memory was delicious but it was time to park that for now.

He dried himself, dressed and packed. He didn't have much, but his rifle was back in his possession, which gave him comfort. He took the last item out to the car, which was his gun and put it in its hiding place under the Jeep's back seat. He placed Rebecca's door key on the hallway table and looked up the passage for the last time, drew in a deep breath and closed the door, the click of the latch a sign that that chapter was closed.

He jumped into the Jeep, readying himself for the fifteen-hundred-kilometre trip back to Adelaide. It was a frosty morning still at 8.00 a.m. as he drove past the police station. Sergeant Jones was unlocking the door and he gave him a beep and a wave as he cruised by. He saw Jones stop to watch him as he disappeared down the Stuart highway.

He arrived back in Adelaide just before dark the following night. It was nice to be back in his city townhouse. He made himself at home and remembered the last time he'd been there was the night before he and Rebecca flew to Dallas to help Greg and Jennifer put her criminal husband in jail.

'Greg and Jennifer,' he said out loud and reached for his phone and sent a text.

Came Greg's reply.

Kara Gilbert? Yes sure. Why not? That will be interesting. I'll book
for 7 p.m.

Ben was going to enjoy his month off. His pot plants were basically dead and he would need to go and get some more and make the place feel like home again in the morning.

Ben woke in the bed he knew well; his custom-made mattress and bamboo fibre pillow were the creature comforts he'd missed for the last few months. Today was a new start. He jumped out of bed, quickly showered and then headed down to his local café that was opposite the Kent Town hotel, another haunt he was looking forward to getting back to. It was cool but the bite of winter had subsided for today. He decided that it was also time to top up his fitness that had probably dropped slightly in the last couple of months. A run around the River Torrens and a session at his local gym was a great way to add to the day before dinner tonight. A jog was like driving a long distance, it gave him time to reflect on things.

His thoughts started from the most recent—Sam Taylor. How someone so innocent and naive could find himself involved in international espionage. He jogged on past the Adelaide Zoo as he remembered running out to save Sam's daughter and how they could have both been shot and killed so easily at that time. He knew the agents never fired a shot at them, not one, although they were sitting ducks. They must have had orders that no one was to be harmed and create an international incident. His mind rallied on as his steps pounded away. One of them had been shot but still no return fire. He wondered how deep this was coming from. He suspected the Serbian government itself knew nothing about this and was just some small war mongering colonel trying to make himself look good and start a war that nobody wanted or needed. But, for Ben, that was over now.

Of course, then his thoughts went to Rebecca. As much as he tried to hide from the vision of her sitting in the upturned chair on that rickety verandah, he couldn't. It was so undignified. He stopped in the middle of the path, placed his hands on his knees and stared at the course, one hundred-year-old bitumen track beneath his Nikes.

A passerby would just assume he was exhausted, but he was far from that. He just wanted to collapse onto the green winter grass that adorned the side of the path and cry for the only girl he had ever loved. He thought he was past this, but the exercise had reduced his resolve and the pain in his heart returned as strong as ever. She could be with him now, jogging along the river as they chatted, planning the rest of their lives, but no! One small American bullet had changed all that.

He stood up straight and looked around. There was no one near on this late winter morning. He turned and walked back the way he came. As he passed the zoo again, he could hear the animals, monkeys he figured. He thought about all the animals that were killed just for the fun of it, just for sport, just for the thrill. Then he thought of the men he had killed. A precision shot that ended the life of someone he never knew, but they would've been bad men, wouldn't they? Sure, they were, that's why the government wanted them dead. One less person to shoot back at him or his team.

He started running again, faster than before. He decided that he would use the next month to clear his mind and slip back into a mainstream lifestyle.

Ben arrived early at the restaurant and ordered a beer. It was probably only ten minutes later when Greg and Jennifer walked up to the table. Ben stood as they arrived, greeting Jennifer with a hug and kiss on her cheek. He and Greg shook hands with the welcoming grip of bonded mates. Kara arrived a minute or two behind them. She looked so much different to the woman he had found in Melbourne. She was Greg and Jennifer's age, with long dark hair, green eyes and a nice figure that probably hadn't changed much since her twenties. She was a very good-looking middle-aged woman.

'Lovely to see you again, Jennifer,' Kara said as she took her hand and kissed her cheek. Before she could even say hello to Greg, he gestured her toward Ben. 'Kara, I think you may have already met Ben, but I'd like to properly introduce you to Ben Woolford,' Greg said with a grin.

Ben turned to face Kara, extended his hand and said, 'It's lovely to see you again, Ms Gilbert.'

'Oh, my God… it's you?! You're the man from Melbourne! I knew it!' She exclaimed. She whipped her head around to look at Greg. 'And you—you're a bastard—a sweet one, but still a bastard! You knew what happened all along, didn't you?'

Jennifer looked confused, while Greg and Ben just looked at each other and smiled.

Kara turned back to Ben. 'I should've realised. I knew it was strange that you knew my name in that kitchen.' She reached out and hugged him. 'That's for Melbourne. Thank you.'

Jennifer said as she took a seat, 'I think I need to hear this story.'

They took their seats and Greg started, 'It's a long story but the mini version is, Kara, as you know, is, my special friend who disappeared last year. She went to Melbourne without telling anyone; and I hired Ben here to find her. When he did track her down, she was in the middle of a couple's big domestic violence situation about to get flattened by this beast of a guy when Ben turned up just in time and dropped the fella.'

'And so, this man,' Kara said, patting him on the arm, 'was supposedly just walking past, before saving me and saying, 'Are you okay Kara?' I spend the next year trying to work out how the hell he knew my name. As for Mr Sheppard here, when we finally caught up, I told him all about what happened… and he didn't say a word about hiring Ben or that he already knew about the incident!'

'I see,' Jennifer said, desperately trying to put all the pieces together. The table fell silent for a moment before Greg and Jennifer perused the menu, chatting about the choices.

The waiter arrived to collect their orders and Kara then turned to Ben. 'So, tell me Ben, do you live here in Adelaide?'

'Yes, Kent Town, not that I'm there much.'

'I'm in Kensington, not far away,' Kara said with a flirtatious smile.

At this point Greg realised that Kara must have thought he'd invited her to dinner as a fourth, for a sort of date and he hadn't told her about Ben and Rebecca. *Damn it!*

'So, Ben, what have you been up to since all that shit in Alice?' asked Greg, now keen to change the subject.

'Well, Peter and I went to Fiji for a little holiday and ended up looking after a family that some Serbians were after and then I went to New Zealand with them and then got myself sacked.'

'Sacked, how did that happen, can I ask?' Greg said.

'Well, I kissed the bloke's wife,' Ben said in a lower voice.

'Really?' Greg asked, smiling.

'Yep, kissed her right in front of her husband, my client, Sam. Well, technically she kissed me, but same result, I guess. I'd just rescued her daughter from being abducted.'

'I get it, I wanted to kiss you too, after saving me from being belted by that woman's drunk husband,' Kara said, as she gently touched his arm.

'I'll remind you about that next time,' Ben said with a grin, enjoying the little flirt.

The meals arrived and relaxed, easy chat between the four consumed the table. Ben shared how he had been offered detective work in Alice Springs, but that he decided it was time for that door to close.

Jennifer knew that she had to bring up the fact that Rebecca had passed. She knew it wasn't the right place but to just ignore the fact would be disrespectful.

'Ben,' she said. 'I'm so sorry about Rebecca. Greg and I could see how much she loved you, when we were all in Texas. Such a tragic loss. It's probably good you are home now and not in Alice.'

'Thank you, Jennifer. I do miss her. But it does feel good to be back with friends—all three of you,' he said, giving Kara a wink.

Kara shot a horror glance at Greg, then dropped her head. *I'm such an idiot. This poor man—and I've been playing up to him like a fool.* She drew herself up, and turned to Ben.

'Ben, I'm so sorry. I had no idea. Losing someone you love, is heartbreaking.'

'Thanks Kara, appreciate that. But it's okay. I'll be fine.'

Suddenly Ben's phone rang. He looked at the number, +64, New Zealand.

'This can't be good,' he said, looking at Greg and standing up to answer. 'Excuse me, I'll take this outside.'

'Hello.'

'Ben, it's Tanya, they have him,' she said so fast he could hardly understand.

'Whoa, Tanya, slow down, they have who? Sam or Jack?'

'Sam, he didn't come home from work yesterday. The security guards who usually collect him from work were found bashed and tied up this morning. I didn't know who else to call, I can't tell the police the full story.'

'No, don't tell the police, whatever you do don't do that. Have you tried 'Find my phone' for his mobile?'

'The police did, came up with nothing.'

'What about an iPad or his computer? He will definitely have that with him.'

'I haven't tried that; I'll do it now and call you back.'

The phone went dead. This was just the scenario, the Plan C that he had been working on. Ben walked inside and sat back down; everyone's eyes were on him. He looked up and said, 'I think I just got that job back. Sam Taylor has disappeared.'

'The Serbians?' Greg asked.

'That's my guess,' he said as the phone rang again.

He answered, not leaving the table this time.

'Oh my God, Ben, he's in Belgrade, Nemanjima street. How did they get him there so fast?'

'Private jet, it would be easy, they could have him there in ten hours. Tanya, please send me that address and any other information you have, however small. I will get onto it tonight. I already have a plan in place in case this happened. I'll be in touch.' And he hung up the phone.

'I'm sorry everyone, I need to go. Hey, what are you doing for the next week, Greg?'

'I can be free, are you okay with that, sweetheart,' Greg said looking at Jennifer.

She wore a look of concern but said, 'Of course, but keep him safe.'

'Great, pack a bag for Serbia, we leave tomorrow morning.'

'Will do,' he said looking at Jennifer to be sure she was still okay.

Ben looked at Kara. Her dark hair, olive skin and gregarious personality could be just what he needed to fill his team.

'Hey, Kara, you're an actress, right? I remember from reading your profile.'

'I did some acting in my younger days, no Hollywood stuff but television commercials and a small film or two.'

'That's perfect, I have a job for you as well if you'd like?'

'As long as you'll kiss me at the end this time, sign me up,' Kara said jokingly, not thinking he was really serious.

'That I will, I promise. Okay, be ready to leave tomorrow morning, travel light, we will be flying into Pristina, Kosovo and sneaking across the border into Serbia.'

'Oh my God, you aren't joking? It sounds exciting—sort of!' Kara said.

'Trust me, it will be the hardest kiss you've ever earnt,' Ben said as he leant over to kiss Jennifer on the cheek. 'I'll make sure he comes home safely to you Jennifer.' Then he looked at Greg and Kara in turn. 'I'll see *you two* in the morning.' He turned and raced out of the restaurant, jumping into a taxi that was just dropping someone off.

CHAPTER TWENTY-FIVE

Sam Taylor had booked a security firm that would pick him up from his house, take him to work and then return to pick up the two children and take them to school. One of the big Mauri guards would escort them to the door of the school and do the same in reverse at the end of the day. It wasn't always the same two men, but Sam felt that he was getting to know them all and was in good hands. The colonel had stopped messaging and although he lay in bed at night imagining the millions he could make if he took up the offer, the thought of a lifetime in jail was enough to wipe the greed from his mind.

Several days had past and there was no mention of the incident with Milena from Tanya, and he wasn't going to bring up the kiss with Ben Woolford either. Life almost felt back to normal and he was starting to feel a little like a celebrity having a chauffeur driven vehicle take him the work and pick him up each day. Jack didn't really understand it, but Bethany certainly did. She knew full well why the guards were picking her up and she never wanted to be in the same situation again. The memory of being dragged across a paddock by an unknown man dressed all in black was still fresh in her mind.

It was Friday and a full week had passed since they arrived back from the farm. Sam had the security firm booked on a per month basis and was seriously thinking of cutting that back. The incident at the farm must have scared them off. He would keep the drop-off for the children till the end of the month but he was keen to get the GT3 Porsche out of the shed again. He closed his computer, tidied his desk and after calling out, 'have a good weekend' to everyone he made his way to his pickup point. There was a small amount of drizzle as he left the building's front door that had been on and off all day. He could see the black Holden Statesman was in the same place it always was. He covered his head with his computer bag and ran to the car. He was a little surprised when the passenger didn't jump out and open the door for him, but it was raining he figured. He slid into the back seat and placed his briefcase on the floor so it didn't wet the leather seats.

'Good evening, gentlemen,' Sam said, reaching for the seatbelt.

The car was already moving when the man in the passenger seat replied.

'Good evening Mr Taylor,' Goran said.

Sam's heart dropped. He reached for the door handle and there was no resistance, he could've made a run for it when they stop at lights, but the child locks were on.

'Where are you taking me?' he demanded.

'Mr Taylor, the colonel is becoming inpatient and is very keen to talk to you but you continue to ignore his invitation, so he has asked us to escort you to his office.'

'In Serbia?' Sam said in shock.

'Mr Taylor, just sit back, we have a first-class flight for you.'

Sam snuck out his phone from his pocket; but before he could even turn it on, it was snatched from his hands. Goran held the phone in front of his face and snapped it in half.

They headed north out of the city. It was almost dark now and the rain had stopped. Goran reached over the seat and before Sam could resist, a black hood was pulled over his head.

'If you leave it on, I will not tie your hands, do you understand Mr Taylor?'

'Yes,' Sam said, in no doubt that Goran wasn't bluffing.

They drove for nearly an hour when he felt the car leave the highway and travel for what seemed another fifteen minutes along a dirt road. The car slowed; Sam sensed they were turning into a driveway. Another five minutes and the car stopped and both men in the front of the car exited. Sam's door opened and he felt a firm hand take hold of his arm.

'This way please, Mr Taylor.'

'My computer?' Sam said.

'My friend will get that for you.'

Goran stopped and Sam took another step that hit something that sounded plastic. The hood was removed and in front of him was a staircase connected to a sleek, black, two engine jet. It wasn't very big but it certainly looked fast.

'Please Mr Taylor,' Goran said, pointing to the open door. He started his way up, appreciating that his hands weren't bound. He ducked his head to enter the luxurious jet. The interior was as extravagant as you could ever imagine, large tan leather seats ran up both sides of the cabin. A timber desk was positioned on one side with two seats facing each other. He was directed to a seat that had no window and was asked to fit his seat belt. The engines on the aircraft were now running and a man with three stripes on his epaulets appeared from the cockpit and pulled the main door closed. He secured the large locking handle and headed back to the cockpit, closing the door behind him. The aircraft made two turns after a short taxi and then went to full throttle. Sam was pushed back in his seat harder than any commercial jet he had ever been in and only seconds later they lifted off the ground.

'Mr Taylor we will shortly land in Wellington, where an immigration official will inspect the plane while we refuel. You and my friend here will hide in a small compartment in the back. He will have a gun at your head. You make the slightest noise; he will shoot you and I the officer. Is that completely clear?'

'Yes,' Sam said nervously.

The plane landed at Wellington airport only a few minutes later and the process went exactly as Goran described. The official was on and off the aircraft in seconds. He heard the main door close and what he imagined was the refuelling truck leave. As the plane started to taxi, the hatch was lifted and Sam was instructed to make himself comfortable and take a seat.

'Would you like a drink, Mr Taylor?' Goran asked.

'What the hell! Scotch please.'

Goran returned with a chunky crystal tumbler that held three large ice cubes and a healthy serving of the Scottish amber liquid.

Sam took a sip, then relaxed enough for the bigger picture to sink in.

'My wife will be freaking out,' he said to Goran.

'I'm sure you will be home soon enough, Mr Taylor. Just give the colonel what he wants, and you could be back at work on Monday.'

Ben gave the taxi his Kent Town address and called Steve.

'Steve, Ben, I need you and Dan in Pristina, Kosovo ASAP. Get there as fast as you can. I know it won't be straight forward but just do what's quickest.'

'Roger that, do we need to take anything?'

'No, if my plan works, everything we need will be supplied.'

'Roger that, over and out.'

Ben hung up and opened the World Time app that told him it was 1.00 p.m. in Pristina, Kosovo's capital.

The taxi pulled up outside Ben's townhouse. He paid the driver and ran inside. He flipped open his computer, found the contact for the minister of defence amongst his notes, grabbed his phone and dialled the number.

After a few beeps and international tones, the phone was answered by a woman speaking what he assumed was Albanian.

'English please,' he said.

'I speak little English,' the woman said back.

'I need to speak to Mr Alimir Azarmi, the defence minister. It's urgent.'

'Sorry sir, you need appointment,' the woman said back.

'Please take down my number and tell him that there is a virus in your military computers that has been put there by the Serbians.'

'Yes, sir I will pass that on. I have your number here.' And she was gone.

This was a critical part of the plan.

Next was to book some flights. He was surprised to see that he could have himself, Greg and Kara in Kosovo within twenty-eight hours leaving at 10.00 a.m. tomorrow morning. There would be airline changes in Doha and Istanbul but the one-day travel was ideal. He knew Kara's details from the job he had of finding her, and Greg's were still on file. He pushed the buy button when his phone rang.

'Hello,' Ben said after the international beeps had stopped.

'Hello, my name is Enis Januzaj. I am the assistant for the Deputy Minister of Defence of the Republic of Kosovo. How can I help you?' the man said in particularly good English.

'Sir, my name is Ben Woolford, I am a private detective in Australia. I have reason to believe that you have a virus in your government and military computers that the Serbs have hidden behind your firewall.'

'I see Mr…'

'Woolford, have you pen?'

'Yes, I writing this down.'

'Get your people to look for two files, one is, program1.exe and the second is, program2.exe. One is a trojan and the other is the worm that is infiltrating your system. Have your experts check that but do not delete it, then call me back.'

'Yes, sir, I will call you back.'

Ben put his phone down and started packing for the trip. He had no idea how long he'd be away, but was hoping he would be back in under a week. Of course, that was if he came back at all. The plan he had was probably as dangerous as anything he'd experienced in Afghanistan.

It was only twenty minutes when the next call came in from Kosovo.

'Did you find it?' Ben asked without any preamble.

'Yes, we did. I have the minister here with me. He doesn't speak English so I will interpret. What is your name sir?'

'My name is Ben Woolford, I'm a private detective in Australia.' Ben said again. 'A client of mine was blackmailed by a Serbian official, Colonel Milovan Simovic, to produce the virus to penetrate your computers.'

Ben waited as the message was translated.

'We know of this man. How long has the virus been in our computers?'

'About two weeks.'

'How do we remove it?'

'Sir, you must under no circumstances try and delete the files, it will have all your computers crashing. The only person that can remove it has been kidnapped by the Serbians and is presently in Belgrade.' Ben hoped he sounded convincing enough.

'How can we get this person?'

'With your help, if you can supply my team weapons, and a way over the border, I will bring him to you and he will not only fix it but prevent it happening again.'

Ben waited as the men discussed the situation.

'What is in it for you, Mr Woolford?'

'The man is my client, and my job is to get him home safely.'

'Mr Woolford how can we trust you?'

'Mr Januzaj, I have shown you that the virus is there. It was uploaded by a spy in your government. I just want to get my asset home safe and all you have to do is lend me some equipment. It's very low risk for you.'

There was a longer pause this time.

'When can you do this?' eventually Januzaj said.

'We are booked on flights and will be in Pristina at ten hundred hours the day after tomorrow, your time, on a flight from Istanbul.'

'Mr Woolford, the Minister is very keen to discuss this further and will meet with you as soon as possible on your arrival.'

'Thank you, Mr Januzaj, I will call this number when we are on the ground in Pristina.'

'We will pick you up sir. How many of you?'

'Five of us,' Ben said.

'Only five?'

'Yes, we aren't planning on starting a war, just preventing one and extracting an innocent man.'

'Okay, and thank you, Mr Woolford, your help is greatly appreciated.'

'Roger that, we'll talk soon, oh, and by the way, you said you know all about this Colonel Simovic, I need everything you have on him, where he works, lives, eats and shits, everything, however small.'

'I will have that ready on your arrival.'

'Thank you.'

Ben hung up the phone and called Steve to see where he was at with flights for himself and Dan. Steve confirmed that they would meet in Doha and be on the same two flights from there to Kosovo. Ben quickly briefed Steve on the details of the mission. Ben explained that he had a basic outline of a plan, but a lot of the gaps would need to be filled in once they were there.

Next was a call to Greg.

'Hello Ben,' Greg said as he answered. 'Are we still full speed ahead?'

'Yes, all good, the first part of the plan is complete and I'll fill you in along the way.'

'Great, let me know if there's anything I can do.'

'Mate, do you think Kara is up for this? I mean, this won't be a walk in the park, these are dangerous people.'

'She would be up for anything. She can certainly act a part, she was a great actress.'

'Great, that's exactly what we need. I'm planning on her flirting with the colonel, who is the one behind this whole mess. She may need to do a little more than just flirt, let's see.'

'Okay, I guess we won't be far away, will we?'

'No, we will be right there at all times.'

'Well, I can't think of a better person.'

'Me either, okay, I'll see you at the airport at zero, eight hundred. Don't forget your passport.'

'Roger that, we will see you then.'

Ben's next call was to Kara.

'Kara, Ben.'

'Hello Ben, you still want me along?'

'Yes, but it's only fair I give you a little heads up about what we will need from you. You can change your mind if you want.'

'Okay, shoot,' she said.

'This will be a dangerous mission, don't underestimate that. But I will be doing my best to keep you and Greg out of any of the major action. Greg's role will be predominately driving; and yours, well… is to have dinner, a few drinks and maybe flirt with a certain person to see if we can get information out of him.'

'I can do that.'

'I have no idea how it may all go.'

She stopped and thought for a moment. 'I've probably done worse, as long as you can keep me safe?'

'That will always be our first priority.'

'Alright, I trust you, Ben. You've saved me once. That's good enough for me. I'm in.'

'Things change as you can imagine, we don't have a full picture yet, but I will brief you on your cover once we are wheels up tomorrow.'

'Okay, I'm nervous but excited.'

'Let's hope it's a good experience for us all Kara. Glad to have you on the team. See you tomorrow.'

As Ben hung up the call, he had a thought and dialled a familiar number.

'Peter, what are you up to?'

'Now?'

'No, the next week or so?'

'Nothing I think, the sarge didn't say he needed me for anything.'

'Do you want to get back on the job, the Taylor's job?'

'You bet. New Zealand?'

'No, Serbia.'

'Serbia, shit yeah.'

'Okay start packing. I will send you flight details. Bring the drone and every battery you have.'

'The airlines are a bit funny with taking lithium batteries on the plane,' Peter said.

'Okay bring what you can and we should hopefully be able to buy some there.'

'Yes, sir, I'm packing now.'

Ben found him an overnight flight to Adelaide that would enable him to travel the whole way with them.

Next was to Tanya. He dialled the +64 number and she answered almost straight away. He checked his watch and realised it would be early hours of the morning there.

'Tanya, it's all in place. We leave first thing in the morning.'

'Oh God Ben, thank you.'

'Tanya, this won't be a cheap exercise and I can't promise you anything.'

'Ben, I have absolutely no choice, you are my best and only option. We have money, don't risk his life trying to save dollars.'

'Yes Ma'am,' he said. 'I'll keep you informed as we progress. Keep searching for the computer, they will be turning it on again at some stage.'

'I will, every chance I get.'

'Okay, talk soon,' he said and ended the call.

Next was to make a list of everything he could possibly need from the Kosovars. He included handguns and rifles, sniper and automatic. Radios with in-ears and plain or Serbian uniforms should they be seen or caught. He tried to picture each scenario as he knew once they were over the border there would be no last-minute deliveries. The list was long, but he preferred to be over supplied than under. He still had no idea how the drone would play and it wouldn't be until they were well into the situation that he would know. All he did know though, was that every time he didn't have it, he wished he did. He now needed some sleep.

He stood and looked out the glass sliding door that displayed the shrivelled dried-up plants that was his garden. He reached for the kettle and went outside and poured the contents onto the only one that had some resemblance of life. He hoped that he would return soon enough to water it again. He turned and locked the door, set his alarm for 6.00 a.m., and was soon fast asleep.

CHAPTER TWENTY-SIX

Sam was snoring in the leather chair, four scotches in, when he felt the jet start its descent. He woke with a start and quickly realised where he was and the dire situation that he was now in. He imagined it would only be hours now before he met with the colonel. He would refuse of course, but then what, would they just shoot him? He pictured his family watching his coffin being unloaded from an aircraft. Then realised how silly that was.

He would just disappear, never to be seen again, no body for his family to mourn or bury.

His children would be raised by another man, hell, it might even be Ben Woolford. He shivered, suddenly icy cold at his isolation. *No one even knows I'm out of the country.* He would just be one of those people that went to work and never came home. *Oh shit.* That's exactly what would happen, whether he helped them or not. They would just dispose of him. He would know too much.

Sam looked out the window of the jet. It was still dark. He knew travelling west would make it a long night. He tried to imagine what time it would be in Wellington, probably morning. He wasn't sure what day, probably Saturday. Tanya would be a mess.

The plane landed and taxied straight into a hanger. He felt the aircraft stop and the pilots shut down both engines. He could see through his window that armed guards flanked the same Mecedes he had ridden in only a couple of weeks ago. The co-pilot appeared again, opened the main door and lowered it down. It also incorporated the stairs.

'Mr Taylor, this way please,' Goran said.

Sam descended the stairs and walked toward the open rear door of the car. He sat down on the soft white leather and the door was closed for him. Goran sat in the front and the man Sam hid with under the hatch on the plane sat beside him.

'Unfortunately, Mr Taylor, we won't be providing the same level of accommodation as last time,' Goran said without turning his head. Sam didn't reply. It was still dark with no sign of the sun rising anytime soon. The car pulled up to a heavy security airport perimeter gate. The man next to him jumped out and opened it with a swipe card.

Again, above the law.

It wasn't long before the car stopped in front of the same building where Sam had conducted the training. He was shown to a room in the opposite wing to the training room. Goran led the way and the other man followed Sam from behind. They walked almost the full length of the wing when Goran opened a door to the room and walked in. Sam followed. It was basically a big hotel room. Timber halfway up the walls, with green wallpaper or paint and the same green carpet as the meeting room. There was what looked like an ensuite and walk-in robe.

I expected worse.

'This is your room. I will come and get you once the colonel arrives. He is here about 9.00 a.m. Please be ready. And, Mr Taylor, don't try and leave the room.'

'My computer?'

'It will be at the meeting.'

Goran turned and left the room, closing the door behind him. Sam heard a lock clunk into place a moment after.

Sam fell back onto the bed. *What am I going to do?*

If he wrote the programs, they would keep him till they were implemented and then kill him. If he refused to give it to them, would they torture him and then kill him.

He imagined the many forms of torture that he'd seen on television. *How long could I hold out? Would I wait until I was maimed beyond repair and then give them what they wanted? Maybe I could give them the virus files and escape, telling the authorities what had happened... but that wouldn't work, these people were above the law. I'm screwed whichever way I go.*

He realised in that moment that it would be very unlikely he would ever see his family again.

Ben was at the airport when Peter arrived into Adelaide from Alice Springs and it wasn't long until Greg and Kara arrived as well. Kara wasn't the same playful person that she'd been the night before. A few hours' sleep and the realisation of what she may be getting herself into had dawned on her. Ben noticed the change.

'Are you okay Kara? It's not too late to pull out and you can at any stage.'

'No, I'm good. I know Greg won't let me do anything too dangerous.'

'I know he won't and neither will I.'

They found a table in the far corner of a café where they could talk and not be overheard.

'Kara, your job will be to get friendly with one of the officials to see what he would be prepared to let slip to impress a pretty woman. You will be English, your eastern suburbs accent would fool them easily, I think. We will have a wire on you, so you won't need to remember anything.'

Kara smiled, a sense of relief overcoming her.

'Greg, you will be our driver of course. What and how we are going to do this, I don't know yet. We need to find where they have Sam, what security and how to get him out. We will start in Belgrade where Tanya found the ping from his computer.'

Ben told them all he knew about the colonel, which wasn't a lot, but this should be easier than the extractions his team had done in the middle east.

It was soon time to head through the immigration and customs terminals and board the Airbus A350 to Doha. Peter would get his second stamp in his new passport. He had no idea what he was in for but the excitement of being involved was hard to control. The first flight was the long one and Ben wanted to sit next to Kara to brief her thoroughly on his plan.

The big widebody Airbus taxied to the hold point and waited for the take-off clearance that would begin the thirteen-hour flight. It turned onto runway two three and was soon climbing on its way to thirty-eight thousand feet. Ben could see that Kara was nervous, he wasn't sure whether it was from the flight or what the hell she had signed up for.

'Are you okay?' Ben asked her again.

'Yes, I just hope I can do what you need.'

'There's no pressure at all. There are a few ways this can go and we may not need you at all and you can just sit back and enjoy a holiday in another country.'

She smiled back at him. 'I want to help if I can.'

'Let's see what we find when we get there. My plan A didn't include a woman being involved but when I saw you at the restaurant, a plan started to form, so I'm glad we have another option, thank you.'

The flight went quickly with them all consuming three movies each. It was 5.00 p.m., when the plane touched down in the Qatar capital. It had been a long day, the daylight extended by seven and a half hours. Steve and Dan were already there when Ben, Greg,

Peter and Kara walked into the international transfer terminal. It was all business with these boys and Ben loved that about them. The three of them knew exactly how dangerous this could be and that they would be the ones in the firing line.

It was a four hour wait for the next flight to Istanbul which would take around four and a half hours and then transfer to a regional commuter plane that would have them in Pristina, Kosovo at 6.00 a.m.

Ben discussed his list of equipment with Steve and Dan while Greg, Peter and Kara cruised the middle eastern Arab airport. Ben made a few additions to the list and then told them all he knew.

'His henchmen have seen me, so I will need to stay low. We need to find this colonel and hopefully he can lead us to Sam. I have the exact address that popped up when his wife did a 'find my computer' search but that has since gone, flat battery on the computer I guess.'

'Are we taking on a government here, Ben?' Steve asked.

'I don't think so. I'm guessing the colonel is doing this off his own back but I can't say someone high up doesn't know something about it. Either way, you can bet it's unofficial.'

'That's better for us,' Dan said.

'Much better,' agreed Ben.

The three men looked at each other, all starting to think the same thing.

Then Steve said, 'This can only end one way Ben.'

'Yes, I know, otherwise they'll keep coming after him,' Ben admitted.

The three sightseers returned and it wasn't long before the six of them were lining up for the Pegasus Airlines A321 to Istanbul. It was dark now and they had all been awake for over twenty hours so each of them slept while they could. They changed planes again after another long wait, and were soon landing into Adem Jashari airport, Pristina, Kosovo at 6.05 a.m.

The six of them slipped through immigration without any question—it was obvious that an instruction had come from above.

Ben was first to exit the airside door and was immediately greeted by a man in a black suit. He was short, not much over five feet, thin black hair that was combed to cover his balding head as best it could. He wore thin framed glasses that Ben was sure he'd seen in movies from the sixties. He held out his hand and looked up to the six-foot-three ex-soldier.

'Enis Januzaj,' the man said with a smile. 'Thank you for coming, you must be exhausted.'

'Ben Woolford,' he said and introduced his team by first name only. The minister's assistant was a little taken aback when Kara was introduced. He clearly didn't expect a woman to be involved in such a dangerous mission.

Mr Woolford, the minister wanted to be here himself but had another engagement this morning. He has asked if you could come to his office and discuss what we can do to help you.'

Januzaj held out a welcoming hand in the direction of a black Mercedes Vito van with dark tinted windows. The six of them with their bags, filed into the van. The door was soon closed and the van departed. None of them had ever been to Kosovo and were surprised at how pretty Pristina was. There was no big high-rise buildings and the traffic appeared to travel smoothly.

The van turned into an underground carpark at the Rilindja Tower, the building that the whole country was run from. The van stopped and the sliding door opened for them by a man that appeared from nowhere.

'Mr Woolford, we have booked you accommodation nearby. I suggest we meet with the minister and our head of state security—he will be the one that will supply the equipment you need. Then you get some rest and tonight we will get you into Serbia.'

'That's great, thank you. Can we please have Greg, Kara and Peter taken to the accommodation as they are tired and not needed for the equipment meeting?'

'Of course,' Januzaj said, and gave an instruction in Albanian to the driver.

Ben turned to Greg. 'Get some rest mate, it will be a long night for you, probably a seven-hour drive via who knows where to get to Belgrade.'

'Will do,' Greg said as he Peter and Kara jumped back in the Mercedes van.

Ben, Steve and Dan looked like warriors with their solid builds, black military pants and boots. They stood in a plush waiting room with looks that crossed somewhere between confidence and arrogance, when Alimir Azarmi, the defence minister, arrived to meet them. Ben noticed the look of approval. Januzaj introduced the minister to the three men along with a tall dark man in full military dress. He was in his late fifties, grey hair and stood with an air of confidence as he qualified the three men. Ben quickly assumed a rank of colonel having no stars on his epilates.

'This is Colonel Dushku of the Kosovo Security Force,' Januzaj said.

They all shook hands; it was an awkward situation and they all knew it. If this went wrong, it could reignite the already delicate situation between the two countries. The six men sat around a twelve-person French polished timber conference table.

'Mr Woolford, the colonel should be able to get you what you need but you must know that no one outside this room knows anything about this and it must stay that way. If you are caught, killed or stranded, we cannot come to your rescue and will deny any knowledge of any of you. The weapons we will supply will be what we have captured from the insurgents and rebel fighters. We can't have any links back to us. Is that acceptable to you?'

'It is exactly what I expected, sir,' Ben said.

The colonel said something in Albanian to Januzaj.

'Do you have the list of equipment, Mr Woolford?'

Ben reached into his top pocket and pulled out the A4 page and handed it directly to the colonel. The colonel took it without saying anything and Ben watched his eyes as he worked his way down the list. He noted an eyebrow raise once somewhere about the middle of the list.

'Mire?' the colonel said in Serbian.

'We can supply this for you,' a relieved Januzaj said.

The minister spoke and they waited for the translation.

'Mr Woolford, can you please outline for the minister your plan and how we will get the virus removed from the computers.'

'I would like to go over the border tonight, if we can. It will take us a couple of days to locate the asset and secure him safely. We hopefully can come back the same way and I will deliver Mr Taylor here to remove the virus for you. Remember, do not try and remove it yourselves.'

Januzaj translated the statement and the minister said something to the colonel, who then stood and left the room. The minister also stood and said something to Januzaj. He reached for the hand of Ben, then Steve and Dan and then also left the room.

'The minister wishes you the best of luck and looks forward to seeing you back here soon with a victorious outcome.'

'So do we, Mr Januzaj.'

'At 10.00 p.m., tonight we will deliver to you two vehicles and an escort that will take you to a secret path that is almost on the Bulgarian border. It hasn't been used since the war with those dogs, so it could be slow going. There will be a man that will meet you with a barge at 12.00 a.m. That will get you across the Danube River and into Serbia. We will include Serbian licence plates so you will fit in.'

Ben looked at Steve and Dan. 'Any questions?'

'How will we contact the barge driver on our return?' Steve said.

'He will give you a contact number and a map for when you are ready,' Januzaj said.

'Okay, we should all get some sleep. It will be a long night,' Ben said.

'Gentleman, the driver will take you to your hotel. Two Land Rovers will be delivered at 10.00 p.m., with what you have asked for inside.'

They followed Januzaj back out to the waiting Vito van. He wished them luck and the three ex SAS soldiers headed for the hotel.

Ben texted Greg, Peter and Kara to be ready at twenty-one hundred hours in the foyer of the hotel. He hated not being able to have a more solid plan, but it was impossible until he got there. The big advantage was that no one knew they were coming and the more he thought about it, Kara could be his biggest asset.

CHAPTER TWENTY-SEVEN

Ben's alarm woke him and for just a second, he had no idea where he was. He looked around the stark white hotel room and his heart accelerated as the jetlag fogginess cleared. He jumped into action, showered and packed his gear. He was again going to battle with some untrained crew but he would do his best to keep them out of harm's way. His main concern was for Kara who would be in the lion's mouth and he wondered whether he would still go ahead with that plan.

Everyone was assembled in the hotel foyer when Ben arrived down from his room. There was an air of excitement among them. Three black Land Rovers were parked outside the hotel. The Kosovar colonel approached Ben and offered a greeting that he didn't understand. The colonel opened the rear door of the second Land Rover and opened three khaki coloured duffle bags. There was everything he could remember asking for. He could see an Israeli Uzi and two AK47's. Behind them were three bolt action rifles, none of them the same but all had reasonable looking scopes. The second bag contained black coveralls and flak jackets that were probably of Russian origin. Ben turned, thanked the colonel and shook his hand and without another word, the man turned and walked away. Ben reached into the third bag and took out two handheld radios and handed one to Greg.

The Kosovar drivers jumped into the first car, Steve, Dan with Ben driving hopped into the second and Greg, Peter and Kara into the third. The first car moved off and Greg and Ben followed close behind. It was dark, the low cloud obscuring any light from the moon or stars. The traffic was light, and the streetlights contributed very little to the vision. The first car turned onto a main road that headed south. Ben knew Serbia was to the north of Kosovo and Belgrade in the north of Serbia which would mean that there would be a lot of driving before they slept again. The lead car didn't mess around and Greg and Ben spent most of the time significantly over the speed limit trying to keep up. He tried to imagine explaining to a traffic cop why his car was full of assault and sniper rifles but figured the two men in front could sort that. They reached a small town called Gjilan and they turned east. Ben had worked out that they would be entering Serbia in its most southwestern corner. It was now 11.00 p.m.; the road had turned into a single lane of broken bitumen which then turned to a dirt road that hadn't seen a grader in years. Ben looked at his watch—the barge would be there at midnight.

Steve had his maps open on his phone and was following the route.

'How far from the Macedonian border are we?' Ben asked Steve.

'About the same distance as we are from Serbia but it looks like dense scrub when I look at the aerial shot.'

'I guess it needs to be or the Serbians would have found it by now.'

The black Land Rover in front stopped and Ben and Greg pulled up behind them. The two men were quickly out and with a roll each of what looked like black duct tape started to tape over the headlights of the two cars. Everyone watched and didn't speak; it was obvious to them all what they were doing. The men left a slit about twenty millimetres wide in each light and then covered the taillights completely. One of the Kosovars went back to the first vehicle and returned with two scary looking machete's and two torches. The first man pointed to a small hole between two trees and said something that no one understood. He pointed to his watch and Ben recognised the word 'twelve'.

Ben nodded and shook both the men's hands.

'Thank you,' Ben said, and he assumed what they said back was something like 'Good luck'.

'After you, my friend,' Ben said to Greg and everyone jumped back into their cars.

Greg turned into the clearing and drove through the bushes. The headlights were only just lighting up the track. It was obvious that this track hadn't been used since the war between these two countries in 1999 which only ended when America commenced bombing raids over Serbia under the loose guise of NATO. He knew that these two neighbours had never kissed and made up and war was always just one argument away.

'How far from the river are we?' Ben asked Steve.

'Probably only one kilometre but at this rate we won't make it.'

It was slow going, with low light and the thick growth. Greg stopped and hopped out and walked up to Ben's window.

'Mate, I can't see shit and I don't want to head off the wrong way and get us lost.'

'We are only about a kilometre from the river, so we just need to average one K per hour to get there in time. Steve and Dan can you guys take the machetes and torches and walk the track for us?'

'Sure thing,' they replied, and jumped out armed with the heavy swords.

'That would be perfect,' Greg said, heading back to the first car's driving seat.

Greg was cringing at the sound of the branches scraping along the side of the almost new cars but figured that if what they were doing was going to stop a war, paintwork on two cars was a small price to pay. They moved on at a fair pace, but it was lucky to be the one kilometre per hour that they needed. Ben watched Steve and Dan studying the ground when the track became invisible.

Only once they needed to back up and relocate the correct position. They all knew if it had of been winter this task would be impossible.

Ben checked his watch, 11:45. He didn't need to ask Steve how much further because they would get there when they could.

Steve held up his arm with a clenched fist, the sign to stop. Greg saw Steve and Dan kill their torches and he switched off the Land Rover's lights. He saw Ben do the same. It was pitch black now, the only light was from the dashboard lights that faintly lit the faces of his two passengers, Kara and Peter. Greg reached up and turned off the interior light switch before he opened the door. He felt as much as saw Ben walk past to where Steve and Dan were standing. Greg hopped out and joined them. There was complete silence except for a small diesel engine that was running at not much over idle.

'Hopefully that's our barge,' Ben said, pulling back the bushes that hid them from the Serbian side of the river.

There were no lights on the barge when it bumped into the bank only metres from them.

'Hello,' Ben called in a hushed voice.

A child's voice replied. 'Hello, are you ready?'

The four men looked at each other. 'Yes,' Ben called back.

A torch from the barge lit up the front of the floating platform. Steve and Dan climbed forward to receive the ramps that would assist in loading. Steve chopped away the last of the bushes exposing the front of Greg's Land Rover. Greg could see that the barge was old and lucky if it was designed to carry the two and a half tonne vehicle. The ramps were long and with that the weight of the car would press further down the barge and reduce the chance of it tipping up. Greg suggested for Kara and Peter to leave the vehicle because if it all turned to shit and tipped over, he didn't want to be worrying about getting anyone out other than himself.

They could now see there was an older man and a young boy. It was obvious the young boy was there to translate instructions.

'My grandfather will hold the boat to the bank with power,' the boy said.

Greg heard the boat's engine revs increase slightly and he selected low range and started forward toward the edge of the bank. He felt the front wheels touch the ramps and he slowly moved along them. Water was lapping over the front of the barge now and he knew if he didn't hurry and get to the middle it would sink. The back wheels touched and he moved swiftly to the middle of the floating death trap. The barge rocked violently as he braked. The old man said something and the boy said, 'We must hurry.'

Greg waved for Peter and Kara to board and Steve and Dan quickly slid the ramps onto the barge.

'Go with them, Steve,' Ben called and Steve jumped the small gap that had already appeared as the old man reversed the boat. Water spilled over all four corners as the top-heavy barge rocked as it crossed the one-hundred-metre-wide river. The old man was as gentle with the controls as a Tai chi expert. He was very aware that any sudden moves would have them all in the river. The young boy handed Greg a map.

'This will get you to the road from Macedonia. It will be much easier than what you just did.'

'Thank you, young fella and thank your grandfather as well.'

'I have been told this is very important,' the boy said.

Greg touched him on the shoulder and said, 'Yes, very important.'

The boy nodded and the barge tapped gently onto the opposite bank.

Steve and Peter had the ramps in place and Greg knew from the loading that it was important to get off quickly. He selected drive and rolled forward till both front wheels were on the ramp. He wanted the weight on them before accelerating off and up the bank. This side must have been shallower than the other side because the front of the barge didn't dip anywhere near as much. He was quickly off and Steve, Peter and Kara followed walking. Steve and Peter pushed the ramps back aboard the barge and watched the barge disappear into the darkness back towards the other side to collect the other car. They heard it clunk into the far side bank and then the metal ramps drag along the steel barge deck and shortly after, the engine started on Ben's Land Rover.

Again, the barge rolled and tipped as the much too heavy vehicle was loaded. Ben stayed in the car which was not the place to be if it all tipped over but he figured he would be out quickly if he had to. Dan had already retrieved both ramps and the barge was reversing back, quicker this time.

The boy approached the driver's window and said to Ben, 'We must be quick; the Serbian border patrol is due anytime.'

The old man had the small diesel engine working hard to push the weight through the water. They were just over halfway across when Ben saw in the distance to the north a light being waved from bank to bank. It was at least a kilometre up the river still but travelling fast. Ben heard the old man call out and he swung the barge sideways nearly sending them over. The old man cut the engine and the front of the barge dipped under the water sending a wave the full length of the unstable vessel. It was silent now and Ben could hear the powerful outboards getting closer.

The barge crashed side on to the bank and rested under a tree. Dan, the boy and the old man grabbed for branches to hold them against the bank. Ben didn't dare open the door and risk an interior light coming on. He looked back—the surface of the water had settled enough that hopefully the patrol boat didn't notice any disturbance. The light was powerful and lit each bank fully. He knew it was going to be a fifty-fifty chance that they weren't seen. He was confident that it would be a shoot first scenario if they were seen. He now wished he had one of the AK's loaded and on his lap, but he wasn't going to move an inch—the slightest movement of the boat would send a quiver across the water and give them away.

The engines on the patrol boat were louder now, screaming two strokes. Closer now, maybe only a hundred meters and coming fast. The sound rang through their ears, there was no other sound, not a bird, frog or traffic. Ben could hear his heart beating as he fought for a plan, should they be seen. If he heard the patrol boat slow, he would run for the rear of the car, grab as much weaponry as he could carry and call for them all to run to the first car. He would call for Dan to help the old man. He doubted they could all get away if the guards had automatic weapons and he was sure they would have.

He could see the wake from the front of the patrol boat, the powerful light was on their side of the bank. If it didn't switch soon—they were gone. The light swung across the water to the far bank and Ben could see the water was as smooth as the rest of the river. The patrol boat roared past and Ben listened for a drop in revs. It didn't happen. He let out a sigh as the scream of the outboards faded softly in the distance. The old man fired up the single cylinder diesel and backed the barge out as if nothing had just happened.

The boy called out, 'They will be back in ten minutes; we must go fast.'

As soon as the barge hit the bank, Dan had both ramps down and Ben had the Land Rover running and in gear.

'Go!' Dan called and Ben drove off the boat much faster than he would have liked, the wheels spinning up the bank. He was soon parked behind Greg's car. Steve and Dan had the ramps aboard immediately and the barge was already backing away and getting back to the Kosovo side of the river.

Ben wanted to thank them but they were already deep into the darkness, only the sound of the old engine putting away told them that they were still out there.

'Okay, let's get the hell out of here,' Ben said, and everyone rushed to their seats. The scrub was much easier on this side and cars had been down this track recently. It would have been a great lover's lane or fishing spot.

They made good time on the track and after about ten minutes Ben was sure that they were far enough from the river to not need to worry about the patrol boat seeing them.

'Greg, let's pull over and remove the tape from the lights,' Ben said over the radio.

Everyone assisted removing the tape as Greg and Ben discussed the route using the map that the boy had given them.

'It looks like we will hit a little town at the end of this track. Let's not drive nose to tail, it may just cause some suspicion should the cops see us.'

'Sure, I'll stay to the speed limit and you keep whatever gap you think,' Greg said.

Ben handed Greg the map and they all jumped back into the cars.

It wasn't long before they were on the bitumen and driving into the town of Presevo. They would follow the main road through the town and turn left onto four lane highway A1 that would take them all the way through to Belgrade. The highway was busier than they had expected on the four-hour trip north. Semi-trailers and trucks moving their freight south to Macedonia, Bulgaria and Greece.

CHAPTER TWENTY-EIGHT

Sam Taylor was awake long before Goran arrived to collect him. He'd showered, dressed and was standing at the window that looked over the courtyard that everyone used when they arrived at the prestigious government building. He turned when he heard the door open and Goran's smug face was not what he needed to see. He thought about how Ben and the Chinese man had flattened the two Serbians and he knew they weren't all that tough. This was the first time he had thought about Ben and wished he'd kept him on, and not been so quick to sack him. *Hell, it was just a kiss.* Nothing compared to the trouble he was in now.

'The colonel is ready to see you, Mr Taylor,' Goran said.

Sam didn't reply, just looked at him and headed for the open door. He turned right down the hall— there was no left, he was in the last room in the left wing. Goran and the guard that had been on the door all night followed him to the same lecture room he'd done the cyber training in. Goran pulled out a seat, one of the seats the two recipients of his talk used earlier in the week. He knew that the colonel would be giving the lectures today. He sat and looked around the room, the same wood panelling, the same green carpet with the same stinking emblem, an emblem he would despise for the rest of his life. The guard had stayed outside the door and Goran stood with his arms folded looking out the window. Goran turned as the door opened and the colonel walked in. He then moved and stood behind Sam.

'Good morning, Mr Taylor. I hope you slept well.'

Sam just looked at him without answering.

'Mr Taylor, I must apologise for the abrupt departure from New Zealand but we just want a small favour and we will have you back there before anyone knows you are gone.'

'They already know I'm gone, you idiot,' Sam said just as something hit the side of his head, sending him hurtling to the floor. He laid there wondering whether his neck was broken or not. His ear rang and a screaming headache exploded in his head. He remained there, stunned, before he was grabbed by the collar and dragged back into the chair. He now knew that calling the colonel an idiot wasn't acceptable.

He was still seeing stars when the colonel spoke again.

'Now, Mr Taylor, we need the same programs for our neighbouring countries. It is only for our security.'

Sam didn't want to talk but he wanted to be hit again less. 'Kosovo is no threat to you; you are ten times their size.'

'Kosovo is run by Albanian swine and it would still be ours if the American pigs had minded their own business.'

'You want to start a war with them?'

'Mr Taylor, what we do is no concern of yours. Just give me what I want and you can carry on your life with your wife and two children on the other side of the world.'

'You will never let me leave, I know that, I know too much.'

The colonel didn't answer, confirming Sam's worst fears.

'Don't you realise that my wife knows everything and will be telling the police that you have kidnapped me? Are you stupid?'

Sam knew he had said too much and clenched as Goran's hand slammed into the side of his head again, harder this time. His world went black.

The first thing Sam knew was that his head was throbbing. His eyes were still closed and the pain was like his brain was trying to expand inside his skull with each heartbeat. He opened his eyes slowly and the pain increased as the out of focus light send shards of piercing spikes through his eyeballs to his fragile brain. He was on the bed in his room. He could see it was dark outside, the last he remembered was that it was just after 9.00 a.m. He'd been out all day. He tried to sit up, his head making him pay the price. He figured that he had severe concussion, he was sure of it, and he knew that was just the beginning. He got to his feet and walked to the door, trying the handle. It was locked.

'I need a doctor,' he called out but there was no reply. The guard wouldn't speak English anyway.

'At least give me some pain killers, aspirin or something.' Still no reply.

He walked to the bathroom and drank some water. His head throbbed as he bent over but seemed better as he stood back up. Everything was still blurry, but the lightning shards had gone. He found the bed again and pressed his hand against his forehead and closed his eyes. The pain was subsiding, and he figured he wouldn't be dying just yet. He checked his watch; it was just after 4.00 a.m.

It was still dark when Greg pulled into a closed petrol station in the outskirts of Belgrade. Everyone got out to stretch their legs. It was still summer but the night air was particularly cool. The chilly wind from the northeast blew in from the low-lying plains of the Danube Delta in Romania. They had made good time and would now need to wait to eat and find lodgings. Ben took out his phone and found a hotel close to the National assembly building in

Nemanjima Street, the same Government building that Tanya had seen the last ping from Sam's computer.

The old Yugoslav ministry of defence building was bombed by the Americans when Serbia last tried to take back Kosovo and never rebuilt—it still sat in ruins. The ministry of defence now had its offices in the National Assembly building, the most prestigious building in Belgrade.

He booked three, two-bedroom suites in the Hotel Union which was next to the location and where Januzaj said the colonel drank each night. Ben booked the three suites for seven days and really hoped they'd be long gone by then. Ben and Peter would share one and Steve and Dan would take the second. Greg and Kara would share a suite and book in as a couple.

Kara and Greg were quite comfortable about sharing a room together. They'd been lovers in the past—well not that long past. They had been on a cruise together a few months ago, just as friends with benefits really, and that was when Greg had met Jennifer, falling deeply for the American beauty. Kara, although knowing she could be losing the 'benefits' part of their relationship, encouraged Greg to pursue the gorgeous Texan lady who had taken his heart, and he did. Greg had been Kara's first kiss all those years ago in school and they shared a bond that would never be broken. She knew Greg would protect her with his life if it came to that, which gave her the comfort she needed going into this adventure.

Ben, Steve and Dan used the time to check over the equipment the Kosovo colonel had given them. Ben had picked out the SVD rifle with a wooden handguard and skeletonised stock.

'This will be mine,' he said, holding up the Russian made sniper rifle. He put the gun up to his cheek and looked through the scope. The rifle was old, but the scope new. Although they would need to dial them in. Ben's plan A would involve that rifle playing a part in the rescue. There was ammunition for each weapon, not a lot, but they wouldn't need much. With only three trained soldiers amongst them, they didn't need to be up against the whole Serbian police force or army. Steve laid five Glock handguns on the tailgate of the Land Rover and picked one up. He aimed at one of two wood pigeons that flew overhead and pretended to fire. He inspected each of the handguns and they looked in fine working order.

The sun was starting to light the eastern sky and along with the light would come some welcome heat. The three soldiers packed the firepower back into the Khaki bags. They didn't need the station owner arriving to open up, and seeing them with enough hardware to start a war and calling the cops. Greg put the hotel address into his phone and once everyone was back in the two cars, they followed the map to the location. They parked near the hotel. The sun was fully up now, and some shops were now open for the early breakfast trade.

The Drinka Caffe bar was at the end of the street and the six of them welcomed the heated venue. Ben could see the government building from the café and wondered if somehow Sam was still in there. *It's a long shot. He's more likely being kept out in the woods somewhere. We probably drove past him on the way up from the south.*

They all ordered a hearty breakfast and ate almost in silence as Ben studied the large ornate building in front of him.

'As soon as we can check in Greg, take Kara and Peter and get some sleep. We will find a spot and sight in the rifles.'

'Roger that,' Greg said.

'Peter, find a power adapter and get the drone batteries charged. Did you bring the thermal camera as well?' Ben asked.

'Yes, and I got every battery I had through.'

'Great, okay, it starts tonight. Kara, I will need you to buy some nice clothes, something that you would wear to work but a little sexy as well. I need the colonel to notice you. In any spare time, I want you to study up on the 1998 war between these two countries. You will be Kara Smithson, born in Serbia and raised in London and married to Roger Smithson. You were born Kara Duric and are greatly opposed to the Albanians running Kosovo, land that truly belongs to Serbia. Show the colonel you're a supportive ally and let's see what he'll let slip.'

Ben handed her a torn-out page from his note pad that detailed all the facts of her cover and she reached for it, her mind was racing with how she'd carry off this role and the first priority of what would she buy to wear. She had to look attractive without looking cheap. Classy without looking unapproachable. She knew that if she dressed the part—she could play it.

Ben left the table and paid the bill for breakfast. He, Steve and Dan took the weapon loaded Land Rover and headed back south along the A1 highway to a dense forest area that he'd spotted on the way up from the border. The trees would disguise the sound of the weapons somewhat and he knew it was hunting season here anyway. They would only need to fire off a few rounds to check and fine tune the scopes of the long guns. A quick burst from each of the automatics and a shot from each of the Glocks would have them back on the highway and into town before any police could arrive.

Ivan Gosnjak arrived at work just before 7.00 a.m. and parked in the carpark furthest from the street so he would maximise the parking for his workshop customers. He was in his late twenties, medium build and short for the average Serbian. He ran the petrol station almost on his own now. His uncle, the owner, was much older and would only wander in occasionally. He had no cousins and his uncle had promised that it would all be his one day, and

Ivan treated the business with that in mind. He had started to replace the worn-out equipment with modern up to date machines that could talk to and adjust the modern automotive computers. Business had improved almost immediately since the equipment purchases and he'd installed a state-of-the-art security system and motion censored infrared security cameras around the building. He unlocked the front door after a quick glance around the perimeter for any sign that his soon to be asset had been visited through the night. It looked good. He punched in the code to disable the alarm and then to the switchboard that would power up the station.

The internal lights of the four petrol pumps lit up, showing that they were ready for business. Then the canopy lights and the big NIS price board that would display today's fuel price. He took a seat at his desk and flipped over the page in the work diary to display today's workshop jobs. He pushed the 'on' button for his desktop PC and read through the bookings as he waited for the computer to run through the start-up process. He entered his fingerprint to the keyboard and the footage from the security cameras filled the screen. He was always amazed at who was around through the night and used his station for a lover's lane, toilet or just to kill an hour or two. A car had triggered the sensors around midnight, a man getting out of the car for a cigarette. He watched him lean against a petrol pump, the glow of the cigarette intensifying as he sucked hard on his addictive drug. Ivan shook his head at the stupidity of the man's choice of location but also was well aware a fire would be almost impossible. The cameras then switched to two black Land Rovers that had pulled in around 6 00 a.m.

Five men dressed in dark clothing, and a woman alighted the vehicles. He watched them go to the rear of the second vehicle and open the rear doors—he could see what looked like guns, lots of them, but it was hard to tell. This had his full attention until a white Peugeot pulled into the station and he left the video playing as he went over to the console to activate the self-serve petrol pump. He wandered back to his desk to see the two black vehicles driving away and back onto the highway into town. He was fascinated to see what they were doing and if he had a chance later, he'd replay the video and see what his unexpected guests had in the back of that car.

Check in wasn't until midday, so Kara, Greg and Peter went clothes shopping. Greg found a shopping centre only two blocks away and they decided to leave the car and walk. Their eyes were starting to burn with the lack of sleep but a second coffee helped. Kara enjoyed shopping with the two men knowing full well that Greg himself was a keen shopper and with two grown up daughters, he'd been on the hunt for 'that special dress' many times. It wasn't too long before Kara had two outfits that fitted Ben's description. A dark green dress, that was almost a little too formal for work but not too over the top for dinner. Then a pair of black dress pants, a dark blue mid-length skirt and two shirts, white and blue that she could mix and match. A pair of black low-heeled slip-on shoes and she was set.

Ben had found a track that led them deep into a forested hill side. Even though he knew both Steve and Dan were excellent marksmen, he was the one that would be making any crucial shots. He took out the Russian made SVD semi-automatic sniper rifle, actioned the firing mechanism a few times, and was happy with how well the weapon had been maintained. He took out the Land

Rover's owner's manual, sat it in the fork of a tree and paced back down the two-wheel track about a hundred metres. He set the Bi-pod legs forward and laid flat on the wet grass that grew between the two tyre tracks. The first shot was close, missing the small book by only a few millimetres. The height was perfect and he adjusted the horizontal one click. He fired again and the book flew from the tree. Steve and Dan fired one round from each handgun and each performed as expected. They decided to not fire off rounds from the fully auto Uzi and AK47's as they doubted they'd need them, and they'd certainly attract more attention than desired. If a farmer heard single shots, he could assume that some kids were hunting illegally in the national park, but an automatic would certainly be reason for concern.

Ben ran back to collect the owner's manual, not that it would be much use now that a 7.62mm round had been blown through the centre of it but he didn't want to be leaving any references around that could be tracked back to Kosovo. They packed up quickly and were back on the highway within minutes.

The six of them met in the foyer of the hotel and sat waiting for the check in time to arrive. Peter was asleep on the sofa, the silver drone box at his feet. Kara showed Ben the clothes she had bought and she could tell that he was impressed with what she had selected.

'Are you up with who you are and familiar with the Kosovo war?' he asked her.

'Yes, I think so.'

Ben and Kara sat and rehearsed what she might say to a question that the colonel might ask. He was so impressed and surprised she hadn't made it as a professional actress. Ben pulled out a round disc not much bigger than two twenty cent coins stuck together. 'I need you to sew this into your clothing, your knickers if you can.'

'What is it?' she asked.

'A tracking device. If for some reason we lose you, we will know where you are. Just extra safety.'

'Sure, most of these hotels have a needle and thread, otherwise the shops are close,' Kara said.

Greg listened in to the whole thing, part of him was so impressed at her enthusiasm and skill to play the part but nervous for what she could be getting herself into.

'When do we start?' Kara asked.

'Tonight. We know he drinks here at the Hotel Union every night after he leaves the office. I want you already in there when he arrives, so he doesn't think you followed him.'

Kara gulped. It was all too soon but she convinced herself that it was best to jump straight in and not sit around overthinking it all.

'Goran knows me so just in case that he decides to join the colonel, Steve and Dan will be there at the bar.'

'Okay, that sounds good,' she said.

The receptionist called them over—their rooms were ready early. Ben took care of the payment, knowing full well that once they had Sam they wouldn't be coming back.

'Why don't you all get some sleep and let's be ready to go at sixteen thirty hours. Let's meet in my room. Steve and Dan, casual dress for the bar. And no unpacking, have your bags packed and ready to grab and go at a minute's notice, all good?'

'Roger that,' they replied.

Sam didn't receive a visit from Goran or the colonel today which surprised him, just a tray of canteen food at mid-morning and the same again around 3.00 p.m. He just wanted out of here and was seriously considering giving them what they wanted. He could then somehow contact the New Zealand police and let them worry about it and then at least be in jail in his own country. He figured he would insist the job was done in a public place so that once the programs had been created and loaded onto memory sticks, he could disappear into the crowd.

Then, the tiny bit of warmth that thought gave him turned into a sickening wave of nausea as he realised that he would never be leaving this country, dead or alive. He wished he had his computer.

He walked to the window and looked out at the sun setting on another cloudy Belgrade day. He looked around the window frame. The window was not designed to open. He thought of smashing the window and how far would he get before the guard came running in and shot him? There was no ledge to stand on. He imagined Tom Cruise in Mission Impossible removing the glass with some special glass cutting tool and walking along the side of the building and up onto the roof as a helicopter arrived to lift him away to safety while bullets flew discriminately through the air around him. But that wasn't going to happen. No one even knew where he was.

Tanya would've called the police when he didn't arrive home and the security guards would have reported the car being stolen—that's if they were still alive. He wondered whether Tanya would tell the police the whole story about the Serbians. *No, probably not.* So, at best the police would be looking for him in New Zealand and he was a long way from there.

He then thought about Jack and Bethany who would also be missing him and what Tanya would tell them about his disappearance. Then his heart stopped. *What if the Serbians killed them all so that no one raised the alarm of me being missing?* They had tried to kidnap both Jack and Bethany, after all, so they weren't beneath harming his family. Fear and fury pummelled him in equal measure. *What have I done to my beautiful Tanya, my kids? What have I done?*

CHAPTER TWENTY-NINE

Kara looked in the mirror of the bathroom of the luxurious suite as she pressed her lips together to even out the lipstick. She'd done a pretty good job with the small amount of makeup that she'd brought along with her. She walked out to show Greg and performed a pirouette in front of him.

'What do you think?'

'You look delicious,' he said in return. 'Are you sure you're up for this?'

'Yes, I think so,' she said nervously.

Greg pulled out the wire that she would wear and she clipped the mike onto her bra and the transmitter into the back of her knickers.

Greg checked his watch; it was time to meet the others. He kissed her on the cheek and took her hand.

'Let's go,' he said. He could feel the nervousness in her hand. He had been over each possible eventuality in his head and with Steve and Dan close by listening via the wire, he knew they would be there with their Glock pistols in seconds should she be in any trouble.

They arrived at Ben's room; everyone else was already there.

Ben stood and walked up to Kara. 'You look great, just remember you can bail at any time. Dan and Steve will be right there listening to the conversation, as will I.'

'I'm excited but nervous. I feel safe, it's just that I don't want to blow it for you, that's all.'

'Anything you learn will be an advantage. Don't do anything you don't want to do and at any time excuse yourself and we will cover you.'

'Okay, I'm ready,' Kara said, standing taller as the words came out.

Steve and Dan were dressed quite casually, not as office workers but a couple of mates catching up for a beer. Ben nodded for them to head down. They sat against the wall and ordered two Heineken zero beers. Steve fixed an earpiece in his ear nearest the wall. It was only minutes when Kara appeared and found a table close to the bar, unmissable to whoever walked through the front door. She ordered a mocktail, knowing full well she may need to drink whatever the colonel bought her assuming it all went to plan. Ben had given them all the information he knew about Goran and the colonel, pictures and their positions in the Serbian defence force.

It wasn't long before the colonel arrived accompanied by a man they all assumed was Goran. Ben from a distance confirmed that it was.

Kara looked up as the two men walked into the bar. She made eye contact with the colonel and let a small smile develop on her face. She looked slowly away and continued to look at her phone. The colonel was fifteen years older than Kara which would make her the perfect age for him to think that he could still have a chance with her. The colonel took a seat at the bar with Kara at his two o'clock. He was able to turn and see her without turning his whole body. Goran and he ordered drinks, vodka she assumed. Kara had them at her twelve o'clock so for her to be looking at him when he turned around wouldn't be odd.

Kara took a sip of her drink, lifting her head, the straw between her red lipstick lips. The colonel turned at that moment and she smiled at him with her eyes. Kara did have seductive eyes.

The colonel smiled back and the first part was complete.

Kara finished her drink and went to the bar to order another before the waiter had time to get her table service. She stood next to the colonel who had his back to her now. He and Goran were speaking in Serbian so she had no idea what they were saying.

They waiter asked her for her order in English as he remembered from her previous drink.

'A margarita please,' Kara said in her best English accent.

The colonel turned slowly around. 'English, are you?' he said in far better English than she expected.

'Oh no, not really, I was born here, Yugoslavia actually, but raised in London.'

'So, you speak our language?'

'No, I never learnt it. It wasn't offered in the boarding school and my parents were here in Yugoslavia and could speak English well.'

'Welcome home then, my dear.'

The waiter returned with her drink and the colonel turned back to Goran and said something in Serbian which made him laugh— she assumed it was some crass comment about her.

Kara sat back at her seat and looked over to see Steve and Dan acting out their roles perfectly, just the right amount of laughing and conversation to fit in perfectly. She took a sip of her drink and the colonel gave her another look and smile. She was doing her best not to over sell it. She saw Goran finish his drink and leave without her looking up. She knew the colonel would either go home or come over to her.

'May I buy you a drink madam?' the balding sixty-two-year-old colonel said as he approached her table.

'That would be lovely. Margarita please.'

She watched him turn back to the bar and she glanced toward Dan and Steve. Dan's gaze skimmed hers and she returned to watching the colonel order her drink. She felt completely safe with the two ex-soldiers there.

The colonel arrived back with the drink she ordered and with what she assumed was another vodka for himself.

'May I sit?' the colonel asked, pointing to the chair opposite her.

'Of course, please.'

'So, what brings you to our beautiful city…?'

'Kara, sorry,' she said, holding out her hand for him to shake. 'Just a holiday, coming back to the country I was born, just to have a look.'

'And your husband is here with you?' he said, looking at the ring she'd repositioned from her right hand to her left.

'No, on my own. He is busy working in London.'

'I see. What have you seen so far?'

'The café across the road and the back of the National assembly building. I only arrived today.'

'That's where I work.'

'Where, the café?' she said, smiling.

He smiled back, appreciating her humour. 'My name is Milovan but people just call me 'colonel', you can please yourself.'

'I like colonel. So, I guess you don't make coffee then?'

'No, my dear, I have someone make it for me.'

'So, you work in that beautiful building next door?'

'Yes, my office is there.'

'May I ask what you do there, Colonel?'

'I am in charge, if you like, of national security.'

'Wow, were you in charge when the Albanians took over part of my country and called it Kosovo?'

Kara watched the colonel carefully for his reaction.

He looked toward the front door, took a breath and looked her straight in her eyes. 'If I was in the position I am now, that would have never happened, and trust me, that land will return to us soon.'

Kara wished she could get some feedback from Ben or someone so she could tell how she was going. She decided to talk about tourist locations and change the subject for now. The colonel ordered another drink for them both and it wasn't long before the colonel was making flirtatious and suggestive comments. After a few more drinks and two hours had past, Kara said that she should get some sleep and that it had been a long day.

'Can I walk you to your room, Kara?'

'Colonel, I'm a married woman but you may walk me to the elevator.'

'As you please,' the colonel said standing up. He helped her chair out and she smiled another seductive look at him. The elevators were tucked around a corner, and she knew she would be out of sight from Steve and Dan. As she reached the elevator, she felt the colonel reach for her hand and she let him take it. He pulled her to him and hesitated as her face was just inches from his. She closed her eyes and felt the Serbian's lips touch hers. It was a surprisingly gentle kiss and she let him guide her back against the wall. She responded with equal enthusiasm but when she felt his hand on her breast, she pulled away. That would be all she needed, him feeling the wire that was attached to her bra.

'Colonel, I'm a married woman,' she said with half a smile.

'May I see you tomorrow night, Kara from England?'

'I would like that.'

'Maybe dinner, 6 o'clock?'

'That would be nice, thank you Colonel.'

She turned and hit the button for the elevator. While they waited, she asked, 'Colonel, you said my land will be returned to its rightful place. Is that true?'

The elevator door opened.

'Yes, it will be, my dear, a plan is in place.'

Kara stepped into the elevator and hit the button for the fifth floor. As the door closed tight, she fell back against the wall and let out a sigh.

'I know you can hear me, I hope that went okay?'

Of course, there was no reply.

Greg, Peter and Ben were at the elevator as the doors opened. The smiles on their faces answered her question.

Ben hugged her first. 'Bloody hell, you should be in Hollywood.'

Greg just placed his hands on her shoulders and said, 'You were fucking amazing.' And then he hugged her tight. The second elevator opened, and Dan and Steve walked out. They started clapping small claps when they saw her and she blushed, her head bowing bashfully.

'Get some sleep everyone, let's meet back in my room at zero eight hundred,' Ben said.

Greg put his arm around Kara and walked her to their suite.

'That was an outstanding performance,' he said, squeezing her tighter.

Sam was woken by a heavy knock on his door and then the sound of the lock opening. Goran appeared at his bedside.

'The Colonel wants to see you. Get dressed.'

Sam moved slowly from the bed checking his watch. It was 9.00 a.m.

'Now!' Goran yelled.

'Okay, Okay, you knocked me unconscious, you bloody thug.'

'If you don't want another, get moving, the Colonel waits for no one.'

Sam put on the only clothes he had and figured they were probably the last clothes that he'd ever wear. He quickly splashed water on his face and wet down his hair with his hands. He collected his glasses from the bedside table and headed out the door. People were busy walking around performing their office jobs. Serbian chatter filled the building. How could they not know a man was living, no imprisoned, in a room at the end of the corridor?

Sam walked into the same room as he was in last time. He hoped that this meeting wouldn't end the same way. He sat in the same seat and again Goran stood behind him, something Sam was not happy about.

The colonel walked in. 'Mr Taylor, I hope you slept well.'

'What do you think? Your thug here knocked me out cold,' he said tailing off the anger, so it didn't happen again.

The colonel ignored his statement.

'Mr Taylor, surely you see that you don't have any choice here. Just give us what we want and you can go home. We will drop you into that little airfield and the black car will be there with the keys in it for you to drive home to your loved ones.'

'How do I know you haven't hurt them?'

'They are completely safe and I am sure waiting for your return. For you to drive into the driveway and back to your normal life.'

Sam thought about how appealing that would be, but he doubted that would be the case. If the colonel planned on attacking Kosovo again, tens of thousands would be killed and why would he even consider trying to get some pain in the arse computer hacker back to New Zealand? The truth is, he wouldn't. Sam would just disappear. But he had to do something—maybe he could find a way to send a signal to someone. He knew they would watch every keystroke he made and opening his email would be a bash across the head, if not a bullet.

'Okay, let me see what I can do. I can't promise anything. Kosovo was easy, their firewalls were weak. The other countries could be much harder and take longer.'

'The sooner you do it, the sooner you go home,' the colonel said with a smile. Then to Goran, he said, 'Get the computer.'

Goran left from behind Sam's chair and exited the room.

'It is just for our national security, I promise you,' the colonel said unconvincingly.

Sam nodded as if he accepted the statement. Goran appeared within a minute with Sam's computer bag. Sam had never been so happy to see anything in his life. Goran placed the bag in front of Sam, his eyes burning into him. The message was loud and clear.

'Goran, if Mr Taylor even so much as hovers his mouse over the internet or email app, shoot him.'

Goran pulled out a pistol from under his jacket and a silencer from another pocket. He screwed the lethal addition to the front of the pistol, his eyes firmly fixed on Sam. Once the suppressor was tight, he actioned the slide and the nine-millimetre shell clunked into the chamber. Sam had no doubt that Goran would use it.

'I will need the internet. I need to see what firewalls these countries have.'

'You will use our secure system only. Goran will help you. And Mr Taylor, he will not hesitate to kill you and that would be a shame, but not a tragedy for me.'

Sam imagined his blood and brain matter soaking into the green Serbian carpet and doubted that would be a problem the colonel needed; but a bashing from the butt of the pistol and taken unconscious to a desolate forest and killed was a more likely scenario. He wanted to be sick.

He opened the bag and retrieved the computer that he spent most of his awake time working on. It was a welcome sight. He opened the screen and used his fingerprint to open Windows. It immediately started searching for an internet source. He hit the Wi-Fi button and many options were presented. Goran lent forward and pointed to a secure in-house option. Sam clicked on it, and it asked for a password. Goran placed a handwritten mix of jumbled numbers and letters in front of him and he typed them in. He saw the Wi-Fi tab light up on the bottom of the screen.

He was in.

He tapped away with Goran intensely watching him, the silenced pistol resting on his right shoulder.

Sam could smell the burnt gunpowder; the pistol and silencer had been fired recently.

Kara woke with a feeling of achievement. She felt like she was back in acting school and had just performed a stellar performance on her opening night. She showered and thought about the tracker that she had sewn into her knickers. Should she resew it into another pair or get another day from the pair she had? She put on the used pair. Greg stepped into the shower while Kara did her make up beside the glass screen. They were comfortable with each other's nakedness, having been intimate with each other many times before but now with Jennifer on the scene, Greg was sadly no longer available. She sighed as her eyes looked away from the naked man she loved and went back to her bedroom to finish dressing.

Steve and Dan were already at Ben's room when Greg and Kara arrived five minutes early and Greg thought that maybe zero eight hundred really meant zero seven thirty. They all greeted Kara warmly and again praised her on the magnificent job she did with the colonel last night.

They all sat down, Ben, Steve, Dan and Peter on the cheap wooden chairs that sat around the even cheaper timber dining table and Greg and Kara sat on the three-seater couch.

'Kara can't be seen with any of us now. She will need to shop, eat and wander on her own. Of course, one of us will be somewhere close but just in case, she needs to play the role once she leaves this room. Have the tracker on you at all times, Kara,' Ben said, looking over to her.

'I will need some more cotton and thread,' she said.

'We have all day so we can arrange that for you.'

'Peter, I want you to go into that building and take some photos like a dumb tourist of what security they have until they throw you out which I guess they'll do pretty quickly, and maybe quickly run the drone over the top of the building. I'd love to see if there's any way in through the roof.'

'Roger that, boss.'

Ben smiled at the 'boss' reference.

'Dan and Steve, I want you to take our Russian binoculars and watch every window in that building and see if something looks unusual, like a captive man looking out a window. Let's all meet here again this afternoon at sixteen hundred before Kara's dinner tonight.'

Dan, Peter, Kara and Steve left the room.

Greg was the only one still with Ben when his phone rang.

'It's Tanya,' he said, and answered the phone. 'Tanya, any news?'

'Ben, Sam's computer just pinged a location in Belgrade, same place as before.'

'The National Assembly building, right?'

'Yes, somewhere near the middle of the building, right hand side looking from the street if the location is correct.'

'That's great news Tanya. We are here now, I will let you know how we go.'

'Thank you, Ben. Please bring him home in one piece.'

'I'll do my best. Let me know if it moves or any changes, even in the building.'

'I will monitor it all night and let you know.'

'Tanya, Sam's passport?'

'He keeps it in his computer case, he always has it there.'

'Great, talk soon,' Ben said, hanging up.

He dialled Steve.

'Hello?' Steve said as he walked through the foyer.

'Sam's computer was just turned on, location eastern side of the building somewhere near the centre entrance.'

'Roger that, will report back if we see anything.'

Ben was feeling good but was it all just a little too easy. It was one thing executing an extraction during wartime, but this wasn't and people could end up in jail if they got caught or dead if it really went wrong. Still, he had a job to do and if he could prevent a war and save thousands of lives, it needed to be done.

Kara had sewn a little pocket into a few pairs of her knickers although she hoped that they wouldn't be there much longer. She had very few clothes and although the boys could survive all week in the same clothes, she would need to wash.

She had dressed for the date with the colonel and was ready for the 4 o'clock meeting in Ben's room. She arrived right on time and sat between the boys. She really felt a big part of the team, a useful asset. She just needed to not blow it or get herself killed.

'Kara,' Ben said. 'How did you go today? Ready for another Hollywood performance?

'Yes, I'm ready, tracker is in and I'm ready for the wire.'

'What happened when you went to the elevator with the colonel? it sounded muffled.'

Kara smiled. 'He planted a kiss on me but when his hand reached my breast, I pulled away in case he felt the wire.'

'Good thinking. Shall we not have the wire tonight; did the little fondle upset you in anyway?' Ben asked with a concerned look.

'That's fine with me, I've had worse lining up for a drink at a bar,' Kara said, sounding like a hardened professional.

'Okay, tonight we will have Greg and Peter in the bar. Steve and Dan will be just out of sight listening for any news from Greg.'

'What do you want me to push for?' said Kara.

'We need to get into that building, and if you can, steal a pass. Peter got some pictures of an airport style metal detector and it appears everyone has a card size pass around their necks. Keep pushing your opposition to the Albanian takeover of Kosovo and the division of the Yugoslav. Insist on a return to the Socialist Federal Republic of Yugoslavia that would rule as one single state of the Slavic people. He'll love that.'

'Will do.'

It was soon time to move and each of them took their place. Kara was to be fashionably late and used the time to study up further on the fall of Yugoslavia.

Kara looked lovely in the black slacks and blue satin top. Her bra was just visible enough in the right light to not look cheap but enough to arouse a potential suitor. The colonel stood and kissed her on the cheek as she walked up to the table. She smiled her seductive smile as she backed away to sit.

'It's nice to see you again, Colonel.'

'And you my dear,' he replied, lamely attempting to avert his eyes from looking down her top as she sat.

A waiter appeared and asked if they would like a drink. He placed a burgundy-coloured velvet covered menu with a gold embossed insignia of the hotel in front of them.

The colonel expressed a look of question to Kara and she said, 'Wine please, red.'

The waiter picked up the menu, flicked over a few pages and handed the menu to her. She scanned the page and landed on the only Australian wine listed, a Penfolds. She wondered how rich the colonel was feeling. She looked up at him. 'I really like the Australian wines,' she said.

'Have whatever you like, my English rose.'

Well, that was corny, she thought, but hell, whatever groping he was going to do tonight wasn't coming cheap.

'The Penfolds Bin 707 please.'

The colonel, not knowing what that was, nodded approval of the wine.

'So, Colonel, what is a man in your power doing about reestablishing the true Yugoslavia?'

'It is a slow process,' the colonel said, stretching back in his chair.

'Is Serbia brave enough to fight for our southern land that the Albanians have taken?'

'Some of us are and almost ready. Why the interest?'

'I was born here and I guess I don't like change. Yugoslavia was a proud strong country when I was born and the in-fighting tore it apart. Maybe I'm just old fashioned but I love my heritage.'

The wine arrived and the waiter treated it with the respect it deserved. He poured a taste for the colonel and he swirled the glass, appreciated the bouquet and was slow to respond to the taste. Kara was impressed, he seemed to know his stuff. The colonel nodded to the waiter, and he filled Kara's glass and then the colonel's.

'Nice choice,' the colonel said as he took a larger taste of the six-hundred-dollar cabernet. 'You know your wines I see.'

'I do enjoy a bottle now and then, my dear Colonel.'

The colonel lent back in his chair, feeling that he had paid for something with that wine. They picked up the menus and nothing on there came close to the cost of the beverage. Kara went conservative with the food and ordered a salad, the colonel a three-fifty-gram steak. They talked about what they did that day and surprise, surprise, there was no suggestion of a New Zealand captive in the conversation.

The meals arrived and Kara watched her date demolish the cow's rear quarter in what seemed like just a few mouthfuls. Her salad was far from finished when he pushed the plate away from himself and stretched out to assist in the process of major digestion. The wine was soon finished and the waiter asked if they would like another. To save the colonel embarrassment, Kara suggested that she had had enough wine. The plates were cleared, and Kara leant forward.

'I would love to have a personal tour of the amazing building that you work in, Colonel.'

The colonel sat with a look of total contentment and arrogance.

'I could arrange that… If you give me a tour of your bedroom.'

Kara was a little shocked but composed herself well.

'Yours first,' she said to give her at least another twenty-four hours.

'Okay, I have a little matter to deal with in the morning. What about we say 11 o'clock?'

'That would be perfect. I can meet you in the foyer.'

'That is arranged then, and tomorrow night?'

Kara almost gulped. 'Let's meet here, have dinner again and I will show you my room, you naughty man.'

Kara felt her perfect role play slipping but she figured all the wine the colonel had drunk would disguise her nervousness.

The colonel ordered a French tokay, and he drank his in one gulp, banging the glass down and ordering another. Kara could out drink most men and if the poor colonel thought that a few liqueurs would increase his chances for some action tonight, he was mistaken.

After the fourth, Kara said that she should head upstairs, and the colonel quickly paid the bill. The liqueur effect surely softened the shock of the bill. Kara stood and was followed by a wobbly colonel. He took her hand and escorted her to the elevator and again once around the corner pushed her gently against the wall and kissed her. His kiss was rushed and forced, nothing like the night before, his right hand finding her breast, squeezing it far beyond any point of enjoyment. She let it go, as while her hands started to grope the front of his pants for his pass, disguising it as a little arousing encouragement. What felt like a pass was in his right pocket. He took advantage of thinking she was feeling him up and ran his left hand up between her legs. She pushed him away.

'Colonel, you naughty man, I'm a married woman,' she said with a smile, hoping that would calm him down. Just then two men walked around the corner and the colonel straightened himself up. It was Greg and Peter. They nodded to the colonel, continued talking and pushed the button to go up to their room. The door opened and Kara slipped out from behind the colonel saying, 'I'll see you tomorrow at 11 o'clock,' and rushed to catch the same elevator as Greg and Peter.

The door closed, with Kara still waving a childish wave at the drunk Serbian colonel.

'Oh my God, I'm so glad you two turned up when you did. I don't think I can hold him off another night.'

'You did great, let's debrief in Ben's room,' Greg said, giving her a hug.

The six of them were there within minutes of each other.

'I have a meeting with him for a private tour of the building tomorrow morning at 11am,' Kara said, slurring her words a little and she knew it. The four liqueurs were catching up on her. 'He had what I think was his passkey in his right pocket. I could get it if I took his pants off but would love to avoid that if we can.'

'We won't let it get that far, but bloody great job Kara, you have been the star of the show so far. Get some sleep and let's meet tomorrow at zero nine hundred,' Ben said, patting her softly on the back.

Greg put his arm around her and walked her back to their suite. As soon as they entered, she collapsed onto the bed. Greg stopped and looked at the woman he knew so well and admired what a great job she was doing.

'Greg?'

'Yes?' he replied.

'Can you just cuddle me for a while? I don't want to fall asleep with that Serbian as the last person who touched me.'

'Of course.'

Greg kicked off his shoes and slipped in behind her. His arm lay over her and rested beneath her breast. He knew her scent so well, it brought back memories of the many times that they had been together, but that was then and this was now. He closed his eyes and within seconds could hear her breathing long and deep. He decided to stay there with her and soon joined her in a peaceful slumber.

The next morning Kara woke with only the slightest fogginess from the drinking the night before. Through her open door she could see that Greg was up, dressed and staring out the window with a cup of something in his hand. He turned to look at her as she stretched and sat up.

'Cup of tea?' Greg asked.

'My God yes, thank you.'

Kara looked at the time and headed straight for the shower. Greg soon appeared with a cup of tea and handed it to her in the shower. She took a sip and handed it back, making all the right noises of appreciation. She loved him seeing her naked and desperately missed the times when they had been lovers, but he was Jennifer's now and she had to respect that. After all she had encouraged their union, but she still loved him more than anything, and knew he still loved her in some crazy, confusing way too.

Greg and Kara arrived at Ben's room still holding their cups of tea.

'Again, great job last night Kara but today you will be out of our reach and into the lion's den. Are you still keen?'

'Keen might be a stretch, but hey, let's do it.'

'Great, you are an absolute champion. We need you to ask about every room, especially the south facing rooms on the eastern wing where Sam's computer has pinged.'

Kara nodded, realising any reference to North, south or anywhere else was wasted on her.

'See if you might find a delivery entrance that we might be able to get in through. How are the windows fixed, how complicated are the locks, or if you can secure a pass, that would be a huge win but don't take any chances.'

'I'll do my best, extracting hostages isn't my forte.'

Everyone smiled and Peter laughed.

'Anything you can find out would be great, thank you,' Ben said.

CHAPTER THIRTY

Sam woke the next morning after a day of writing a dummy virus that would never work. He knew Goran would be there at 9.00.a.m., to take him back to his computer and he'd spend another day tapping keys that would never do anything. He was showered and waiting when Goran arrived and again, he was escorted to the same room, table and conditions. But Goran was distracted today and when the colonel arrived to question Sam on his progress, Goran pulled out an iPad tablet and spoke to the colonel in Serbian.

'Colonel, sir, we may have a problem. The police have sent me footage from a security camera in a petrol station from two days ago. Two black cars, with five men and a woman.'

'So?' the colonel asked.

'The car appeared to be full of heavy weapons, sir, and I know that man,' he said, pointing to the frozen screen. 'He was with this Sam Taylor in Fiji.'

They both looked at Sam and he recognised his name being spoken; something was going on.

The colonel reached for the screen and enlarged the picture after noticing a woman in the background.

'And I know that woman,' he said slowly. The colonel looked up from the tablet with the realisation that he was being conned by the woman and she would pay for that, but worse—this group were here and close by. Only he, Goran and a select few knew about his plans to invade Kosovo and he needed the time to be right to convince the generals to take back the land that was rightfully theirs. He looked back at the screen.

'How many of them are there?'

'Six is my best guess, five men and the woman.'

'At 11 o'clock, have Taylor and his computer ready to move. I will have that woman downstairs in the loading dock just after that. Let's take them to the safe house and I'll decide what to do from there. Our plans may need to be moved forward.'

Sam hadn't touched a key on his keyboard as he did his best to interpret what was going on. He heard his name twice and whatever it was on that screen worried them, so much so, that the virus didn't seem all that important now. Goran reached over and took the computer from Sam and placed it back into Sam's black bag. Sam wondered if maybe this was it, his last day as a living person, to be taken off and disposed of like a broken toy that the colonel didn't want to play with any more.

'Back to your room,' Goran said, half lifting him from his chair.

'What's going on?' Sam insisted but knew full well that he would not get a reply and he didn't. He was pushed into his room and the door locked behind him.

Kara arrived at the foyer of the Serbian National Assembly Building at 11.00 a.m. and waited for the colonel to arrive. He greeted her with a smile but no kiss on the cheek. He took her hand and it didn't feel right—his grip was much tighter than the times he'd led her to the elevator. He walked her to the metal detector and without a word offered the test. She felt something wasn't right, she stood in the chamber, her arms outstretched like the painted diagram in front of her. The scan picked up a metal object below her navel and the colonel checked the screen. The female guard lifted her shirt and could see the metal buckle at the top of her skirt and waved her through. The colonel walked straight through. The buzzer sounding and red lights flashed—he must be armed. The guard cancelled the warning and the colonel took her hand again.

'Shall we start at the bottom, my dear?'

'Okay, it's up to you,' she said nervously. If she had her wire on, she would be saying her safe word; but she didn't and a sickening feeling fell over her.

'I'm not feeling very well,' she said to the colonel as he squeezed her hand tighter and pushed the elevator button for down.

'You can rest down here away from the crowd.'

She felt that she might faint but tried to convince herself that she was just imagining it. *Maybe this is how he is at work.* He didn't speak to her in the elevator and once the door opened, he dragged her out. His right hand squeezed her left and his left hand went to her throat. He clenched it tight and she struggled to breathe. She couldn't scream and who would hear her anyway.

'What are you doing here in Serbia?' He let go of her hand and slapped her face. It wasn't as hard as he could have but enough to sting and make her eyes water.

'On holiday,' was all she could get out.

'You are a lying bitch. Who are the five men you are with?'

'There are no men, my husband is in London,' she struggled to say.

He stepped back and struck her again, much harder this time.

'I don't have time to play games. Are you here to rescue Sam Taylor?'

Kara didn't reply as she looked down, which answered the question.

'Who are you with, government or private contractor?'

She was about to receive another hit when the elevator opened and the tall Serbian that she'd seen the colonel with on the first night appeared, pushing a handcuffed man ahead of him. Kara recognised him as Sam Taylor. Goran fitted handcuffs to Kara and then pushed them both into the back of a black Mercedes Van. They each found a seat as best they could with their hands behind their backs.

'Who are you?' Sam asked Kara.

She slowly raised her head to look at him, a look of defeat on her face. 'We came to rescue you.'

'Rescue me? Who is we?'

'Ben Woolford. There were six of us,' Kara spoke as if that was all past tense, and for her and Sam it could well be.

'Ben came to rescue me?' Sam looked around the van trying to piece that scenario together. 'Well that's great news but from where I'm sitting his plan doesn't seem to be going too well because I'm sorry to tell you my dear, today could well be our last day alive.'

Ben hated that the tracker had disappeared when Kara had obviously stepped into an elevator and been taken below ground. Greg, Dan, Steve and Peter all watched on as the screen on Ben's phone went blank.

All of a sudden, the red dot reappeared. 'Shit!' Ben yelled. 'She's on the move. Let's go, get your bags, we may not be coming back here.'

The five men ran to their rooms and collected their kits and were all back outside Ben's room in under a minute. Greg grabbed Kara's bag. Her passport was in it and really that would be all she needed. They rushed down to the Land Rovers in the underground carpark and had the engines started and on the A1 highway south. Ben followed the red dot; they were at least twenty kilometres behind them. Ben, Steve and Dan were in the weapon loaded car and Steve and Dan were busy loading the guns with the small amount of ammunition that the Kosovars had given them.

Peter who was riding with Greg had the drone on his lap and fitted the first of the charged batteries just in case. The infra-red camera wasn't attached but ready. They were thirty kilometres out of Belgrade now and the red dot still about another fifteen ahead of them.

'They're turning off,' Ben said as he studied the phone screen.

He watched it disappear from the highway and head west on a track that didn't show up on his map. He memorised the entry point. Ten minutes later Ben slowed, looking for the entry point from the highway. There it was—disguised by overgrown trees. Ben stopped and called for Greg to back up. The dot was moving slowly now and only two kilometres ahead. Ben concentrated on the bush track driving now and Dan watched the phone screen.

'They've stopped,' Dan called.

Ben found an area off the track and he and Greg turned the two cars around for a quick exit. He could see that they were stopped about a kilometre away. They placed the keys behind a rear tyre and he, Steve and Dan climbed into the black Serbian army coveralls and armed themselves with as much firepower as they could carry.

Peter was setting the drone up for take-off and Greg stood by watching, the nervousness about his friend obvious. Steve handed him a Glock pistol.

'It's only got six in it, mate, but let us do the shooting okay? We'll get her back,' Steve said to Greg, placing his hand on his shoulder.

'Thanks Steve,' he said, looking at a weapon he had never fired in his life.

'Peter, get that drone up and tell me what you can see. Don't let them hear it.' Ben called.

'Roger that, Alpha one.'

They all had their Alpha designations from the last time that they all worked together to rescue the millionaire's daughter. Ben was Alpha one, Steve two, Dan three, Greg was four and Peter five.

Peter sent the drone up with the navigation lights covered over with black tape. Ben was over Peter's shoulder watching the small screen as a small timber house came into view. A black Mercedes van was parked in front. Behind the house was a clearing, purpose built for what Ben assumed was a helipad. A sense of urgency hammered his chest, he couldn't afford to let this get ahead of him.

There was no sight of anyone.

'Bring her back and fit the thermal camera Peter, quickly, I have a feeling that this might be a departure lounge.'

The drone was soon back and the larger camera fitted. Peter soon had it up again and after an orbit of the dwelling could see what looked like two large men and two other people with hands behind their backs.

'Let's move out,' Ben called.

'Peter, swap the camera back to HD and keep an eye in the sky and tell us anything you see.'

Peter brought the drone home and swapped the camera back to the conventional 4HD unit. It was hard going as they jogged along the narrow two-wheel track. The green grass was high in the centre and the vegetation thick on each side. Ben, Steve and Dan were fully dressed as Serbian Special forces and had a sniper rifle over one shoulder, a fully automatic machine gun in their hands and a fifteen shot Glock in a thigh holster. Greg ran along behind in jeans and a shirt; he didn't need to be a part of the rescue. He had no holster for his half-loaded pistol so he carried it pointing to the ground.

'Alpha one, you are two hundred metres away, the house is around that next bend,' Peter said over the radio.

Ben held up his arm with a clenched fist and everyone stopped behind him.

'Roger that Alpha five,' Ben said back.

Ben pointed to the thick forest and they made their way slowly through what appeared to be an old pine forest that had been abandoned and overgrown.

'We need to get between the house and that clearing, we can't let them leave here,' Ben said over the radio.

'Roger that,' came back from Steve and Dan. Greg knew he was only a spectator in this and was desperate to not get in the way or killed.

It took more time than Ben liked for them to shuffle through the thick undergrowth of the tall trees but they were soon in a location that Ben decided would give them a clear shot, whichever way they decided to leave. The three retired special air service warriors set out the sniper rifles, flicking down the bi-pods and getting themselves comfortable and ready for whatever may eventuate. Ben had pre-set his scope for one hundred metres and this was about half that. He gave the vertical a click down but knew the difference would not be much. The automatics shouldn't be needed here as they were too indiscriminate as to their targets and they didn't want Kara or Sam getting hit.

'Any news, Alpha five?' Ben asked.

'No, all quiet.'

'Roger that, keep me posted.'

Ben was desperate to know what was going on but the longer they sat, it appeared they were waiting for something and given the clearing, it had to be a chopper. Ben looked to the treetops to check the wind direction—a chopper would land into the wind and take off the same so he knew that they would have a clear shot at the cockpit.

The colonel had to be eliminated. Ben was confident that this whole invasion of military computers was confined to this small group. If the colonel lived, Sam and his family would never be safe and neither would the innocent people of Kosovo. The colonel would be his target.

'Chopper from the east,' Peter called over the radio.

'Roger that, Alpha two and three, that chopper is not to leave here.'

'Roger that,' they called back.

Ben actioned the SVD. He had filled the magazine but hoped he would only need the one shot. Goran's decision making at this time would determine his future on this earth.

Peter had lowered the drone to tree level, so it was out of line sight of the two pilots. The French made H145M helo came into view above the trees. It was military, painted in camo colours. It had no obvious weapon pods. They didn't need a fifty-calibre machine gun spraying the tree line. It circled the house and touched down into the wind as Ben suspected. The engine revs slowed slightly but with no intention of shutting down.

Steve called, 'Alpha two has the pilot to the left.'

'Alpha three, the right.'

Greg stood behind a tree, quite a few metres back from the three sniper rifles. He not only wanted to stay out of the line of fire but he was also not wearing black like the other three.

The back door of the house opened and Sam, still with his hands cuffed behind him, was pushed out and the colonel followed, still shoving him stumbling toward the helicopter.

'Hold your fire,' Ben said softly over the radio. He wanted Kara and who he assumed was Goran to be outside and vulnerable before they opened fire. If Goran could get back to the house, he could call in the whole army and they would be done. No escape, and no Kara. They seemed to know what they were doing, the colonel pushed Sam into the chopper and the colonel sat next to him before Goran and Kara left the cabin. Ben could see that it was a five-seater chopper and Kara made six, so *how was that going to add up, they had no intention of taking her.*

Kara was pushed from the door with Goran behind her. She fell to her knees and Goran dragged her up by her hair. Greg saw this and wanted to shoot the Serbian brute. Ben focused his sights on the colonel, his bald head filling his scope. He turned, his head moving from Ben's crosshairs and yelled something to Goran in Serbian. The colonel sat back and his head again filled Ben's scope. Goran nodded and pushed Kara hard making her fall face first to the ground. With her hands behind her back all she had time to do was turn her head and hit the firm, dark soil breaking the fall with the side of her face. Goran lifted his pistol to her head.

Ben saw the pistol lifted towards Kara and he spun his rifle toward Goran but the second needed to focus wasn't available. Then, the first shot was fired.

Kara lay flat on the ground not moving.

In the corner of his eye, he saw a gunman burst from the trees firing shot after shot from a pistol, bang, bang, bang, bang, bang, bang, then click, click. Two of the six bullets from Greg's gun hit Goran in the chest and he dropped to his knees. He decided to use the last few seconds of his life to finish off Kara and slowly lifted the pistol again towards the back of her head, but Ben now had him in his sights.

The head shot had him collapse onto the back of Kara's legs.

Kara started to cry. All she could see was the man that she loved more than anything standing out in the open, his arm still raised holding the pistol that had ended the life of the man who'd almost been her killer. Another shot fired, and the inside of the helicopter cabin was sprayed with a red mist. The colonel slumped forward onto the back of the pilot's seat with the back of his head missing, his reign of deceit and evil now over.

The engines of the helicopter started to increase and Steve and Dan ran out from the trees to either side of the cabin, their pistols held high at the two pilots' heads. Steve indicated to the captain to shut the engines down with a sideways action across his throat. The pilot hesitated and Steve moved forward to shoot him. That was enough for the pilot to shut the fuel to the two turbine engines. The engine noise faded and the main rotor started to slow. Ben took out his pistol and ran to the cockpit.

Greg, in shock and disbelief, walked slowly toward Kara, the smoking pistol dangling lifelessly at his side. He could see her sobbing beneath the tall dead Serbian who had fallen face down on top of her from Ben's last fatal shot. He dropped the pistol onto the dark moist soil and took a handful of Goran's blood-stained shirt. He dragged the dead man from her with the disregard he deserved.

Calmly, Greg sat down on the dirt next to her and pulled her muddied face to his chest. He was oblivious to the other three men running around securing the area.

Without even a thought of removing her restraints, he caressed her face with his fingertips and picked bits of grass from her hair. He didn't say anything and neither did she, he just held her tight. Kara's eyes closed and her crying subsided, she knew she was safe and loved. Greg looked up at the empty pistol laying on the ground trying to come to grips with the fact he had just contributed to killing the man that now lay only a few inches away.

Steve and Dan had dragged the two pilots that were dressed in their air force flight suits and helmets from the aircraft and soon had them tied up on the ground.

Ben walked up and squatted down in front of Greg and Kara. 'Are you both okay?' he said, touching Greg on the shoulder. Neither answered, he then reaching into Goran's pants for the handcuff key.

He unlocked Kara's cuffs, gave her a wink and went to remove Sam's.

As soon as Sam's hands were free, he held out his right to shake Ben's. 'I don't know how you're here, but boy am I happy to see you!'

Ben just smiled back. 'We need to go, Sam. Grab your computer and can you see if the keys are in that van?'

'Steve, put the cuffs on the two pilots, linking them together around the skids. Search and rescue will find them in an hour or so.' He looked at Colonel Milovan Silovic, his eyes open and staring lifelessly at him. Ben reached in and closed the colonel's eyes for the very last time. An evil war monger had been eliminated and he didn't want to look at that any other way. He took the handcuff key and showed it to the pilots and then placed it on the front seat of the chopper. He wondered how they would spend the next hour or so trying to reach it.

Sam came running back. 'The keys are in the van,' he said.

'Okay let's get the hell out of here. Grab all the weapons.'

'Alpha five, did you get all of that?'

'My God yes, would make one hell of a movie.'

'Well Spielberg, pack it up, we're heading back.'

Greg helped Kara to the van. Her knees were bleeding and Goran's blood was congealing on the backs of her legs. The left side of her face had the scuffs from the dark soil and her hair was a mess, but he thought she'd never looked more beautiful. Steve was the last one in and slammed the side sliding door closed. Dan was driving and headed quickly back to where Peter and the two Land Rovers were parked. Dan turned into the clearing and everyone transferred to the black English made, four by fours.

Greg had by now come to grips with the emotion of his good friend's near death and the fact he himself had killed a man; but he was back behind the wheel where he felt most at home. Ben asked Dan to drive the second car while he contacted Kosovo for their best way back across the border.

'Mr Januzaj, Ben Woolford, we have our asset and are on our way south on A1. What do suggest for our border crossing?'

'Mr Woolford, it is very nice to hear from you and the success of your mission. There is a small border crossing at Merdare. Come that way and I will ensure a smooth passage.'

'Thank you. Weapons—shall we dump them or bring them with us?'

'You can bring them through Mr Woolford, you won't be hassled, just have them out of sight.'

'Roger that, I will call you once through the check point,' Ben said, ending the call.

He was happy that he didn't need to be on that barge again. They settled in, sitting on the speed limit and avoiding any unwanted attention. It was nearing peak hour and the traffic had increased slightly. The two black Land Rovers would be just two more commuters on the drive home from work.

CHAPTER THIRTY-ONE

Ben and his team had no idea that the Serbian police were still fiercely looking for the two black Land Rovers that had been recorded by a petrol station security camera; full of assault rifles. The registration number was clear on the rear vehicle, they were Serbian plates but not coming up on the motor vehicle department computers.

Greg watched as a white police Skoda drove past heading north before the blue flashing lights burst into life.

'We have a problem,' Greg called over the radio.

'Yes, standby,' Dan said.

Ben grabbed the handheld radio from Dan. 'Greg, I don't know if this will work, if we were at home I would do it the other way around, but I guess these chaps would be after some excitement. We have all the weapons; your car is clean and you're the best driver we have. I think if once they catch us you take off, we will try and block them and then let them through. They will assume that you are the car we don't want caught and chase you. I don't know how it will go, but it's worth a try.'

'Roger that,' Greg said. He could see in his mirror that the police car had crossed the highway and was now on its way at high speed after them.

'They'll know we're trying to get to the border and that'll be quickly shut off to us,' Ben said.

'Roger that, tell me when to go,' Greg came back.

The police car was closing in fast, the turbo charged VW powered Skoda weaving recklessly through the traffic. Dan straddled both lanes as the police car arrived behind it.

'Go now,' Ben called, and Greg floored the Land Rover. The police car was weaving from side to side attempting to get past and Dan blocked each attempt.

'Better idea,' Ben said to Dan. 'Take him out as he goes past.'

'Roger that,' Dan replied. The technique was part of the training that everyone did in the Australian armed forces and Dan knew exactly what to do.

Greg was well down the road when Ben called to let them pass. Dan pulled to the left and let them through. As the police car accelerated past, Dan swung the wheel hitting the Skoda in the rear and turning the small car sideways at well over a hundred kilometres an hour. The police car slammed into the barrier on the left side of the road and then violently bounced across the road hitting the righthand barrier backwards. The car was still spinning out of control as Dan, now in the emergency lane, passed them and accelerated down the busy highway.

'Greg, we've got rid of the police car for now but I'm sure there's many others on their way. There's a road to the right that heads southeast. Let's head that way, we need to dump these cars,' Ben said.

'Taking this next exit to Nis,' Greg called.

Ben knew they had to be out of Serbia before the officials tracked down the helicopter and the two dead men. The A1 highway led to Bulgaria and Macedonia as well as Kosovo, so the destination of the black Land Rovers would be uncertain.

'Turn left toward Sofia,' Ben said. 'Let's make them think we are going to Bulgaria. We'll grab another car and double back.'

'Roger that,' Greg said.

Ben was wracking his brain. 'What did I miss? How did Kara get made and why are the cops after us?'

He ran through each stage. It had to be to do with the Land Rovers, the way the cops immediately turned around as they passed. *Did someone squeal on us? No, it can't be that.* Then he remembered taking the guns out at the petrol station.

Sam, who was sitting in the back seat behind Ben spoke for the first time since leaving the forest.

'Goran showed the colonel something on an iPad and it shocked him. That's when I was dragged off downstairs.'

'Damn it,' Ben yelled. 'The petrol station! We didn't check for cameras and there we were waving guns around everywhere. That's what nearly cost Kara her life and now our smooth exit! Damn it, I should have known better.'

'We all missed it, Ben,' Dan said.

'We were tired and keen to see what we had,' said Steve.

'Okay, well at least we know why,' Ben said.

Ben picked up the radio, 'Greg, we need to dump these cars fast, the cops are going to be all over us.'

'Roger that.'

'First shopping centre, get underground, if possible. I'm sure they'll have a helo up by now.'

'On to it, looks like something ahead,' Greg came back.

Greg turned into the Forum shopping centre. The parking was ground level and the shops above. Good cover from above and would give them time to find a way out of this country. Greg parked in a parking spot away from the shop escalators. He gave Dan the details over the radio and the second Land Rover appeared a few moments later. They parked side by side and the seven occupants jumped out, collecting their bags and waiting for Ben's next instruction.

Ben handed Dan his Leatherman and asked him to swap the rear numberplate of Land Rovers with two nearby cars.

'Greg, can you see a loading dock, there must be one?'

'I'll go and check.'

'What are you thinking?' Steve asked.

'Let's nick a van or small truck from the loading dock while the driver is around the back. We can change the plates as soon as we can and hopefully get the two hours to the border.'

'That shouldn't be too hard,' Steve said back.

'Ideally one with no signage.'

'Roger that.'

Greg returned. 'Theres a loading dock around the far side. A ramp down to an underground storage section. Trucks and vans consistently in and out.'

'Okay, Steve and Dan, it's up to you,' Ben said, and watched the two take off in that direction.

The occasional police car raced past the carpark but it wasn't until one turned in, that Ben knew that they only had a minute or two before they were spotted.

Steve and Dan watched as several trucks and vans came and went from the busy loading dock. They watched the procedure—the driver would back into the bay down a steep ramp, he would get out, more often than not with a docket, and disappear momentarily through a slatted doorway. The driver would then open the rear of the truck and unload most of the contents. Steve and Dan figured a truck wouldn't really be any good, as it would be too slow and hard to hide.

It wasn't long before a Fiat Ducato van pulled in and waited for the present unloading truck to leave. The van was white with no signage and would be their best option. They watched the truck driver jump into his cab and make his way up the ramp, before disappearing from sight. The Ducato driver quickly backed his van in and jumped from the cab heading for the office door. Steve ran to the van. Not only were the keys in the ignition, he'd left the engine running. Steve nodded to Dan who then ran for the passenger side as Steve opened the driver's door and hopped in. He quickly selected drive and roared up the ramp, a quick look in his mirror confirming that the driver had not yet emerged from the plastic slatted doorway.

Steve turned quickly and headed toward where the rest of the team were now nervously waiting as a police car patrolled the carpark. Steve pulled up with a slight lock of brakes and Ben slid back the sliding door. The bags and team were loaded in seconds and then they were all making their way to the exit when the police car found the two Land Rovers. They knew it would only be seconds before the van's driver had contacted police and the stolen van would be pursued by every available police unit.

Steve swapped seats with Greg, knowing full well that if there was to be a car chase, he would be the best man for the job. Ben took the passenger front seat as the other four made themselves comfortable between the small cardboard boxes.

They left the carpark and headed east back toward the highway. The van had been delivering pastries and it wasn't long before Dan was offering the French treats to the staving team. No one had eaten all day.

'North or South?' Greg asked Ben as the highway entry approached.

'South will get us close to our exit but they will be expecting that, so we'll need to go North, we have no choice,' he said, looking over at Greg for some sort of assurance.

'North it is,' Greg said, indicating for the next exit.

Ben took out his phone and opened a map app. He could see that they were so close to the Kosovo border but it would be crazy to try and cross at the two main border points. He knew roadblocks would be in place by now and their only way out would be to sneak across the river border somewhere quiet. Two police cars flew past heading south and Greg saw their brake lights glow as they disappeared in the distance.

'We've been made,' Greg said.

'Yeah, not surprised,' Ben said, not looking up from his phone. 'Take the next exit to Krusevac.'

'Roger that,' Greg said, seeing the exit sign approaching.

Greg took the exit as fast as the van could without running wide or tipping over. A sense of urgency filled the van. Ben searched the grey sky, the sun now low in the west. A dark spot appeared in the distance.

'Shit, there's a chopper coming from the north,' Ben called.

Greg put his foot down—there was no need to try and blend in anymore. He looked over at Ben.

'What are you thinking?'

'We need to split up. We need to get the five in the back out of the van without that chopper seeing us.'

Ben concentrated on his phone maps while Greg raced down the road passing cars at well over the limit. Krusevac was now only ten minutes away. Greg needed to get there before the local police could set up a roadblock or spikes.

Ben turned in his seat to talk to the five in the back of the van. The pastries were now scattered around the floor.

'On the way into town, we'll pass through a small tunnel that runs under a railway line. We will stop in the tunnel, I want you to leave everything—guns, vests, radios, and drone, just bring your bags, and make sure you have your passports. We'll turn around and head back north hopefully luring the police back toward us. Sam, take your computer.'

Sam nodded back. 'It's all I have.'

'Peter, make sure you take the memory card out of the drone.

Steve, there's a national park called Kopaonik. It borders with Kosovo, it's a ski resort in the winter. Get a bus there, it's just a five kilometre walk to the highway once you cross the river out of Serbia. Greg and I will meet you all in Pristina.'

'I can see it coming up,' Greg yelled, and there was a rush of action in the back of the van. Steve tossed Ben's and Greg's bags over the front seat between them. Steve put his hand on Ben's shoulder and said, 'Good luck my friends.'

Ben turned back to him and said, 'Keep them safe buddy, we'll see you soon.'

The traffic was light, really no cars at all entering the tunnel. Greg hit the brakes hard and the side door flew open. Five seconds later, the door slammed closed. Greg turned the steering to full lock, dropped the clutch and exited the tunnel with tyre smoke streaming from the inside rear tyre.

'What now?' Greg asked, looking at Ben.

'I haven't worked that part out yet,' he said, looking over at him with a smile.

'We just needed to get Kara, Sam and the guys' safe. It'll be much easier with just the two of us.'

Greg nodded as the chopper filled the windscreen of the van as it emerged from behind a large tree. Ben studied the map on his phone.

'Company ahead,' Greg called and Ben looked up to see the blue flashing lights of two approaching police cars.

'There's no way off this road—spin us around again and let's hope the others are clear and safe when we shoot back through that tunnel.'

Greg braked hard and swerved through a very convenient break in the road's divider. The van hit the raised centre and the French pastries flew through the air in the back, splattering all over the van's floor. The small four-cylinder diesel pulled well once the turbocharger spooled up, and they'd managed to still maintain a gap ahead of the police, but they were closing in.

It was almost dark and the high intensity spotlight from the helicopter splashed across the van's dashboard. They were almost back to the tunnel where they had dropped off the five others. Greg had the lights on high beam and there was no sign of their friends. Hopefully they would book into a hotel shortly. The police car behind them had closed the gap and Greg knew that more would soon arrive to join the chase.

'We're going to need to lose this van,' Greg said, swinging the car onto the main street of the small Serbian town.

'They are too close for us to dump and run,' said Ben.

'The chopper will have a thermal camera onboard so no running through backyards,' Greg said.

'That's true, can you get this bloke off our arse?'

'Yeah, but it won't be pretty,' Greg offered, taking a sharp righthander into a smaller road. Greg slowed slightly, weaving through the back streets as Ben tracked their location on his phone that was running very low on battery.

The Skoda police car had now tucked in close behind the bulky van, but was still the only police car in sight. The helicopter was still following from a height of what Ben imagined was two hundred feet. Greg turned into a smaller road and the Skoda accelerated up behind him again.

'Hang on, put your head back on the headrest,' Greg said.

He could see that the police car would close up behind when he was on the straight sections of road and drop back as they approached the corners. Halfway down the next street he hit the brakes hard—all four wheels went into ABS. Both of their bags flew from the front seat where Steve had placed them and ended up by Ben's feet. Then the almighty thump as the Skoda police car slammed into the back of the van. Greg hit the throttle again and turned left at the next corner. He looked back to see steam and air conditioning gas pouring from the front of the police car.

'Can you find us something underground, carpark or something?' Greg asked as the helicopter's spotlight again flashed across the dash.

'Trouble is everything is probably closed and we can't just blend in with the crowd,' Ben said. 'I've got it! The central railway station is underground, take the next left and left again.'

Greg did as instructed, turning onto the main street as the flashing of a blue light in the distance from the north became evident. He was on the wrong side of the road to just pull up in front and they had no time to turn around. Greg stopped heavily across the road from the station entrance. Just a few people were ascending the stairs, a train must have just arrived and would most likely be gone by now. Ben and Greg grabbed their bags and ran across the empty road. The spotlight from the helicopter lit their way as they ran. Ben glanced toward the approaching police car as he reached the top of the stairs—they probably had only thirty seconds on them. They both ran down the stairs and scaled the turnstiles like a pair of athletes. Ben reached the platform first and looked both ways. It was deserted except for one elderly man, homeless, Ben figured. Ben would have loved to check to see how far it was in each direction to see which way they should run, but he didn't have the time or phone reception underground.

'This way,' he said as Greg joined him. He knew the mountains were to the west and for no real reason figured the tunnel would be longer before it broke through to the outside. The other way would push them deeper into Serbia, but at the moment, not getting caught was the biggest priority. They ran as fast as they could and Ben jumped off the platform and onto the train tracks. Greg followed and they were soon in total darkness. Their running slowed to a jog and then to a walk as complete blackness surrounded them from both directions. They appreciated that the builders of the tracks had spaced the wooden sleepers perfectly apart, so despite the darkness they could travel quite quickly stepping from one to the other.

'How much battery have you got?' Ben asked Greg.

'Nothing, it's dead,' he replied. 'You?'

'Two percent,' Ben said, stopping to check. He used the dim light to check the layout of the tunnel and then pushed the phone back into his back pocket. 'There could be inspection points along the way and the cops ambush us as we get there.'

'Or they could just be waiting for us at the end of the tunnel,' Greg added.

They both felt it at the same time—the movement of air in front of them. A train was coming. They then heard the noise and then the tunnel started to light up in front of them.

CHAPTER THIRTY-TWO

Steve, Dan, Sam and Peter kept a close watch on Kara as they sat safe and comfortable in the shared room that Steve and Dan had booked. Sam and Peter had a room together and Kara had one on her own. They could see she was worried about Greg, especially knowing he wasn't a soldier or a professional criminal who'd spent his life being chased by police or foreign militants. He was a businessman, a racing car driver. If he didn't get shot by the police, he could easily spend the rest of his life in a Serbian prison for killing a government official. She knew if it wasn't for him, she would surely be among the dead back there at the forest house.

She was almost as white as a ghost when Dan stood and walked to comfort her. His touch was all she needed to let it all out. Kara's head rested on his shoulder as the tears poured like a tap onto his shirt. The stress of the whole event, a man shot inches from her who'd then lay dead across her legs as he bled out from the bullet wounds that had saved her life. The sight of the man who had forcibly kissed her the night before, with half his head missing, slumped against the helicopter pilots' seat and of course the fate of Greg and Ben—that was if they were still alive. Dan patted her back and his soft voice comforted her with positive stories of Ben's amazing ability of survival.

Sam and Steve sat at Sam's computer and planned their way out of Serbia. None of them had a visa or an entry stamp in their passports so crossing conventionally at a border point wasn't an option, plus for all they knew, their faces could be on the Serbia's most wanted list by now.

'As Ben said, let's book bus tickets to the Kapoanik ski resort, there won't be snow but it will be cold, that will get us within two kilometres of the border. We could hopefully hike from there into Kosovo, then another five k's to the highway and we can plan what we do from there if we haven't heard from Ben and Greg,' Steve suggested.

'We can't just leave Greg and Ben here,' Kara said. Her crying had stopped but her eyes were still red and swollen.

Steve smiled at her. 'Trust me, they'll beat us to Pristina. They're probably sitting on a train now in first class sipping champagne.'

Dan was the only one who smiled at that. Everyone else was stressed and tired.

'Why haven't we heard from them?' Kara asked.

'Their phones are probably flat. I'm sure by morning we'll hear something.'

'Okay, let's get some sleep; bus leaves at zero eight hundred.'

Everyone stood and Sam packed up his computer, shook hands with both Steve and Dan and left with Peter to their room.

'Run, back to the station!' Ben yelled. 'Get ready to dive to the side once the light comes around the corner, we don't need the driver seeing us!'

Greg didn't answer, he just ran, the light from the train illuminating the tunnel just enough for him to see each sleeper. As the headlight broached the corner, Ben yelled, 'Down now!'

Both he and Greg threw themselves to the track's edge, their bags just in front of their heads. Neither knew if there was enough gap between the wall and the train for a man to lay, but in seconds they would find out. Maybe a protruding hydraulic fitting would tear their bodies apart like a cutting tool on a lathe as it flew past at speed; before the unknowing driver slowed for the Krusevac station. Greg would be the first to know if they would live or die. He lay as flat as he could, his rucksack in front of him. He decided that keeping his head turned might just give him a few more millimetres of clearance. The noise of the train was increasing louder and louder, the squeal of the metal on metal wheels was deafening. The train had lit the tunnel fully now and Greg could see Ben was just ahead of him. They could only hope that the driver wasn't focused on the track ahead at that second. Greg had faced death a few times in car racing accidents but had never been in a circumstance like this where he was waiting for what seemed to be forever to learn his fate.

He took a deep breath and could now feel the train almost on him. He closed his eyes and the sound of the train was brain numbing as it flew only millimetres above him. He knew he wasn't safe until the last carriage had gone past. The clack of the heavy wheels as they hit each join in the track pounded his head.

As the last carriage finally past, Greg lay there wanting to celebrate the fact he was still alive, but Ben yelled, 'Let's go, now. We need to catch that train.'

Greg jumped to his feet and pulled his rucksack over his shoulders, knowing he had wasted precious seconds. With the residual light from the train, they could both run at their best speed. Ben was slightly ahead and pulling away, he was fitter and ten years younger. Greg knew the train would only be at the station for the few seconds that it would take for the few passengers to disembark. Ben was now a good ten metres ahead of him and the train was almost stationary at the platform. The light of the station made the track more visible but time and fitness worked against him now. The train had stopped and was still a hundred metres at least away from him, a bit less for Ben. He now pictured Ben making it and him leaving him standing on the tracks in front of the alighted passengers as his teammate accelerated away to safety.

The whistle blew, the guard indicating that the passengers were clear.

The train started to move. The electric train would accelerate away much quicker than a diesel locomotive. Greg was still catching up, but the closing the distance much slower now.

Ben had reached the train and threw himself at the chrome handles that were mounted alongside the rear door. Ben turned to see where Greg was, still five metres away and only making a small gain on the accelerating train.

Greg knew if he didn't make it in the next few seconds, Ben and the train would be gone and out of sight. He was exhausted from the sprint but he had to find that little more. And he did. Ben held out his hand stretching out as far as the chrome handle would allow.

'Push!' Ben yelled. If Greg didn't make it, it would be too dangerous for Ben to jump from the train now and Greg would be left behind.

Greg did push and he felt Ben's hand wrap around his wrist. Greg found the strength to wrap his exhausted fingers around his forearm. His feet could no longer match the speed and his legs now dragged behind him banging on each sleeper as the train powered up to its cruise speed. Ben's grip was now the only thing between him living and dying. One of Greg's shoes came off as his feet bounced dangerously from sleeper to sleeper. The speed was now so fast he was flying then banging back against the tracks.

Ben seemed to find some amazing strength and lifted Greg enough so his left hand could also grab hold of the chrome handle. Ben let go of his right wrist and wrapped his arm around Greg's body, lifting him to the small ledge that sat below the rear door. The train was travelling fast now and the wind buffered them wildly. Ben tried the handle on the door—it was locked. No passengers were in the last carriage which saved them from being seen and reported. Greg was heaving, he had nothing left. Ben kept his arm around him just in case he passed out from the exhaustion. Greg was recovering quickly though, enough to start feeling the pain from his left foot that had lost the shoe. He looked down, his sock was torn open and he could see a lot of skin was missing from the top of his foot and the pale white colour of the bones were visible. Blood was flowing onto the step that was only wide enough for the balls of their feet.

'Well done mate, that was close,' Ben yelled as his hair blew everywhere, his arm still firmly around Greg.

'Yeah, can we not do that again.'

Ben smiled. 'Let's buy a ticket next time, hey?'

Greg smiled back, before shouting, 'What's the plan now?'

'I'm guessing we're heading north, away from where we need to be but away from the cops, so let's hop off the next time we stop.'

The train burst from the underground tunnel and the muggy, oily smell was replaced by an icy wind which made them both tighten their grip. Greg still had his rucksack on and Ben had an arm through each handle of his duffle bag.

Ben knew the next town was a long way, he could see the map that was affixed to the overhead panels inside the carriage. The stations were close in the other direction but in this direction, he could see the next stop was a town called Kraljevo. A dot indicated their position on the track and after ten minutes of freezing wind and only a step of about one hundred millimetres to stand on, they were only a third of the way. The blood had made the step slippery for Greg's left foot and Ben knew it was going to be tough for Greg with all his weight on only one leg. Ben saw a conductor appear from the carriage in front.

'Shit, company,' Ben yelled, and without looking, Greg knew to move to the side of the glass window that filled the top half of the door. The conductor had seen that there was no one in the last carriage and turned to leave. Ben watched him disappear through the door. He indicated for Greg to take off the rucksack and put his back against the door. Ben swung Greg's rucksack over one shoulder and with his body, held him tight against the door.

Greg could now use his heels on the step. It was a nice change. Greg slipped his arms through each of the chrome handles and with the pressure from Ben found it much easier. Greg was shivering now. He had a coat in his rucksack but that would just be too hard to retrieve.

He could see Ben looking at the train's position on the map overhead and asked, 'Much longer?'

'Nearly there, five more minutes,' he said, knowing it was at least ten.

Greg for the first time thought about Kara and the four men with her. She was in safe hands, but he knew she'd be worried sick about him, wondering if he was arrested or had been shot dead by the police. He closed his eyes and thought about Jennifer, the new love of his life. Such a beautiful person that he planned on spending the rest of his life with. Warmth at the thought of her paused his shivering, as he felt the welcome slowing of the train.

They could see the lights of the outer streets of the town as it slowed further. Neither had any idea what would greet them at the station—police, railway staff or passengers that would inform officials of the stowaways. The platform appeared on the left side of the train. An old concrete edge that was chipped and cracked flew past. The train stopped and Ben jumped onto the track. He turned quickly and Greg almost fell into his arms. They both quickly tucked in behind the opposite side of the train away from the platform. Ben helped Greg up onto the opposite platform and he limped to a seat and sat. Ben jumped up as the conductor blew his whistle and the train departed. He sat next to Greg and handed him his rucksack. He quickly opened it and took out a coat and wrapped himself in it. He wished he had another pair of shoes, but he didn't.

'Are you okay to walk?' Ben asked Greg.

'Yeah sure, my soles are fine but no left foot drop kicks for a while.'

Ben smiled. 'Okay let's find a bed, charge our phones and check that our friends are safe.'

'I won't argue with that,' Greg said standing and placing his left arm over Ben's shoulder.

Greg's limp was exaggerated by the fact that he only had one shoe as well as the injured foot. It was only two blocks from the railway station when they stumbled across the Hotel Botika. It was getting late and the chance of finding a room was certainly a worry. Fortunately, this hotel appeared to have a twenty-four-hour reception. It was a very nice hotel and Ben looked at himself as he paused at the door. His clothes were dirty, black from the back of the train and laying on the side of the track as the train flew past only millimetres above them.

He brushed himself down. It didn't improve his look much. Not speaking Serbian wasn't going to help either. He dropped back out of sight and took out a clean shirt from his bag. His pants were black in colour and would hide the oily soot. With the clean shirt he might just pull it off. He brushed his hair down and wiped his face with the inside of his dirty shirt.

'Presentable,' Greg offered.

'Let's hope. We could really do with cleaning up that foot and getting some sleep.'

Ben pulled the door open and marched over to the counter with confidence. A lady in her mid-thirties looked up and smiled at him as he approached. Greg looked a mess—not only was he filthy from the railway line, he had one shoe missing and a foot soaked in blood. Greg headed for a seat and sat smiling toward the counter at the curious attendant.

'Hello, do you speak English?' Ben asked.

'Yes sir, how can I help you?'

'That's great, could we please have a room for myself and my friend. My friend here was just hit by a speeding car which slightly injured his foot and knocked him to the ground.'

'Oh, that is awful. Does he need a doctor?'

'No, I have checked it and it's just a scratch, some sleep tonight and a shower and he will be fine.'

The lady showed no more interest in Greg and typed away on her computer.

'We only have a twin room available.'

'That will be great, thank you.'

'Can I have both your passports please?'

Ben found his quickly in his leg pocket and held it up for Greg to see that he would need to show it. By the time Ben reached Greg he had it in his hand.

'All good?' Greg asked.

'A twin room, it's all they have.'

'Well given that I was expecting to spend the night in a cell, I'm happy with that.'

Ben smiled and returned to the counter.

'Thank you,' the receptionist said as he handed the passports over. 'Long way from home Mr Woolford.'

'Yes, a quick trip to meet someone and we thought a little sightseeing on the way home. We thought Pristina next. What's the easiest way there?'

'The train will take you to Kosovska and then you need to catch a bus from there to Pristina.'

'That's great, do we go through immigration here or at the other end?'

'Sometimes there is an inspector on the train to check passports but not always. We believe that Kosovo is still part of Serbia.'

'Yes, I've heard that, okay, that's great, thank you.'

The lady typed the amount into a credit card machine and spun it so he could tap his card. She then handed him a key card. Third floor room 312. He gathered up the passports with a smile and walked back to Greg who stood, not without some effort. Greg managed to play down the limp but just having one shoe made that awkward.

'I'm pretty sure I've broken something,' Greg said, stepping into the elevator.

'Do you want to go to the hospital?'

'Nah, let's just get out of Serbia as soon as we can. It might just be bruised but it hurts like hell to walk on.'

'Okay, first stop once we get to Pristina.'

The elevator stopped and the shiny stainless-steel doors slid open. Ben stepped out and found the room was two to the left. Greg limped heavily, trying to keep his weight off his left foot. It was getting worse; he could see it was swollen and going a shade of blue. He was sure something was broken. Ben opened the door and held it open for him.

'Are you sure you're okay?' Ben asked.

Greg smiled back at him as he sat on the first bed he came to. 'I wouldn't be if you hadn't kept hold of me! Imagine going face first on that railway line at the speed that train was going.'

'I wasn't going to let go, you didn't need to worry about that,' Ben said, taking out two bottles of beer from the mini bar and wrapping them in a tea towel.

'Let me have a quick shower first and let's have a look at how bad it is.'

'Good idea, we could both do with one,' Ben said, placing the two bottles in the freezer.

'You do that while I get my phone on charge and see that the others are okay,' Ben said.

'Sounds like a great plan,' Greg said, hobbling to the bathroom.

Ben plugged in his phone charger lead and waited for the charge to reach two percent. Holding a button had the phone bursting into life. He could hear the shower running and couldn't wait for his turn to wash away the black soot from the train track. As soon as the phone started up, a string of messages came through. Several from Steve and Dan. He tapped the ring icon to call Steve.

'Oh boy, I'm glad to hear from you,' was the first thing Steve said.

'I'm bloody glad to be calling you. So, you found somewhere safe?' Ben asked.

'Yes, we're in a hotel in the main street of that town where you left us. Are you here somewhere as well?'

'No, we caught a train to a town about fifty K's north, I can't remember what it's called. Greg might have a broken foot though; it looks pretty bad.'

'Roger that, what's your plan?' Steve asked.

'In the morning, I'll get some crutches for Greg and either some shoes or a bandage so he looks like someone with a sore foot rather than someone out of a war zone and blood everywhere.'

'Shit, what happened?'

'Let's just say we were running late for a train.' Ben could imagine Steve smiling at the comment.

'What's your plan for getting out?' Ben asked.

'As you suggested, catch the bus to the ski resort and slip across the border somewhere.'

'Apparently, from this town there's a way to Pristina via train and bus. The girl at reception said that the border checks are only random.'

'That sounds like a better option than we have. Can your man in Kosovo help us with that?'

'That was going to be my first call in the morning. Get some sleep and I'll call back once the sun's up.'

'Roger that,' Steve said, and was gone.

Ben heard the shower stop and he sent Kara a message, knowing she would be worried.

Hi Kara, all safe in a town to the north. Greg's in the shower, we will call in the morning.

Thank God.

That was all that came back, she was obviously still awake.

The bathroom door opened, and a much cleaner man appeared with a white towel around his waist.

'I think that was the best shower I've ever had.'

'I can't wait. Sit back and let's get some ice on that foot.'

Ben jumped up and retrieved the cold bottles from the freezer and the couple of ice cubes that were there. Now that the blood was washed off, he could see that a lot of skin was missing including the nail from his big toe.

'The others are safe in a hotel back in that town. I sent Kara a message as well.'

'Thanks for that, she must've been stressing; it certainly has been a big day for her.'

'Yeah, that's for sure,' Ben said, placing a pillow under Greg's foot that was now wrapped in the blue striped tea towel that held the ice and bottles against his foot.

'All good? My turn for that shower.'

'Could you grab me a drink and I'll go you halves in that packet of chips?' Greg said, pointing to the mini bar selection.

'They are all yours,' Ben said, throwing them like a Frisby to him. 'Orange juice, coke or beer?'

'Orange juice, thanks.' Ben passed the cold bottle over and disappeared into the shower. Greg reached for his rucksack and took out the phone charger lead and plugged in his phone. After a minute he turned it on and sent Jennifer a message. It would be mid-morning there but he needed some sleep, so he decided to message and not call.

> All gone well, on our way home, will call tomorrow. Love you x.

Greg was fast asleep when Ben returned from the shower. His foot was elevated on the pillow that Ben had arranged and the ice pack he had made was still wrapped tightly around it. Ben knew they were lucky to get out of trouble as easily as they did.

He sat on his bed and thought back through the events. He knew that the helicopter pilots and the two dead Serbian officials would have been found by now and that they were probably the prime suspects. He also knew that they were still far from home and a safe base. They were still well inside enemy territory and could in no way relax. He ran through the scenarios of whether they sit tight and have the other five join them in Kraljevo, or if they were better off staying split up. *The conversation with Januzaj in the morning will help.* He figured that the authorities had pictures of them from the service station cameras. *But are the images good enough to recognise our faces or just the vehicles? No, the colonel picked out Kara from the pictures, so it isn't going to be just be a simple train ride out of here.*

CHAPTER THIRTY-THREE

Ben woke to see Greg inspecting his foot.

'How is it?'

'I think the ice helped reduce the swelling. It looks worse than it is. Well, I hope anyway.'

'Have you tried walking on it?'

'Not yet, but I won't be running anywhere.'

'Let's hope we don't need to.'

Ben checked his watch. It was 7 a.m. local time, still too early to call Januzaj. He pulled the covers back and went to the bathroom. When he returned, he dressed and headed for the door.

'I'll get coffee.'

'Sounds bloody good to me,' Greg said.

Greg also dressed in much cleaner clothes than he'd had on the night before. He fitted a sock and shoe to his right foot but left the injured one bare. He tried to put some weight on it, and thankfully, he could. His unprofessional opinion was that it may well not be broken after all, just badly sprained with lot of skin missing from the top of his foot.

Ben returned after half an hour with a bandage, a pair of crutches and two coffees in a cardboard holder.

'Coffee first,' Greg said, and he took one from the holder and immediately took a sip of the caffeinated frothy milk. 'The world is good again,' he said, holding the cup up.

Ben opened a large gauze patch and unrolled the bandage.

'Are you ready for me to wrap it up?' Ben asked.

'Sure am, Doc.'

Ben could see that the wound had dried and was in the process of forming a scab. He placed the gauze on the top of Greg's foot and wrapped the bandage around it firmly.

'Feeling okay?'

'Feels good. It's better that I can't see it,' Greg said, taking another sip of coffee.

Ben took his phone from his pocket; it was time to call Januzaj.

'Hello Mr Woolford, looks like you have stirred up a bit of trouble. Are you all okay?'

'Yes, two of us are in Kraljevo and five in Krusevac.'

'The Serbians have police on every exit, road and rail, looking for Albanian terrorists who ambushed and killed two government officials.'

'What do you suggest we do?' Ben asked.

'I will talk to the minister and call you back,' Januzaj said and was gone.

'How's it looking?' Greg asked.

'I don't think it'll be simple; it would be much easier if we knew what they knew, but we don't.'

Ben sat down on his bed facing Greg.

'Maybe only the colonel and Goran had the pictures of us, maybe not. Are they looking for two people or seven? We can't risk just walking into a team of police that might have pictures of our faces.'

Ben's phone rang and he answered it before the second ring.

'Mr Woolford, can all of you get to the Kopaonik ski resort to the south of you?'

'Yes, that was my initial plan but it looks hilly.'

'If you can catch a bus to the resort, it's all downhill from there. I will message you the exact tracks to take you to the border which is only a simple fence. At that point, we will have someone there to meet you.'

'Thank you, I hope to see you soon.'

'Yes, Mr Woolford, I will see you in a day or two.'

'Okay we have a plan,' Ben said to Greg after hanging up. 'We all meet at the ski lodge and walk to the border from there. It won't be fun for you mate, sorry.'

Ben called Steve.

'Steve, get yourselves to the Kopaonik ski lodge, we will meet you there and we'll have to walk down the mountain to the border from there.'

'Roger that,' Steve came back.

'We'll be there as soon as we can. How is everyone?'

'Everyone is good, I think it's been hard on Kara but she is toughing it out.'

'Yeah, copy that,' Ben said, hanging up the phone and turning to Greg.

'You'll be one of the few people going to a ski lodge on crutches. Normally people leave on them.'

Greg smiled and stood up. His first few steps were painful but with the crutches he felt it was all possible. They both packed their bags and were in the elevator ten minutes later. The receptionist was a different lady and Ben asked her about the best way to get to the resort. Her English wasn't as good as the girl from the night before, but it was pretty clear that a bus was the only way and she pointed out the station to him on a small map of the town. He thought that the other five would beat him and Greg there.

'Would you like ticket?' the girl asked.

'Yes, sure,' Ben said, looking back at Greg.

The girl looked at her watch. 'Bus leaves in forty-five minutes.'

'Can we make that on crutches?' Ben asked.

'Yes, just ten minutes down road.'

'That would be great, thank you.'

After a few computer keystrokes and a couple of simple questions like their names and credit card number, two A4 printed tickets emerged from the hidden printer. The lady handed them to Ben with a smile and they both thanked her. Greg made good time with the crutches and with his foot bandaged and no sight of blood or ripped and dirty clothes the two of them blended in perfectly. The driver directed Greg and Ben to have the front seat of the bus so he could straighten out his leg.

The bus took off down the highway that was straight and flat but it wasn't long before the road became steeper and wound its way up the Balkin mountains. Two hours later the bus arrived at the terminal and Greg and Ben were the first off. The air was cold but the summer sun was a nice contrast. Although it was primarily a ski resort it was also a great get away destination for the summer and there were plenty of people everywhere. Ben took out his phone and sent Steve a message.

Kara sat staring out of the window of the Balkin Bus Lines coach as it wound its way up the luscious hillside. The last few days had been amazing but the scariest of her life—all in one. She was a tough woman, she knew that, everyone did, but in this moment, she felt alone and needed a hug from the only person on earth that could somehow turn her darkest hour into a sunny day.

She needed no more than that from Greg, just his closeness and his arms around her would put the much-needed smile back on her face. He was only an hour or so from giving her the reassurance she needed. The amazing four men that were accompanying her continued to watch over her and make sure she was okay and she was, sort of. However, the trauma of watching a man prepare to end her life only to be killed by her guardian shepherd, and then lie dead and bleeding on top of her, was more than the average woman could handle in a day.

The road soon flattened out and the bus started to slow. A large carpark came into view which also doubled as the bus drop off point for the Balkin ski district. Kara's eyes searched for her saviour until it was time to leave the bus. She grabbed her bag from the overhead shelf and all five of her fellow travellers waited for her to leave first. She stepped from the bus looking in the direction of the bus terminal. There were many people in front of her and almost like a parting of the seas, Greg and Ben appeared in front of her. Tears started to form in her eyes at the sight of the two men, each of whom on different occasions had saved her life. She could see Greg on crutches and his bandaged foot. Her heart felt a stabbing pain. With wet eyes but a smile on her face she fell into Greg's arms and stayed there until she felt her life was perfect and complete again.

Ben shook the hands of the four men that had just arrived and he suggested they stay the night here as the walk down the hill could take a full day with Greg on crutches. No one complained and being the ski off season, it wasn't hard to find rooms for them all. Sam insisted that everyone had their own rooms. They all checked into their accommodation and most were quickly back out buying some warmer clothes.

Sam had been messaging Tanya from Peter's phone along the way confirming all was going well and seemingly out of danger, but now it was time to call. He purchased a phone from a shop—it had enough charge out of the box. He walked out to a seat that had a view to Kosovo to the south. He could see they were a long way up from the valley below that tomorrow they would all descend. It was the most beautiful colour of dark green and the trees rocked from side to side in the cool breeze that caressed the mountainside. It was nearly lunchtime and with the time difference, nearly midnight in Wellington.

'Hello,' a sleepy voice said.

'Hey babe.'

'Sam, where are you, are you okay?'

'Yes, we are nearly home free. We are on the Kosovo border and will cross tomorrow.'

'We've been so worried! Is everyone okay?'

'Greg has an injured foot but all good other than that. I can't say the same for the Serbians.'

'What do you mean?' Tanya asked.

Sam immediately knew he shouldn't have said anything. 'Let's just say that they won't be coming after us again.'

'Did Ben kill them?'

Sam paused, desperate for the right answer. 'Let's not talk about it now but there was a shootout and the two baddies didn't make it.'

'Oh my God.' Neither said anything for a few seconds. 'Well, I guess that's a good thing.'

'Yes, it is,' was all Sam offered back. 'Get some sleep babe, I should be home in a day or two.'

'Okay, love you and be careful.'

'Love you too,' Sam said back and closed the cheap flip phone. He looked up at the view again—steep green mountains as far as he could see. In only a few months it would all be covered in snow and what they had planned for tomorrow would be impossible. He stood up from the bench, looked once more at the breathless view and headed back toward the hotel. He could see Ben, Peter, Steve and Dan sitting at a table outside a bar, a large beer in front of each of them. They were all sporting brand new ski jackets. He was the only one that had no clothes. He survived with only his computer bag which included his wallet and passport—he was grateful for that.

'Nice coats,' he said as he walked up to the table. 'I'll be back for a beer as soon as I change my wardrobe.'

Clothes shops were not very plentiful, but he found one that could supply a full change of clothes including underwear. He changed and then threw everything he'd been wearing in a rubbish bin. He didn't need to be carrying anything other than his computer down the hill tomorrow. Ben and his team were relaxed and in good humour when Sam returned.

Ben was confident that they were past the worst of it and other than Greg's foot, they'd achieved a difficult extraction successfully without any casualties to his team. He knew the cost for Sam financially would be huge but he truly believed that Sam would never have seen his family again if they didn't do what they did. He was pretty sure Sam knew that as well. Greg and Kara soon arrived and two extra chairs were added to the table. Kara had changed the bandage on Greg's foot and it seemed to be healing well.

'How's the foot?' Steve asked as Greg placed the crutches against the nearby wall and sat at the table.

'It's looking good, really. Not as swollen but still pretty sore to walk on.'

'How will you go on the climb down the hill?' Dan asked.

'I think I'll dump the crutches and maybe a walking stick… or you SAS chaps could carry me on a stretcher?' Greg said, smiling.

'Walking stick sounds good to me,' Steve said, and everyone laughed.

The laughter softened and Ben looked at Kara. 'How are you going, Kara?'

She looked up from the menu she was perusing. 'I'm good.'

Ben continued to look at her. Everyone was now.

'Really? That was a pretty frightening situation,' Ben said, softer now.

'I can't say I won't be having nightmares in the weeks to come but I won't be needing any therapy, that's for sure. We're all safe and we got Sam out and that's all that matters.'

Everyone was smiling at her now with a genuine look of admiration.

'Well, we couldn't have done it without you,' Steve added.

'And what about the Sundance kid here,' Dan said, looking at Greg. 'Bursts out into the open with his point shooting, putting us to shame.'

'I have it all on here,' Peter said, holding up an SD card.

Greg smiled a half smile back at the compliment but he knew it was reaction only. He knew that Ben had his sights on the colonel and Dan and Steve the pilots. His eyes were on Kara and was probably the only one to see Goran raise his weapon directly at her after the command from the colonel was given.

They ordered a meal which would be their lunch and dinner. Ben had said that they would head down the path at daybreak. He had a map from the ski lodge plus the one from Januzaj that showed where to meet their pickup once over the border.

They ate and laughed through the meal and soon found themselves in their rooms for a much-needed early sleep. Greg and Kara went to the in-house ski shop and bought two ski stocks as the crutches would be impossible on a downhill path. He also purchased a pair of sandals that he could use as a sole for his injured foot. He'd grin and bear it tomorrow, but privately, getting home to his leather lounge couldn't come fast enough.

CHAPTER THIRTY-FOUR

It was 6.00 a.m. and bitterly cold outside when the seven of them met in the hotel foyer. Greg was the last to arrive with his foot freshly bandaged by Kara and the sandal taped on. He looked like an injured skier as he walked toward them with the two new fluro green ski stocks.

'I'm ready,' Greg said.

'How's the foot today, mate?' Ben asked.

'It's better than yesterday and much better than the day before but I suspect the five K walk will blow it up.'

'We won't be in a rush, we are all happy to cruise along at your pace,' Ben offered. 'Shall we head off?'

Everyone swung their bags and rucksacks over their shoulders and walked out into the cool pre-dawn breeze. The track was clearly marked and well-trodden as it was the peak hiking season for the mountain. Greg was keeping a good pace where the decline wasn't too steep but steps were a very slow process and he didn't want to damage his foot any further. It was starting to swell slightly and they stopped to loosen the bandage after about an hour into the walk.

Ben checked the GPS on his phone and could see that they had travelled about two thirds of the way to the pickup point. The actual border would be nearby and they would be climbing a fence and changing to a smaller unused track.

'Keep an eye out, the track we need must be somewhere soon,' Ben said, studying his phone.

Steve who was out front stopped and pushed back a bush that revealed what appeared to be a once well-worn track that hadn't been used in years. It was wide on the ground but the bushes and trees had grown over the path, in some spots completely blocking the way. Ben knew he had to be on high alert here because if the Serbians were serious about catching whoever it was that killed Goran and the colonel, they could be covering every possible escape route.

Steve pulled up at a six-foot-high chain mesh fence and said softly, 'This must be the border fence.'

Ben took out his Leatherman and made short work of the wire.

They marched on in silence, confident that they were now well inside the Kosovo border. Ben, the second in the line, held up a closed fist indicating for all to stop. He touched Steve on the shoulder for him to stop as well. He could hear a car engine running. Ben pointed to his ear and then ahead. He pointed for Steve to go and check it out. Everyone stood in silence while they waited. Two minutes later Steve returned.

'I think it's our ride,' Steve whispered to Ben. 'Kosovo government number plates.'

'That'll do me,' Ben said as he turned to Dan. 'Wait thirty seconds and then follow us.'

Ben and Steve walked off toward the black minivan. They crouched down behind a thick bush and recognised one of the men as the one that they had followed to the border crossing in the Land Rovers. Ben emerged from the bush and held a hand up to say hello. The man in the van smiled and the passenger door of the van opened. He immediately slid open the rear sliding door. This all added up to it being their ride. Ben went to the van and shook hands with the man he recognised, and Steve waited to direct the other five. Greg had discarded the stocks and now had his arm over Dan's shoulder.

The soft leather seats of the Mercedes van were a welcome relief for everyone but no one more than Greg. His foot was swollen and trying to burst from the bandage. He sat sideways on the middle row, Kara next to him and Peter alongside her.

'Pete, can you get that bloody bandage off before my foot goes green?' Greg asked him.

'Sure,' Peter unwrapped his foot with the care of a father dressing a newborn baby for the first time. Kara and Greg smiled as they watched him work with such delicateness. As the sandal fell away and the last of the bandage that was stuck slightly to the wound left his foot, Greg sighed with relief. The wound was pretty horrendous and Peter hadn't seen it before. He had to look away and used all his effort to not throw up. It looked like it had been through a grater.

It was a good two-hour drive back down the rest of the mountain as the car wound its way to the freeway and then into Pristina. The van pulled up in front of the same building that their first meeting with the minister was held. They all alighted the van, with an overwhelming sense of relief. They'd done it. They had saved Sam from what was probably a very short future and possibly prevented war between the two countries.

Ben whispered into Sam's ear, 'Make it look complicated, I told them you were the only person in the world that could remove it safely.'

'I will,' he said, and winked back at Ben.

Januzaj emerged from the elaborate building's front door and he stepped down the six steps with his hand held out to Ben.

'This is Sam Taylor, Mr Januzaj.'

Januzaj stepped forward and shook Sam's hand. 'This way please, Mr Taylor.' Januzaj turned, not wanting to waste not another second before erasing the virus from their computers.

The driver of the van invited the rest of them inside.

'Can we get a doctor?' Steve asked as he pointed to Gregs exposed wound.

'Yes of course, sir,' the Kosovo security man said. He held out his hand for Greg to get back in the van. Dan and Kara went with him.

Peter, Ben and Steve took up the offer of relaxing in the ministry of defence building while Sam did his stuff.

Ben now sipping a cup of tea, told Steve and Peter the finer details of them escaping from the Serbian police and the whole detailed steps of the train encounter. Peter sat mesmerised and sat on the edge of his chair. But to Steve it was nothing more than what he expected from his former sergeant and mentor.

Ben's phone rang.

'It's Greg,' he said looking at the caller ID.

'Hello, what's the news?'

'Just a broken big toe and the plastic surgeon said he can sew the skin back together without any skin grafts, so happy with that.'

'Good stuff, will they do that today?'

'Yes, we should be able to leave tomorrow, Kara and Dan are on their way back as I will be here a while.'

'Okay, good luck and see you soon,' Ben said hitting the end call button on his phone.

Sam sat in front of the computer that ran the Kosovo military. It wasn't a large military, it didn't need to be, because they had a big tough ally in the United States. The last time Serbia tried to take back the disputed land now called Kosovo, the US arrived, bombing the Serbian capital and immediately bringing an end to the hostilities.

Sam spent a few minutes looking through some of the program files on the mainframe and could see that they were quite vulnerable to cyber-attacks. He could see whose computer had uploaded the files and forwarded that little bit of information onto Januzaj. This rescue mission was going to cost him personally a lot of money once he had paid Ben and his team. So maybe a trip back sometime soon to upgrade their system might just help pay some of that bill. He eventually pushed delete on the two files and the computers were secure again. He doubted that anyone else other than the colonel was hacking the Kosovo computers anyway.

Januzaj and Ben had arranged accommodation for them all and their flights back to Australia. They would all leave tomorrow on a zero nine forty flight to Istanbul, then onto Kuala Lumpur where Greg, Ben, and Kara would fly direct to Adelaide, Peter to Alice Springs via Darwin, Sam to Wellington via Sydney and Auckland and Dan and Steve to Melbourne direct. The Kosovo foreign minister wanted to thank Ben personally and met with him in the Pristina office before he departed. The minister spoke in Serbian but Ben could feel the appreciation without the translation from Januzaj. The minister knew that not only with the virus deleted but more importantly with colonel Milovan Simovic's demise and his Kosovo mole arrested, his country would be a safer place.

The six members of the rescue crew were sitting in the bar of the Swiss Diamond Hotel when Greg arrived on a new set of crutches. Ben stood to make room for him at the table.

'How'd it go, buddy?' Ben asked.

'All good, the broken big toe will fix itself and they sewed the top back together. A full recovery is expected, plus a good-sized scar to remind me of how much fun this adventure was.'

There were laughs and smiles all round.

'Can you have a beer, mate?' Ben asked.

'You bet I can!' Greg said, falling back into a chair.

Then Ben turned to Kara. 'Now, about that kiss, Kara.'

ABOUT THE AUTHOR

Gary Baxter's journey as a wordsmith began in his youth, where his natural gift for articulation and entertaining storytelling captured the attention of those around him.

With an unwavering love for action novels and a burning desire to create stories that would enthral readers, he embarked on a mission that had been simmering within him for years.

As an accomplished car and motorcycle racer, instructor, entertainer and an esteemed figure in movie action vehicle coordination and stunt driving, Gary's thrilling life has fuelled his imagination and inspired his writing.

From the roaring engines on the racetrack to the heart-pounding stunts on the film set, he channels his experiences into words that leap off the page.

Gary's writing is extensive spanning an assortment of genres, including short stories, adult fiction and crime novels that captivate.

Ben Betrayed is Gary's second action story, now the sixth of his published novels.

Gary continues to entertain crowds with his V8s and perform stunts and precision driving for the film industry across the country—while catching every spare moment to write.